Praise for the Sophie Katz novels of
KYRA DAVIS

SEX, MURDER AND A DOUBLE LATTE
"Part romantic comedy and part mystery, with witty dialogue
and enjoyable characters...the perfect summer read."
—*The Oregonian*

"A thoroughly readable romp."
—*Publishers Weekly*

"A terrific mystery. Kyra Davis comes up with the right mix
of snappy and spine-tingling, and throws
in a hot Russian mystery man, too."
—*Detroit Free Press*

PASSION, BETRAYAL AND KILLER HIGHLIGHTS
"A witty and engaging blend of chick lit, pop culture, and
amateur-sleuth whodunit [that] will appeal not only to
female readers but to any mystery fan who has an offbeat
sense of humor.... Laugh-out-loud funny."
—*Barnes & Noble*

"Davis spins a tale full of unexpected turns and fun humor."
—*Romantic Times BOOKreviews*

OBSESSION, DECEIT AND REALLY DARK CHOCOLATE
"Wry sociopolitical commentary, the playful romantic
negotiations between Anatoly and Sophie and plenty of
Starbucks coffee keep this steamy series chugging along."
—*Publishers Weekly*

KYRA DAVIS

LUST, LOATHING
AND A LITTLE
LIP GLOSS

MIRA®

Recycling programs
for this product may
not exist in your area.

ISBN-13: 978-0-7783-2736-3

LUST, LOATHING AND A LITTLE LIP GLOSS

www.MIRABooks.com

Printed in U.S.A.

This book is for my son,
who has taught me more than I thought it was possible to learn.

PROLOGUE

I DIDN'T ALWAYS BELIEVE IN GHOSTS. MY SKEPTICISM WAS BASED ON MY religious and philosophical beliefs. I believe that there are only three things that we can count on to make this world bearable: good friends, a loving family (even when they're as crazy as mine) and certain mood-altering substances, mainly caffeine and vodka. I also believe that God is good. So why would a good God force the souls of the dead to stick around in a world where they can no longer talk to their friends, be comforted by their families or drink espressotinis? That just doesn't seem right.

But now I'm beginning to question myself. What if the souls of the dead don't need to exchange words with those they love in order to be comforted? What if ghosts have access to better drugs, ones that don't lead to insomnia or hangovers? And ghosts don't have to deal with mortgage payments. Perhaps heaven is free quality housing.

Then again maybe good people get to move to a more celestial address and it's only the bad people who become ghosts. Is it possible that it's the souls of the evil that are forced to stay here, doomed to an eternity of loneliness?

If that's true then I have a problem because I think the house

I just bought might be haunted. That's what I get for making a deal with the devil, aka my ex-husband, Scott Colvin. He's the Realtor who sold me my beautiful San Francisco Victorian.

But whether this place is haunted or not, I'm not leaving. I *love* my house. It has oak floors, crown moldings and, most importantly, two-car parking. This is my home now and I'm willing to fight to the death to keep it.

Unfortunately, I think it might come down to that.

There are men worth dying for and others who really just need to die.

—*The Lighter Side of Death*

WHEN OUR MARRIAGE ENDED TEN YEARS AGO, I FIGURED THAT WAS IT. I would never see Scott Colvin again. I certainly didn't expect him to be at the open house for this Marina District $1.4-million fixer-upper. But there he was, standing right in the middle of the living room, making it impossible for me to concentrate on the water-stained ceiling or broken light fixture. His body was angled away, so I could only make out a partial profile, but I had no doubt about his identity; that was Scott and the very sight of him brought on a slew of conflicting emotions. One of them was hope. Hope that someone had secretly dropped acid in my Frappuccino and that the thing that looked like Scott was nothing more than a messed-up hallucination.

I had taken hallucinogenics once before, during my freshman year in college. Perhaps if I hadn't allowed a magic mushroom to trample all over my brain cells I might have had the presence of mind *not* to get married at nineteen. Fortunately my brain cells were working again by my twenty-first birthday and I celebrated their recovery by getting a divorce.

But this moment didn't have the feel of a hallucination. The Frappuccino in my hand tasted real. The hopelessly out-of-date faux-wood paneling looked real. The mildew on the windows smelled real. And Scott looked like a real real-estate agent trying to convince a real middle-aged Japanese couple that the house we were all here to see really wasn't contaminated with asbestos. People on drugs see diamonds in the sky and riders on the storm; they don't see real-estate agents and overpriced four-bedroom houses that need new flooring. That meant that what I was hearing, seeing and smelling was all horribly real.

But the good news was that he hadn't seen me yet. I pivoted and tried to lift my wedge heel off the floor so I could quietly tiptoe out.

"Are my eyes deceiving me or is that the beautiful and talented Sophie Katz?"

Shit! I turned around again and was confronted by Scott's teasing smile. "What do you know, it is you!" he continued. The Japanese couple was now climbing the creaking staircase to check out the second floor. "Of all the open houses in the world you had to walk into mine."

I grimaced and made a sweeping gesture with my hand. "You're the agent representing this mess?"

"Apparently you didn't read the ad I ran in the paper." He handed me a promotional flyer detailing the house's few saving graces. "It's not a mess, it's an *opportunity.*"

I almost smiled. Almost. "Save your BS for the couple upstairs. I'm out of here."

Once again I turned to leave, but Scott quickly jogged in front of me so that I had to stop to keep myself from slamming into his chest. "Sophie, we haven't seen each other in over ten years. You can't still be angry at me."

"I'm pretty sure I can be."

"Nah, you just think you are." Scott's hazel eyes were twinkling with mischief. That's usually what they did when they weren't red from getting stoned. "You're really mad at the old Scott. The kid you were married to. But we're both grown-ups now, old enough to understand the value of forgiveness. Remember, grudges always have a greater effect on the lives of those who carry them than on the lives of those they're carried against."

"Wow, that's pretty deep, Scott," I said solemnly. "So let me think about this. During the time that I've been holding this grudge, I've become an internationally published bestselling author. I have wonderful friends. My family is healthy and reasonably happy. I have a fantastic cat and a boyfriend whom I adore. I'd say this grudge is working pretty well for me. I think I'll keep it."

"Don't you want to know why I've been calling you?"

After ten years of no contact, Scott had, as of five months ago, taken to calling me every few weeks and leaving messages on my answering machine. Of course I wanted to know why, but I wasn't going to give him the satisfaction of admitting to my curiosity. Instead I shrugged and retorted, "Don't you want to know why I haven't been returning those calls?"

He chuckled, apparently finding humor in my irritation. "I think the answer to your question is a lot more obvious than the answer to mine," he said.

I hesitated a moment and studied the countenance of this new "grown-up Scott." He had the beginnings of crow's-feet, but other than that he looked exactly the same. He had the same blond wavy hair that was always a little mussed, and of course he still had one dimple in his left cheek and that golden skin tone that suggested he spent his days surfing off China Beach. Once upon a time I had thought that his looks were the perfect complement to my darker, more exotic appearance. My father was black and my mother has the fair complexion common to her Eastern European Jewish ancestry. People were always confused and delighted by my ethnicity. They usually don't know exactly "what" I am yet they find my very existence to be a sign of hope for the improvement of race relations everywhere. However, the attention I get now is a pittance compared to the attention I got when I was with Scott. Together we were a walking Benetton ad. Of course I get a certain amount of attention when I go out with my current fair-skinned, Russian-born boyfriend, Anatoly Darinsky. But our differences are less visually dramatic thanks to Anatoly's dark hair and brown eyes.

"I got your latest book, *The Lighter Side of Death*. It's good." He inched a little closer. "I've also been reading about you in the papers. Sounds like you've become quite the amateur sleuth. According to the *Chronicle* you apprehended your own stalker, you helped figure out who killed your brother-in-law, and you even had a hand in bringing down the guy who killed that political aide in Contra Costa County." He gave me an approving once-over. "Sounds like you've turned into a real-life Charlie's Angel. Of course, you've always been an angel in my eyes...."

"Ugh." I wrinkled my nose in disgust. "I think I've just been slimed. I'm going now."

I started to walk around him, but Scott quickly sidestepped in front of me. "What if I told you that I had a brand-new listing for a recently renovated Ashbury Heights three-bedroom Victorian."

I hesitated. "How recently renovated?"

"Five years ago."

Only five years ago? Not bad. "Floors?"

"Hardwood. The owner has a thing for Persian rugs so the floors have been covered and protected."

"Seriously?" I was still focused on the door, but my feet didn't follow my gaze. "Okay, I'll bite. Who's the owner, and why is he selling?"

"The owner's name is Oscar Crammer, and he's selling because he thinks the place is haunted."

"Why's that?" I asked. "Was anyone ever murdered in the house? Because if it's a site of a recent homicide it should be selling for at least ten thousand below market."

"Sophie, the owner's only asking for $980,000."

I broke out in a full laugh. "Yeah, right, a renovated, three-bedroom Ashbury Heights Victorian selling for under a million? Tell me, Scott, does it come with its own leprechaun, too?"

"I know it doesn't sound possible, but it's true." He hesitated before adding, "I think the guy selling may have the beginnings of Alzheimer's."

"You want me to take advantage of some guy with Alzheimer's?" I snapped.

"It has a two-car garage, Sophie."

My heart skipped a beat, but my sense of morality would not allow me to be tempted by this alluringly wicked proposal. "I won't scam a sick man, Scott. Not even for parking."

"Oscar's old money. He's got at least ten to twenty million in the bank and his son, Kane, has made millions more in the stock market. He sold off his investments in 2007, before the Dow got squirrelly. Plus I know for a fact that Kane has been trying to get Oscar to sell the house and move into a retirement home ever since the old man became a widower. So by buying this place you'd be doing everybody a favor."

I turned all of this info over in my mind. It still wasn't ethical to take advantage of an old man with a possibly fatal illness but...*it had a two-car garage!*

The Japanese couple came down the stairs and headed into the kitchen just as an Armani-clad gentleman stepped into the entryway. Scott smiled at the latter and nodded at the former before leaning in a little closer and whispering, "I just got the listing this morning. If you want to be the first to see it we could meet there at eight-thirty tonight."

"Eight-thirty?" I asked in a voice much louder than his. "What kind of real-estate agent shows houses at eight-thirty at night?"

"One who is trying to get his ex-wife to give up an outdated grudge," Scott said. "Tomorrow I have to tell all my other clients about this, and at that price you know they're going to descend upon it like a bunch of hungry hyenas. But since I do kinda owe you..."

"You *kinda* owe me?" I parroted. "While we were married you spent my entire inheritance on gambling, alcohol and the various sluts you were screwing. You more than *kinda* owe me."

"I'll show it to you before anyone else," Scott continued, ignoring my brief tirade. "If you're the first to make an offer the old man might take it before a bidding war has a chance to break out. The guy is motivated with a capital *M*."

I chewed on my lower lip and glanced at the Armani guy who was now knocking on one of the walls—probably testing to see if it could withstand the impact. This is what $1.4 million could buy you in San Francisco. I had written six *New York Times* bestselling novels and yet I could barely afford to buy this moldy rat hole with a view. With that in mind how could I *not* take Scott up on this once-in-a-lifetime offer?

Another couple walked in and Scott flashed them one of

his most charming smiles while whispering through his teeth, "So, we on for tonight or not?"

I squeezed my eyes closed and forced myself to make the only rational decision available to me. "We're on. Give me the address and I'll be there at eight-thirty."

I drove my Audi through the residential streets of Ashbury Heights. Victorian after Victorian blurred into one another as I sped by. There were few pedestrians out although there were probably more than you could count several blocks over where the local shops and restaurants populate Cole Street. I was tempted to turn my car around and head that way now. I could play quarters with some bartender and laugh at the knowledge that my evil ex was standing around an empty house waiting for me. It would be petty, though perversely sweet entertainment. But as I brought the car to a halt at each stop sign, my mind came screeching back to the conversation Scott and I had earlier. I didn't have a problem with being petty, but stupidity was not something I was comfortable with. I had to at least see the place.

It was 8:40 p.m. when I found the address Scott had given me. He'd told me to park in the driveway, but for a moment I found myself idling my car in the middle of the quiet street and staring at the building to my left. The windows were all dark, but the streetlamp illuminated the details of the exterior. It was no bigger than the houses to the left or right, but still, it was superior. Unlike its neighbors, this house was not painted in pastels, but in a color that hovered between tan and a muted lilac. Its gabled shingled roof shielded its angled bay windows from the hazy evening sky. It was beautiful and oddly familiar. I must have passed it before and somehow taken notice of it. As my eyes traveled from the roof to the foundation I spotted Scott huddled between the Greek-styled columns bordering the front entrance. Watching me and toying with the zipper of his insulated brown suede jacket, his presence surprised me. When I had been married to Scott we had both considered *punctuality* a dirty word. Slowly, I pulled into the driveway, which was so narrow that it barely accommodated the width of my car.

"How long have you been waiting?" I asked as I slipped out of the car and trotted up the front steps.

"Got here at eight-twenty." He got to his feet and brushed some nonexistent dirt from his jeans. "I figured you'd be late, but I thought I should get here early just in case you'd changed." He smiled, bringing his dimple into view. "I'm glad to see that you're still the same ol' Soapy."

I let out a disdainful puff of air. Soapy was the pet name he had assigned to me after we had gotten into a soapsuds fight while washing my old car. It brought back irritatingly fond memories.

"Let's see the house," I said coolly. As front doors went, this house had a pretty nice one. Tastefully carved without being too ornate or flowery. "Where's the owner staying?"

"Hotel Nikko," Scott said as he fiddled with the key.

"Really? Why doesn't he just stay here until it sells…oh, Scott!" I exclaimed as he opened the door to reveal the foyer. "Are those crown moldings?"

"Better believe it, baby. Crown moldings fit for a queen." As we stepped inside he sniffed the air suspiciously. "That's Pine-Sol," he said slowly. "Oscar must have cleaned before leaving."

I barely registered Scott's comment. I was in the living room looking at the bay windows and the lovely upholstered window seat. The furniture wasn't my style, very flowery in a Victorian kind of way, but I wasn't buying the furniture. The gorgeous built-in mahogany bookcases though, *those* would be mine!

"That's strange."

I turned at the sound of Scott's voice behind me. I had almost forgotten he was there. "What's strange…wait, that doesn't look fake." I pointed at the fireplace behind him. "It's not just decorative? It's real? A real honest-to-God fireplace that you can set fires in?"

"Gas starter, too," Scott confirmed. "But that's not what's weird. What's weird is that Oscar seems to have rearranged all the furniture. This place has been totally redecorated since this morning."

"Oh, yeah, that's weird…is that a formal dining room?" I ran past Scott into the next room. Sure enough, it was a dining room, and it was stunning. Not huge, but certainly bigger than anything I'd ever had. Right now it contained an antique oak sideboard complete with carved winged griffins and a beveled mirror. It also held a table that was long and rectangular and covered with a white lace tablecloth. In fact, the table was set as if someone had been preparing for a dinner party of six. There were two beautiful silver candleholders holding long, tapered cream candles, and each place setting shone with Victorian rose-patterned fine china.

"He set the table?" Scott choked.

"Guess he thought that setting the table would give the place a little more ambiance or something," I muttered, glancing over at the door that led to the kitchen. There had to be a problem with the kitchen, right? No house was perfect.

I carefully stepped inside and broke into a grin—a totally charming kitchen. The cabinets were white, and while I usually prefer a natural wood finish, this white actually worked well with the Victorian ambiance. There wasn't a huge amount of counter space, which would be a problem for Anatoly, who loved to cook almost as much as I loved to eat, but I could always put in an island or something.

The thought tickled me. Last month, Anatoly and I had been

on the Marina watching the ferries riding over the bay. He had kissed my cheek and then my neck while mumbling about the way the salt water tasted on my skin. Then, out of the blue he had taken my hand and suggested we move in together. He wanted to wake up with me in the morning...every morning. Only a year ago he had expressed discomfort with the level of commitment implied by the words *boyfriend* and *girlfriend* and now he wanted to share his life with me. It had almost made me cry.

Almost. The truth was that I didn't want to move him into my apartment, and I sure as hell wasn't going to move into his. I have come to believe that domestic partnerships have a higher chance of success when they exist within spacious houses. Conversely, cramped quarters and limited closet space is a recipe for domestic violence. But Anatoly made significantly less money than I did, so if my dreams of romance and elbow room were going to come to fruition I was going to have to find a house that fit *my* budget. He could help me with the mortgage if he chose (and I knew he would), but the down payment was a burden I would have to bear alone. I hadn't detailed my objections for Anatoly, knowing that he would have dismissed them. Instead, I had stalled for time with whispered abstract promises of future arrangements. He hadn't argued, but he hadn't been happy, either.

I glanced at a paned glass door in the back of the room and was hit by yet another wonderful revelation. "Scott, *this place has a yard?* Why didn't you tell me?" I ran to the door and flung it open. Yes, the yard was about the size of your average master bathroom, but in San Francisco any house that came with grass was a huge commodity.

"He took his small appliances with him." Scott was now standing in the doorway. "The man took his appliances to the Nikko."

"Or maybe he moved them into a storage unit," I suggested,

not really caring what had happened to some soon-to-be ex-owner's toaster oven. I walked across the room and opened a door discreetly adjacent to the pantry. "Or maybe he put them in here with the washer and dryer."

"Huh?" Scott peeked inside and noted the coffee machine, blender and a few other basic kitchen tools on the floor of the laundry room. "Why would he do this?"

"Why are you so freaked out by it? The guy wants to sell his house so he spruced it up a bit. That's normal, Scott. As a real-estate agent I would think you would know that."

"Sophie, the reason I got this listing is because I know the owner. Oscar and I...travel in some of the same circles."

My eyes slanted in suspicion. "*You,* the man who once speculated that life after sixty wouldn't be worth living—*you* travel in the same circles as a seventy-year-old with the beginnings of Alzheimer's."

"He's a friend of...a friend. He called me at, like, six this morning all agitated and upset, insisting that I come over immediately and help him sell this place. I made him wait until eight and then I sat and listened to him rant about the ghosts who were driving him out of his house. He's not well, Sophie. In addition to the mental stuff he's got a heart condition. There's no way he has the physical strength to move the furniture around. This is just weird."

"Maybe he just called another friend...someone who travels in his eclectic circles, and asked him to help fix the place up. Really, Scott, for a man who has mastered the fine art of lying you sure don't have a very good imagination." I shut the door to the laundry room. "Show me the bedrooms."

Scott's expression morphed again, this time into something that made my stomach churn. "Soapy, I thought you'd never ask."

He showed me the one downstairs bedroom (which would

make a great office) and half bath, then led me up the staircase and brought me to the second bedroom and full bath. They were both beautiful. The house was so underpriced it was *sick*. But sick in a good way. I could deal with this kind of sick.

With each room Scott made another comment about how everything was different from this morning. When we looked at the second bedroom he shook his head and pointed to a ceramic vase that hadn't been there before. "It's weird," he insisted again. "It's like he tried to make this place look more…" He snapped his fingers a few times as if trying to command the word he was looking for to pop into his mouth. *"Victorian,"* he finally said. "He made the place look more Victorian."

"It's a Victorian house, Scott. What did you expect? That he would try to make the place look art deco?"

"I didn't expect *anything,* that's the point! I thought he was just going to leave and let me deal with fixing it up for the sale. You should have seen him this morning. He didn't even feel comfortable hanging around here to talk. Now I'm supposed to believe that he spent the day here redecorating and cleaning?"

"Are you going to show me the master bedroom or are you going to just stand here flipping out over a vase?"

"Right, the master bedroom…let's just hope he didn't get rid of the bed, I'd really like to show you that…." But the flirtation lacked conviction. Oscar the redecorator had thrown Scott off his game.

The door to the master bedroom was closed and for a second I entertained a disturbing thought. "You don't suppose he's in there, do you? Maybe he's been sleeping the whole time we've been wandering around his house."

"Oscar assured me that he would be out of here by six at the latest." He reached forward and opened the door to reveal a charming, if somewhat foul-smelling, room with delicate moldings and paned glass doors that were left open to reveal a pretty little deck—and there was Oscar…sitting on the bed…mouth wide-open…face tilted up toward the ceiling. It didn't look like a natural position and he didn't acknowledge us.

He didn't move at all.

"Oscar?" There was a slight tremor in Scott's voice.

I crept toward him. "Hello?" I whispered, although I had an ugly suspicion that I could scream and not get a reaction out of Oscar. Something crinkled under my foot and I realized that I had just stepped on a bunch of antique photos. They had that lovely golden glow that always made me think of horse-drawn wagons and Ellis Island immigrants. But these photos weren't of people, they were of rooms. I was tempted to take a moment to examine them more closely, but I knew that was just my natural inclination to put off the inevitable. "Oscar? I'm Sophie…can you hear me?" I got a little closer and very carefully checked for a pulse. Nothing.

I pulled my hand away and stared at the two white prints the pressure of my fingers had left on the corpse's flesh.

"Scott, I think he's dead."

"You *think?*" Scott asked.

I looked down at Oscar's lower half and realized his pants were wet with urine, which explained the smell. "He's definitely dead."

I waited for Scott to respond and when he didn't I turned to look at him.

"Scott?"

He held up a finger as if to indicate that he needed a minute, then ran to the attached bathroom where I could hear him promptly regurgitate whatever it was that he'd had for dinner.

And now I was alone with a dead stranger. Hesitantly, I

turned back to Oscar. I didn't see any blood or sign that he had struggled with someone, although the expression on his face was anything but peaceful. He looked kind of horrified, like he had seen the grim reaper. My eyes traveled to his left hand. His fingers were curled around a piece of jewelry. I leaned over, not wanting to touch him again, and realized that the jewelry was actually an antique brooch with a cameo. Little goose bumps materialized all over my skin and I tried to suppress the anxiety building within me. I wished Scott would pull himself together and handle this. But I expected that would take a while. Scott liked to deal in fantasies and what-ifs. Death was one of those things that was just too real for him.

I turned my back to the body. Actually, this was a little too real for me, too. With shaky hands, I gathered up the photos I had stepped on. One Victorian room after another...a bedroom, a dining room...*this* bedroom, *this* dining room. These were pictures of the house as it once was. The furniture had been different, obviously, but not the placement. Oscar had rearranged his furniture to fit the images in these pictures. Even the table setting was similar. Mechanically, I turned back around.

"How did you die, Oscar?" I whispered. I reached over and tentatively touched the brooch in his hand. It was cold, colder than the dead hand holding it. The colorless depiction of the woman on the cameo was surely meant to be flattering, but to me her sharp chin and unseeing eyes appeared sinister. It was then that I became vaguely aware that I was frightened.

At that moment Scott stumbled out of the bathroom and looked purposely at the floor. "So," he said in a scratchy voice, "do you still want the house?"

"Report this," I said pointing to the phone on the nightstand closest to Scott. "Dial 911 and tell them we found a dead man."

Scott looked up at the phone, noted its proximity to the bed and then quickly looked away. "Didn't I read that you discovered a body in Golden Gate Park a few years back?" he asked hopefully. "You have more experience with this kind of thing. Why don't you call?"

"Oh, for God's sake, be a man, Scott," I said, once again inching away from the body.

"I am a man! I just happen to be a man who suffers from necrophobia."

"What?"

"I have a fear of dead things. I'm working on overcoming it. Still, this," he waved toward the bed without looking at it, "is a bit much for me to deal with."

"You weren't necrophobic when we were married."

"Yes, I was, we just didn't talk about it. Remember how upset I got when we went to that restaurant and they served us the fish with its head still on? That was a traumatic moment for me, Sophie."

"Wow, Scott. I didn't realize. I'm so sorry you had to go through that. Now suck it up and call the police." I stared at the floor. The urine was getting to me. The smell had been bad when we first entered the room, but now that I knew what it was and why it was there, it had become unbearable. I had to get out of the room.

Scott swallowed hard and then pulled his cell phone out of his jacket pocket. "I'll call from this." He walked over to the bedroom door and motioned for me to exit with him, which I gladly did. I left the pictures where I had found them.

As we walked down the stairs Scott dialed 911 and I used my cell phone to dial Anatoly's number.

"Hey there." The lightness of Anatoly's tone was jarring considering my circumstances. "I was just thinking about you. A minute ago I accepted another case and it turns out my new client is a huge fan of your books." Anatoly was a P.I. and lately it seemed that everybody in San Francisco wanted his services. Businesses wanted to prove that their employees were stealing, wives wanted to prove that their husbands were cheating and so on and so forth. But right now all of those problems seemed paltry and inconsequential.

"Anatoly, I'm in Ashbury Heights." It was amazing how I could keep my voice smooth even as my hands shook. "A Realtor was just giving me a tour of this Victorian he's representing and—"

"Now? It's almost nine o'clock."

"Yeah, I know it's unusual, but that's not why I'm calling. Listen, the owner's here and he's sort of…dead."

There was a moment of silence followed by a Russian curse. "You found another dead body."

"It would seem that way, yes."

"Are you safe?"

"Yeah, I'm here with the real-estate agent and he's calling 911." Scott and I had now reached the bottom of the stairs and he was standing by the bay windows answering some dispatcher's questions. "The owner was old so he probably died of natural causes. Still, could you come over? I mean, it's not like I've never been through something like this, you know that and…well, you'd think it would get easier, but…"

"Tell me how to get there and I'll come over immediately."

I looked up at Scott. He was describing the state of the body to someone on the phone and gagging between sentences. Thank God for Anatoly because I was pretty sure Scott wasn't going to be that big of a comfort to me.

2

Smart Agoraphobics Invest in Real Estate.

—*The Lighter Side of Death*

LESS THAN FIVE MINUTES LATER, A POLICE CAR AND AN AMBULANCE arrived. The paramedics and one of the two officers immediately went upstairs to check out the body while the other officer, a sergeant with salt-and-pepper hair and a face like Paul McCartney, lingered in the living room to ask Scott and me a few questions. He introduced himself as Sergeant Poplar, but in my head he was Sergeant Pepper. After giving him a quick rundown of why we were there and what we had found, his partner (a cute blond woman who looked more cheerleader than cop) appeared at the top of the stairs and said something about it looking like "natural causes," at which point Sergeant Pepper asked us to stick around while he took a look for himself. Once both officers were out of sight, Scott and I simultaneously collapsed on the couch and stared up at the vaulted ceiling.

"Well," Scott said dully, "I've never had a house showing like this before."

"Did you know Oscar well?" I asked. The cushions on the

couch were overstuffed to the point of discomfort, but neither Scott nor I moved to find a better seat.

He shook his head and ran his fingers through his hair. "He's more Venus's friend."

"Who's Venus?"

But before he could answer Anatoly burst through the door. His hands were still encased in the thick black gloves he so frequently wore while riding his Harley, and he creased his forehead in concern. Without a second thought I went to him and he received me with a tight embrace. "You seem to have a talent for being in the wrong place at the wrong time," he scolded, but his tone was gentle and comforting.

"I just wanted to see the house," I said, my words muffled by his shirt.

Anatoly pulled back slightly and took in his surroundings. "Nice," he noted before his eyes landed on Scott. "I take it you're the Realtor?"

Scott nodded and wiped his palm sweat on his designer jeans before extending his hand to Anatoly. "Scott Colvin, Sophie's Realtor, friend and ex-husband."

Anatoly's smile of greeting froze midhandshake.

"He's lying," I said quickly. "At least about being my Realtor, or my friend for that matter."

"And the ex-husband part?" Anatoly asked, keeping his eyes on Scott. He hadn't let go of his hand yet, and judging from Scott's expression, Anatoly's grip had gotten a little tighter than necessary.

"That part's true."

Anatoly released Scott and turned to me. "You came to this house in the middle of the night with your ex-husband?"

"Eight-thirty's the middle of the night?" Scott asked. "Guess you must be an early-to-bed guy. Sophie and I have always been night owls."

"We haven't seen each other in ten years, Scott," I hissed. "You have no idea what my sleeping habits are like now." The cool damp breeze coming in from the open door was beginning to get to me and I rubbed the back of my arms in an attempt to increase my circulation.

Scott cocked his head to the side, and shot me the first real grin since we had discovered Oscar. "There's no way you've turned into an early bird. Not my Soapy."

"Soapy?" Anatoly raised his eyebrows.

"You didn't tell him about that nickname?" Scott chuckled and refocused on Anatoly. "Man, you're going to love how she got it. We were washing her car and she was wearing these Daisy Duke shorts and this sheer white tank top—"

"They were *regular denim shorts* and the tank was not sheer," I snapped. "I can't believe you're trying to play juvenile head games while the paramedics upstairs are trying to determine the cause of death of one of your friends."

"Whose friend is dead?" a Kathleen Turner–type voice demanded.

We all turned toward the front door and standing there was a human hanger.

Actually "human hanger" was my friend Dena's term. She used it for runway models and those who looked like them; in other words, women who were too skinny, angular and narrow in the hips to look sexy in lingerie, but managed to make clothes look fabulous. This particular hanger was hanging a delicate off-white long-sleeve top under a spaghetti-strap charcoal-gray empire wool dress. The outfit would have made me look like a matronly dwarf. She, on the other hand, looked ethereal. She glided over to Scott and wrapped her arms around his neck.

"Scott, darling, who's dead?"

"Venus, what are you doing here?" he croaked.

She pulled back, her height enabling her to look him in the eyes without tilting her head. "Perhaps you didn't hear me, darling. I asked you who was dead. That *is* what you said, isn't it?" she asked, whirling around to look at me. "You said that there were paramedics upstairs determining the cause of someone's death."

"I think you should answer your girlfriend's questions, Scott," Anatoly suggested. "This woman is your girlfriend, right?"

Scott nodded mutely.

"Then why don't you explain to her what Sophie was talking about. Fill her in on what's happened and what it was you said that got Sophie so irritated."

"Your name is Sophie?" Venus asked. She truly was beautiful. Her skin was a creamy-white and her chestnut hair, which was pulled into a loose, low ponytail, had enough sheen to make an Herbal Essence model jealous. Her features were kind of perfect, to the point that I had to wonder if she had been crafted by genetics, or a very talented plastic surgeon. When I stared directly at her I could see that she was wearing makeup, perhaps a lot of it, but everything was so perfectly blended and the tones so muted that it managed to look natural. The only things that didn't quite fit were her hands, which were a little too big to match an otherwise delicate figure. However even this inconsistency served her well, making her seem a bit more powerful than her heart-shaped mouth would suggest.

But she wasn't nice. I could just tell. Something about the icy sheen in her green eyes hinted at a foul temperament.

"What's your last name?" she demanded, not waiting for me to answer her first question.

I inched a little closer to Anatoly. "My last name is Katz."

"This is your ex-wife, Scott," Venus said slowly. "How interesting." Her mouth curved into a wry smile. "Now, someone is going to tell me why we're all here and why there's a police car and ambulance outside. I know Oscar's staying at the Nikko tonight so—"

Scott put a firm hand on her shoulder and turned her back around to face him. "Venus, Oscar didn't get to the Nikko."

I couldn't see Venus's face, but her body had gone absolutely still.

"I'm so sorry, love. We found him in his bed and—"

"Stop." Venus's voice was shaky and discordant. She moved away from Scott and farther into the house, pausing before the fireplace. As skinny as she was she still had the presence to fill up the spacious room. "I don't want to hear this from you. I want to hear it from Oscar."

Anatoly and I gave Scott a questioning look. "Right…" Then Scott looked longingly at the door. "Venus, um, sees dead people."

"Feel," Venus corrected. "I can feel them. The circumstances in this room aren't right for a ghost to actually make an appearance right now."

Anatoly stared at her for a few seconds before pulling me closer so my ear was near his lips. "Why don't I take you home and we'll let your ex deal with the crazy woman."

"I heard that," Venus called over her shoulder. She turned around again to face us, her posture upright and her head high. A single tear trickled out of the corner of her eye and she allowed it to slide down her cheek, unchecked. Most people are uncomfortable with the idea of shedding tears in front of strangers, but Venus wore hers like a badge of honor. The effect was disconcerting because instead of making her seem vulnerable, the pride she seemed to have in her own grief made her appear stronger and maybe even a little bit unnatural. She reached a hand out to Scott and he was instantly by her side as she whispered, "I knew he wasn't well, but I thought he had more time than this. It was a…natural death, wasn't it? No one did him harm?"

"I think it was natural," Scott said quietly. "Venus, why did you come here?"

But before she could answer, the police and the paramedics came down the stairs. The paramedics went out to the ambulance to fetch a stretcher while the police officers stayed to talk to us. "It was most likely a stroke or a massive heart attack," Sergeant Pepper explained after establishing Anatoly's and Venus's identity and collecting all of our phone numbers and addresses. "We'll need to do an autopsy, but there's no evidence of homicide here."

"Someone needs to tell his son," Venus said. "Poor Kane will be devastated. I don't believe he's ever even recovered from the death of his mother."

"Do you know how we can reach Mr. Crammer's son?" the female cop asked.

"I have his number stored in my cell phone." Venus glanced down at her hands as if expecting to find the cell there. "I must have left it in the car." She gestured toward the door and a moment later she had Scott and both officers escorting her to her parking spot.

"So if Scott isn't your real-estate agent, why did you come here with him?" Anatoly asked as we stepped aside to allow the paramedics to come in with a stretcher.

"He was the agent representing the open house I went to this afternoon," I said once the paramedics were upstairs again. "It was a total coincidence."

"That still doesn't answer my question, Sophie."

"He told me about a house that just went on the market this morning and when he described it I knew I had to see it. I mean, look around you! This place is so *me!*"

Anatoly scanned the living room with disinterest. "Real-estate agents usually don't give tours after dark."

"He wanted to show me the house before anyone else and I agreed because he said that if I made the first bid I might be able to get it for nine-eighty."

Anatoly's head snapped in my direction. "This house is worth a million-seven easy."

"Oscar wanted out of the house." I walked over to the bookcases and fingered a hardbound edition of Jean-Paul Sartre's plays. It was the most contemporary of all the literature held by the mahogany shelves. "He said it was haunted."

Anatoly snorted. "Didn't Scott tell him to up the price?"

"My guess is he was planning on making the suggestion, but probably not if I was the prospective buyer. Apparently Scott grew a conscience in the ten years since our divorce and now he wants to make up for all the wrongs he's committed against me by setting me up in my very own Ashbury Heights three-bedroom." My voice faded off at the end of my sentence. I had been so disturbed by the discovery of Oscar's body I hadn't yet thought about how his death was going to affect the deal. This house now belonged to Oscar's son. What if he didn't want to sell it? And even if he did, he probably wouldn't want to do it for only $980,000. My hand moved from the book to the bookshelf and I clutched it so hard my thumb began to cramp, as if I could make this house mine if I just held on to it.

"It's for the best," Anatoly said, correctly reading my thoughts. "If you were to buy this place it would come with strings attached. By not convincing Oscar to sell at market, Scott was giving up on at least $20,000 of commission. Men don't make those kinds of sacrifices because they want to make amends for the past. Those kinds of sacrifices are only made when men think they will be repaid with power or sex."

"Well, obviously." I spun around to face him. "That's what makes my possible inability to buy this house all the more painful. How fabulous would it have been if I had been able to cheat Scott out of a huge commission and then turn around and reject him? Do you have any idea how much I wanted to inflict that kind of pain and suffering on that bastard? He used my distress over my father's death as a way to worm his way into my life and then he screwed me over in every way you can think of. Do you know that he sold a diamond pendant my father gave me to a pawnshop just to keep some bookie from breaking his legs? And the bookie's name was Vinny! Everybody knows you're not supposed to borrow money from bookies named Vinny! He was not only a bastard, but he was a *stupid* bastard!"

Anatoly opened his mouth to respond, but then abruptly closed it when the paramedics reappeared. They were carrying Oscar on the stretcher and his body was covered in a white sheet. With his face hidden, the corpse took on an anonymity that scared me. The body being carried down the stairs could have been anybody. In fact, my father's body had looked just like that when they put a sheet over him and carried him out of my parents' house twelve years ago.

That isn't my father, I reminded myself. I pulled up the image of Oscar's countenance and held it in my mind as Anatoly and I watched the stretcher go out the door. This was the body of a stranger who had been foolish enough to rearrange all his heavy furniture despite his age and reportedly bad health. No wonder he had a stroke.

My eyes moved to the couch. When I had first seen it all, I could think of was how unstylish it was. But I hadn't thought about its mass.

I walked over to the armrest and threw all my weight into trying to push it forward. It moved, but only a half of an inch.

"What are you doing?" Anatoly asked.

"I couldn't move this," I said slowly. "Not by myself."

"So don't," Anatoly wisely suggested.

"I won't, but Oscar did. He had to have had help."

"Excuse me." Sergeant Pepper was standing in the doorway looking bored and irritated. "I'm afraid I'm going to have to ask you both to leave the house."

"Why?" I asked.

"Because it's not yours," he said. "If you stay you'll be trespassing."

With that statement my potential loss hit me with renewed force. I had already fallen in love with this place. I wanted it, and I wasn't good at walking away from things that I wanted.

3

One of the unfortunate side effects of my medication is that it hinders my ability to act crazy.

—*The Lighter Side of Death*

"HE DIED OF A HEART ATTACK. WHAT'S THE BIG DEAL?" DENA REACHED around the wood pole that held the yellow oversize umbrella above our outside table and handed me back the obituary that I had brought along for her to look at during our lunch date at MarketBar. She took a moment to peel off her fitted leather blazer before continuing. "You know you're just obsessing over this to distract yourself from the fact that you might not get the house."

"Bite your tongue," I muttered, even though I knew she was partially right. It's not that Oscar's death hadn't actually affected me. It had. I had seen Oscar's pale, dead face in my dreams on more than one occasion since I'd found him. The cameo, the smell, the photographs…it all came together to create a scene that was as harsh as it was ominous. But I had seen worse and I had learned how to tuck my fears away into the dark corners of my mind that I rarely explored. But the house…that house had dominated my thoughts ever since I had laid eyes on it.

In a few minutes Scott would be here to tell me my future. Would I be buying the home of my dreams from Oscar's son, Kane, at a price I could afford or was I fated to buy some $1.4-million-dollar rat hole on a fault line? I had called Dena and asked her to join me for lunch before this pronouncement of destiny, and to stay with me during its actual telling. My reasons for this were obvious to both of us. I needed my best friend for support and I needed her to help me stay grounded despite my agitation.

Dena took a sip of the cappuccino she had ordered in place of dessert and then licked the foam off her burgundy painted lips. "I don't suppose you ever found out why Scott was calling you before?"

"Nope, and I'm not going to ask him about it." I let my gaze linger on the clock tower that soared above us only fifty feet away. Time seemed to be passing slower than usual. "The goal here is to get the house and then get Scott out of my life—for the second time."

Dena nodded and took a moment to ogle the cute Eurasian busboy who was clearing off a nearby table. He wasn't really my type, although I recognized his beauty. He was tall and sinewy, almost feminine in his grace. She reached forward and emptied her previously untouched glass of water in three consecutive gulps.

"Okaaay." I reached forward and tapped her empty water glass. "Are you suffering from diabetes or something?"

Dena smiled wickedly. "I have my reasons." Just then the busboy crossed to our table to refill her glass. "Thank you," Dena purred. "I was hoping you'd come over here and quench my thirst."

The busboy looked up from the glass, surprised, and then, noting Dena's expression, his eyes widened with understanding. "No problem," he said uncertainly, glancing over his shoulder, presumably to ensure that he wasn't the cause of the giggles coming from the women at the nearby table. But the women were deeply involved in their own conversation and he turned back to us with more confidence. "I'm Kim. Just call me over if you need anything else."

"What a wonderful invitation, Kim," Dena said. "It seems only right that I should reciprocate." She pulled a business card out of her purse and wrote her home number on the back. "Obviously I'm attracted to you," she said simply. "However I'm not looking for a serious relationship and I don't tolerate chauvinists. If you're okay with casual and you're not a sexist then *you* can call *me* over and I'll...show you what's on my menu." She slipped her card into his hand and added, "If you're opinionated and smart I might even take you out for a nice dinner first."

The busser flushed and then turned even redder after noting what it was that Dena did for a living. "Sole proprietor of Guilty Pleasures? Is that a...you know...a—"

"We sell upscale lingerie, sex toys and things like that," Dena said matter-of-factly. "Some of it's rather tame and romantic. Some of it would make Fergie Ferg blush."

For a moment it appeared that Dena had rendered Kim speechless. "I think you may be the most amazing woman I've ever met in my life."

Dena lifted her thick Sicilian eyebrows in amusement. "We've only just met."

"Yeah, but you just basically told me that you want to... to...have an affair!"

"So all I had to say was that I wanted to mess around with you and I become the most amazing woman you've ever met? That doesn't say a lot for your sex life, Kim."

"No, I mean...most women are more coy and, you know..."

"I don't do coy, and I don't play games."

Kim turned his gaze to me.

"Yes," I said, reading the question in his eyes. "She's for real." Kim's shock was a totally natural reaction. I should have been shocked, too. But I had become so accustomed to Dena's brand of insanity that it honestly didn't faze me anymore.

"Okay," Dena said, running her hands through her short dark hair. "You have my number both literally and figuratively. What's yours?"

"You mean my phone number or..."

"Who are you? What's your story?" Dena clarified.

"Right," he said grinning sheepishly. "I guess I'm sort of smart. I'm in my last year at SF State."

"What are you studying?" Dena asked.

"I'm a radio and television major with an emphasis on audio production and recording."

"Really?" Dena asked. "So what's it going to be, radio or television?"

"I'm thinking about music production. I DJ a couple nights a week now and I'm always mixing my own stuff. I think maybe I can make a real career out of it. I'm going to try anyway. Either way it's a hell of a lot of fun."

Dena threw an arm over the low back of her chair and nodded approvingly. "See, that's a conversation topic that could get us through a long dinner at a three-star restaurant."

Kim lit up and then caught sight of a man watching him from the other side of the restaurant and immediately straightened his posture. "My manager's watching me, but I'll call you tonight," he whispered. I noticed Dena didn't bother leaning back when he reached for her plate, thus causing him to "accidentally" brush her right breast. He blushed again before hurrying away under his manager's watchful eye.

"I arrived with the expectation of meeting with one incredibly beautiful woman, but here I find two!"

Dena and I both looked up to see Scott standing a few feet away. He stood with his left hand tucked away in the pocket of his dark denim jacket and the bulk of his weight on the corresponding leg, a still figure against the hustle and bustle of the sidewalk and street behind him. The passing tourists probably thought he was pausing to admire the outdoor café, but I knew he was posing for the benefit of the women in the area, and the knowledge made me queasy. Perhaps he noted my disgust because he broke into a self-conscious chuckle and strode over to our table. "Dena Lopiano," he boomed, "I haven't seen you in years."

"Yeah," Dena said wistfully, "those were great years."

Scott laughed again and sat down between the two of us. "Any chance you two would agree to a few drinks and small talk before we get down to business?" he asked hopefully.

"No," Dena and I said in unison.

"Very well." He contorted his face into an exaggerated frown before relaxing back into his trademark Rembrandt-White smile. "Here's the deal with the house. If Kane has to list it, he's going to list it for $1.75 million with the expectation of having to reduce it to as low as $1.6. Personally, I think he stands a good chance of getting the full listing price."

"Shit!" I seethed. I did some quick math in my head. I might be able to swing it if I got a really big loan from a bank at an extremely low interest rate. I gazed at my wineglass. Goodbye fine wines, hello cheap wine coolers.

"But if *you* buy it," Scott continued, "and you make an offer right now, he'll sell it to you for the original price of $980,000."

Dena and I exchanged confused looks. This was fantastic news, but it didn't make sense. "Scott, are you playing a game with me?"

"Kane is sentimental about that house. He grew up there, and when he heard his father had died, he briefly considered moving back in. But as it stands he's already living in the house he inherited from his grandparents. He doesn't want two houses and he doesn't want to be a landlord or deal with property managers. Still, he doesn't want to sell to just anyone."

"But *I'm* just anyone," I pointed out. "I've never met Kane. I have no relation to him. Nothing connects us at all."

"On the surface, you're right," Scott said. "But Kane doesn't see it that way. He knows that under normal circumstances I wouldn't give a potential buyer a night tour of a residence. And normally you wouldn't come within fifty feet of me, in the day *or* night. Hell, I haven't even been able to get you to return my calls. But then, out of the blue, Oscar calls me up and tells me he wants me to sell his place ASAP. On that same day you show up at the open house I was holding in the Marina, and I convince you to come to see Oscar's place at eight-thirty that night, the night Oscar died."

"So?" Dena asked.

"So Kane thinks that means something," Scott explained, still addressing me. "He knows you want the house, but he also thinks the house wants you."

I brought my fingers to my temples in an attempt to massage away the headache that was beginning to form there. "If I understand you correctly," I said, "you're telling me that Kane is crazy."

"Poor people are crazy, Sophie," Scott corrected. "Kane is eccentric."

"I see. Are his eccentricities ones that can be medicated?"

"Probably, although I don't think Kane approves of drugs that aren't recreational. But that's neither here nor there. What's important is that you can have the house, and you're getting it for a song—at least by San Franciscan standards."

"This is too good to be true," Dena said. She was looking at Scott, but her eyes had become so narrowed with suspicion that it was questionable if she was able to see anything beyond her own eyelashes. "There's got to be a major catch."

"A major catch?" Scott scoffed. "He wants to sell you a house for over $600,000 below market. There are militant vegetarians who would eat a truckload of Big Macs just to get a crack at the deal I'm offering you. All Kane wants from you is a one-month escrow, your word that you'll treat the house well and your commitment to become a lifetime member of the San Francisco Specter Society."

"Excuse me?" Scott had said the last part so fast that I wasn't sure I had heard him correctly. I certainly hoped I hadn't.

On the sidewalk some man was screaming obscenities, but none of us turned to see what the problem was. "It's not as bad as it sounds," Scott said in a voice that was something less than convincing. "It's a group of people who get together twice a month for about an hour or so just so they can hang out, schmooze and, um, try to talk to ghosts."

Dena burst out laughing while I tried to digest this unexpected request. "Scott," I said slowly, "please tell me this isn't a deal breaker."

"You won't have to go to every meeting," Scott quickly assured me. "Just go regularly for the first year or so and then if you can only make it to a meeting every two or three months after that I'm sure Kane will be okay with it. The group really isn't as weird as its name implies. Venus is a member and so is Kane. Even Oscar came to a few meetings, although he hasn't for a long time."

"That's what you meant when you said Oscar and you traveled in the same circles," I said slowly as I pieced everything together. "Your current circles consist of a bunch of ghost-loving freaks. Really, Scott, isn't it a little bizarre for a necrophobic to hang with people who are trying to raise the dead?"

"First of all, they're not freaks," Scott said defensively. "I'm not even convinced that all of the members believe in ghosts even though they all say they do. They just like listening to ghost *stories*. I've been to over twenty meetings with Venus and they haven't been able to channel a single disembodied spirit. Trust me, if they had, I wouldn't attend no matter how much Venus insisted. And Sophie," he paused to wave a hovering bee away from his face, "it *is* a deal breaker."

"But that's ridiculous! Why is it so important to Kane that some stranger joins his precious society?"

"I keep trying to tell you, Sophie, Kane doesn't see you as a stranger. He thinks your discovery of his father connects you in some peculiar way and he thinks…okay, try not to laugh, but he thinks that if he's going to successfully channel his parents' spirits the people who found his father right after his death need to be part of the séance."

"Really?" Dena asked, her curiosity overcoming her mirth. "Is that some kind of Wiccan rule?"

"I have no idea," Scott grumbled. "What I *do* know is that I'm stuck going to these meetings for at least another year. But really, they're not that bad," he said switching back into salesman mode. "And Enrico Risso is a member so we usually get to sample some dish that he's thinking about adding to his menu."

"Hold up." Dena's chair audibly scratched against the concrete floor as she scooted forward. "Are we talking about Enrico Risso, *the executive chef at Sassi?* The man who was just voted one of the nation's twenty best chefs in *Gourmet Magazine?*"

"The one and only."

Dena blinked and then turned to me. "I'm not saying you should join, but if you do you should invite me to one of the meetings. Enrico's risotto is enough to make you cream your panties."

Scott shot Dena a bemused smile. "You really haven't changed at all, have you?"

"Before I agree to any of this I'm going to need to have a contractor come out and look at the pipes, foundation and whatnot," I interjected. I really didn't want to dwell on Dena's panties remark.

"Naturally," Scott agreed. "You can have a contractor come out anytime. Kane's already moved all his father's things into storage so it'll be easy to check out all the floors and walls."

"He's already moved everything out?" I asked. "That was fast."

"Kane's efficient. But before you call a contractor you should take another look at the place. Make sure you really want it."

Scott said the last words suggestively, implying that I might want more than just real estate from him. I didn't. But I'll admit I was pleased to know he still desired me. It put me in a position of power, and with Scott it was always important to keep the upper hand. "When can I look at it again?"

Scott glanced at his watch. "What are you doing right now?"

After saying my goodbyes to Dena I got in my car and followed Scott to Ashbury Heights. Well, *follow* isn't really the right word because Scott got a significant early lead on me thanks to his Tango. It was the same electric vehicle George Clooney drove. Scott said he got it last Christmas—it was Venus's version of a stocking stuffer. Apparently Venus's parents owned and ran Organically Yours, the food product line that sold energy bars and whole grain cereals all over the country. That bit of information explained their entire relationship to me. Scott was a gold digger and Venus was his sugar-mommy. They were a perfect match.

So by the time I got to the house Scott had already parked and was presumably inside. I pulled my car into the driveway and climbed the steps. My hand was shaking with excitement as I pushed on the front door that was already open a crack. The place no longer smelled of Pine-Sol. The floral couch and overstuffed armchairs were gone and the beautiful mahogany bookcases were empty. It took me a moment to adjust to the change. I hadn't liked the furniture, but I didn't realize how much it had detracted from the strength of the architecture. The vaulted ceilings felt higher now and the wide, dark wood staircase had a boldness of design that I hadn't noticed before. In fact the whole house felt bolder…no, *bold* was the wrong word. Power. That was better. The house seemed to have a power all its own. Yet its power had a magnanimous quality. The ambiance of the room seemed to embrace me and despite what I had found upstairs only weeks earlier, the place made me feel safe. I almost believed that the house was going to take care of me—like a father.

Suddenly I was struck with a sense of déjà vu. I had been here, not weeks before, but years before; before I had ever heard of Oscar or even Scott.

But that was impossible. My mind had to be playing tricks on me. Yet the sense of déjà vu didn't go away and oddly enough made me want the house more than ever. It was calling to me.

And then I heard the footsteps of my father. He was walking through the dining room toward the living room. But that, too, was impossible. I turned my head in the direction of the sound.

It definitely wasn't my father. Scott was standing next to a guy with an army-camouflage T-shirt and brownish-red hair cut close to his scalp. He was wearing rubber-soled sneakers, which explained why I had only heard the one set of footsteps.

"Sophie, this is Kane," Scott said, patting the man on the back.

I smiled and shook his hand. "I didn't know you were going to be here."

"And I didn't know *you* were going to be here," he said. "Seems fate wanted us to meet. More proof that this is all meant to be, don't you think?"

"Sure." I struggled to keep the sarcasm out of my voice. I was one of those people who firmly believed in coincidences.

I started to pull my hand away, but Kane held on to it firmly. His expression had become serious and I found myself unable to break eye contact. "Do you feel anything?"

"Umm…the palm of your hand?" I said, unsure if he was playing some kind of game with me.

Something crossed Kane's face. I couldn't read the emotion, but I had a feeling it wasn't a good one. But before I had a chance to come up with a better answer he released me and eased his mouth into a lazy grin. "Guess my parents aren't around right now. But they'll make an appearance soon. I'm sure of it."

"Right, well, if I see them I'll be sure to let you know," I assured him.

"So there you have it," Scott said with what seemed to be forced enthusiasm. "Sophie's the person you should sell to. Not only is she a believer, but she's willing to notify you if she makes contact."

What the hell was he talking about? But one look from Scott told me that if I wanted the house I'd be wise to play along—at least for a while. I swallowed and stepped around them into the formal dining room. "This really is a great property." I flicked on the light switch and watched the chandelier illuminate.

"You still want it?" Scott asked hopefully.

"I'm going to do a walk-through," I said absently as I furnished the room in my mind. "But yeah, I want it. I'll have a contractor out here in the next few days."

Kane walked over to one of the windows and peered out into the street. "You should move in soon, before escrow closes."

I did a quick double take. "Um, wouldn't that sort of complicate things?"

"I have a sense about you, Sophie," Kane said. "I do *think* you'll treat this house with the care it deserves. I just have to be sure of that."

"What are you suggesting?"

"Yeah," Scott said, suddenly uncertain, "What *are* you suggesting, Kane?"

"Just one more stipulation written into the escrow agreement. Nothing major, but I think it would be a good idea if you stayed here during that month that we wait for escrow to close. If you don't treat the house with respect I'd like to have the option to back out of the arrangement."

I opened my mouth and then closed it before slamming the back of my hand against Scott's arm. "You knew about this, didn't you! You just brought me here to fuck with me!"

I whirled around and started for the door. Scott reached out and held me back and I made a halfhearted attempt to pull away, but I was afraid that if I put too much effort into fighting him I wouldn't have enough strength left to hold back the tears. So I just stood there, stoically facing the door.

"Sophie," Scott said urgently, "no one is fucking with you...not that I wouldn't like—"

"Don't even start!" I snapped.

"Right, what I meant was that everyone here is serious about the sale, *right, Kane?*" he said, pronouncing his question like a warning. "You don't expect Sophie to agree to move in here and go through all the trouble and stress of escrow knowing that you could call the whole thing off and throw her out at any moment for something as ambiguous as her not *respecting* the place. That would be crazy and we all know you're not crazy. You're a businessman. A reasonable businessman."

I heard the house exhale in a roar as hot air rushed through the vents. Central heating. Was there anything that this place didn't have? I imagined myself standing up against those vents on the coldest of days, letting the air press against my feet and ankles until they prickled from the heat. Somehow I had to make this work.

"I'm sorry you think I'm being unreasonable," Kane said, seemingly nonplussed. "I certainly don't want you to think I'm not earnest in my intent to sell to you. How about this, we'll let an attorney find a word that's more to your liking than *respecting.* I'll pay for all the utilities during that month…in fact, why don't we cut escrow in half and make it two weeks. And we'll put in a clause stating that if I do put an end to our deal before escrow closes I'll have to pay you…how about twenty grand? That should cover the rent for your apartment for almost a year, right?"

Now I did turn around, but for the life of me I couldn't remember how to speak.

Scott had no such problem. "Yeah," he said, his voice an octave higher than normal, "that'll work."

Kane beamed. "Great! Then get the contractor out here so you can start moving in."

"I feel there has to be a catch," I choked out.

Kane laughed. It was the least contagious laugh in the world. "Sophie," he said, "I may be a bit different, but I'm not so peculiar that I relish the idea of giving huge amounts of money away at the drop of a hat. If I thought there was a good chance that I would need to pay you the $20,000 I wouldn't be making the offer. But this was once my mother's house. It was her dream home. I just need to be assured that whoever ends up here will love it the way she did and not just flip it the moment the market improves. Can you understand that?"

No. I didn't understand anything about Kane. But how could I say no to this? "When's the first Specter Society meeting?" I asked.

Kane's grin widened. "In three weeks," Kane said. "Why don't we have it here? It could be your first social gathering in your new home." Kane ran his hands along the wall with the gentleness that one usually reserves for a lover. "It would be a great way for you to introduce yourself to all the members…and to anything else that might make an appearance."

Any*thing* else. I understood his meaning, but it didn't bother me. It was, after all, the most conventional thing he had said in the five minutes I had known him. "I'm going to want my own lawyer to go through this escrow agreement with a fine-toothed comb," I said.

"Of course, Sophie," Kane said. "Whatever it takes to get you to trust me."

I tried not to smile. I'd sooner trust my ex-husband. But if a lawyer gave me a thumbs-up it really was a spectacular deal. If I could get a contractor and a lawyer to work with me right away, I might be able to start the escrow process in about two weeks, which meant that in four weeks I would either get a fantastic house well below market or I would get $20,000.

What did I have to lose?

4

Dinner parties would be so much more fun if you were allowed to actually *throw* your dinner at the guests!
——*The Lighter Side of Death*

I DIDN'T WASTE A MOMENT. I HAD A CONTRACTOR COME OUT TO THE HOUSE and a lawyer storm Scott's office. And as soon as I was told that both the house and the escrow agreement were in good condition I signed on the dotted line. I had moved over the furniture from my apartment, and although many of the pieces didn't really suit the new space at least they were mine. In a fit of optimism, I had put the bulk of my belongings in boxes and brought them over, as well.

During the first week of escrow Kane had come over for a visit, and while he seemed slightly disappointed that I hadn't heard any thumps in the night, he did praise the passion I had for the house. I was just one week away from officially owning my own home, and now I was preparing to pay for it. Not with money, but with a combination of time and lies; time that I would spend at my first Specter Society meeting and lies that I would tell to convince my guests and fellow members that I desired their company. Scott had explained to me that if I wanted escrow to go through I had to pretend to believe in ghosts and the mystical power of the séances that supposedly called them to this world. It was a stupid but acceptable compromise of my integrity.

Of course the gathering required some planning and for that I had called in the big guns—or to be more accurate, *the* big gun, my sister and special-event-coordinator-extraordinaire, Leah. At my request she had spent most of the afternoon (and the better part of the past week) setting up for the séance I would be holding that evening. All my unpacked boxes had been moved into the bedrooms and the garage and there was a rented round table in the middle of the living room covered with a white linen tablecloth. In its center were three thick beeswax candles that Leah had strong-armed me into buying despite their ridiculously high price point. And in front of ten antique wood dining chairs there were metal place-card holders molded into the shape of fallen leaves. Many of the names they held were foreign to me and the few that I knew— Venus, Scott and Kane—didn't exactly make me feel warm and fuzzy. Enrico was the only person I was looking forward to meeting. I had spoken to him on the phone several times in the last few days, and now Leah and I were waiting for him to arrive before the others, with trays of delicacies that would undoubtedly make the rest of the evening a bit more tolerable.

Mr. Katz let out a mew of protest as Leah removed him from one of the chairs and dropped him unceremoniously on the floor.

"Hey, be careful with my baby," I admonished.

"The only baby here is sitting on the couch," she said distractedly as she rearranged the candles one more time, pulling at their wicks until they stood up like little soldiers trying to impress a drill sergeant. Of course she was referring to her two-year-old son, Jack, who was at that moment quietly watching her every move. It was unclear to me if his gaze was one of admiration or calculation. His pudgy little hands looked innocent enough while they rested on his lap, but they had often been used as the instruments of destruction and torture, like the time he had tried to clean my cat with Clorox or when he pulled out a fistful of hair from his swim instructor's chest.

"It's a shame I can't stay for the actual event," Leah said, although we both knew she was grateful for the exclusion. Scott had explained that the number of people in attendance had to be an even number and if Leah took part in the proceedings there would be eleven of us. Leah couldn't have handled the quiet meditative atmosphere of a séance anyway. We were both sure that spirits could not be summoned, which meant that any communication with the dead would be imaginary. The imaginings of other people cannot be monitored or predicted and Leah didn't like events that she couldn't control.

"At least you'll get to taste the appetizers. Enrico promised me he'd make enough so that you could bring a few home with you."

"Sweet of him." She glanced at the metal hands of my walnut-finished clock and the smooth skin between her eyebrows wrinkled in disapproval. "He should have been here by now. We want to make sure that we have time to clean up after any last-minute preparations before the guests arrive. Nothing undermines a party as quickly as a messy kitchen."

Clearly the parties Leah attended were a lot tamer than the ones I went to. "I'm sure he'll be here soon," I said sweetly.

"Mmm, well, since we can't do anything else until he arrives, let me take this moment to give you your housewarming gift."

"Housewarming gift?" I repeated. Visions of Pottery Barn throw pillows danced in my head.

She grinned and crossed to the large UPS box she had

placed on my window seat. Full of props and decorative items upon her arrival, I had assumed it was now empty. But from it she pulled out a carefully wrapped large rectangular gift.

The paper was a pale gold and gleamed in the dwindling light coming from the window. I found a weak spot and pierced the paper with my fingernail then tore into the wrapping. Shreds of gold fell to the floor like oversize confetti.

And when the covering was gone I was left with a black-and-white photograph of myself as a little girl. My hair was the same unruly challenge it was now and my features hadn't changed much, but the eyes of the child-me lacked the cynical skepticism that I had cultivated over the years. It was me in my own age of innocence. My arms were wrapped around the neck of the man who gave me that hair. His own curls were cut short and a cluster of them embraced his chin in a well-trimmed beard.

"Thank you. I forgot about this picture," I whispered, although this very photo had graced our mother's dresser for at least ten years. "I'll have to find a good place for it." I turned it over and touched the cool black metal that held the photo in place. A silver wire stretched from one side to the other, waiting to be draped over a nail.

"There, over the side table with the other pictures," Leah said without hesitation.

I looked at the newly mounted images on the wall. There was a small picture of a blue jay swooping down to snatch a peanut out of my friend Mary Ann's hand. Next to that a framed newspaper article, the first critical review my work had ever received. I had highlighted the words *highly enjoyable* and then blacked out *but at times trite.* Then the nighttime picture Dena had taken of our friend Marcus, his hand extended up into the air so that it looked like he held the moon in the sky. There was also a picture of Leah holding Jack shortly after his birth. In that picture my mother bent over the swaddled infant, her lips shaped into an exaggerated kiss. But all these people were alive. Even the review referred to a book that I still had access to. What I held in my hand was a tribute to a man who was gone. It felt like the Sophie-child in the picture was laughing at me, saying, "Remember this? Remember what it was like to touch him? Remember what it was like to feel safe?"

I did remember, and it made me heart-achingly sad and I had no desire to hang my grief on my living-room wall.

Leah waited a respectable amount of time for me to come up with an excuse for why the picture shouldn't be placed with the others before taking it from me and holding it up above the fireplace. "Fine, we'll put it here. He's been gone for twelve years, Sophie. It's time you said goodbye to the man and hello to your memories. Besides," she glanced at the staircase and pressed her full lips together as if working out some complicated equation, "he belongs here. I don't know why, but it just feels like some part of him should be here."

"Some part of him?" I repeated. "That sounds like the premise of some part of a poltergeist movie."

"Not literally a part of his body, but this." She pressed the picture against the wall and admired it. "This belongs here."

"I'll think about it."

"There's nothing to think about. Give me a hammer and a couple of nails."

"I only have one left," I said. "Wait 'til I go to the hardware store later this week. You know how hard it is to hang a picture straight with just one nail."

"Well, we'll just have to try to make it work. Bring me the one nail."

I suppressed a couple of swear words and reluctantly brought her what she asked for. I turned away as the hammer struck the nail and reached for my cell phone. Leah was right about one thing; Enrico should have been here by now. He picked up on the second ring.

"Yes?"

It took me a second to respond. Enrico had always been warm on the phone and the question he had used to replace a greeting jarred me. "Enrico?"

"Yes?" he said again, this time with even less patience. Behind me Leah was banging the hammer in a quick but steady rhythm.

"Um, it's Sophie Katz. I was just wondering if you were on your way?"

"What? Is it so late? I did not realize." I could hear his irritation, but whether it was directed at me, himself or something else was anybody's guess.

"Sooo, are you? On your way, I mean?" I didn't want to be pushy, but he was only one of nine people coming over and the only food I had in the house was made by Kellogg's.

"Yes, I come. Things have happened that are not so good, but still, I come."

The pounding of the hammer stopped and I turned to see Leah's handiwork. The frame was crooked, not horribly, but enough that anyone looking at it would note the imperfection. Last time I had spoken to Enrico his English had been similarly imperfect, but now it was considerably worse. Was he drunk? Tired? Or were the "things that had happened" so disconcerting that he had literally forgotten how to speak English? "Enrico, is everything okay?"

"No, everything is not okay. Today I am…how do you say…I am haunted. Yes, this is right, I am being haunted by the past." His voice sounded weak and far away. He must have been speaking into the phone, but I had a feeling that he was really talking to himself.

"Uh-huh…so when you say haunted, do you mean that

something you've done has come back to haunt you? Or do you mean that you've been visited by Casper or one of his not-so-friendly associates?"

"Casper? The cartoon character? Are you mocking me?"

"I'm sorry," I said quickly. "That was insensitive."

"What—? But...you fucking bitch!"

"*Excuse me?* That was totally uncalled for!" I waited for Enrico to explain himself, but instead he must have thrown the phone down on the ground. I heard it clatter against a hard surface and in the background I thought I heard another noise—a squawking, like the sound of a distressed bird. "Enrico?" I yelled. "Are you still there? You owe me an apology!"

But he said nothing. I heard another squawk, a loud thump and then the line went dead. "He hung up on me!" I snapped.

"Well, what did you expect?" Leah shrugged and adjusted the frame once again. It was still crooked, but now it leaned toward the left rather than the right. "I heard your end of the conversation, Sophie. You were flippant with him."

"I was trying to engage him in friendly banter! And he didn't just hang up on me, he also called me a fucking bitch!"

"That's extreme," she admitted. "But...well, he is a chef. You know how they are—artistic temperaments and all."

"So what are you saying? That it's okay to call women you've never met before bitches as long as you can make a good pâté?"

"No, of course not, but— Where's Jack?" We both looked at the empty couch. I immediately scanned the room for Mr. Katz and sighed in relief when I spotted him on the window seat. At that moment Jack came toddling out of the bathroom, buoyant and seemingly unharmed. "Mommy, Mommy! Auntie Sophie has sandbox and she hides chocolate in it!"

"A sandbox?" Leah threw me a questioning look.

"Um, noooo, but I do keep Mr. Katz's litter box in there."

Jack's mouth spread out into what might actually have been a shit-eating grin.

"Call poison control!" Leah snapped.

"But there's nothing in his teeth," I pointed out.

"I save it," Jack explained, still beaming. "See, I save for dessert." His little fist removed and offered a cat turd to Leah, who stumbled back, aghast.

"Put it back," she screeched, "before you get some kind of weird cat disease!" She grabbed his arm and dragged him back into the bathroom, screaming something incomprehensible about antibacterial soap. I went to the doorway and watched her scrub his hands as he struggled to free himself.

"What if Enrico doesn't show up?" I asked.

"Waiters on Wheels," Leah said, too busy to look at me while she spoke. "Call and have them deliver appetizers from Sassi. But call him back first and try to smooth things over. Apologize to him for being insolent."

"Are you kidding me? He called me a fucking bitch!"

Jack giggled and jumped up and down. "Auntie Sophie has potty mouth!"

"Oh, yeah?" I said. "Well, I'm not the one who tried to eat out of a litter box."

"That's it, we're leaving." Leah swooped Jack up in her arms and headed for the door, pausing briefly to retrieve her jacket and purse from my coatrack.

"Don't go," I pleaded. "If Enrico doesn't come there will only be nine of us and we need ten. You could be part of this."

"Thanks, but no thanks. Why don't you call Mary Ann, I'm sure she'll come."

"Mary Ann's in Italy. She scored a killer assistant makeup artist job for Milan's Fashion week and when she's done with that she's going to take a few extra weeks to do some Cathedral hopping around Europe. You, on the other hand, are right here. Come on, Leah, it could be fun."

"Sophie, I love you, but I absolutely refuse to make merry with a bunch of people at a séance."

"Fine, but if they call up the ghost of Emily Post you'll be sorry!"

"Emily Post isn't dead," Leah yelled over her shoulder as she walked out.

I watched her carry my nephew down the stairs like a sack of potatoes. As a general rule I preferred to limit my time with the two of them to a couple of hours a week, but now I would have done almost anything to get Leah to stay. Bad things happened in threes, the unpleasantness exponentially increasing in severity. I was counting Enrico's obscenities as one and I had a horrible feeling that bad thing two and three were going to pop up before the day was done.

I tried to call Enrico back, but all I got was the steady and grating pulse of a busy signal. He had seemed so normal when we talked on other occasions, but apparently he had a dark side. I ordered food from his restaurant and it was delivered within an hour. After setting it up there was nothing to do but sit on the window seat and watch the colors of a sunset try to struggle through the dense fog. When the sky finally went black my doorbell rang. I hadn't seen anyone walk up the steps. At that time I had been focused on my cat curled up on my lap. I pushed him off and he repaid me by dragging the tips of his claws across my thighs. It was exactly six-thirty. Whoever had come was punctual.

I opened the door unsure if I was going to be greeted by Kane, Scott, Venus or a stranger. But all those predictions were wrong. The man in front of me wasn't Kane or Scott, but I did know him. His pointed goatee and piercing eyes had made an impression on me years ago.

"Jason Beck," I exclaimed. "What are you doing here?"

Dena had so many exes it was hard to keep track of them all, but Jason had been more memorable than most. Perhaps it was his penchant for velvet (right now he wore velvet jeans and an open, untucked white dress shirt over a T-shirt that read Chaos *Rules*. But as original as his look was, it was his belief in vampires that had held my attention. Jason thought that Anne Rice was not a novelist but a biographer, and that Count Dracula was a lot more than a dead SOB who had earned himself a dubious place in Transylvanian folklore.

"You're the Sophie who's buying this house?" he asked, sounding just as surprised as I was.

I looked past him at the empty sidewalk and the silent street and tried to find the logic in our meeting. "You didn't know I lived here?" I asked. "You came—to visit the house?"

"I came for the Specter Society meeting."

Of course. I nearly slapped my forehead in a vaudeville demonstration of my own idiocy. "They told me a Jason was coming," I said. "I have your name on a place card, but I would never have guessed it was you."

"And I never could have guessed that you would be hosting a séance. You're not a believer."

I smiled wryly. "You want to know if I've ditched my…what did you call it? Oh, right, my spiritually closed-minded, excessively materialistic world view."

Jason smiled and cocked his head to the side. "Have you?"

"It's a long story," I hedged. Scott had insisted that all of the members of the group must think that I'm a believer, but Jason had come through for me in the past, and despite our years of separation I counted him as a friend. I didn't lie to my friends.

I ushered him inside. He walked to the center of my living room and stared at the table. A cold breeze tickled the back of my neck, and I felt my skin prickle with goose bumps. For a second I thought the temperature had dropped for no reason, but that of course was not the case. I had been so overwhelmed by the surprise of Jason that I had forgotten to close the door behind him. I turned to do so, but my doorway was no longer empty. Framed by the streetlight was a character from the musical *Hair.* At least that's how she appeared to me. Her mountains of untamed curls fell to her waist and her rainbow rayon skirt grazed her ankles, revealing Birkenstocks and pink toenails.

"I'm Amelia," she said, not waiting for my question, and without warning pulled me into a hearty embrace and pressed her lips against my cheek. "Thank you so much for inviting us into your home!" she gushed, then broke away and skipped to where Jason stood. She pressed herself into his back and encircled his waist with her arms. "Whoa, this is one of the fanciest séance tables I have ever seen! Who are we trying to summon? Rockefeller?"

"My sister helped me put this together."

"Leah," Jason said and I saw the spark of memory twinkle in his eyes. He had never met Leah, but had heard about her from both me and Dena. More to the point, he had heard tales of her devious offspring.

I closed the door and led them to the food and wine. Before I had even finished pouring the first glass the doorbell rang again. I excused myself and went to welcome my next visitor. This time it was Venus, Scott and Kane. Venus was boldly ignoring the weather by going coatless in a knee-length pencil skirt and an asymmetrical sleeveless top made of a material that resembled crinkly paper. Her hair was pulled into the same low ponytail she had worn on our first meeting. Kane was less adventurous in chinos and a wool sweater that had the look of being handmade. Scott looked like Scott—well dressed, hair purposely and attractively disheveled, an impish smile. Later I would notice that he only aimed his smile in my direction when Venus had her back to him.

It was Venus who said hello first as she stepped inside, letting her massive presence ooze into every corner of my home until the room was so full of her that I wondered if there would be enough space for the rest of us. She raised her arms, her fingertips touching like a ballerina preparing to dance. She then gracefully spread her arms wide, inhaling deeply. But that's where the dance ended. She coughed and brought her hands to her flat chest. "This is all wrong."

"What's wrong?" Kane asked anxiously. But Scott didn't seem perturbed by her announcement at all. If anything he looked bored.

"The arrangement of the furniture," she explained. "The feng shui—it's not right."

"My mother never decorated in accordance to feng shui," Kane snapped. "And she still felt the spirits."

"But she didn't *see* them," Venus said evenly. "She didn't know how to direct the energy of the house."

"There were reasons why the spirits couldn't come to my mother." Kane stepped in front of Venus, invading her personal space. "But those reasons had nothing to do with interior decorating. Feng shui means nothing to those in the world beyond."

A light laugh escaped her lips. "Kane," she said, cupping his chin with her workmanlike hand. "You are not an expert in these matters. You can barely summon your own dog, let alone a ghost."

Kane didn't move and for a second I thought that Venus might be in danger. I shot a questioning look at Scott. He no longer looked bored, but neither did he seem to have any intention of intervening.

But then Kane stepped back, just out of her reach. They continued to stare at one another, not speaking. From the dining room I could hear Amelia's cheerful chatter, and then she rushed into the room, her eyes dancing with a vivacious energy that seemed incongruous with the mood of the other guests. "Hello!" Her salutation echoed in the silent room. Then she went around to each of the three new arrivals and gave Kane and Scott the same hug and kiss she had given me. Kane tolerated this with what appeared to be strained patience, but Scott clearly enjoyed the close female contact and their hug lasted a half a minute too long. It was Amelia who broke away first. She then smiled nervously at Venus. "Did you get a load of that séance table?" she asked, her joviality suddenly seeming a little forced. "Those candles are beeswax, Venus. I haven't seen anything this fancy since the last time *you* hosted an event."

"You weren't at the last event I hosted," Venus said.

"No, but I was at the one before that." She then turned toward the male guests. "Come to the dining room. Enrico outdid himself this time." She paused right before disappearing back into the dining room and tilted her head in my direction. "Where is Enrico anyway? Did he go out for the perfect wine or something?"

I winced. I hadn't yet told them that while the food was from Enrico's restaurant it wasn't actually made by Enrico. I wasn't entirely clear on where I stood with Kane, but I was pretty sure that I was on Venus's shit list. If she found out that Enrico and I had exchanged words she would blame me for his absence, even if I was the one in the right.

But before I could figure out how to address the situation the doorbell rang again. I sent up a quick silent prayer that it was Enrico, but to my disappointment it was a family of three. The man introduced himself as Al and the woman and Goth teenage boy as his wife, Lorna, and son, Zach. Three more names from my place cards.

They were a family, but as far as I could tell the only thing that unified them was proximity. The man was a clean-cut blonde with thinning hair. He wore a polo shirt and chinos and he appeared more resigned than happy to be there. His son was a whole other story. His hair, his clothes, his nails, all colored black. Even his eyes were outlined with a harsh black eyeliner, made all the more dramatic by his white powdered face. Around his neck he wore a velvet ribbon choker, and I was tempted to reach out and see if its unraveling would result in decapitation.

But it was the woman who interested me. Like her husband, she wore chinos and her cotton shirt was a pale pink. Her hair was a graying brown and cut neatly in a style that you would expect to see on the stereotypical suburban homemaker. Totally normal, yet, on her, the outfit, the haircut, even the mild-mannered smile, it all seemed like a costume: her hair too thick for such a neat cut where it should have been long and unruly, her skin too olive for the light-colored clothing, the determination in her eyes too strong to gel with the timid pink of her lip gloss.

But I didn't say any of that. Instead I just ushered them in and closed the door behind them. Jason reentered the living room, a glass of red wine in his hand. "Looks like almost everybody's here," he said. "As soon as Enrico shows up we'll have ten."

This was the time to tell them. Venus already suspected something was amiss. I could tell by the way she was looking at me, her stare hinting at an underlying hostility.

I cleared my throat and went to the place card that bore Enrico's name, fondling it like it had some kind of voodoo power that could call him forth. But of course that didn't work. "I don't think Enrico is coming," I finally said.

"Not coming?" Scott asked. "But hasn't he already been here? Isn't he the one who brought the food?"

"Um, no. I ordered the food from his restaurant. See, I

talked to him earlier today and he seemed a little...out of sorts."

"How so?" Venus lowered herself onto my armchair with practiced casualness.

"He said he was, um, haunted."

"Haunted!" Kane was immediately by my side, encasing both my hands in his. "Did he see something? Was he visited?"

"I...I don't know. He just said he was haunted and that things were not so good."

"Whoa, okay, this is really heavy," Amelia said, taking a moment to examine each of our faces to make sure we all shared her sentiment. "Maybe he summoned something and he can't make it go away. Maybe we should take this party to him and see if we can be of help."

There was a chorus of protests although Kane and Scott both remained silent.

"I know Enrico better than the rest of you," Venus said, her eyes still on me. "If he wanted us in his home he would have told us to come."

"But maybe he didn't think we'd accept the invitation," Kane offered. "After all, he must know that some of us blame him for Maria's departure from the group."

"I didn't say he would have invited us," Venus said evenly. "I said he would have *told us* to come. There is a very big difference. Enrico may or may not have been aware of your feelings, Kane, and they are *your* feelings, but whether he was aware of them or not he would have still expected us to yield to his celebrity."

"He's a chef!" Amelia said with a laugh. "Not a movie star."

"I think people in San Francisco like chefs more than movie stars. They're more real," Zach said. It was the first thing I'd heard him say and his voice sounded too young and innocent for his somber attire. I tried to get a sense of his age. It was hard to gauge considering all the white powder covering his face, but my guess was that he was around fifteen.

"Maybe we should just give him some space," Lorna said softly. "Of course, there's still the problem of our number. Someone will have to leave."

Lorna leaned over and put a hand on Al's knee. "I know you don't really want to be here, darling. Why don't you go get a beer at that pub you used to go to? The one around the corner. What's its name again?"

"Jax, but I'm not going anywhere," Al said shortly.

"But I just thought…"

"I know what you thought, but you were wrong," he snapped. "Now is someone else going to leave or are we going to call this damn thing off?"

Lorna seemed to shrink into herself and Zach scowled at his father.

"I guess I could—" Amelia began, but she was interrupted by the doorbell. "Maybe it's Enrico!" she exclaimed and rushed to see.

When she opened the door she revealed a woman dressed head to toe in Calvin Klein with her hair cut in a severe, short style. She peeled off her overcoat and threw it into Amelia's unexpecting arms. "Tell Enrico I'm here."

"Maria," Kane said in a soft voice.

She blinked at the sound of her name and grabbed onto the door frame as if she expected someone to try to push her out. "Whatever you're going to say about numerology or whatnot just…just save it," she said. "I'm giving him our condo, our house in Tuscany, I'm even giving him the damned parrot, but I'll be damned if I'm going to give him my friends." She glared at the occupants of the room. "You're supposed to be *my* friends! *I'm* the true believer, not that fat, self-important, fet-tuccini-eating snob! How could you not invite me to this?"

"Some of us wanted to," Kane whispered, then sent a scathing look at Venus who stared blankly back.

"Enrico's a no-show, Maria," Amelia said, struggling to give her a welcoming hug while holding her coat. "He's being haunted."

"Is that what he told you?" Maria said with a bitter laugh. "The only thing haunting that man is the last review he got from Michael Bauer. Did you read it? Three and a half stars. Not four, three and a half. That's why he's not here. The bastard is sulking, probably teaching that bird how to destroy a newspaper clipping."

"That shouldn't take a lot of training," Scott said, somewhat bemused.

"I see that the table is all set up," Maria noted. "Can we start this then? Or are you afraid I'll taint the proceedings with my bitterness?"

"Nothing wrong with bitterness," Scott said. "Just look what it does for chocolate, right, Soapy?" As soon as he said it you could see the regret spread across his features. It was as blatant as Venus's scowl.

"Soapy," she said slowly. "How adorable. Don't you think it's adorable, Kane?"

"We'd love it if you'd join us," Kane said, directing his comments to Maria and ignoring Venus. "All that matters is belief."

"And numbers," Jason added, perhaps a bit sarcastically. "And candles and colors and fucking feng shui."

"Feng shui has nothing to do with any of this!" Kane snapped.

"Hey, guys, remember Sophie got white candles so if this is going to work we're all going to have to get in a peaceful state of mind!" Amelia chimed in. "At this rate we're going to have to go out and buy some pink candles just so we can manage *that*, right, Sophie?"

"The pink candles are lame," Zach sighed. "They never work."

I raised my fingers to my temples. I had no idea what any of these people were talking about. Maria was Enrico's ex, that much I understood. I also understood that Enrico had a parrot and Venus didn't like me, but I was beginning to suspect that Venus disliked pretty much everybody. Other than that, I had no idea what was going on.

"I suggest we skip the meal and get right to the séance," Venus said, staring at Scott. "Unless you would like some more time to chitchat with your Soapy."

"I'm cool with skipping the meal," he replied meekly. "It's hard for me to think about food when I'm with you anyway, sweetie. All I can focus on is how flat-out gorgeous you are."

Jason started to laugh, but managed to silence himself before Venus had a chance to whack him over the head with one of my candlesticks.

"Sophie," Kane said, "you are the official host of this event and it sounds as if you bought the food yourself. Are you all right with our skipping the meal?"

"Absolutely, no problem at all." I would have paid double the amount of the meal's cost if it meant that I could have these people out of my house any more quickly.

"Well, I'm for it," Zach said. "I think we'd all be better off talking to the dead than to each other."

"Wise man," Jason muttered, taking a seat next to the boy.

"I'm taking Enrico's chair," Maria declared.

We all took a seat and Venus announced that she was the medium. She looked at me, daring me to argue, but I didn't. Let Venus call up her demons, I just wanted to get the whole thing over with.

Venus picked up one of the candles and held it up for everyone's inspection. "As noted, all of the candles are white," she said. "White symbolizes peace. Before I light them I will pass each candle around the table and when you hold it in your hands you must charge that candle. Visualize its power; visualize peaceful smoke curling from its wick, a warm peaceful glow emanating from it."

She passed the first two candles to the left and one to the right. I shot Scott a look, but for once he wouldn't meet my eyes. I had a feeling that he was suppressing a laugh.

Jason and Al looked equally skeptical. It was only Amelia, Lorna, Kane and Venus who appeared to be clearly enrapt. Zach's expression remained unreadable under the white powder and Maria was still too angry to convey a different emotion. I let the first two candles pass from my hands without a second thought. But when my palms pressed against the third candle, thicker and heavier than its companions, I found myself wanting to follow Venus's instructions. Not because I believed it would do any good, but because it was fun. I was hosting this damn thing so I might as well do it right. But the candle didn't look like an instrument of peace. It was made of beeswax, for God's sake. Bees are not peaceful. I passed the candle to Maria. Perhaps she would be able to charge it for both of us. Then again, when you consider her state of mind, I might have more luck finding peace in the Middle East.

When all the candles had been "charged" Venus lit each of them. She left the table long enough to turn off the other lights in the living room then returned to her seat.

"Join hands," she instructed. "Now, breathe. In through your nose, out through your mouth. Clear your mind of everything. Absorb the peace of the candles."

I did as Venus asked and watched the shadows cast by the flames alter the appearance of my guests. Zach's powdered white face, which only moments ago had seemed humorously overdone, now looked preternatural and shocking. Lorna's dark circles disappeared and the light reflected in her eyes seemed to illuminate an emotion that I hadn't noted before. Determination? Desperation? It was impossible to say. Kane, on the other hand, was easy to read. His breaths were deep and resonating, but he was not calm. No, Kane's excitement was mounting with each second.

"Our beloved Andrea," Venus began after several minutes had passed, "we ask that you commune with us and move among us."

None of us said a word as we waited for some kind of response. I didn't know who Andrea was. I had thought that we were going to try to call Oscar back, but the surprise didn't bother me. She could have tried to call Elvis back for all the good it was going to do us.

Of course, Andrea didn't make an appearance, so Venus repeated her request again and again. Eventually she rephrased the question, asking the spirit to rap once if she was among us. She was answered with silence. The wax from the candles dripped down in little molded teardrops, reminding all of us of the painfully slow movement of time. Kane's mouth turned down with frustration. His eyes met mine and I realized that without speaking he was talking to me, trying to convey some kind of message that I could not decipher. An inexplicable chill ran up my spine and I felt an ache in my chest, dull and fleeting as it was. And then there was warmth, comfort and for a second I felt the peace that Venus had tried to get me to visualize.

"Say goodbye."

My breath caught and I looked to Maria and then to Zach to see which of them had just spoken. But both of them were looking at the candles, distracted and oblivious to my change in mood.

"This isn't working," Venus said with a sigh. "Someone blow out the candles."

"We're giving up?" Lorna asked. "But we've only just begun! We could at least try to call Deb!"

"If this was going to work there would have been some kind of sign by now. Time is not the problem." Venus looked pointedly at me as if to silently say that the problem lay with me, but I was too discombobulated to care about Venus's deference of blame. I was still trying to figure out who had spoken before. Kane? Scott? Amelia? And then another disturbing realization hit me. I didn't know if it had been a woman or a man who had spoken. The words had been completely clear, but the voice that said them had been completely abstract. What was that about? Fifty million questions were swirling around in my head and yet those questions didn't make any sense even to me—and I was the one forming them! I gently touched my hand to my heart where I had felt that dull ache only moments before. The ache was gone, replaced with a rapid beating.

"Sophie, what is it?" Kane was leaning across the table, agitation gleaming in his eyes. "Did you feel something?"

The entire room fell silent as everyone focused on me, waiting for me to give them some kind of hope that their séance hadn't been a complete waste of time.

"I didn't feel anything," I lied. "Just a little heartburn. I ate a lot of spicy food for lunch."

A cloud of disappointment descended on the group, but I didn't care. I had much bigger problems. After all, I was beginning to suspect that I might actually be losing my mind.

5

Life is like a box of chocolate, and I'm allergic.
—*The Lighter Side of Death*

have to. Once it was decided that the séance was a failure everyone left with the speed and enthusiasm of an audience who had just sat through a bad three-hour movie. Jason took the time to give me his number so we could "get together for coffee sometime." Kane was the only one who lingered. He kept pestering me with questions about why I thought the séance didn't work and if I knew who the disbeliever in the group was. He even asked me if I thought it would have helped to have red candles since it was Andrea's favorite color. Like I was some kind of expert on all this. I didn't say so, but I was pretty sure that the séance failed because séances don't work and ghosts don't exist.

But what about those words:

Say goodbye.

But I didn't tell Kane about that and eventually he left, too, leaving me alone in my new house. It was just as well, Anatoly was supposed to come over later. I hadn't asked him to move in yet—I had decided to wait until after escrow closed, but still, that didn't mean he couldn't help me keep the bed warm. And he could also distract me from what had turned into a rather disturbing evening.

Now alone, I turned on all the lights in every room and tried to focus on the more mundane aspects of life. I desperately needed to do laundry, but in order to physically reach my washer I'd have to relocate several heavy boxes. Then there were the boxes in the garage. Normally I would just leave those there and park my car on the street until I had a little more energy, but now I had Venus to consider. I knew from experience that it was impossible to be with Scott and not see other women as threats, fidelity not being his strong suit. Now Venus knew that Scott had been with me, after dark, in a house that he had expected to be empty, and to make matters worse he had called me Soapy right in front of her. Add that to the fact that she was obviously completely out of her mind, and I had to conclude that parking my car on the street might lead to a few slashed tires.

So when Anatoly finally showed up at 10:30 p.m. with his sexy half smile and a bottle of Merlot I was sweaty, exhausted and doggedly filling my living room with all my packed-up odds and ends.

"Interesting decorating choice," he said as he navigated through a field of brown boxes with cryptic labels such as "Knickknacks" and "Miscellaneous."

"I don't know how I managed to collect so much stuff," I said, wiping my hands on my clothes before leaning in for my kiss.

"Why did you move everything all at once? You still have your apartment until the end of next month. Why didn't you take a little at a time?"

"I don't know, anxious to get started, I guess."

"Yes, you were quick to pack," Anatoly acknowledged, taking in the scene. "It's the unpacking that seems to have slowed you down." He threw his jacket over one of the boxes and then found his way to an empty chair. "Is that because this isn't your place yet?"

"Don't be ridiculous, of course it's my place. I signed the papers."

"For an escrow that won't go through for another week, if at all. If you ask me, $20,000 is worth showing your new residence a lot of disrespect."

"But I'm getting the house for hundreds of thousands of dollars below market, so it's not like six of one, half dozen of the other," I pointed out.

"Has Kane even transferred the utilities over to you yet?"

I swallowed and looked away. "He's insisting on paying them until escrow goes through, but that doesn't mean…"

"Sophie, you're practically squatting."

"Are you purposely trying to piss me off or do you really not get it?" I snapped. "I don't want his $20,000. This is my house! I have always wanted to live here and now I finally do!"

"'Always?'" Anatoly repeated. "'Finally?' Sophie you first saw this place five weeks ago."

"Seven," I said stubbornly, but I did see his point. Why did it feel like I had been fighting for this place for years? And why was I jumping all over Anatoly for pointing out the obvious? I did some quick calculations in my head, but that didn't give me an explanation for my temper tantrum; I wasn't due to get my period for another two weeks.

Anatoly considered me for a moment then lowered his gaze to the wine bottle as he shifted it from hand to hand. Something was bothering him, but instead of opening up he said, "So tell me, Sophie, how was the freak show?"

"What?" I asked, not following him at first. "Oh, the séance.

Well, it was…weird—but I suppose weird's normal for a freak show. You're not going to believe this, but Jason Beck was there. He's a bona fide member of the Specter Society."

Anatoly looked at me blankly. "Who's Jason Beck?"

"You remember Jason. One of Dena's GBCs…you, know, Mr. Velvet Pants."

"Right." Anatoly laughed appreciatively. "How could I forget him? And GBC stands for…?"

"Glorified Booty Call."

"Right. It makes sense that he would be part of that group, he was crazy enough." He looked back down at the wine. "Did Scott give you any trouble?"

"No, he was fine. I still can't believe he's with Venus. I mean, yeah, she's got money, but they're such a mismatched couple. It's like if Owen Wilson hooked up with Greta Van Susteren. It's just strange." Anatoly continued to study the wine bottle as if I hadn't spoken. Something about his demeanor made me nervous. I took a few steps toward the window seat before changing my mind and converting one of the boxes closer to him into a temporary stool. "How was your stakeout?" I asked, grasping at the one question that I knew could get him talking again.

"Boring," he sighed. "My client hired me to see if her ex is using. There's a custody thing going on and she's looking for ammunition. But as far as I can tell all his vices are legal. Women, alcohol, that kind of stuff. Nothing that will cost him his visitation rights."

"It may be legal, but too much alcohol tends to hamper people's ability to parent," I pointed out. "That's why I've chosen to remain childless."

He laughed and I immediately relaxed. "Speaking of which, why don't you open that wine," I suggested.

"I can do that." I waited as he went to fetch a corkscrew

from the kitchen. My corkscrew and glasses were the first things I had unpacked. I had my priorities.

"Wine for two," he announced as he returned with a couple of filled glasses.

I smiled gratefully. "Leah put some logs in the fireplace in case my guests wanted more ambiance. Shall we light it?" I asked, turning toward the fireplace as he came to my side. But then my smile froze on my face as I noted the photo above the mantel.

Anatoly turned to see what I was looking at. "What's wrong?"

"That picture of me and my father..." I whispered.

"It's new, right? I don't remember seeing it before."

"It's new, but it's also...straight."

"I don't understand."

"It was crooked by, like, half an inch. And now it's not."

"Someone at your party must have fixed it for you." Anatoly handed me the glasses before crouching by the fireplace and picking up the long matches that Leah had conveniently left there.

"I don't think they did," I said.

"Then perhaps it wasn't crooked at all." The fire sprang to life and Anatoly quickly closed the curtain as the sparks reached out for him. "Maybe you were just looking at it from the wrong angle."

"No, I know it was crooked. Leah was the one who hung it and she was trying to even it out before she left."

"And she succeeded."

"No, she didn't," I said firmly.

"Sophie, what are you trying to say?" Anatoly straightened up and took his wineglass from me. "Do you think the picture was crooked and then it just magically corrected itself?"

I finally tore my eyes from the wall and looked at Anatoly. "No...no, of course that's not what I'm saying."

"So what *are* you saying?"

"I don't know," I admitted. "All I do know is that I'm going to need more than one glass of this."

"You haven't even started your first one."

In three large gulps I downed my entire glass of wine.

Anatoly laughed appreciatively. "All right then, why don't you take my wine and I'll pour myself another. And then maybe I can talk you into a few more indulgences." He tucked a lock of my hair behind my ear before gently nibbling on the lobe. "A full body massage? I'll start here—" he carefully cupped my left breast and let his fingers graze my hardening nipple "—and work my way down."

"You just assumed that I invited you over for sex?" I asked with mock indignation. "Maybe I wanted to talk."

"So talk," he murmured. He slipped his hand under my shirt and resumed the massage.

I smiled and took another sip of wine, this time from his glass. "All right, I will. How was your day, Anatoly?"

"I already told you it was boring," he reminded me. "The night looks a lot more promising."

I laughed softly and drank more of his wine. I thought of the séance, of what I had heard, but hadn't heard at all. I could talk to him about that. But as his other hand began to work its way up my inner thigh, the warmth of his skin burning through my jeans, I quickly dismissed the idea. I didn't really want to talk or think. Right now I was content to just feel whatever it was that Anatoly planned to do to me.

And just as I began to relax, the wine and his touch finally lightening my mood, the doorbell rang. It was a melodic chime, but it might as well have been the obnoxious scream of a smoke alarm for all the irritation it provoked.

"Were you expecting someone?" Anatoly asked.

"Just you."

He furrowed his brow and then reluctantly removed his hands

and went to see who had interrupted us. He peeped out the little leaded, textured glass window built into the top of the door and frowned. "It's a woman. Italian, I think."

"Sophie?" I heard a muffled voice come from the other side of the door. "It's Maria Risso. May I please come in? I must speak to you."

Confused and slightly inebriated, I walked to the door as Anatoly opened it. "Did you forget something?" I asked as I acknowledged Maria.

"No, I…may I come in for a moment? I promise not to be long."

I glanced at Anatoly who looked more than a little peeved at this point. Reluctantly, he stepped aside as I waved her in. She was frowning, intensifying the few wrinkles in her face.

"Maria, this is my boyfriend, Anatoly."

Maria either didn't hear me or didn't care. "Did Enrico call and tell you why he wasn't coming?" she asked, glancing at the round, rented table, now the only piece of furniture not holding a box.

"No," I said carefully, not really wanting to relive that particular phone conversation. "He just said he was having a bad day."

"Did he say he was going somewhere?"

"No."

"Did he say he was feeling ill?"

"Why are you bothering me?" I asked bluntly. I was required to attend these people's séances, but there was nothing in my escrow that stipulated that I had to play twenty questions.

She sucked in a sharp breath and toyed with the belt of her trench coat. "I went to see him."

"So?" Anatoly asked impatiently.

"I still have the key to the building, so I let myself in, and when I was standing outside the door to his condo I smelled food and I could make out the sounds of Gabrieli playing on the stereo, but he didn't respond to my knock or to the doorbell. When I called out to him, the only response I got was from that damn parrot."

"Maybe he doesn't want company tonight," Anatoly suggested. "Maybe he has a guest over and he's in the middle of enjoying some wine and other pleasures and your presence would have been an intrusion."

I suppressed a smile. Subtlety was not something that Anatoly was comfortable with.

"I didn't see any evidence of a guest."

"How could you see evidence of anything when you're standing outside a door?" Anatoly continued reasonably.

"Because I have the key to his apartment," Maria admitted after a moment's hesitation. "I tried to let myself in, but the chain lock was on. Enrico may want to avoid me, but my trying to come into the condo on my own accord should have thrown him into a rage. I expected a confrontation of some kind. But he didn't scream at me or even acknowledge my attempt. I'd say that he might not have been home, but then he wouldn't have left the CD player on."

"And he wouldn't have been able to chain lock the door," I pointed out.

"Well, that would be explainable, but the music…"

Her voice trailed off and Anatoly and I exchanged looks. Last I checked it was a lot easier to leave a stereo on than chain lock a door from the outside. But I didn't really want to argue the point.

"Maria, I don't know where Enrico is or why he has his music on," I said slowly. "All he essentially told me was that he was having a bad day. His exact words were that he was being haunted, whatever that means. He said he was going to be late and then we kind of got into it."

"You got in an argument? What could you two possibly argue about? You don't even know one another." Then her eyes widened in horror. "You didn't insult his food, did you? Or did you praise another chef? Perhaps you said something nice about Wolfgang Puck. Enrico is very jealous of Wolfgang Puck."

"Wolfgang never entered into our conversation. I was just a little flippant when he said he was being haunted."

"Enrico doesn't believe in ghosts," Maria said firmly. "He comes to the Specter Society meetings because he finds them amusing…although now I suspect his reasons for coming have more to do with me than anything else."

"I don't know anything about any of that," I said. I was beginning to lose patience with this line of questioning. She was uninvited and she was preventing Anatoly from ravaging me. "All I know is that he told me he was haunted, I made a joke about that and then he called me a fucking bitch and hung up on me."

"What!" Maria gasped. "But he only uses such profanity for food critics and diet gurus!"

"Yeah, well, I'm neither," I said drily.

Maria now looked even more agitated than she had when she walked through my door. She started wandering around the room, weaving in and out of boxes like a confused rat aimlessly exploring a maze. "Something is amiss."

"It might be," Anatoly agreed. "But it's not our problem. Now if you'll excuse us."

Maria glanced down at the empty wineglasses on the box near where I had been standing and comprehension spread across her countenance. Unfortunately, the comprehension didn't seem to be mixed with even the slightest bit of acquiescence. "If you're right," she said, directing her comments to Anatoly, "if Enrico isn't answering the door because he specifically doesn't want to talk to me, then I'm going to need another person to act as my decoy."

"Forget it," Anatoly and I said in unison.

"I'll pay you," she said quickly. "A hundred dollars. All you have to do is pick up the phone and call him."

"And if he doesn't answer?" Anatoly asked.

"I'll pay you two hundred more to go over to the house and find out what's going on."

"Excuse me, but I'm about to invest in a million-dollar property. Three hundred dollars isn't even enough to pay for the sales tax on my upcoming furniture-shopping spree. If you want a decoy you're going to have to find someone who is a little more desperate."

"Me for instance," Anatoly said.

"*You?*" I squeaked. "But you already have more business than you can handle!"

"This is a one-night job, correct?" Anatoly asked.

"Yes," Maria said uncertainly. "Do you do this kind of thing often?"

"I'm a P.I."

"Like Magnum," she exclaimed.

I rolled my eyes. "You just gave away your age."

Maria flushed, but kept her focus on Anatoly. "This is perfect," she continued. "You can call him and if he's not available then sneak over, break in and—"

"No," Anatoly said quickly. "I'm not going to break the law for you. But I will find out if he has a guest."

"You can do that without breaking in?"

"Of course." Anatoly smiled. "Magnum did it all the time."

"You shouldn't have come," Anatoly mused as we followed Maria through the winding traffic.

Enrico hadn't answered his phone, not even while Anatoly was leaving a message on his answering machine telling him that he believed someone was in the process of breaking into his restaurant. After that the three of us piled into two cars, Maria into her Mustang and Anatoly and I into my Audi, and we all went over to Enrico's condo on Telegraph Hill. Since I had been the one doing all the drinking, I had given Anatoly the keys.

"I thought you wanted me to," I lied. The truth was that I couldn't stomach the idea of sitting home alone, thinking about the sex I wasn't having. At least this was distracting. "Besides, it's not like we're trying to hunt down the Zodiac Killer," I noted. "Maria basically hired you to knock on a door and ask if anybody's home. I don't see how I could screw that up for you."

I saw the flash of white teeth as he laughed in the darkness. "You're underestimating yourself. I'm sure you could screw up anything if you put your mind to it."

I groaned as he pulled into a spot located only one block away from our destination. "I really hate you, you know that?" I asked lightly.

"I hate you, too," he whispered. He kissed me and I felt his rough hands gently but firmly pulling my hair back from my face. Anatoly had incredible hands. Watching him knead bread dough was the equivalent of watching a porn flick.

We walked to the condo and found Maria in her car blocking the complex's garage. She rolled down her window just low enough so she could reach her arm out and shove a set of keys at us. "The silver one's to the building, the gold one's to the condo itself. Come down and let me know what he's up to as soon as you can."

"No," Anatoly said simply.

"No?" Maria repeated. "No, what?"

"If you want us to go in there you're going to have to open the door for us."

"But that's preposterous! You yourself suggested that the

whole reason Enrico didn't answer the door earlier is because he didn't want to see me. If he knows I'm there what's to keep him from hiding out again?"

"I didn't say you had to call out to him. But you have to be there. I'm assuming that the reason you have these keys is that this was, until recently, your home. You can argue that you have a legal right to burst into this condo unannounced. Sophie and I can't make that same claim, not unless we're there with you, as your guests."

Maria lowered the window farther and glared up at Anatoly. "No one is that paranoid! What's the real reason you're insist-ing I accompany you?"

"That is a real reason," he said. A streetlight flickered above us as if struggling to stay awake. "Another real reason," he went on, "is that I find your motives for hiring me questionable. You're divorcing Enrico, so why are you so concerned with his well-being? Do you still have feelings for him or did you do something to him and now you want someone else to find him and clean up the mess...or even take the blame?"

"I came to you for help and now you're accusing me of some kind of crime?" Maria shrieked. "I have never been so insulted! How dare you! You're completely full of..." Maria shook her head violently, too angry to continue.

"I believe the word you're looking for is chutzpah," Anatoly said with a smirk. "Are you coming or should Sophie and I go home and leave you to stew in your Mustang?"

Maria let out something that was between a scoff and a growl before raising her window and thrusting open her door. She didn't even bother to look at Anatoly or me as she marched to the entrance of the building and unlocked it. She walked in without holding the door open for us.

"What have you gotten us into?" I muttered.

"I got myself into this," he countered as we followed Maria

up three flights of stairs. "I take no responsibility for your decision to come."

When we reached the top floor of the four-story building, we paused. From the look of it there were only two apartments on this floor, and, as promised, the music of Gabrieli could be heard coming out of one of them. Maria went up to that door and pressed her hand against the wood. "Now what?" she whispered. I started to raise my finger to my lips, but then realized that the volume of the music would allow us to whisper without the fear of being overheard.

"Do you expect me to break through the chain lock for you?" Maria went on.

Instead of answering, Anatoly reached into his pocket and took out a small black object that looked like the kind of magnifying-glass used by jewelers. "What's that for?" I asked.

"See for yourself." He gestured for Maria to step aside and then put the object against the peephole. Silently, he invited me to look through it. Upon doing so I discovered that the device reversed the optics of a peephole, making it possible to look into the condo in the same way someone inside would have looked out into the hall. Little gizmos like that always delighted me. It was so very 007.

Anatoly smiled at my obvious pleasure and then took a turn looking through it.

"Well?" Maria asked in the same whispered hiss she had used before. "What do you see?"

"A parrot."

Maria squeezed her eyes shut in an expression of disgust. "I hate that damn bird. Enrico's trained it to torment me, you know. He used to instruct it to steal my soy nuts."

I did a quick double take. "You're not serious."

"This would be a good time to open the door," Anatoly said, locking eyes with Maria.

"I told you, the chain lock is on."

"It *was* on," Anatoly corrected. "There's no reason to assume that's still the case, unless you know something you're not telling us."

Maria's glare became a little more venomous. In one swift movement she stuck her key in the lock and pushed the door open...or at least she opened it as much as possible, considering that the chain really was on.

"*See?*" she said with an I-told-you-so smirk. Anatoly shrugged and reached into the pocket of his jacket again. This time he took out a thin rectangular mirror that was roughly as long as his palm. He leaned against the doorjamb and stuck the mirror through the slit in the door.

"Can you see anything beyond the bird?" I asked.

"Not much—a sofa, the television. I can see the doorway leading to the kitchen and...uh-oh."

"Uh-oh?" Maria and I said at the same time. We were no longer whispering.

Anatoly withdrew the mirror and stood up. "Does Enrico usually take naps on the kitchen floor?"

"Of course not!" Maria replied. "Why do... My God, is he lying on the floor of the kitchen?"

Without waiting for Anatoly to answer she began to pound on the door. "Enrico! Enrico, answer me! This isn't funny anymore. Open this door!" Then, she pursed her lips and whistled. "Giovanni, sweetie, open door. Open door, Giovanni."

I looked at Anatoly. "Is she talking to the parrot?"

Anatoly didn't answer. Instead he pushed Maria out of the way, took three steps back and in a rush of motion broke the chain on his first try.

Maria rushed past him to the kitchen where, from the front door you could see the loafered feet of a man lying on his back. For a split second I hoped that maybe Enrico was just passed

out in a drunken stupor, but Maria's scream put an end to my
optimism. Anatoly went to her and when I heard him swear
loudly in Russian I knew we had trouble.

Maria let out another penetrating scream and a man from
the condo next door stepped out into the hall. "What's going
on?" he asked. A wet mat of gray hair clung to his scalp as he
tightened the belt of his terry-cloth robe.

"Nothing good," I said quietly. I reluctantly stepped in and,
passing the impassive parrot, walked into the kitchen. Maria
was hysterical and Anatoly was trying to drag her away from
what was on the floor.

It was a body, presumably the body of Enrico. There was
little question that he was dead. No one could lose that much
blood and live. And the way that it caked on his throat, bringing
grim attention to the gash that had been made there—it was
too sick. And there was the murder weapon, lying beside him
caked in the blood it had spilled. Not a knife, but an honest-
to-God scythe. The kind that you would expect someone to
carry while dressed up like the grim reaper on Halloween,
except this blade wasn't plastic. Above the globs of crusted red
blood there was the unmistakable gleam of real steel.

"Maria, we have to call the police," Anatoly was saying as
he struggled not to slip in the pool of body fluids on the floor.
"We don't want to disturb the crime scene any more than we
already have." His hands were around her waist and, considering his significantly bigger size, he should have been able to
pull her away easily. But Maria was flailing like a panicked
swimmer on the verge of drowning. She was knocking things
off the counter, a large bowl of washed arugola, a plate of
half-made hors d'oeuvres, it all fell into the blood as she
clamored to get free. I stepped around Enrico and grabbed one
of her arms just as she reached back in an attempt to claw at
Anatoly's face.

"Let me go!" she cried. "I have to help him!"

"You can't," Anatoly breathed as he finally got a firmer hold of her and together we dragged her out of the room. "All you can do is calm down and call the police."

She tried to claw at him again, but he managed to pin her to the floor. "Call the police, Sophie."

"I think someone else may have already done that." I gestured to the staircase and now, in addition to the little man still standing in his bathrobe, there was a small collection of people standing in the stairwell, looking aghast. "Did any of you call the police?" I asked.

It was a moment before anyone spoke, but eventually an elderly woman who couldn't have weighed more than ninety-five pounds, stepped forward with her hands on her hips. "Why is your friend assaulting that poor woman?" she asked.

"I'm *not assaulting her*," Anatoly yelled back. "I'm trying to keep her from messing up the crime scene. Now, if it hasn't been done already, call the damn police!" But he clipped the last word short and his head immediately jerked up and he stared across the apartment.

"What's wrong?" I asked.

"Sophie, when you came in, did you see any open windows?"

"No. My guess is that if there was an open window the bird would have found it long before us."

"But the bird didn't find it," Anatoly muttered. "And the chain lock was on the door."

Maria wasn't yelling or struggling anymore, and when Anatoly carefully released her she curled up in a little ball and began to sob.

"Do you think he's still in there?" I asked.

"Who's still in there?" screeched the old lady from the stairwell. "Was somebody robbed? We all didn't haul ourselves out of bed for nothing, we want to know what's going on!"

"Should we go in and check it out?" I asked. I was praying that the answer was no. I liked investigating crimes, but I didn't like confronting murderers. It had been my experience that they weren't very friendly people.

"That depends," Anatoly said. "*Has* anyone called the police?"

"I have." I turned to see a tall, heavyset man with small wire-rimmed glasses push his way past the other people. With effort, he managed to sit on the ground by Maria's side. "Maria, they should be here soon. Are you all right?"

"Toby?" she croaked.

He let out a gentle laugh. "You lived here for years and never remembered my name. Now you've been out of the building for two months and it rolls off your tongue."

"Can anyone tell me if there's any other way out of this condo other than this door?" Anatoly called out.

"Just the door," bathrobe man confirmed.

"Good, and I can see the fire escape from that window so no one can get on it without my noticing." Anatoly pointed to the window at the other end of the hall. "If the killer's in there he's trapped. We'll wait for the authorities to arrive. They'll handle it."

The word *killer* was echoed in a series of whispers throughout the stairwell.

"They murdered Enrico," Maria whimpered. She was still in the fetal position and Toby was rubbing her back. "Some-one…someone took my beloved *amore* from me!"

"So that's it then?" Toby asked, looking up at us, "Enrico's really dead?"

Anatoly nodded just as we heard the sounds of sirens in the distance. I silently prayed that the murderer was still around, hiding in the dark corners of Enrico's condo. As creepy as it was to think that someone so violent could be so close, I was also aware of how all this was going to look to the police if they *didn't* immediately catch the killer. If the fact that I had discovered two dead bodies in a short period of time bothered *me,* it was sure to bother the police even more.

"You fucking bitch."

I jumped and then peered into Enrico's apartment from where the voice came…not a human voice, but the voice of that seemingly mild-mannered bird now perched on top of the sofa. He stared at me with his sharp avian eyes and repeated, "You fucking bitch."

The bird went out of focus as did everything else. For a moment all I could see was blurred colors and the vague forms of the things and people around me as I was transported back hours earlier to that phone call. "Anatoly," I finally managed. "I heard it."

"Heard what?" he asked.

"The murder. I heard Enrico die."

6

People frequently claim to be going insane, but I've never heard anyone say they were going sane. Perhaps it's because sanity isn't a desirable destination.

—*The Lighter Side of Death*

THE KILLER WASN'T THERE. THE POLICE RUSHED INTO THE APARTMENT AND searched every room and examined the windows, all of which were locked from the inside. The police questioned me, Anatoly and Maria separately, grilling us about every detail of our discovery. I knew they considered us to be suspects, how could they not? But no one was arrested or even detained down at the station. Maybe it was because all of our stories were consistent, or maybe it was because none of us looked stupid enough to make up a story that involved a chained locked door when we didn't have to. After all, it would have been easier to say that the chain lock had been broken before we showed up.

In the end they let us go with the promise of more questions in the near future. Toby offered to let Maria stay at his place since she was "clearly unfit to drive," but she refused and opted to take a cab home instead. She didn't want to be in the same building in which her husband had been killed. We all walked out together and waited on the sidewalk for the taxi that Toby had called.

For several minutes we stood there in silence, the other neighbors now back in their own apartments, with furniture barricading their doorways, no doubt. There were plenty of police cars double parked along the street, but most of the officers were inside dusting for prints.

It was Maria who eventually broke the silence. "I know who did it," she whispered.

I let out a little noise of surprise, and Anatoly snapped his head in her direction.

"It was Jasper Windsor."

"Who's Jasper Windsor?" Anatoly asked.

"He's the owner of that scythe."

Impulsively, I reached out and grabbed her arm. "You *did* tell the police that, right?"

"Yes, but they didn't take me seriously."

"Why the hell not?" I asked. "If he was the owner of the murder weapon I'd say that's pretty damn serious!"

"You're right," Maria agreed. She had become so pale that her skin seemed to actually glow. "It's very serious.... Even more serious, considering he's dead."

Anatoly and I exchanged looks. "Maria," Anatoly said gently, as if he were speaking to a panicked child, "I don't understand what you're talking about. When you say he's dead, are you referring to Enrico?"

"No." Maria's eyes seemed to be focused on an invisible object before her. "I'm referring to the man who took Enrico's life. Jasper Windsor is dead. He's been dead for over three hundred years."

Anatoly and I both gave her silence as a reply. The cab came, and in less than a minute she was gone.

"Do you think she's crazy?" I asked quietly.

"She's not sane."

I agreed. I had to I agree because disagreeing would require me to change my entire outlook on life and death. I watched the steam of Anatoly's breath float into the night. I was losing my bearings. I needed to get back to my own turf, where I could feel safe. "Take me home, Anatoly."

He draped his arm over my shoulders. "We're going. I'll be by your side all night long."

I pretended to sleep until I was sure Anatoly was dead to the world, then I allowed my eyes to pop open and laid there, staring at the ceiling. Mr. Katz had planted himself on my stomach as usual, but like me, he seemed to be holding on to at least some semblance of consciousness. His yellow eyes blinked at me and I could feel the gentle vibrations of his body as he purred. He hadn't had any problems adjusting to his new home. I hadn't, either, not really. Yes, I was having a little difficulty resigning myself to the fact that I was going to have to spend time with Venus twice a month for a year, but even after that disastrous séance I still thought it was a fair price to pay for the house.

This evening I had seen something truly horrible, gruesome and undeniably frightening. I had expected to carry that fear with me into the morning hours. Hell, I had expected to carry it well into next week, but the minute I had walked into the doors of my home it had dissipated. This place was my haven. And yet my sense of security was mixed with an odd sense of agitation. There was something I was supposed to do…but what?

Say goodbye, Sophie.

I froze, literally unable to move. It had been that voice again…or at least it had been the words, because, as before, I couldn't actually identify a voice. It was like the words had been pushed inside my brain, but they weren't exactly my thoughts. I knew that…but then…I couldn't know that because that wasn't possible.

Anatoly was still fast asleep. I glanced at Mr. Katz. He wasn't purring anymore. In fact, his hair was sticking straight up and his eyes were wide with alarm. He had heard it, too. Me and my cat.

My eyes slid from side to side. No one was in the room, and there was no evidence that there had been anyone in the room other than me and Anatoly. Except for that scent…what was that? Strawberry air freshener? No, it was way too faint for that…it was more like…like flavored lip gloss, the kind little girls wear when they're trying to look grown-up. Strawberry lip gloss.

But I didn't have any strawberry lip gloss.

Without warning, Mr. Katz jumped off of my stomach onto an unpacked suitcase and then onto the floor. In the bedroom doorway he paused, looked back at me and then continued on his way out. Careful not to wake Anatoly, I climbed out of bed and followed him. I don't know why I did that, but it seemed like the right thing to do. No, more than that. It felt like the thing I was *supposed* to do. Mr. Katz was now standing at the top of the stairs. When he saw me he started his descent into the living room. Carefully, quietly, I followed him, the odd fragrance hovering around me making me calm but alert. He walked through the living room and then stopped—right in front of the picture of me and my father.

I was beginning to feel a little unsteady on my feet. I actually pinched myself because the only way that any of this made sense was if I was dreaming. But I wasn't. I was awake and seriously confused. I squatted down next to my pet and studied him carefully. "Mr. Katz, what's going on?"

I talk to my cat all the time, but this was the first time I had ever spoken to him half expecting a verbal response. But if there was a response it wasn't from him. It was from the upstairs floorboards where I heard a very distinctive thump.

All sense of safety left me. The fragrance was gone, if it had ever really been there at all. Suddenly being down in the living room alone didn't seem like such a good idea.

There was another thump, in a different place this time.

It was pretty obvious that Mr. Katz had heard these noises, too, but this time he reacted by fleeing under the coffee table.

A third thump in yet another place on the ceiling above me.

"Sophie?" Anatoly called from upstairs, his voice groggy and puzzled.

I brought my hand to my cheek as if checking to make sure I still had a head. Of course it was Anatoly. What was I expecting? "I'm down here," I called up.

A minute later Anatoly was slowly making his way down the stairs wearing nothing but a pair of boxers and mussed hair. As he got closer I could see that his eyes were slightly red with exhaustion and somewhat bewildered. "You *are* down here."

"What, you thought I was lying?"

"No, but I thought I heard…" His voice trailed off and he lifted his eyes up to the ceiling. "Never mind, I must have been dreaming."

"What did you think you heard?" I tried to keep my voice calm, but I was getting worried again.

"I thought I heard you walking around upstairs," he said, nonchalantly. "But now that I've found you…" He reached to pull me toward him, but I stepped away.

"You thought you heard me upstairs?"

"Yes, but clearly I was mistaken. Sophie, what's gotten into you?"

"I thought I heard *you* walking around upstairs."

"I *did* walk from the bedroom to the staircase so…"

"I think someone's in the house."

Anatoly met my eyes. I knew he was trying to gauge if I was joking or just suffering from a brief bout of hysteria thanks to the earlier events of the evening, but something in my expression must have told him that neither was the case. Quietly, he crossed to the corner of the living room where he had left his duffle bag from work, and from it he pulled out a .45. "Stay here," he whispered, and with a sharpness and stealth that most of us can't pull off at three o'clock in the morning, he crept up the stairs. Watching him do this in boxer shorts was kind of a surreal experience. Daniel Craig couldn't have been better.

In a moment he disappeared from sight. Mr. Katz continued to crouch under the coffee table. When I had followed him down the stairs a few minutes earlier, he had seemed like he had some kind of clarity of thought and was trying to communicate with me. Now he just seemed like…well, like a cat.

I tore open one of my many boxes and dug my hand into a sea of crumpled newspaper and Bubble Wrap looking for something heavy. My hand settled on a crystal vase. Dena had used a similar vase to defend both of us from an attacker once and ever since I had grown an affinity for them. This one was heavier than the one Dena had used. Obviously it wasn't a gun, and the taped-on Bubble Wrap might soften the blow, but still, it served the purpose of making me feel a little tougher. I may not have bullets, but I do have Lalique.

According to the wall clock, Anatoly was up there for a full four minutes before coming down to give me the all clear. "It probably was just me you heard after all," he reasoned. "The mind can plays tricks in the middle of the night."

Yes, but can the mind make your cat start acting like a small, laconic version of the Lion of Narnia? And what about the voice? But I didn't say any of that. Instead, I collapsed on the couch and motioned for Anatoly to join me.

"I take it you couldn't sleep."

"I was pretending for your sake."

"You need to improve your acting skills. I knew you were awake."

"Then why did you fall asleep?"

"Am I required to have insomnia every time you do?"

"On the nights that I discover a dead body, yes, you're required to stay up with me."

"Sophie, that's at least eight or nine nights a year."

I smacked him on the thigh and he laughed softly. "I *am* sorry you had to see that," he said with a slightly more somber tone. He pulled me to him and I rested my head on his shoulder. "You've had a tough time of it lately."

"Yeah, but I do have a new house."

"Almost have it," Anatoly said softly. "It'll be yours in about a week."

I didn't argue this time. I mean, technically, he was right. How was I supposed to explain that this house belonged to me in a way that completely transcended any technicality?

"I think," Anatoly continued, "that this house is too big for one person."

I turned my face away. I had planned on asking him to live with me, but…but there was something I was supposed to do first. There was that sense of agitation again. What *was it?* What was I forgetting? Or had I ever known?

"Sophie? Are you all right?"

"What? Oh, yeah, I'm okay. I'm just…thinking."

"About Enrico?" Anatoly nodded without waiting for my answer. It was one of the few times he had ever misread me. Well, there was that short period of time right after we met when he thought I was a serial killer, but other than that small error he had pretty much had my number from the get-go. But since he had brought Enrico up…

"How did the killer get out?" I asked. "I don't get it."

"Neither do I," Anatoly said. "And nobody commits suicide by slitting his own throat with a scythe. I'm not even sure it's possible. Besides, he was in the middle of cooking a meal. That's not usually the time people choose to end it all."

"Yeah, but he was a chef. Maybe his soufflé didn't rise and he got a little emotional…oh God, I can't believe I just said that. I'm a horrible, horrible person."

"No, you're just a normal person," Anatoly assured me. "A person who has had to toughen up due to life experience and several close calls. But to get back to the point, suicide doesn't make sense here. It also doesn't seem possible that someone could get out of an apartment and then lock it from the inside."

"Did you ever watch *The X-Files?*" I asked.

"No."

"Well, there was this one episode where there was a murderer who could sort of change his genetic makeup in order to squeeze through otherwise prohibitively narrow openings…"

"I don't think that's what we're dealing with."

"Neither do I, but it would be interesting if it was."

"No doubt." He smiled at Mr. Katz, who had finally come out from under the coffee table and was making a pillow out of Anatoly's feet. "Who knows, maybe the police will find fingerprints, catch the killer and this whole thing will be over in the morning."

"If it doesn't play out that way we're going to remain prime suspects."

"For a while that's true," Anatoly agreed. "But not for long. We have absolutely no relationship with Enrico and we just met Maria today. Establishing a motive for murder would be nearly impossible. And the idea that we would break into the apartment of a man we didn't know with a woman we didn't know and then sit idly by while she took out a scythe…that's beyond the suspension of disbelief."

"I hope you're right." As I let myself become enveloped in his warmth, my eyelids became significantly heavier. Maybe my mind *had* been playing tricks on me. There had been no voice; Mr. Katz had not had a moment of depth and complexity; there had been no inexplicable thumps in the night. "I think I'm getting sleepy now," I offered.

"Good, because I really don't want to stay up with you tonight. Let's go to bed."

He took my hand and led me back up the stairs. Everything was going to be fine. The police would catch Enrico's killer, and once the shock of the whole thing wore off, I'd no longer get spooked without a good reason.

And eventually I'd figure out what exactly it was I was supposed to do. When I did, I might be able to get rid of the nagging sensation that Enrico's comments about being haunted now applied to me.

7

Men love their freedom, unless you give it to them.
—*The Lighter Side of Death*

THE NEXT MORNING, I MANAGED TO GET UP IN TIME TO CATCH THE second half of the eight o'clock news. Anatoly was already awake and showered since he had a case he had to tend to. He brought me a cup of coffee and a Spanish omelet. There are major benefits to dating someone who loves to cook.

The news shows were dominated by the story of Enrico's murder. They didn't have all the details, but they did know that it had been Maria, Anatoly and me who had found him. Apparently we were all unavailable for comment. I suppose that was the benefit of relying solely on a cell phone.

"The police won't tell the press who their suspects are," I called out as Anatoly went back into the kitchen to refill his travel mug.

"Reporters aren't stupid. They're going to figure it out."

"I'm supposed to bring my mom over here this evening to see the house. I so don't want to have to tell her about this."

"Then don't. There's a fifty-fifty chance she hasn't seen the news yet."

"Are you kidding? She's probably been on the phone with every single member of Hadassah by now, kvetching about her daughter, the Angel of Death. I'll be lucky if she even waits 'til tonight to ream me. She may show up on my doorstep any minute with a rolled-up newspaper and a bagful of Jewish guilt."

As if on cue, my doorbell rang. Anatoly came back into the living room and threw me a questioning look. "You want me to get it?"

I gave him a what-do-you-think look before gathering up my breakfast and moving it into the dining room where I could hear without being seen.

Anatoly's irritated groan should have been a hint as to who was at the door, but it wasn't until I heard Scott's voice that the pieces came together. "Is she here?" he asked. "I need to see her."

"You're not invited in," Anatoly said sternly.

"I saw her on the news!" Scott retorted, as if that somehow entitled him entry.

"You're not coming in, Scott."

"I just want to talk to her!"

"Sorry."

"I brought Frappuccinos!"

"It's all right, Anatoly. He can come in, but just for a minute," I said, putting my plate onto the small dining table and moving into view.

The scowl Scott had been wearing a second earlier transformed into a huge grin as he saluted me with a plastic Venti cup. Anatoly's scowl stayed firmly in place. He glanced at his watch and his jaw twitched in frustration. "I have to get going," he said. "Are you sure you'll be okay?"

"I'll be fine."

Anatoly regarded me skeptically. "Why don't I wait while you get dressed," he suggested.

Scott turned on him with apparent exasperation. "For Christ's sake, man, she's wearing leggings and a T-shirt. What do you want her to wear around me? A burka?"

Anatoly moved toward Scott with obvious menace, but I quickly stepped in between the two. "Scott's not a threat," I said, placing a hand on Anatoly's tensed shoulder. "He's not even a distraction."

Anatoly hesitated for a moment before nodding. "Call me if you need me."

"Absolutely," I agreed. "But then, I always call on you to satisfy my...needs." That last comment was for Scott's benefit, but it seemed to mollify Anatoly. He leaned in for a long, lingering kiss. He tasted like coffee and Tabasco, my favorite flavors. Behind me I could hear Scott shuffling his feet. The reminder of his presence motivated me to slip my hand into the back pocket of Anatoly's jeans. I felt the laugh that he was stifling as he gently pulled away.

"I'll see you later."

"Absolutely," I agreed and watched him collect his duffle bag filled with various spy stuff and walk out my door.

"Quite a show," Scott said. While still behind me, he had taken a step closer so that his voice seemed to be coming from directly over my head. "Was it for my benefit?"

"In part. If you hadn't been here there would have been less kissing, but more groping." I turned to face him and took a step back for breathing room. "Thanks for the Frappuccino. If there isn't anything else, you can go."

Scott hesitated for a moment and then turned and went over to the dining-room window where he stared out at the street. "Is it true, Sophie?" he asked. "You really found Enrico...dead?"

"It's true," I said, suddenly aware of my insensitivity. "I'm sorry...for your loss I mean."

"It wasn't *my* loss. Enrico and I were never more than reluctant acquaintances. He thought I was obnoxious."

"Really?" I took a long sip of my drink. Apparently Enrico and I had a lot in common.

"I'm still tripping out on this," Scott continued. "We just found Oscar a few weeks ago. Now Enrico?" He turned around, his eyebrows raised in question. "What were you doing over there anyway?"

"How is this your business?" I asked. "Especially if Enrico wasn't even a friend?"

"Yeah, but you are!"

"Since when?"

"Fine, whatever, you hate me, but I don't hate you." He looked around for something to sit on and when he noted that every chair was holding the stuff I hadn't found a place for yet, he leaned against the wall. "I actually like you a lot and that's why I want to warn you."

"About?"

"About Kane. He saw the report, too. He called me this morning to talk about it."

"So?"

"So he's not so eager to sell his house to someone who is a suspect in a murder investigation. And escrow is still six days away from closing."

"No!" I cried. "He can't take my house!"

"Look, I don't think he's going to do anything drastic, not after I talked to him, but he has questions."

"Whatever he wants to know, I'll tell him. All he has to do is ask."

"Fine, fine. But we need to sit down and talk this out. I need you to tell me exactly what happened and then if there's something we need to spin for Kane's benefit we can brainstorm on how to do that together."

"Why together? Neither one of us has ever had a problem spinning on our own."

"I know Kane. I know what he wants to hear and you know what actually happened and what he's likely to find out through Maria and the press. We need to work together if we're going to ensure that he never finds his way to the no-spin zone. Besides," he said, his mouth curving into an insidious smile, "I like spinning with you."

Suddenly I wished Anatoly was still there. "Look, this is stupid. We don't need to come up with a story because the truth is totally innocent. Maria came over last night because when she went over to Enrico's place, he wouldn't open the door and it freaked her out. She wanted to know what Enrico had said to me on the phone and then she hired Anatoly on the spot to go over to Enrico's to find out what was up. I tagged along and then we all found Enrico's bloody dead body lying next to an antique scythe. That's it, end of story."

Scott stared at me blankly for a minute before breaking into a full laugh. "You don't actually expect Kane to buy that, do you?"

"It's the truth!" I snapped.

"Maybe so, but it smells like bullshit."

"Yeah, well, so do you. Why don't you just go back to your Goddess of Love and leave me alone so I can have some peace and calm?"

Scott tilted his head to the side. "Peace and calm? Why, Soapy, are you unable to stay calm when I'm around?"

"Okay, that's it, we're done." I marched to my front door and flung it open. "Get out now!" I swung around, prepared to stare Scott down but disappointed to discover that he wasn't anywhere to be seen.

"Wow, this Spanish omelet is great!" he called from the dining room.

I slammed the door and marched right back to where Scott was. "Stop eating my food!" I demanded, pointing accusingly at the plate in his hand.

Scott took two more bites. "That is seriously good," he said, his voice muffled by eggs. "When did you learn to cook?"

"Never. Anatoly made this for me."

"Did he now?" The mocking tone was unmistakable. "What a good little wife he'll make."

I stepped forward and snatched my fork from his hands. "He's more of a man than you'll ever be." As soon as I said the words I slapped my hand over my mouth. "I can't believe I just said that."

"I know. It was right out of a bad soap opera."

"But I never sound like a bad soap opera! I'm a writer!"

"Who do you think writes the bad soap operas? Chimps? Wait a minute, was it you? Were you the writer responsible for Erika Kane's near-death experience?"

"Shut up," I said, whacking him lightly on the chest. "And what does it say about you that you are aware of Erika's brushes with death?"

"It says that there was a time in which I lacked sufficient employment."

I laughed, and Scott's eyes crinkled in the corners. "I've missed that," he said softly. "I've missed that sound."

I stiffened immediately and took my plate back. "You told me that Kane had questions. What are they specifically?" I sat down on the floor cross-legged and plowed into my breakfast, careful to keep my eyes on the eggs and not on Scott's grin.

Scott sighed and sat beside me, a little too close. "He wants to know what drew you to Enrico's last night."

"I told you. I wasn't drawn, I was hired to go. Well, Anatoly was hired. I was hired by association."

"What I don't understand is why Maria would hire Anatoly to pay her ex a visit. What exactly does your boyfriend do?"

"He kills people."

"Really," Scott said drily.

"Yeah, so you may want to stop flirting with me. He has little secret cameras all over this place so he can keep track of me while he's at headquarters. You saw *Mr. & Mrs. Smith?* It's just like that."

"Sophie…"

"Okay, fine. He's a private detective."

"Hmm." Scott pulled off his jacket and folded it beside him. It wasn't a casual gesture. The T-shirt he was wearing flattered his well-built torso and he was trying to draw my attention to it. The guy was so transparent it was almost funny. No, it *was* funny. "On the news they said that Enrico's condo seemed to have been locked up from the inside when you found him. How can that be true?"

"Dunno," I said, chewing on my last bite of egg. "But that's exactly how it was. Anatoly had to break the chain lock in order for us to get in."

"You know, she was going to get nothing in that divorce. Venus told me their prenup was ironclad."

"Why were they getting a divorce in the first place?"

Scott sighed and stretched out his leg, putting one ankle on top of the other. "Maria used to be old school. She was a real Italian, you know? That's why Enrico fell in love with her. She reminded him of home."

"So what, she's not Italian anymore?"

"No, but she's assimilated. She no longer speaks wistfully of siestas and promenades. She prefers Calvin Klein to Versace. Enrico could have handled all that, but then she went a little too far."

"What'd she do?"

"She gave up carbs. Enrico was one of this country's most prominent Italian chefs and suddenly his wife was refusing to eat pasta."

"Wait a minute, are you telling me that the South Beach Diet ended Maria and Enrico's marriage?"

"I don't think it was South Beach, but still, it was a diet that destroyed their love."

"Unbelievable," I muttered.

"Yeah, we all thought it was nuts. And then things got predictably bitter. She wanted the parrot, one of the few things *not* covered in the prenup. I don't think she ever liked that bird, but Enrico loved it, and she wanted to hurt him. In return he tried to steal away the things that were important to her."

"Like?"

"Like the Specter Society. Ghosts were always more Maria's thing than Enrico's. He came to the séances with her, but I don't think he ever fully bought it. He *said* he did, but that was probably to appease Kane."

"Why would Kane care?"

"Kane won't let anyone in the Specter Society who isn't a believer. Remember that, Soapy, keep your doubt to yourself. But believer or not, Enrico wasn't gonna stop coming to the meetings. Not if attending meant pissing off Maria. Twice in the last few months Maria wasn't even invited because she would have been an odd number and Venus made sure Enrico got preference. Venus loved Enrico."

"I didn't think Venus was capable of human emotions."

"She displays a few on occasion. Apparently it depends on the cycles of the moon."

I started to laugh, but then, remembering what that had led to the last time, forced myself into silence.

Scott grinned anyway, correctly reading my discomfort. "Look, I believe you about how it went down, and if I had to bet on who killed Enrico I'd put money on Maria, but I really don't think your story is going to be enough to calm Kane down."

"Well, what will be enough?" I asked.

Scott rapped his knuckles across the hardwood floor in lieu of response.

"Look, Scott, if you can't help me with this then…" I gestured toward the exit as a way of ending my sentence.

"I can help, but I'm not sure you're going to like my methods."

"Oh, this is going to be good. What exactly do you expect me to do?"

"Change the story. Kane won't care if you're guilty or not if he thinks you…you know, communicated with Enrico after he died."

"What do you mean he won't care if I'm guilty? We're talking about murder here! How can some bogus medium shit compensate for slashing some guy's neck with a scythe?"

"You do remember who we're talking about, right?" Scott asked. "Kane? He's not normal. Look, he thinks that some people are more connected to the next world than the rest of us and right now he's inclined to think you're one of those people."

"Why the hell would he think that?"

"He thinks there's a possibility that the reason you've found so many dead bodies in your life is because, on *at least* a sub-conscious level, you knew that these people were going to die. You were allowed to find their bodies first because you needed to make that contact with the spirit world."

"So he thinks I'm like a *clueless* medium?"

"Yeah, that's about right."

I dropped my head back, inadvertently banging it against the wall. Scott put his hand on my hair as if to soothe the pain, but I slapped him away.

"Tell Kane that on Enrico's way to heaven or wherever, he stopped long enough to give me some cooking tips. I can now make tiramisu that is literally to die for. Okay?"

"He's not going to buy that, Soapy. He's going to want some kind of proof, like information you could only have gotten from Enrico."

"What, he gives his tiramisu recipe to everybody?"

Scott gave me a look and I felt my fingernails dig into my palms as I reflexively clenched my fists.

"Obviously I don't have that kind of information, Scott. I never even met the guy. So just hold Kane off until I figure out who killed Enrico—"

"What?" Scott snapped his head in my direction. "You want to find a murderer now? Who died and made you Angela Lansbury?"

"I don't want to find a murderer, but what else am I going to do? I can't lose this house!"

"Then *tell Kane you saw a fucking ghost!* If not Enrico, then somebody else. His mother used to live here, say you met her. Let's figure out a way to put one over on him!"

"But you just said that telling Kane I saw a ghost won't be good enough! So if I can't fulfill his paranormal fantasies I'll at least have to relieve his suspicions by catching the killer. Anatoly will help me. Really, it'll be fine."

"No, this is not fine." Scott got to his feet and glared down at me. "I've been doing some research on the Internet. There are, like, eight articles in the *SF Chronicle*'s archives detailing events in which you purposely put yourself smackdab in the middle of insanely dangerous situations and acted like an idiot!"

"I have never acted like an idiot!"

"You have invited suspected killers into your home!"

Now I got to my feet. "I only did that once, and as it turns out he wasn't a killer and that's why I'm dating him now!"

"Anatoly? You used to think he was a killer? And now that you know he's not, you're dating him? That's your standard?"

"Hey, well, they can't all be philandering con artists like you, Scott."

Scott stammered for a minute before throwing up his hands in defeat. He turned his back on me and paced the room, his boots leaving footprints in the dust. Eventually he stopped and pivoted in my direction.

"I don't know how to talk to you. Not about this."

"Then don't talk," I said, simply. "Leave."

At that moment Mr. Katz entered the room. He took one look at Scott and did a quick 180. Scott watched his retreat, his face the picture of frustration.

"Okay," he said finally. "I'm going. But this isn't finished. I didn't go through all this just to lose you again."

And before I had a chance to remind him that he didn't actually have me to lose, he was gone and I was alone. I picked up my now-empty plastic Frappuccino cup and crushed it in my hand.

8

When it comes to our relationships it's hard to see the forest for the trees. Better to invest in some emotional deforestation. That way you don't have to acknowledge any of it.

—*The Lighter Side of Death*

I TRIED TO WASH AWAY MY CONTACT WITH SCOTT IN A LONG, HOT shower, but the pounding of the water only reminded me of how much I wanted to hit something. Part of me realized that my primary problem was with Kane, not Scott, though in this case the idea of killing the messenger had a lot of appeal. I tried to come up with a plan to solve Enrico's murder, but I couldn't seem to come up with anything. I'm frequently more focused after writing, so I put the Enrico dilemma aside for a while and took my laptop to Starbucks, where I spent the better part of the day writing a synopsis and the first chapter for a new book. In this one, a woman would be given the opportunity to rescue her ex-husband from a burning building, but would pass it up when she realized that there wasn't enough time to save both him and her cat.

I wasn't any calmer that evening when I pulled up in front of my mother's house. I sat in my car for a full five minutes, earnestly trying to absorb the quiet serenity of the streets of the Sunset District, but I couldn't quite manage it.

I stared up at the heavy fog that seemed to be perpetually present in this area, a constant reminder that the beach was only a few blocks away and beyond that an ocean infinitely bigger than the problems of any single human being. And my problems really were relatively small. I could afford to put a down payment on a $980,000 home at a time when people all over this country were going into foreclosure. But this wasn't just any house, and that was my difficulty. In some weird way this house was a part of my family and the total illogicality of that statement didn't make it any less true. I didn't want to lose it no matter what.

I exhaled loudly and made faces in the rearview mirror until I came up with a smile convincing enough to hide my aggravation. And that's what I wore as I rang my mother's doorbell. But the minute I saw her face I knew my efforts were wasted.

"Another body!" she howled. She glared up at me, her round, wrinkled face red with frustration. "What are you now, a traveling mortician?"

"Mama, if you could just hear me out—"

"All the ladies from the Jewish senior group think you're cursed!"

"If I'm under a curse, then why is it that I'm never the one to get hurt? Maybe I'm blessed, ever think of that?"

"This doesn't happen to regular people, Sophie," she pointed out. "So why must it always happen to you? You look for trouble, that's why. Always sticking your nose in other people's business. You want to give me another ulcer already?"

"You don't even have one ulcer!"

"So now the mortician's a doctor?"

"I—" But I stopped myself, realizing the futility of this argument. "I'm sorry that I worried you," I said carefully. "And I promise to keep my nose where it belongs. So, are we done? Can I show you my new house now?"

"Listen to the way she talks to me," Mama said, although there was no one other than me to hear her. She opened the door wider and I stepped inside her wallpapered foyer long enough to help her into her favorite purple wool coat. She was a little over five feet tall, if you counted her halo of white curly hair. She reminded me a bit of an aging hobbit. I like hobbits. In the whole *Lord of the Rings* trilogy it's the hobbits who always outperform expectations despite their various neuroses, and they have a fierce love of home and community, but still—nobody wants to look like them. Once upon a time my mother had looked so different. She had been a little thinner when I was younger, but always curvy. Her hair had been brown, and she would style it into smooth waves that fell down her back. She never, ever went unnoticed. Once, when I was a teenager, my father had brought home a dozen of Noah's jalapeño bagels and presented them to Mama like a gift. He said they reminded him of her: spicy, Jewish and irresistibly delicious.

"What's with the daydreaming?"

I blinked in surprise and tried to bring my focus back to my mother, who was now waiting to leave. "What is it, mamaleh?" she asked, her tone gentler than before. "Is there something bothering you?"

"No," I said quickly. "I just realized that I forgot to stop at Noah's earlier. I haven't eaten much today and a bagel sounds perfect."

"So we'll order pizza after we get to your new home," she

said decidedly. "I want to see the fancy house. Nine hundred and eighty thousand dollars! They should make these places out of gold for what they charge."

Mama carried the conversation for the entire car ride. According to her, I was too skinny, the low cut of my jeans made me look like one of those shiksas that lived with that "Heffner character," and if I didn't stop treating my cat like a child he'd be expecting a bar mitzvah in a few years. I responded with mmm-hmms and uh-huhs and tried to be chastened rather than complimented by her rebukes.

I parked my Audi in my driveway rather than the garage and went around the passenger side to open her door. But she didn't get out. Instead she simply stared at the house with her mouth open. "This," she finally said, still firmly in her seat, "*this* is the house you bought?"

"Well, sort of. I'm really still in the process of buying it, but I'll have the deed soon."

Mama finally got out, but she didn't walk toward the door. "You...you picked it out yourself?"

"Well, yeah, Mama. It's not like you can hire a personal shopper for this kind of thing."

The corners of her mouth began to tremble and I would have sworn I saw her blink away a tear.

"Mama? Mama, what's wrong?"

She turned to me and placed a dry wrinkled hand on each one of my cheeks. "You're just like your father, that's what you are."

"Um, okay," I muttered, not sure of what to make of my mother's non sequitur. "Do you want to come in and see the place?"

My mother removed her hands and slowly turned back to the house. After a moment's thought she shook her head and sat back down in the car. "Not tonight, mamaleh. *This* I need to work up to."

I stared at her blankly. "What are you talking about? You were in a major rush to get the grand tour a few minutes ago and now you have to work up to it? It's a house, not a roller-coaster ride!"

As I finished my sentence I heard the sound of Anatoly's Harley pull to a stop several yards away. I glanced nervously at my mother. She never failed to make a comment about Anatoly's bike whenever she saw it. It was, to her mind, too dangerous, too loud and too much of a spectacle. But this time her mouth remained closed as she continued to stare up at my home. Anatoly strode up to me, a small, blue shopping bag in his hand. Seeing my mother in my car, he bent down and offered his free hand in greeting. "Mrs. Katz, it's always good to see you."

My mother accepted his hand with a distracted smile. Her silence was as deafening as the roar of the ocean, but Anatoly didn't seem to notice. He straightened back up and placed his lips against my ear. "I forgot she was coming," he whispered. "Any chance I could talk to you alone for just a minute?"

"What?" I asked, still focused on my mother. Finally I pulled my eyes to Anatoly's and saw the urgency there. "All right," I finally said. "I think I'm about to take my mother home. Can it wait until after that?"

"I don't need to be anywhere for over an hour," he replied. "If you let me in I'll wait for you here."

I pulled out my key chain and held up two identical gold keys. I removed one and placed it in his hand. "It's yours."

A smile flickered across his face and I watched as he opened my front door and then closed himself inside my house.

I cast another glance at Mama, only to see that she was still in a partial trance. Without another word I got in the driver's seat and drove her home. I wanted to ask her again why she hadn't gone inside, but I kept my mouth shut. For one thing I sensed that she didn't want to talk; for another I wasn't at all sure that I wanted to listen. I had the irrational fear that she knew some secret that would explain my attachment to that house. I wanted to believe that my feelings of attachment were natural. Just the normal passions of a first-time home owner and that consequently those passions were rooted in the present, despite my growing, nagging suspicion that this particular passion was directly connected to me in a way I didn't understand yet.

So I pretended she was tired and I brought her to her door with tenderness and left her with a kiss. She didn't argue, which in and of itself should have been cause for alarm…if I had allowed it to be.

When I got back home Anatoly was waiting for me on the couch, the blue shopping bag now folded up by his side. He didn't get up to greet me, but instead gestured to a box that he had used to hold what looked to be a small cocktail and a box of chocolate. I took a few steps forward to get a better look. The chocolate was from CocoaBella, my absolute favorite chocolatier. Either he was about to deliver me a blow or he wanted something from me.

"Maria contacted me today," he said. "She wants to hire me to find out who killed Enrico."

"I thought she believed a ghost did that."

"She still believes that, but her sister convinced her to hire a P.I. anyway on the off chance that she's wrong," he said with a soft laugh. "She's not the only suspect the police have, but she is the main one and she wants to take all possible steps to prove her innocence."

"Well, you should definitely take the case," I said, lifting the glass to my lips. It was a Cape Cod…double shot. "I was about to hire you to investigate the same thing anyway."

"Why do you care who killed Enrico?"

"Maria isn't the only suspect, you know. We were there, too."

"As I said, I don't think we'll be suspects for long. We just need to give them time to check our alibis and all that. After all, you were with Leah for most of the day. While you were with her I met with two different clients and later I bribed a bartender to tell me about the guy I was following. We'll be in the clear soon."

"But they'll have to check the credibility of our witnesses. After all, my sister has plenty of reasons to lie for me and God knows I've lied to the police in the past. They'll need to assure themselves that I'm being honest this time and it could take them over six days to do that."

"Is that a big deal? I would think you'd be used to this kind of thing by now."

With a sigh I joined him on the couch. "Kane doesn't want to sell this place to a murder suspect. I need to be sure I'm not one by the time escrow closes."

Anatoly absorbed this and then gestured to my drink. "Have another sip."

"Anatoly, what's going on?"

"I'm going to take the case," he said, "not because I'm worried about either of us being suspects or because you need to close escrow, but because Maria is offering me a lot of money."

"Fair enough."

"But before I begin," he continued, "I need you to promise me something."

"What sort of promise are you looking for?"

"I want you to promise that you will not try to help me."

"Anatoly—"

"I mean it, Sophie. I want to get through this without having to worry about you getting yourself maimed, shot or killed."

I was tempted to argue that I was actually very good at detective work and that I didn't attract disaster, but Anatoly didn't look like a man who had been suddenly struck with amnesia. "What if I just did a little research on the Internet into Enrico's life—"

"No," Anatoly said definitively. "No helping."

"Fine," I said. "But you better find out who did this quickly. You can't expect me to sit on my hands for long, not when this house is at stake."

"That's the other thing I need to talk to you about," Anatoly said, slower this time. His eyes moved from box to box until they finally fell on the bookcase now half-filled with some of my recently unpacked books. "I don't want you in this house."

I felt my shoulders drop with the weight of my exasperation. "I know moving in before escrow is closed is unusual, but Kane insisted. Besides, it would be a pain in the ass to move all this stuff back to the apartment."

Anatoly finally met my eyes. "I didn't say I wanted you to move out temporarily."

The words ran around my head until they finally found the part of my brain that could interpret them. I leaned forward, transferring my weight onto the balls of my feet until I had enough balance to stand up. "What you want," I said in a voice so low it sounded foreign even to me, "is not important."

Anatoly didn't leave his seat. "I spent some time talking to Maria about Enrico's other friends and acquaintances, particularly the ones in the Specter Society since those are the ones you have to deal with. Kane may be dangerous."

"He's just eccentric."

"He also may be up to something with Scott."

I paused, feeling thrown a bit off track. "Scott?"

"Scott starts calling you out of the blue, then he just happens to be at an open house that you attend," Anatoly said, counting the incidents off on his fingers. "Then he takes you to Kane's family home and introduces you to a corpse—"

"He didn't know that was going to happen," I pointed out.

"And then," Anatoly continued, without regard to my correction, "Scott tells you that if you want Kane to sell you this house you have to join the Specter Society, and shortly after that the throat of the society's most famous member is slashed on the exact day you were supposed to meet him. Don't you find any of that strange?"

"Strange, yes, but not particularly relevant."

Anatoly raised an eyebrow. "Maria told me that neither Scott nor Kane particularly liked Enrico. Maybe they had reason to hate him. Sophie, what if Scott is behind all of this? What if his getting you into this place was part of a strategic plan?"

"You think Scott is behind Enrico's murder?" I broke into a full laugh. "Not in a million years."

"You're defending him," Anatoly said flatly.

"No, I'm explaining him. Scott is capable of doing a lot of horrible things, but not this."

"Before that open house you two had been out of touch for ten years. You don't know what he's capable of."

"I know I can handle him and I know I'm not moving."

Anatoly rose to his feet, eliminating my height advantage. I glared up into his face, my fists clenched at my sides. "I don't want you in this house," he said again. "I won't let you put yourself in danger again."

"Let me?" I scoffed. "Who says you have the power to *not let me* do anything? I, on the other hand, don't have to *let* you talk to me like this." I walked to the door and threw it open. "It's time for you to go."

Anatoly's jaw was extended by at least an inch. I waited for him to argue, to throw something, to tell me I was behaving like a child, but instead he picked up the keys to his place and cavalierly tossed them in the air. When he reached the door he stopped less than an inch away from me. I tried to focus on my anger, but the faint scent of his aftershave was amazingly distracting. He put a hand on my waist. "I don't own you," he said, his hand now slipping up my back, "but you *are* mine. I'm going to find out if Scott is a threat to you and if he is…"

His voice trailed off as his eyes slowly made their way up and down my figure. He pulled me closer and used one hand to lift my face up to his. *Give in to this,* my body screamed. *Argue with him tomorrow or later tonight, but this is a make-love-not-war kinda moment, just go with it!* But when he brought his lips to mine I whispered, "You're wrong. He's not a threat."

Anatoly dropped his hands to his sides. "I hope you're right," he said. "It's been a long time since I've had to resort to violence."

I watched him walk into the cold and eventually ride off in the distance on his motorcycle. I had essentially kicked two men out of my house in less than twenty-four hours. I hadn't had the opportunity to do anything like that in years.

I looked over my shoulder to see that he had left his jacket draped over a box underneath my father's picture. The fact that the cold night air hadn't immediately reminded him of his forgetfulness proved that he had been more troubled by our exchange than he had let on. I sighed and closed the door. All I wanted to do was get as comfortable as possible so when I finished the drink Anatoly had made me (and perhaps three more just like it) I would be able to pass out in my jammies. Mr. Katz approached and rubbed himself against my leg in a plea for attention.

"Later," I said apologetically. "Let me change first." He glared at me and I stuck my tongue out in response before trotting up the stairs.

With the flick of a switch I realized to my great irritation that the hall light had burned out. The hallway was pitch-black but it was manageable since there weren't any boxes or other items blocking my way to the bedroom. Fortunately, the bedroom light worked fine. I slipped out of my shoes and went straight to the bathroom to wash the makeup off my face. I was working up a worthy lather when the lights in my bedroom went out.

"Hello?" I called out. No one answered, but that didn't mean there wasn't anyone there.

I looked at my reflection, the foam of my cleanser now sliding down my cheeks. "This," I whispered, "could be very bad."

9

It was once accepted belief that if a corpse didn't decompose right away the deceased individual was either a vampire or a saint. Now it just means they had a good plastic surgeon.

—*The Lighter Side of Death*

FOR A FULL MINUTE, I STOOD THERE, FROZEN, TOO FRIGHTENED TO EVEN turn off the faucet. I looked again into the mirror to see if I could make out anything through the open bathroom door. The bathroom light was enough to cast a very pale glow over my room, but the shadows were almost worse than pure darkness. Keeping my eyes on the mirror I opened the drawer and fumbled around for something sharp. All I could find was my Tweezerman. I glanced down at its sharp tip and decided it would have to do. At least I might be able to gouge out an eye. I turned slowly and walked into my room. No one seemed to be there. I went to the light switch. It was pointing up, exactly as I had left it. I flipped it down and up and the light immediately went back on. A relieved laugh bubbled up my throat. A short circuit, that's all it was.

God, when had I become so paranoid? I went back to the sink and rinsed the soap off and of course the light went out again, but this time I knew it was nothing to worry about.

I went back to the room to try to once again rectify the problem when I saw it. The brooch that had been in Oscar's hand was now pinned to my pillow.

Had that been there when I walked in the room a minute ago? It was possible; it's not like I had been looking for it. I stared at the darkness of the hall beyond my room. Was there someone waiting for me there? I glanced toward the bedside table, but of course there was no phone. In fact, the only working phone in the house was my cell and I had left that downstairs. I turned my gaze back to the brooch. Maybe the person who had placed it there wasn't in the hall after all? What if they were under the bed? *Lift the bedskirt and find out,* my inner voice yelled, but I couldn't get myself to do it. Instead I carefully backed up into the bathroom and reemerged with a plunger. I knelt down quietly, as far away from the bed as I could and still do what I needed to do. Then, with a sudden thrusting motion I shoved the plunder under the bed, jabbing it this way and that, ready to suction up the face of any intruder who might be lying there. Nothing.

The closet was crammed with boxes, so unless the person who had been in my room had been able to transform himself into that *X-Files* villain, he wasn't going to be able to fit in there.

Still, the brooch didn't walk into my room by itself.

Just then the chime of the doorbell echoed through the house. I jumped as if I had just heard an explosion. I had to get the door. Maybe it was Anatoly. God, was I regretting kicking him out now. But getting to the front door meant walking through that dark hallway.

I pressed the base of my palms against my eyes and cursed.

I didn't want to be afraid. In fact, I wouldn't be afraid. I lowered my hands. This was my house! No one was going to make me afraid of being in my own house!

Armed with both a plunger and a Tweezerman, I forced myself to start my journey down the hall. I stopped at each room so I could turn the light on, increasingly illuminating my path. I couldn't see any evidence of another person being there, but I kept my weapons raised, just in case. It occurred to me that the plunger would be more dangerous if I held it by the rubber end and swung the stick, but I was pretty sure that I would rather die.

When I reached the top of the stairs the bell rang again and this time I decided that speed was my friend.

I ran down the steps and practically launched myself at the front door, but I checked myself before opening it. "Anatoly?" I called, putting the plunger to the side.

My only answer was the sound of the doorbell ringing a third time. I backed up. If I walked to the window in my living room I could see who was there…and they'd be able to see me. And if they had a gun I'd be providing them with a perfect shot.

But really, what else was I going to do? I counted quietly to three and then rushed to the window, fully prepared to rush away if I saw anything sinister.

No one was at my door. I stared at the empty spot where I had assumed a person would be. And then the doorbell rang again.

It rang and there was no one there to ring it.

"Another electrical short," I said quietly. I glanced back at my couch, hoping to get a look of agreement from Mr. Katz, but all I saw was the swish of his tail as he rushed from the room.

"Coward," I whispered, although I was tempted to flee myself. I turned back to the window…and screamed. There was a woman there now. I stumbled back and almost screamed again when I realized who it was. Venus stared at me through the glass and raised her hands as if to show me that there was no need for alarm.

Something about the forced innocence of the gesture infuriated me. I went back to the door and threw it open.

"Why on earth are you screaming?" she asked, her silky brown hair loose around her shoulders.

"It was you, wasn't it?" I demanded.

"Was what me?" she asked warily.

"You were the one who put that thing in my bedroom. Why?"

Venus cocked her head ever so slightly and for the first time I noticed the tiniest little scar right on her throat. "I assure you, I didn't put a thing in your bedroom." She pushed past me and walked into the living room. "I simply thought I'd stop by and find out how you're settling in."

I opened my mouth to speak, but couldn't find my voice. She was every bit as cold as that brooch.

"You haven't unpacked much," she went on, running a slender finger along the mantel of my fireplace and then making a face as if disgusted by the dust she had found there. "I suppose that's practical since it's not actually yours yet, is it?"

"I'm still in escrow, but it's mine," I said, my vocal cords finally popping back into action. But my legs were still shaky. "Why did you break into my house earlier?"

"I still don't know what you're talking about. But I do know that until you have a deed you can't really claim ownership of a property," she said, offering me an evil little smile. "But Scott's going to make sure you get that, I suppose. It's so nice that you two have been able to rekindle your friendship after all these years."

I swallowed and looked up at my staircase again. It had to have been her. Her showing up now...it was too big of a coincidence.

"Anyone with eyes can see that the two of you care for one another," Venus continued. "I suppose it's natural considering that you were married...what was it, ten years ago?" She smoothly maneuvered around the boxes and then lowered herself onto my sofa. "My goodness, I was still in puberty ten years ago. I always forget how much older you are."

"Guess that's because your complexion is so much duller than mine," I growled.

If my remark had stung she showed no sign of it. Instead she stretched both arms out to the side and looked up to the ceiling as if she was offering herself up for crucifixion. It was a tempting idea.

"This house has such a rich history. Do you know it?"

I didn't answer.

"Oscar was here for quite some time, but before him there were many others. Have you heard of Cecile Mercier?"

I shook my head mutely.

"Ah, and it's such an interesting story. You really must hear it. You see Cecile lived here at the turn of the century, having bought it with her inheritance. Quite scandalous at the time, a woman buying a home without the benefit of being married. But Cecile didn't care about social conventions or rules. She was independent and reckless and quite frequently foolish."

"And you know this how?" I asked. What the hell was she up to, anyway? First the brooch and now this story that sounded more like an urban legend than a historical account.

"I have studied the history of San Francisco's more beautiful old Victorians. I'm not as interested in the architects or the workers who built them as I am in the people who lived in them and the spirits that remain in them to this day."

"The only spirits in this Victorian are alcoholic," I snapped. Was she actually trying to gaslight me? Did she think I was that stupid?

"You're wrong, Sophie," Venus said. "You are never alone

here. Oscar may visit periodically, but Cecile lives here. She's the one who really owns this house."

"Well, according to you, you can't own a home unless you have a deed, so I think poor dead Cecile is shit out of luck. Plus, she's dead."

"But I told you, Cecile has never cared for rules. Not when it comes to houses, and not when it comes to men."

"Men," I repeated.

"Cecile was having an affair with Vincent Davincourt, a man who was promised to a woman named Miranda Whit-worth. Cecile thought she had the right." Venus's eyes narrowed and her voice lowered to something that resembled a hiss. "She thought she had the right because he had wooed her once before, when they were both too young to see that they were ill suited for one another. The romance between Vincent and Cecile died before it had ever really begun, but she actually thought she could reclaim him whenever she saw fit."

And right away Venus's motivations became crystal clear to me. They should have been clear the moment she mentioned my so-called renewed friendship with Scott, but I had been too shaken to immediately read the writing on the wall.

"You know," I said slowly, "old stories usually get a bit altered in the retelling. I bet Cecile wasn't having an affair with Vincent at all. I bet she was more than happy to let some other woman deal with him so that she could get on with her life."

"No," Venus said quickly. "Cecile was foolish, but not stupid. She saw Vincent for what he was."

"An asshole?" I offered.

"A charming, intelligent and handsome man…. But not strong. Cecile was able to lure him to her bed easily enough. He still loved Miranda, of course, but men will be men. They lack the discipline and resolve of a woman."

"Seriously?" I asked. "You think that if a guy strays it's the other woman's fault? *Seriously?*"

Venus waved my question away with a flick of her wrist. "It doesn't really matter how much fault lay with Vincent. We are talking about Cecile and she was hardly an innocent."

I rolled my eyes. "Fine, whatever. I assume Cecile got caught, otherwise you wouldn't know about it."

"She did get caught," Venus confirmed. "By Miranda."

"Yeah? And how did Mandy take it?"

Venus smiled. "She stabbed Cecile to death."

"You have got to be kidding me. You did not really come here to tell me this."

"Cecile did try to fight back. She must have grabbed at Miranda's throat because she managed to rip off the brooch that Miranda always wore on her collar."

The anger was rumbling inside me like a storm.

"In fact," Venus went on, "it was the same brooch Oscar had in his hand when you found him. Yes, I know about that," she said, responding to a question that no one had asked. "Scott told me all about it. I contacted the hospital Oscar was taken to, but oddly enough no one had any idea what I was talking about. It's as if the brooch just vanished...or has been re-claimed."

I visualized myself getting her into a headlock and slamming her into the wall over and over again. But instead I swallowed hard and looked away. "You're trying to mess with my head. You come into my house, *my* house and try to scare me with your brooch and your stupid story..."

"It's not my story and—"

"Did you actually think I would buy it? Any of it?" I asked. "Have I done something to make you think that I'm a total moron? I've had people try to convince me that I'm crazy before, but you really thought you could make me believe in ghosts?"

"But you do believe in ghosts, *Soapy,*" Venus said. "At least that's what you told Kane. It was a requirement for moving in, wasn't it?"

I sucked in a sharp breath. I couldn't let her goad me into giving her the rope to hang me with.

"Anyway, I do love stories that one can learn from," Venus continued. She stood back up, moving her body with the grace of a ballerina. But it was practiced, everything about Venus felt practiced. The way she moved, the way she talked, even the way she cried. It was like humanity was something she had studied and mastered, but never internalized.

"The lesson here," she said, "is to never try to steal another woman's man. The woman wronged might not be very forgiving."

I craned my neck back in order to meet her eyes. "Are you threatening me, Venus?"

Venus blinked and then the corners of her lips curled up in amusement. "I'm simply telling you a story. One that I hope you will find useful." She stepped back and glanced at her watch. "Is that the time? I must get going. If that brooch shows up again I'd be happy to take it off your hands. I'd like to have something of Miranda's. I believe the two of us have a lot in common."

I laughed. I couldn't help it. "You want it back? Sorry, but you're the one who broke in here and pinned it on my pillow. That makes it a gift. So thank you and goodbye."

For a few seconds Venus didn't move or speak, but I could sense that her mood was getting darker and that was saying something. "There was no gift." Her voice was different, so different that I found myself looking behind her to find the ventriloquist. "If you have found the brooch, if it was left here by some*thing* then you should give it to me. I understand what it is and you never will."

"There's something familiar about this," I mused. "Oh, I know! You're the gatekeeper from *Ghostbusters!* You're Sigourney Weaver! Now all we have to do is get you a pet gargoyle and a perm and you'll be all set to film the remake."

She turned on her heel and marched to the stairs.

"Where do you think you're going?" I asked, grabbing her arm. She yanked it away with unexpected strength and went up the stairs. I ran after her, my legs having to work double time to keep up with her longer ones. I watched as she entered my room. She looked over at my bed and let out something between a growl and a curse before snatching up the brooch, literally tearing the pillowcase it was attached to in the process. She walked past me again, and this time I didn't try to stop her, but simply followed her back down the stairs. Her audacity was literally awe-inspiring. Before leaving she dropped a few twenties on the sofa. "For the pillowcase," she said. "If it's more than that, save the receipt." She stopped again just as she was about to step outside. And peered at me over her shoulder. "I almost forgot, Scott sends his love."

And then, at last, she was gone.

Mr. Katz reentered the living room and stared at me with his tigerlike eyes. "Yeah, I know," I said. "I should have ripped her hair out."

Mr. Katz swished his tail, his way of saying "Well, *duh!*" And really, who would have dared to suggest that the assault wouldn't have been justified? The bitch broke into my house! She tried to scare me with those pathetic ghost stories! It had just been luck that the lights had started short circuiting just minutes before she arrived. Luck, nothing more.

The doorbell had been weird though....

I shook my head fiercely, trying to force the last remnants of fear to release their grip. Over the years I have faced down thieves, murderers…politicians, for God's sake! I wasn't going to be spooked by a short circuit and Scott's jealous girlfriend.

It's just that Venus really had seemed taken off her guard by the fact that I had the brooch and I've never heard of a doorbell short circuiting….

I walked over to the box holding the cocktail Anatoly had made me and finished it in three consecutive gulps before turning on my heel and marching into the kitchen. A little food and I'd be thinking clearly again. Ten minutes later I reentered the living room with a freshly heated cup of chicken noodle soup and a tumbler full of liquid courage. I gently lowered these items onto the box already holding the chocolates before turning on my flat-screen TV, one of the few appliances that I had plugged in and ready to go. Another example of my traditional, American priorities. I sat on the couch next to Mr. Katz and started flipping though the channels. A *Will & Grace* rerun, a new episode of *Access Hollywood* and…

I dropped the remote in my lap and stared at Maria's face. She was shifting her weight from foot to foot as she stared at the camera in front of her.

"It was a scythe," she said in a halting voice.

The reporter standing next to her shook his head in amazement as if he hadn't been given this information from his producers hours earlier. "Had you ever seen the scythe before?"

"It's not mine," she said a little defensively. "And it wasn't Enrico's…. I don't believe it belonged to any…*living* person."

Mr. Katz got up and then made his way over to my dinner. "She really thinks a ghost killed her husband," I said.

Mr. Katz brought his nose close to the soup bowl and sniffed in disbelief.

"And why are all these ghosts so friggin' sloppy?" I asked him. "Everywhere they go they're dropping scythes and brooches…."

My voice trailed off. Venus had been the "ghost" with the brooch, so was it so far-fetched to believe that she could have been the ghost with the scythe? I flattened my hand against my chest. "I can't believe it, Scott may actually be dating a murderer…! And he used to have such good taste in women."

Mr. Katz leaned a little too close to the soup and then darted back, a bit of noodle dangling off his nose.

"I should warn him," I said as I gently removed the noodle. "I mean, I've wished him dead enough times, but in my fantasy it was always me doing the killing. It seems somewhat immoral to let Venus do it."

But then again Scott probably wasn't the one in danger. After all, he wasn't the one finding ugly old brooches in his bedroom. And then there was the matter of how Venus got into my bedroom in order to put the brooch there in the first place. She didn't have a key…of course, Scott had a key at one point. He said he had turned all the keys over to me, but maybe he hadn't. He *would* get off on the idea of having the key to my place. I shook my head in disgust. "You know what?" I said to Mr. Katz. "I'm not in such a hurry to tell Scott about Venus anymore. He'll figure it out on his own…when she pulls out the ice pick."

Maria wasn't on the TV anymore. The newscasters were now reporting on Oprah's half-eaten pancake, which had apparently sold on eBay for $12,000. Perhaps crazy was a relative term.

I wasn't hungry anymore and my soup probably had cat hair in it anyway. I picked up my drink and went up to my bedroom once more. The lights were working again, but I knew they could short out at any moment. I dug around in a suitcase until I came up with a clean pillowcase to replace the ruined one, threw on an oversize T-shirt, crawled under my extrasoft sheets and pulled the comforter up to my chin. My bed, my bedroom, my home. Any fear I felt within these walls would be fleeting—

at least that's how it felt at the moment. My eyes went to half-mast then closed completely.

My last conscious thought was of the inspection I paid a contractor to do of the house. Funny that he hadn't noticed a problem with the wiring.

10

Of course I married a submissive. Now if I want to have sex without messing up my hair I just tie him to the bed and don't worry about it.

—*The Lighter Side of Death*

WHEN I OPENED MY EYES THE NEXT MORNING, THE CLOCK READ 10:05 A.M. and light was pouring in through my uncurtained windows. That was late even for me. But I had been having such intense dreams…something about being a child running up and down a beautiful staircase, and someone had been with me….

With a sigh I gave up the effort of recollection and propped myself on my elbows, upsetting Mr. Katz, who had been curled up on my chest. I was feeling more alert and focused than I normally do before my first cup of coffee, and as I studied the way the particles of dust danced in the sunlight, I was hit by the realization that Maria was a potential problem. If she was innocent, then she was of no real concern to me. But if she wasn't, then she had gone out of her way to make me complicit in the murder of her husband. Why exactly would she want to do that?

And like Kane and Venus, she belonged to the Specter Society.

Of course there were other members of that group, as well, members who had known all three of my current nemeses longer than I had and might be able to provide me with information and clues as to how to deal with them. I could turn to Scott and we could "put our heads together," as he had suggested. But I really didn't want my head anywhere near him if I could help it. There was also Jason Beck. When he had been with Dena I had gotten myself into some serious trouble and he had earnestly tried to help me. There was no reason to think he wouldn't do so again.

I swung my legs over the side of the bed ready to retrieve my cell phone that I had neglected to take into the bedroom with me the night before....

Or at least I thought I had neglected to take it up, but obviously I was wrong because there it was on my nightstand. I tried to remember doing that, but then chalked it up to having a highly efficient subconscious. I skimmed through my contacts looking for Jason's number, which I had punched in on the night of the séance, and pressed the send button the moment I found it.

"Hello?" His voice was hoarse with undisguised sleepiness.

"Hey, Jason, it's Sophie. Did I wake you? It's after 10:00 a.m."

"You forget—I'm a creature of the night."

"Are you? Last I heard you were still looking for Mrs. Good Bite to help you cross over."

"Funny," Jason yawned. "So what's up—wait—" his voice took on a much more urgent tone "—why *are* you calling? Did someone *ask* you to call me?"

"Nooo," I said uncertainly. "I called of my own accord. That okay?"

There was a moment of silence on the phone. "Sure," Jason finally said. "So you called to talk and get reacquainted."

"Well, I really do want to catch up with you," I hedged, "but I was also hoping you could help me get some stuff sorted."

"Stuff?"

"There's a chance Kane will evict me if I don't produce a ghost for him, or, if I can't do that, then prove that I'm not a murderer."

"I don't know, Sophie. The latter request seems reasonable."

"Yeah, well, I'm not a murderer and it would be nice if people would just take my word for it." I ran a finger across my bottom lip, lingering over the dry patches of skin. "I also have a problem with Venus. She's jealous. She thinks I'm after Scott."

There was another long silence on the line before Jason asked, "Can you get yourself into the witness protection program?"

"Excuse me?"

"Venus is wicked, Sophie. If she was a vampire she'd be Claudia."

"Claudia…is she from the Anne Rice series?"

"Yeah, she was the childlike sociopathic vampire. Venus has that same energy."

I watched Mr. Katz leisurely walk toward my paned-glass window as I tried to figure out what differentiated a sociopathic vampire from the run-of-the-mill bloodsuckers. But I skipped that question in favor of another. "Can you fill me in on what you know about Venus and Kane? And Maria, too, I have some questions about her."

"Sophie, last time I helped you it didn't turn out so well."

"I'm just asking for a little info, here."

"Yeah, how much is this info worth to you?"

I sat up a little straighter. "Seriously?"

"Is it worth a haircut?"

"You want me to cut your hair? Jason, I can barely cut out a paper doll without decapitating her."

"Not you. Marcus. Think he can fit me in?"

"Oh." From the corner of my eye I could see Mr. Katz

curling up in a patch of sunlight, the fur on the left side of his body pressed flat against the glass. "That's probably doable. I'll give him a call. You want to see him in the next few weeks?"

"I was thinking about today."

"You want to see Marcus *today?*" I sputtered. "Do you know he's become one of the most celebrated hairstylists in the city?"

"Whatever. I don't dig on the pop-culture trends or the what's-hot-what's-not-crowd. I just want the man to cut my hair. I know he's good."

"Right, well, I'll see what I can do."

"Sure, that's all I ask. And when I get my haircut you can tag along and I'll tell you all about Venus, Maria and Kane."

"Not before?"

"Fair is fair."

"Oh, this is so not fair," I seethed, but then I stopped myself before I said anything more. I hadn't spoken to Jason for years and I was already asking him for favors. All he was asking for was a hair appointment with one of my closest friends. Was that really out of bounds?

"Like I said, I'll do my best," I said, trying to be more conciliatory. "I'll call you back as soon as I know something." I hung up and immediately punched Marcus's number in.

"Well, well, if it isn't the upwardly mobile Ms. Katz," Marcus sang upon picking up. "I was beginning to think you had gotten too big for your rent-poor friends."

"Yeah, I know I've been a bit out of touch."

"A bit?" he quibbled. "Honey, there are agoraphobics who have been more sociable than you've been this last month. But you can make it up to me by telling me all about the fabulousness of your new casa. Are we making bold new decorating decisions or are we trying to stay true to the whole Victorian thing by channeling Laura Ashley?"

"I'm kinda going with the deconstructionist look right now. You know, scattered, half-full boxes, clothes hanging out of suitcases, lots and lots of dust…it's very avant-garde."

"And you're calling me in hopes that I'll share my fierce artistic vision before you go furniture shopping? How very pro-active."

"I'm calling because one of Dena's former lovers needs a haircut."

"First of all, I don't cut, I style. Secondly, I'm afraid you're going to have to whittle this one down for me. Dena's slept with half the straight men in the city, which would put her number at…let's see, thirty? Thirty-five, maybe?"

"I'll have to check the latest census report, but this particular straight guy is Jason Beck."

"Vampire boy! Oh, how fun! How are the undead wearing their hair these days?"

"I don't know, but I'm sure you'll come up with something that works. Any chance you could fit him in today?"

"You're joking of course—I'm booked for the next two months."

"But today's Saturday, and you don't come in until 1:00 on Saturdays, so if you got there at noon…"

"And why exactly would I do this for someone I barely know?"

"It's a trade-off. I get him in to see you and he gives me some information. I don't know if Dena told you this, but the Realtor for this place is—"

"Scott, your demonic ex," Marcus finished for me. "Dena did tell me. I hear he's dating a planet."

"Her name is Venus, but the name doesn't fit. She seems more like a Pluto or something."

"You mean she's cold, distant and barely legitimate?"

"Something like that." I filled him in on what had gone down with Maria when she had dragged Anatoly and me to

Enrico's and on Kane's threats to take away my home and Venus's subtle threats to do something vaguely horrible and Jason's connection to all of them. "It's all a big mess," I finished.

"Obviously. And you don't think Jason will help you with any of this if I don't do his hair?"

"I don't know, I might be able to finesse it out of him without your artistry, as you call it, but I'd rather just meet the demands. I do kind of owe him."

"Not as much as you owe me," Marcus pointed out. "I'm sorry, love, but I have no desire to come in early today. And I can't keep doing favors for friends. As it is, I already agreed to fill in my one o'clock cancellation today with one of Dena's friends."

"Which friend?"

"Don't remember, it's written down at the salon. Some girl with a *K*."

"Hmm, I think she hired a salesperson named Kendra a few months ago."

"Could be, but for some reason I don't think so. Anyhoo, if Jason really wants to come in, tell him I can squeeze him in at the end of next week. That's my best offer."

Mr. Katz got back up and in a moment he was on my bedside table. With his paw he batted at a cheap silver bracelet that I had bartered for while visiting Mexico. I smiled as a new idea popped into my head. "Remember that cute barista from the Nob Hill Starbucks?" I asked.

"The one who looks like Clark Kent?"

"Yeah, him. He transferred to another Starbucks and he also broke up with his boyfriend. And he *also* told me he thought you were cute."

"Seriously?" Marcus asked eagerly. "Which Starbucks does he work at now?"

"I'll tell you at noon today, while you're styling Jason's hair."

★ ★ ★

Jason met me outside Ooh La La at exactly ten to noon. He leaned against the sleek, black-tiled wall of the salon, his legs clad in straight-cut ripped jeans, his motorcycle jacket open and his arms crossed over a T-shirt featuring an artistic rendering of Barack Obama.

"You're an Obama man?" I asked as I approached, somewhat surprised.

He shook his head distractedly. "I don't believe in politics. The Democratic and Republican parties are just organizations designed to brainwash us into embracing an establishment mentality."

"Uh-huh," I said. I had no idea what any of that meant, but I wasn't all that interested in finding out. "So what's up with the T-shirt?"

"It's an iconic portrait of our times."

"Okay."

Jason smiled slightly. "Dena would get where I am coming from with this. She has a very existential view of life."

"Okay," I said again. Dena wasn't an existentialist, but she did like dating lunatics. "Shall we go in?"

Jason eyed the exterior of the salon doubtfully. "I usually get my hair cut in the Lower Height."

"Well, this will be a change for you," I said, visualizing the grungy teens and panhandlers who frequent the area. "You'll see, it's fun getting your hair done by someone who's not on acid."

"I'm philosophically opposed to what this portion of Fillmore Street represents."

"Of course you are." I draped my arm over his shoulder. "But perhaps we can soften your opposition with a mimosa."

As we entered, Jason's eyes flitted from the art deco painting on the wall to the chic reception desk while I tried to read his face for some hint of what was going on. If Jason didn't want to get his hair cut in an expensive salon, why were we here? And why today?

The woman at the front desk had hair the color of an autumn leaf with copper highlights expertly woven into her locks. She smiled politely at both of us, but before she could open her mouth Marcus appeared behind her. His perfect mocha skin seemed to project a natural glow, although my money was on bareMinerals powder foundation.

"The name of the Starbucks?" he asked while carefully rolling up the sleeves of his cotton shirt, which was just sheer enough to draw your attention to the well-cared-for torso it covered.

"After you cut his hair," I said coolly.

Marcus rolled his eyes. "God, I'm such a whore. How many mimosas do we need?"

I held up two fingers and Marcus imitated the gesture for the benefit and instruction of the receptionist before leading us forward.

We entered the main room, which was much more expansive than the greeting area. Men and women, all managing to be hip without following any particular trend, snipped away with their scissors as their clients' tresses floated to the bamboo floor beneath their feet. Marcus gestured to his station and Jason awkwardly climbed into his chair just as the receptionist appeared to serve us our drinks. By the time she was in retreat, Marcus was already playing with Jason's hair and studying his face in the mirror.

"You do have fabulous bone structure," he said to Jason. "If we go short we can do a bit of a George Clooney thing."

"Not short," Jason said quickly. "Do you remember how my hair looked last time you saw me?"

"Vaguely," Marcus said with an expression that said no.

"I want it to look exactly like that. And I want to get rid of the gray."

"Gray?" Marcus repeated. He began to pick through Jason's hair with the meticulous and somewhat appalled manner parents employ while checking their child's head for lice. "Honey, you've got maybe five or six white strands. That doesn't exactly make you Anderson Cooper."

"Then just dye the five or six strands," Jason said desperately. He fumbled in the pockets of his leather jacket until he found his wallet and pulled out a picture. Marcus and I both leaned over to better examine it. It had been taken in front of Fog City Diner and Jason had his arm wrapped around Dena's waist as she toyed with his hair. "I want that haircut again," Jason said firmly. "I know the picture doesn't really show the cut well but I was hoping it would jog your memory."

"It's rare that someone comes in saying they actually want hair that is so three years ago," Marcus said, leaning in a bit closer. "What else do you want back from that year? The fashion, the music, the girlfriend perhaps?"

Jason flushed.

"Oh my God," I exclaimed. "Is that what this is about? You're trying to look the way you did back when Dena had a thing for you? You're planning on making a move on her again?"

"I don't make moves," Jason corrected. "I connect with people and Dena and I were connected."

"Yes," Marcus agreed, "but then she hung up. Poof!" He made a grand gesture with his hands. "Connection gone."

"But not forever. I don't think it has to be gone forever."

Across the room a woman broke into peals of laughter, her voice carrying over the sounds of Death Cab for Cutie. I looked down at Jason and found myself oddly touched by the wistfulness of his expression, but the sad truth was that Dena rarely ate her own leftovers.

"Nothing's impossible," I said carefully. "She *could* decide to give it another go. But you could also move on to someone else. Someone who doesn't think monogamy is a social anxiety disorder."

"Dena doesn't believe in commitments," Jason acknowledged, "but there are some forces that are stronger than our most dearly held convictions. I think the connection that Dena and I share could be that kind of force."

Marcus chuckled and shook his head, causing all his short, neatly groomed locks to wag from side to side. "Okay, Obi-Wan, I'll recreate the old look for you and I'll make you fabulous." He wrapped a towel around Jason's neck and then a dark apron. "But don't expect it to help you on this quest of yours. I'm an artist, not a magician."

He turned to me. "I'm going to take him over to shampoo and condition. Find yourself a stool and we'll be back in a snap."

I nodded and went off to search for a stool while Marcus and Jason moved toward the sinks in the opposite direction. By the time we were all back at Marcus's station I was comfortably seated and Jason had a towel wrapped around his head and looked a bit like an Arab sheikh...wearing an apron.

"Just so you know," Jason said as Marcus removed the towel and began to snip, "you didn't have to do this."

Marcus stopped cutting and made eye contact with him through the mirror. "From what I understand we absolutely did have to do this. That's why I came in early despite the Bravo *Project Runway* marathon."

"It does mean a lot to me," Jason said quickly. "I needed this for confidence, you know, it's like Sampson and Delilah—I need hair that will give me strength."

"If Dena is Delilah, you've got trouble," Marcus muttered, but resumed cutting.

"What I'm saying is that if you absolutely weren't able to fit me in today then I still would have told Sophie about Venus." He turned his focus back on me. "You need to know about her."

"What exactly do I need to know?"

"She practices voodoo."

Marcus stopped cutting again. "Are you saying that somewhere out there there's a little Sophie doll getting acupuncture?"

"I don't know.... Sophie, have you had any odd pains lately? They would be sharp and sudden."

"Wait, you don't actually believe in this?" I asked.

"Look, when I met Scott and Venus last year things were tense. Scott was screwing some mortgage broker...well, that was my take on it. According to Scott—"

"According to Scott they were just affectionate friends. Very affectionate." I finished for him. "I've heard that one before. So why didn't Venus leave Scott?"

"Venus doesn't always have an easy time of it when it comes to finding and keeping men," Jason said. "Maybe she's desperate. Or maybe she just seriously digs on Scott. That guy doesn't just kiss her ass, he uses tongue."

"Oh, okay, that was not a visual that I needed to have," Marcus groaned.

"So Venus didn't leave him," I said, getting us back on track. "What did she do?"

"She went to a fucking voodoo priestess. It was some seriously sketchy shit."

I shook my head. "If by sketchy you mean patently ridiculous then, yeah, sketchy."

"Don't be so quick to dismiss it," Jason warned. "If I were you I'd be getting myself a gris-gris about now."

"A gris-gris?" Marcus asked. "That sounds rather wicked, do tell more."

"It's kind of like a protective amulet," Jason explained. "It's a small cloth bag you wear around your neck containing stuff like herbs, oils and pieces of cloth soaked with perspiration. It really works." He paused before adding, "It doesn't always smell so good though."

"I think I'll pass," I said, finishing off the last of my mimosa. "Besides, I don't think Venus is commissioning any dolls in my likeness right now. Her strategy seems to be to convince me that my house is haunted so I'll get the hell out of Dodge."

Jason looked at me blankly for a moment and then broke into a full, rich laugh, loud enough to make the clients in the nearby station briefly look our way before their respective hairdressers yanked their heads back in place. "She's telling you your *house* is haunted?" Jason said when he was finally able to speak again. "What kind of moron would believe anything that far-fetched?"

I stared at him for half a beat. "Gee, I don't know, Jason. Maybe the kind of moron who believes in vampires and the power of the gris-gris."

"That's different," he said, still chuckling. "Vampires and voodoo makes sense. Haunted houses don't."

"Wow, I am getting such an education," Marcus said. "Can we talk about unicorns next? There's something about the symbolism of a big stallion with a long, hard horn on its head that appeals to me."

"I'm serious," Jason said. "See, voodoo is a West African religion brought over by the slaves. It began with the Yoruba people. They were more in touch with spirituality and the force of nature than any of us puritanical white-breads will ever be. Stories of vampires can also be traced to Africa and countries all over the globe."

"And you're going to tell me that stories of ghosts don't have long-standing international appeal?" I asked. "Because if so I suggest you start watching the late-night programming on the History Channel."

"No, sightings of ghosts have been reported all over the world. But stories of *buildings* that are haunted are a Western phenomenon. It all comes back to our inflated sense of materialism. We actually believe that those who travel to the next world can't shed their attachment to a man-made commodity. It's stupid."

"Totally silly," Marcus agreed, shooting me an oh-my-God-can-you-believe-this-guy look.

"The only bond that cannot be broken by death is love and loathing," he explained. "Love for your soul mate, a child, a sibling, even a best friend. That kind of bond can extend into the next world. A spirit might choose to hang out on earth for something like that, but a piece of architecture designed by some sellout hack?" He shook his head emphatically. "Not likely."

I was more than a little peeved by the implication that my house was designed by a hack, but considering where the criticism was coming from it seemed wise not to take it too seriously. "What about the hate part?" I asked. "You said that spirits might hang out for that, too."

"Nah, I said they might stay because they *loathe* someone. For a spirit to actually resist the draw of the next world it has to have a connection to someone on earth that is a lot stronger than the hate you might feel for some politico who wants to raise your taxes. A spirit has to be so repulsed by you, so offended by your very existence that it can't rest until it completely destroys you."

"Wow. That's comforting."

"I wouldn't worry about it. From what I understand, the only people who truly loathe you are still alive."

Marcus bit back a laugh.

"Okay, okay," I said irritably. "Truth is, I'm not at all convinced that Venus believes in haunted houses, either. But she definitely wants *me* to believe in them. That's the issue here and I think she might have actually broken into my house and staged a haunting in order to turn me into a believer."

"I can't believe she broke into your house," Marcus said. "That's so 2005."

"I know, how messed up is that?" I asked as the music switched from Death Cab to Flobots. "So you tell me, Jason, is this woman dangerous?"

Jason didn't say anything. His eyes were wide and he was staring at an image in the mirror. Both Marcus and I followed his gaze. A few steps out of the reception area on the salon floor was Dena with Marcus's 1:00 p.m.—Kim, the tall Eurasian busser from MarketBar Café. This time he was wearing a denim jacket and his hair was slicked back in a way that could have looked greasy, but on him was oddly dashing.

"Wow," I murmured. "That is so not Kendra."

They say you have to be cruel to be kind. I'm going to be so kind to my ex he won't know what hit him.
—*The Lighter Side of Death*

ALTHOUGH I COULD TELL THAT DENA WAS LOOKING AT US, I COULDN'T actually see her eyes very well from her position across the room. But I could feel them. I could feel the questions they posed and the uncertainty…particularly the uncertainty. That was an emotion Dena rarely indulged in. She stood still by Kim's side as he blithely took in his surroundings. She said something to him and then, while he stayed where he was, she marched toward us. Up until that point, the cheerful chitchat of the other clients around us, the occasional ringing of cell phones, the sound of the hair dryers and water running from the sinks, had all blended together into a pleasant humming background noise in which no individual sound was clearly discernable from the other. But now the resonance of Dena's stiletto heels moving toward me was as clear and distinguishable as the scream of a smoke alarm. In seconds she was standing by my stool.

Marcus, the only one of us who didn't seem the least perturbed, offered Dena a bemused smile. "Hi, honey, how—"

"Explain," she said. Not a complete sentence, but clear
enough in its meaning, particularly since she wasn't looking at
Marcus or Jason, just me.

"Jason is in the Specter Society, so we kinda reconnected,"
I said meekly. "He asked if I could get him in for a haircut."

"Style," Marcus corrected. "He came in for a little of my style."

"Marcus mentioned that a friend of yours would be coming
in after us," I continued, "but I didn't think you would be
coming, too, and I didn't think your friend would be...well, I
just didn't think period, did I?"

"No, you sure as hell didn't," Dena snapped.

"Hi, Dena!" Jason swatted Marcus's hands away and got to
his feet. It's amazing how quickly he could shift from vampire
to puppy. "It's been eons. I didn't know you would be here!"
He stopped short and then his smile widened even more. "We
got those earrings on University Avenue! I was actually with
you when you picked them out. Remember, we were going
to see that indie band playing at Cal and—"

"Jason," she said, completely cutting him off, "you know
I'm not fond of memory lane. I'm more of a Tomorrowland
chick."

Marcus let out a low whistle and I winced on Jason's behalf.
I knew that if I were to confront her about her rudeness she
would tell me that Jason was clearly not over her and that he
was the kind of guy who could (and would) misinterpret even
the smallest civility. Dena's belief was that it was kinder to be
brutal than misleading.

"Dena," Jason whispered, clearly unsettled, "you just used
a Disneyland metaphor."

Marcus burst out laughing and Dena's mouth dropped open
slightly. Then she shook her head in utter frustration. "Shit,

this is what happens when I'm totally unprepared for something."

Jason tried to smile, but it was shaky. He made a small gesture in Kim's direction. "A friend?"

Dena looked over her shoulder and sighed. "He's my tomorrow," she said in an apologetic voice. "Probably not my next week, but who can think that far ahead, right?"

Amazingly, Jason seemed to see that as a sign of encouragement. He lifted his chin ever so slightly and sat back in his chair. "Introduce me," he instructed.

Dena did a quick double take. "You're not going to try to challenge him to a cockfight or something, right?"

"Dena," Jason said solemnly, "my cock is for love, not war."

Dena chuckled despite herself, but still I doubt she would have introduced Kim if he hadn't walked over on his own. He smiled and extended his hand to me. "Hey, how you doing…um…"

"Sophie," I reminded him. "And this is Marcus and Jason."

"I'm a friend of Dena's," Jason said. The fluorescent lights reflected off his upturned face.

"Great!" Kim looked to Marcus. "Are we too early?"

"I'll be done in ten," Marcus answered. "Fifteen tops. Why don't you two lovelies get something to drink from the receptionist while you wait. I think she may have put together an hors d'oeuvre plate, as well."

"Dena, remember the time you used my bare stomach for a plate?" Jason interjected, while looking at Kim. "I still remember how cold that ice cream felt. I don't think I would have been able to deal if you hadn't licked it off as quickly as you did."

I stared down into my empty champagne glass and tried to wish it full. But Kim seemed inexplicably cheery.

"You, too?" he asked Jason eagerly. "She used sorbet with

me, I really thought I was going to end up with frostbite! Hey, I want to let you know that I'm not weird about meeting Dena's exes. Dena's told me about how she likes to stay on good terms with the guys she's gone out with, and I think that's totally cool." He wrapped his arm around her waist and pulled her to him as he planted a kiss on the top of her head. "You really are awesome, you know that?"

Mimosas weren't going to be enough. Clearly it was time for shots.

"Good terms?" Jason said in a low growl. "I haven't even gotten a phone call!"

Kim dropped his arm. "Oh, hey…I didn't mean…I just thought…well, you know how Dena always talks so casually about her sexual experiences…I thought maybe this was just friendly banter, but I didn't mean to start anything or…"

"Damn it, Dena," Jason went on, completely ignoring Kim. "I knew you'd be screwing guys after me, but how could you cover another man's stomach with ice cream? That was *our* thing!"

"I switched it to sorbet!" Dena pointed out.

"So you cut the fat!" Jason shot back. "That's all I ever was to you, huh? The fat that you can casually discard! Remember, Dena, the fat may not be good for you, but it makes everything taste a lot better! There are a lot of women out there who would love to lick my fat!"

Marcus's comb barely made a noise as he dropped it to the floor, but his suppressed gag was clearly audible.

"Okay, I'm done," I said as I got to my feet. "Jason, thanks for all the info on the ghosts and voodoo stuff. I'll pay the receptionist on the way out."

"Sophie," Marcus said in a warning voice.

"Laurel Village," I said quickly. "That's the Starbucks, right on the corner of California and Laurel."

"You're not leaving me yet," Marcus said firmly.

"Tell you what, I'll bring Starbucks-man to you! I'll deliver him with a big bow and a bottle of exotic oils. I'll get right on that."

"Sophie," Marcus said again.

I sat down sullenly.

Marcus smiled triumphantly before turning back to Jason. "Let's finish you up, and you two," he said, pointing at Dena and Kim, "go wait in the reception area until I'm ready for you. You're bothering my client. And *you*," he said pointing at me, "are going to give me a thirty-percent tip for this."

I nodded. The only part of the plan I objected to was that it didn't include more mimosas.

Kim looked like he wanted to disappear. Dena, on the other hand, just looked pissed. She grabbed Kim's hand and dragged him back to the reception area as Jason slumped in his chair.

"She never even called," he whispered as Marcus resumed clipping. "I told her...I told her how much she meant to me and she just cut me out of her life!"

"Jason," I said carefully, "Dena may say that she likes to stay on good terms with her exes, but that only really works for her when the ex was never all that attached. She probably thought that being friends wasn't going to be enough for you so——"

"It wouldn't have been! God, we have such great physical chemistry. Have you ever read *The Multi-Orgasmic Man?*"

"Jason, sweetie," Marcus cooed, "there are some details that we don't really need to know."

"All right, then I'll just say that the book only made sense to me after I met Dena. And with no warning, no warning at all, she just ended it!"

"Yeah, well, Dena doesn't like long goodbyes or, you know, emotional complications," I said, trying to be as gentle as possible.

Marcus gently tilted Jason's head to the side. "Don't worry, sweetie, by the time I'm done with you the ladies will be lining up with the ice cream scoopers."

"But I don't want *ladies,*" Jason sighed. "I just want Dena."

"Okay, but, Jason?" I took his hand and smiled at him with the same gentle condescension I would have used with a distressed child. "Dena doesn't *just* want you."

Jason stopped talking after that. Marcus fulfilled his promise and made him look fairly fabulous, deviating slightly from the picture he had shown him in order to better complement Jason's features. Jason didn't object, or approve, for that matter. He just sat there dully looking at his reflection in the mirror.

"I insist you comment on my work," Marcus finally said as he pulled the apron from Jason's neck.

Jason stood up and took a step closer to the mirror. "It's good," he acknowledged. Then he turned and cast his gaze in the direction of the reception area. "I'm just not sure…" he started, his voice heavier now, "I'm not sure it's going to be good enough."

Marcus put his hand on Jason's shoulder. "Honey, no hairstyle is that good. Do yourself a favor and find yourself a nice supermodel. They're more accessible."

Jason didn't answer and after a moment Marcus removed his hand.

"Come on," I said to Jason, "I'll walk you out."

Jason walked by my side, his head lowered and his feet shuffling. Part of me felt that I should shout out, "Dead man walking!" but instead I simply linked my arm through his and tried to hurry him along.

In the reception area Dena and Kim were flipping through a *Rolling Stone.* They both looked up as I walked up to the reception desk, checkbook in hand. Out of the corner of my eye

I saw Kim try to get up, his countenance full of apology and regret, but Dena held him back. I paid as quickly as I could and dragged Jason out of there.

We walked along the street for a few minutes. Fillmore was teeming with its usual crowd of trust-fund babies and dot-commers looking for trendy and socially responsible avenues for their consumption. The store to my right boasted sheet sets made from organic Egyptian cotton for the low price of $550 and to my left there was a woman admiring the "cruelty free" diamond brooch designed to resemble a skull and crossbones in another store's window. Quintessential San Francisco. The scene was reassuringly familiar enough to strip away the anxiety that had been building up during the course of the last hour. I closed my eyes and breathed in the clean, damp air. Everything was going to be okay.

Then I opened my eyes and looked at Jason and realized that our surroundings had only managed to soothe one of us.

"I knew she'd be sleeping with other guys," he finally said. "I'm cool with that. Human beings are primates. We're not meant to only mate with one partner."

"Gee, Jason, that's romantic."

"But the ice cream," he moaned. "She told me she had never done that before. That *meant* something, you know?"

I didn't know. How could dumping food all over your lover's stomach be interpreted as a tender expression of love? I scooted aside as a passing Chihuahua strained against his pink leash in an attempt to sniff my shoes. "Are you giving up on her?" I asked.

"I don't know, man." He reached into his inside pocket and pulled out a pack of cigarettes.

"Ew!" I recoiled. "You smoke?"

"Only when I drink," he said, reaching for a lighter, "or when I'm seriously depressed."

I snatched the pack away. "These will kill you, and you don't want that."

"Yeah?" he said sarcastically. "How should I get myself killed then?"

"You could hang out with me some more," I suggested. "I attract homicidal maniacs like mosquitoes, baby."

Jason cracked up and then stopped suddenly in his tracks. "You know what we need to do?"

"Is this still about Dena?" I asked warily. "Because if you want my help getting her back, there really isn't a lot I can do."

"No, this has nothing to do with Dena. This is about Venus and Amelia."

"Amelia? The happy hippy chick?"

"Yeah, that's her. We should talk to her about Venus. She knows her brother."

A series of sonic booms coming from a car stereo caused our conversation to pause until it passed. "Venus has a brother?" I asked once I knew I could be heard again.

"Yep. See, Amelia says she knew Venus's brother, William, from Carnegie Mellon. Not well, but they were part of the same study group once. Only she didn't know he had a sister. When she found out who Venus was and who her family was she got all excited and asked after him, and Venus got all uptight."

"Why?" I asked.

"Turns out William's dead. He checked out six years ago."

I sucked in a sharp breath. I didn't want to feel sorry for Venus, but to lose a sibling…

I looked up at the darkening sky, all those rain clouds making their intentions known. Despite the craziness Leah brought into my life, I never wanted to face a world that didn't have her in it.

"Thing is," Jason continued, "Venus was seriously sketchy about what went down. Was it a car accident, suicide, some weird illness—no way to know because Venus wouldn't say."

"Too painful to talk about?"

"I don't think so. You didn't see her face or hear the way she said his name. Venus *hated* her brother. You could feel it just emanating off of her. Amelia and I talked about it and we both wonder if maybe…" His voice trailed off.

"Maybe what?"

"Maybe Venus had something to do with it."

And there you had it, problem solved. Now, not only did I not have to feel sorry for her, I could hate her even more than I already did.

"I remember Amelia saying she was going to look into it," he added.

"Do you have Amelia's number by any chance?"

"Yeah, but not her work number and that's where she's at right now. She works for a florist south of Market. Forgot the name of it, but I know where it is. You wanna pay her a visit?"

I whipped out my car keys. "Absolutely."

Jason and I took two cars, which was convenient in that we could both go our separate ways when we were done talking to Amelia, but inconvenient in that it took what would have been a thirty-minute search for parking and turned it into one that lasted nearly an hour. You would think that with all the talk of energy conservation and fewer people driving there would be more parking spots. Unfortunately, the reverse is true. People don't drive now, they park. And then they leave their cars in that parking spot for an entire week while they catch the bus to their various destinations. I was bitching about this to Jason, but quickly forgot my complaints when we stepped into O'Keefe's, Amelia's place of work.

O'Keefe's was of significant size and from the ceiling the green leathery leaves of the Swedish ivy mingled with clambering branches of the more sumptuous purple passion vine. On the floor and on the shelves were exotic bouquets of bird of paradise, anthurium and dendrobium orchids, each flower adding its own signature to the perfumed air. And among it all was Amelia. In her tie-dyed skirt and purple T-shirt she was every bit as colorful as the flora around her. As she danced among them, sprinkling the plants with water like Tinkerbell with so much pixie dust, it was hard to remember that she wasn't meant to simply be part of the decor. It was while she was watering a gardenia that she first noticed us.

She pushed her mane of brown curls off her shoulders and greeted us with open arms. "What a fantastic surprise!" she exclaimed after she had given us both lingering hugs. She stepped back and examined Jason's hair with an approving nod. "Groovy new look! I'm totally into it!" But then her smile faded and a small line materialized on her forehead. "You didn't come for a pickup, did you?" she asked, her focus still on Jason. "I told you I wouldn't be able to get the stuff until Friday."

"Nah, I got enough to last me the week. It's cool." Jason turned to me and explained, "Amelia supplements her income by dealing marijuana and hash."

And just like that my Tinkerbell metaphor was blown to smithereens.

"Then you came by just to say hi!" she suggested, instantly brightening. "Or maybe you want some flowers? I just put together a killer bouquet of Gerbera daisies and chrysanthemums. You know both those flowers are major air purifiers. Gets rid of the carcinogens."

"Yeah, that's not why we're here." Jason looked to me, signaling that it was my job to broach the subject.

"Right," I said awkwardly. "Well, we actually came here because I wanted to ask you about Venus."

A moth flitted in front of Amelia's face and she forcefully swatted it away. "Why ask me about Venus? I barely know her."

"Yeah, well, neither do I, but she kind of has a problem with me, and Jason here says that there's a small chance she's a murderer, so, you know, it just seemed like something I should check into."

"This is about William then," she said. A few more lines popped up on her face and I suddenly realized that she might be a little bit older than I had first assumed.

"You said that you were going to check into that whole thing," Jason reminded her.

"Yeah," Amelia said slowly. "And *you* said we weren't going to just be a one-night stand. I guess people just say things, huh?"

Amelia took in a deep breath and turned to me before I had a chance to mask my surprise. Although I probably should have taken this new revelation in stride. After all, it wasn't like they were talking about the sexual possibilities of Ben & Jerry's.

"Sorry about the negative energy," she said. "I shouldn't have gone there. Anyway, I did look into how William died and it wasn't murder. He went in for elective surgery and, you know, sometimes those things don't work out the way they should."

"Meaning?" I asked.

"He died under the knife."

"Good God." I took an involuntary step backward, almost knocking over a ficus. "Why was he getting surgery?"

"It was cosmetic." Amelia started watering plants again, although her earlier enthusiasm for the task had dissipated.

"What exactly was he getting done?" I pressed.

"I didn't take the time to get all the details. All I know is that he died in surgery and it wasn't murder."

Amelia's tone was measured. No word bore more emphasis than any other, making it hard to interpret her real meaning. What was clear was that she wasn't going to tell me anything more. Something about Amelia's demeanor told me that she just didn't think it was her place.

I glanced over at Jason, but his eyes were now back on Amelia. He walked over to one of the more exotic bouquets. "Are these dendrobium orchids?"

"You know your flowers," Amelia said, seemingly relieved by the change in subject.

"They have to be imported from Thailand, don't they?"

"During the winter, yeah. We can get them from Hawaii during the summer."

Jason dropped his hand and exhaled loudly. "That sucks," he declared. "We use how much fossil fuel for this shit? And why? So some bourgeois socialite can say she got the most expensive bouquet to decorate her oversize table in her oversize, energy-inefficient mansion?"

Amelia smiled. "You are so raw, Jason. I just love that about you."

"Yeah?" He took a step toward her. "I'm sorry I haven't taken you out in a while. I'm still having a hard time getting over Dena. Remember, I told you about her."

"And I told you that I was cool about that," she said as she leaned over to water a monkey tree. "I just like hanging with you, Jason."

"Yeah? You want to hang out tonight?"

Amelia immediately came back to life. The wrinkles in her forehead were replaced with ones that appeared around her eyes and mouth and she graced Jason with a brilliant smile. "I would like that."

Jason smiled down at the floor. "Should I pick you up after work or did you drive?"

"I don't drive, remember?" Amelia said, turning back to her plants. "It's either my bike or the bus for me. Today it's the bus."

"I'll pick you up then—I just got a Prius," he added quickly.

Although I was glad Jason was picking up on someone other than Dena, watching him do it was not what I had come for. As they continued to make plans I began to slowly make my way toward the door, stopping here and there to smell a star-shaped flower or admire a bonsai tree. I was just about to announce my exit when Amelia broke away from Jason and caught up with me. "Hey, I hope it's okay, but Scott told me about your problems with Kane."

It was so out of left field that it took me a good minute to process what she had said. "Scott came to you with that?" I finally managed. "Why? I didn't even know you two were close."

"We're not," Amelia said emphatically. "But sometimes I think he'd like to be."

"Of course he would." I let my fingers run over the soft flowers of a silver sage and imagined how fun it would be to rip Scott's face off. So now he was using my problems as a pickup line. No wonder Venus was so insanely jealous. The only way Scott could ever be trusted around other women was if someone had the decency to turn him into a eunuch.

"You won't tell Venus I said that, will you?" Amelia asked, as if reading my thoughts. "She kind of gets agro about that stuff."

"I won't say anything." God, I wish I *could* tell Venus. How great would it be if I could direct her attention to another target?

"Thank you," Amelia said, rather emphatically. "The only reason I bring it up is…okay, I do believe in ghosts, so if you could channel Oscar and Enrico that would be supercool, but if you can't then maybe you should talk to Maria."

"You mean to try to figure out if she killed Enrico? Remove myself as a suspect?"

Amelia shook her head. "I can't believe that anyone would think you're a suspect. Anyone who knows anything about energy and auras knows that you could never kill anyone."

I kept my focus on the silver sage. It wasn't silver at all, really. More like a cool green. Not like the silver of the gun I had used when I actually did kill a man. That had been over a year ago and it had been in self-defense. I had no choice. Still, a man was dead because of me. You would think that the guilt would set in at some point. You would think it would have at least altered my *aura,* right? I was still waiting for that to happen.

"Maria isn't a killer, either," Amelia said. "But she did know Enrico better than anyone else. I bet she knew things about him that no one else did."

I looked up from the plant, beginning to get her meaning.

"If you could get her to give you that information and then have her promise not to tell anyone she gave it to you—"

"I could fool Kane into thinking that Enrico's ghost gave it to me personally," I finished.

Amelia nodded enthusiastically.

"I understand she's been kinda a homebody since you guys found Enrico, so it shouldn't be hard to get in touch with her. I'll get my cell. I have her number and address in my contacts."

As she ran off to another room to get her cell, Jason took her place by my side. "I'll find out what she's not telling us about William tonight," he said in a conspiratorial whisper.

I did a quick double take. "That's why you asked to spend time with her?"

"Nah, I dig Amelia. She's cool. I just know how she is. Tonight she'll bring out the ganga and start talking. She just needs to loosen up, that's all."

I didn't have a chance to respond because Amelia was back with an index card filled with all of Maria's information.

"Thank you." I pulled the card from Amelia's delicate and

unmanicured fingers. "I'll try to make this work for me. In the meantime, do you think you could vouch for me to Kane? Tell him that I have the power to summon ghosts or—"

"Sophie," Amelia interrupted, "I have about as much sway with Kane as he has with me, which is zilch. Don't tell anyone else, but both him and Venus freak me out a little. I mean, I'm sure that deep down underneath they're good people, but they both have murky auras. Never trust anyone with a murky aura."

"Umm…right, well I'll try to remember that," I said, as I studied Maria's number and address. I considered calling her right there from the flower shop, but decided against it. She didn't have any qualms about barging in on me without notice, so why shouldn't I extend her the same courtesy?

I left Jason to continue his flirtation with Amelia and stepped out onto the sidewalk. In front of me was one of the wider streets in San Francisco, this one actually built for cars, not carriages. For a few seconds I just stood there, trying to peek inside the windows of the vehicles zooming past me, wondering if even one of those drivers had a life as complicated and convoluted as mine. Eventually my gaze was drawn to the other side of the street.

Standing there, in front of a black Mercedes, was Kane. He was staring at me.

My mouth dropped open, although I had no plans to speak. Kane continued to stand there, impassive, staring at me. What was he doing here? Was he following me?

A big rig rumbled in front of me and as the light at the end of the block turned red it stopped, blocking Kane from my view.

He had to be following me. There was no other explanation. Unless he wanted flowers or a plant from Amelia. Could that be it? Could this really be a coincidence?

The light turned green just as I was making up my mind to cross the street and confront him. But when the big rig moved, Kane wasn't standing in front of his car anymore.

I stood there in bewildered silence as I watched the Mercedes pull out onto the street and drive away.

Without explanation he had simply moved on. And I could see no other alternative than to do the same.

12

As a little girl I believed in all sorts of ridiculous things like fairy godmothers and functional families.

—*The Lighter Side of Death*

MARIA RISSO LIVED IN A PENTHOUSE ON THE OUTSKIRTS OF THE FINANCIAL district. That fact in and of itself surprised me. I knew from my own housing market research that the prices on these places weren't that much less than many of the city's nicer houses and it was hard to imagine a location less ethereal than a condo that was marketed as "luxury living for the new millennium." If the exterior of Maria's building was any indication, new millennium living was very sterile. Kind of like living in a fancy office complex.

I stepped up to the gate keypad. Maria's name was printed in small, bold, print letters against a strip of black. I pressed her number into the intercom system. Seconds later I heard Maria's voice come through the speaker. "Yes?"

"Maria?" I asked uncertainly. "It's Sophie Katz."

"Magnum's girlfriend," she said coolly.

"Can I come up, Maria?" I asked. "I'll only stay a minute."

There was a brief pause before I heard the buzz of the gate being released from its lock. I pushed my way in and took a moment to orient myself. Before me was the courtyard that was only a little better than the exterior of the building itself. Everything was symmetrical and neatly cared for and the grass was so shaped it was practically forbidding, like a misplaced footstep might destroy the landscape's forced perfection.

When I reached the door of her place Maria was already holding it open. She was wearing a pair of slim-cut Rock & Republic jeans with a Donna Karan button-down top and two large diamond stud earrings. "Magnum told me that I shouldn't talk to you," she declared. "He said you were not trained in detective work and that if involved you would mess up the investigation."

Immediately, my fists clenched. "He shouldn't have said that," I said, trying to take the insult in stride.

"Perhaps not, but what do you expect? He's a man and men are condescending jerks. It's their nature." With that, she ushered me in and quickly closed the door behind us, taking care to double lock it before turning her attention back to me. "It seems that today is the day for visitors. Lorna and her son, Zach, just stopped by, as well. A complete surprise. Lorna usually works on Saturdays, but she managed to sneak out. They're in the study waiting for us now."

I had to repeat the names before I was able to recall the people they belonged to. This was a major inconvenience. I had been hoping to get some information out of Maria about Enrico and then somehow convince her not to tell Kane about my visit. I hadn't been sure how I was going to manage all that, but now it was all a lost cause. After all, I couldn't expect all three people to keep their mouths shut, could I?

These thoughts were clanking around in my mind as I followed Maria up the stairs. Her place was immaculate. But the furniture was no more interesting than the home it was in. Nothing had personality. There were no antiques or anything else that looked to be more than six years old. It didn't seem to fit the colorful woman walking in front of me. Evidence of her interest in the paranormal was nowhere to be seen.

Not surprisingly, the study was a perfect study of beiges and muted pastels. The whole place acted as a visual sedative.

But breaking up the monotony were Lorna and Zach, two totally incongruous individuals sitting side by side on a tan love seat. Zach no longer had his velvet choker, but he still had the black nails and dyed black spiked hair. His eyes were outlined in dark liner and he kept them firmly pointed toward the floor. Lorna, on the other hand, was wearing chinos again, and this time instead of wearing a pink polo top it was pale blue. She, too, had been looking down at the floor, but when she heard us come in her eyes shot up and met mine. They had all the clarity and fierce focus of an eagle zoning in on its prey.

"Lorna, Zach, you know Sophie, our host from last week," Maria said. "I've hired Sophie's boyfriend to help me with my...situation. He's a P.I., like Magnum."

"Magnum?" Zach asked incredulously. "Like the LifeStyle condoms?"

"Trojan," I corrected automatically. Maria and Lorna both jerked their heads in my direction looking respectively amused and horrified. "I'm sorry," I faltered, not entirely sure what I had done that was so wrong, "but Trojan makes Magnums, not LifeStyle."

The eagle eyes of Lorna were now shooting laser beams at my head. "Of course, abstinence is best," I added lamely.

"I'm sorry, Sophie," Lorna said, her voice much more timid than her glare, "But Al and I don't think we should talk about those kind of things in front of children."

My gaze lowered to Zach's Slipknot T-shirt featuring a gagged man who was about to get his head punctured.

"I'm not a child, Mom," Zach growled. "And I'm the one who brought it up!"

"That's true, he did!" I said eagerly. Then immediately regretted my words and tried to backtrack. "I mean, actually, it was Maria who brought it up and I was just trying to, um…"

"I was referring to Tom Selleck," Maria interjected.

Zach shrugged. "I don't get it. What does Tom Selleck have to do with Magnums?"

"Zach," Maria said, apparently shocked. "Does your generation really know so little?"

Zach blushed and looked away, undoubtedly thinking he was missing an obvious sexual innuendo. This display of embarrassed innocence seemed to soothe Lorna and the tightness of her smile softened.

"I'm sorry if I snapped before, I'm just protective of my children," she said. Zach's blush deepened.

Maria smiled in obvious amusement, but, perhaps out of sympathy for Zach, tactfully changed the subject. "What brings you here today, Sophie? Are you here to offer your support? You see Sophie was with me when I found…" The humor slipped from her voice. You could almost see it falling away, revealing the despair that it had been hiding. "My God," she whispered, "it's all too much."

Lorna reached her hand out to her, but Maria seemed not to see it.

"How can the police think that I could have done this to my Enrico? Don't they know that I loved him?"

Lorna and Zach seemed to balk at this sudden change of mood, but as far as I was concerned Maria had just given me the opening that I had been looking for. I crossed to her side. "It's not like it was in Magnum," I said as gently as possible. "It can't all be wrapped up in an hour, but they will figure it out. All anyone has to do is look at you to see how much you cared for him."

Maria collapsed into a nondescript beige armchair and offered a soft sob in response.

"Do you think you and Enrico were headed for reconciliation?" I asked.

"You must be joking!" Maria said with a bitter laugh. "Each of the last nine months has represented its own individual circle of hell! Enrico's refusal to accept my new healthy Californian lifestyle, our arguments, our separation, the lawyers, the fights, being thrown out of my *home* and forced to reside here in this prefurnished bastion of depression!"

"Oooh, it was prefurnished," I said, finally understanding. Once again every one took a moment to gape at me. "I just couldn't figure out the décor here because it didn't seem to suit your tastes, not that it's not lovely," I stammered, "I mean, it's great, it's very clean and, um…I really like the use of beige." I stuffed my hands into my jeans. "Anyway, you were telling us about the nine circles of hell?"

"Ah, what difference does it all make?" she replied. "The police will never understand what everyone here already knows."

"We know something?" I asked.

"We know this was a death brought on by the supernatural," Lorna said. "Maria thinks it was a ghost named Jasper Windsor."

We all turned at the sound of Lorna's half-whispered words. Zach snorted as if his mother had said something perversely amusing. "Don't laugh, it's very serious," Lorna said, much sharper this time. Zach immediately shrank into himself and resumed his staring contest with the floor.

"You've mentioned Jasper Windsor before," I said, still directing my questions to Maria. "Who is he…or was he…do you use *is* or *was* when referring to the identity of a ghost?"

"Was," Maria said softly. "I don't know that his name is really Jasper, it's just what Lorna and I call him, isn't that right, Lorna?"

Lorna nodded sagely. "If he wants us to know his name, he'll tell us, don't you think, Maria?"

"I don't know what I think anymore," Maria said with a laugh bordering on hysteria. "Do you remember when we first saw it, Lorna?"

Lorna looked away. "Maybe we shouldn't talk about this."

"Talk about what?" I asked. "What did you see?"

Maria hesitated for a moment and then looked up at Lorna. "Will you make us some espresso? And Zach, perhaps you can help your mother and find us something to taste. I have some almonds and perhaps you could wash off the cherry tomatoes and cut a few pieces of celery. I don't believe I've eaten since breakfast."

Lorna didn't looked thrilled by this and Zach didn't react at all, but they both did as they were told and left Maria and me alone in the beige room. Maria waited until she was sure the other two were out of hearing distance before turning back to me. "I want to trust you," she said softly. "I would like to make a friend of you. I don't have many friends anymore. I lost them in the divorce. You expect to lose your stereo, your vacation home, the *things*. But no one tells you that your friends will be divided up right along with all the other possessions and it seems that Enrico claimed almost every one of them."

She sighed and looked out the window. The clouds had now completely blocked off the sun, enveloping the city in an early darkness. "Now that he's dead they still cling to his celebrity," she went on, "because really that's what they loved, not the man himself."

"Is that what you loved?" I asked, only realizing after the words had left me how tactless they were.

"No, but maybe I should have." Maria ran her thumb over the inside of her fingertips as if stroking an imaginary cloth. "The fame he had was tangible. You can still find evidence of it in the way his murder is being reported, in the way the people still flock to his restaurant. But the man that I loved...he's just gone. Sometimes I wonder if he ever truly existed at all."

For a brief second I considered calling Jason. If he thought *Dena* was existential he would be eating this up with a spoon.

"You and your boyfriend," Maria continued, "you helped me that night. And then you didn't let me pay you for your service."

"Well, you were pretty upset—it didn't seem right—"

"But others would have taken the money anyway," Maria insisted. "Only now that I have hired Magnum to do a more detailed investigation will he accept my checks. I want to make a friend of you, Sophie, but how can I trust anyone when the rewards of betrayal are so high?"

"The rewards of betrayal?" I asked. Her vulnerability was touching. It would have been even more touching if she could demonstrate that she knew my boyfriend's name.

"It's easy to take something out of context," Maria explained. "I could say something that you think sounds incriminating and then you could run to the police with it...or to a journalist. Either way I'm sure you would be compensated, if not in money then in some other way. Hurting me is so profitable these days."

I walked over to the couch Lorna had been sitting in and took her place. Maria was a little dramatic and more than a little flowery in her speech, but underneath all that there was something quite likeable about her. I hadn't seen that during our first meeting. "I'm not here to hurt you," I said truthfully. "I've never hurt anyone who hasn't at least tried to hurt me."

Maria met my eyes and in an instant I knew she had made

some kind of decision about me. Lorna came in at that moment with a silver tray filled with four small ceramic espresso cups, and Zach followed her with a bunch of cherry tomatoes in a bowl in one hand and a bag of almonds in the other. I stood up to give them back their seat and went to sit on a cushioned stool that undoubtedly doubled as a footrest.

"The tomatoes are organic," Zach said as he dropped the food unceremoniously on the coffee table. "They don't need to be washed."

"But I made him wash them anyway," Lorna said quickly. "I'm sorry he didn't arrange the food on a plate, he's never been very good at things like that."

"They're tomatoes, Mom. You can't arrange them, they roll."

Maria smiled distractedly, accepted the espresso and held it daintily in her hand. "Lorna is one of the few people who sided with me when Enrico and I first separated. She came to me at the hotel and she listened to me rant. I did rant for a while, didn't I, Lorna?"

"You were upset." Lorna handed an espresso to me and then placed the tray with the two remaining cups next to the tomatoes. "Anyone would have been if they were in your shoes."

"And then I decided we simply had to drive, do you remember that, Lorna?"

Lorna didn't answer this time. She took a seat on the couch next to Zach and reached for his hand. He pulled it away.

"I insisted that Lorna come for a ride with me," Maria explained, "and we drove and we drove...Highway 5, 46, 58...the highways we took read like a locker combination and I wouldn't stop for anything but gas and water. I wouldn't stop until there I was in nowhere. And I thought I found nowhere in Topock, Arizona."

"You drove to Arizona?" I stammered.

"To the border. Topock is a little ghost town. There's nothing there but abandoned buildings, desert and stars. More stars than you have ever seen in your entire life. I fell in love with that sky. Do you remember, Lorna?"

Lorna was now scratching the back of her arm with the urgency of a dog with fleas. "I didn't know we were going to Arizona," she said, more to Zach than to Maria. "If I had known, I would never have gone. Al wouldn't have let me. He was so mad."

"But that's the whole point, Lorna! That night we didn't answer to men! We only answered to the stars." Then Maria paused and turned back to the window. "That's where we found Jasper's scythe."

"Jasper's…wait, are you talking about the murder weapon?" I exclaimed. I turned to Zach to see if he was as confused as I was. Zach was watching Maria intently with something that bore an odd resemblance to respect. Lorna was still scratching.

"We don't know that it was the same scythe," Lorna said carefully. "There must be plenty of scythes around…maybe not in San Francisco, but in other places. This one was next to a rusted old belt buckle with the letters *JW* engraved into it. Maria decided that both things belonged to a man named Jasper Windsor, but we don't really know that."

"I made up a whole story about good old Jasper, a ghost story," Maria said. "Of course, whoever owned those things had to be a ghost, they were so old. It was an awful story, filled with violence and revenge…but maybe I didn't just make it up. Maybe something was whispering into my subconscious. Maybe Jasper followed me here and he tried to get the revenge that I said I wanted. Maybe I am responsible for Enrico's death in that way."

Zach snorted derisively. "You people are high," he said. "When are you going to get that when someone kicks it, that's it? In the end the only thing any of us turns into is a feast for the worms."

Lorna slapped him across the face. The sound echoed through the room as we all watched in stunned silence. "Never!" Lorna said, her voice hoarse with rage. "Never the dead."

"I'm just saying it how it is, Mom!" Zach shot back, apparently unfazed by her outburst.

Lorna raised her hand again, but stayed it just in time. "You believe, Zach," she said. "You just don't like to admit it in front of strangers, but you told me. You told me you're a believer."

"I told you I might believe in life after death and you heard what you wanted to hear, just like you always do," he muttered. His posture was slackening now, turning him once again into a sulker rather than the confronter he had been a moment earlier. Lorna, on the other hand, looked like she was the one who had been slapped. Her breathing was irregular and she was visibly shaking.

A psychiatry student could write an entire thesis on mentally disturbed behavior based on the subjects in this room.

The worst part was that Zach didn't freak out when his mother whacked him, which meant that he had probably gotten used to it. That little detail immediately changed my perspective of the kid. He was no longer the weird rebel without a cause. He was a teenager that seriously needed help.

"Perhaps Zach's right about Jasper," Maria said in what was clearly forced joviality. "After all, we don't know if he was ever real. But with this death we have to at least face the fact that Enrico had to have been attacked by something otherworldly. You saw the windows," she said, directing her words to me. "They were locked. The chain lock was engaged. No human could have gotten in there, and then what you said you heard Enrico say into the phone…" Her voice broke off and she blinked her eyes rapidly. "He saw something. He had so many flaws, but he didn't deserve this." She looked at Lorna beseechingly. "I swear he didn't. I didn't wish it on him."

Lorna stood up and walked to the side of Maria. The image of them was hard to dismiss: Lorna with her unflattering attire and unnaturally peach cheeks and Maria sitting by her side, all glamorous and distraught. It was like they were posing for a promotional photo of an ill-conceived play in which the playwright tried to channel both Tennessee Williams and Neil Simon simultaneously.

"This is stupid!"

I jumped, startled by Zach's voice.

"Enrico wasn't murdered by a stupid ghost." He continued, "He was killed by some totally mortal person who managed to get away with it. And you know what? It's not sad at all! Enrico was a big fat fuck and I bet that whoever took him out was only paying him back for some major shit he pulled on them!"

"*Zach,*" Lorna snapped, her voice stronger than I had ever heard before. "I know you didn't like Enrico. We all had hoped that he would use your father's services when he opened his other restaurants, but that certainly doesn't mean that he deserved to die! He was a human being and he was loved." She turned to Maria again and said, more softly this time, "He was loved."

Zach chose not to answer. Lorna's hand on Maria's shoulder tightened and then relaxed a few times until she had eased into the steady rhythm of a slow massage.

I stole a quick look at Zach, who was back to glaring at the beige carpet. Lorna and Maria were now quietly talking about how awful Enrico's murder had been, but I was only half listening. I was focused on Zach. This visit had been a lot more revealing than I had anticipated. I didn't know anything that would help me convince Kane that I had spoken to Enrico's ghost, but I was beginning to think that I might have found a strong suspect for his murder. Feeling my gaze on him, Zach finally looked up and examined his silent inquisitor. The two of us remained like that for at least a full minute, with Zach seemingly daring me to ask the questions that I refused to ask in the presence of this particular audience.

"Oh Lord, is *that* the time?"

I blinked, Lorna's voice jerking me out of my thoughts.

"Al's supposed to pick me up at my work at five-thirty and it's almost five now! Zach, we have to go!"

"I'm walking home," he said, rising to his feet.

"Don't be ridiculous! I told Dad that you would be coming to the office to do your homework!"

"Tell him I flaked," he said offhandedly. "Or I could tell him that you left work without checking in with him and came here. Your choice."

Lorna looked positively panicked. Maria shot her a sympathetic look and took her hand in hers. "Al just worries about you, Lorna," she said. "He doesn't mean to be so impossible. He simply can't help it. He's a man."

"I know, but I really can't be late and he can't know I was here. He'll be furious!" She rushed to the couch where she collected her purse. "You sure you won't come with me, Zach?"

He shook his head, not budging an inch.

"Well, then, I'll tell Dad you didn't show up. But please, don't come home too late. Your father worries about both of us, you know."

"Whatever," he mumbled. Lorna cast him a desperate look before giving me a halfhearted wave and running out, leaving me alone with Maria and Zach.

"Are you all right, Zach?" Maria asked. Then, without waiting for an answer she continued, "If one is to be creative at all, one must have parents who are at least a little bit crazy."

Zach laughed humorlessly. "A little bit crazy? Did you just see the shit that I saw?"

Maria simply smiled. "I believe you will grow to be a true beacon of creativity. How can you not?"

Zach wasn't even a little amused. "I'm out of here."

I did some quick calculations in my head. I did want to talk to Maria alone, but now I wanted to talk to Zach, too, and while Maria seemed amenable to future conversations this might be my last chance to catch a few minutes with Zach. "If you like, I could give you a ride to where you're going, Zach." I offered.

"How do you know we're going in the same direction?" he asked.

"I don't, but I'll give you a ride anyway." I went over to Maria and gave her a quick hug. "I'd love to stop by for a visit again soon. Maybe even in a few days?"

"That would be fine," she said with a sigh. "But do call first."

"Absolutely." I hesitated a moment before continuing. "Do you mind if I ask what did you do with Jasper's scythe after you found it in the ghost town?"

Maria smiled coolly. "Not a thing. Lorna and I left it in that little city of nowhere—right in the middle of the desert. If it *was* the murder weapon, it was Jasper that brought it here, not me."

I nodded, not sure what else to say, and walked out with Zach. "That may have been the most bizarre social call I've ever been on," I said as we entered the courtyard.

Zach didn't answer.

"Have your mom and Maria been friends long?" I asked.

"I dunno, I guess," he mumbled. "They got closer after Maria split with Enrico."

We walked through the front entrance without another word. It had gotten considerably colder in the short time I had been at Maria's and I found myself picking up the pace to get to my car parked down the block. Once both Zach and I were inside my Audi, I turned to him, our proximity making it impossible to avoid eye contact without looking like he was being purposely rude. As I expected, he chose rudeness. "Can I ask you a question?"

He shrugged and stared stubbornly out the window.

"Is The Cure staging a comeback tour?"

Finally Zach snapped his head in my direction. "I'm not trying to look like the singer from The Cure! I'm making a visual statement!"

"Right, does that statement have anything to do with the weird excesses of the eighties? Because I'm pretty sure that was the last decade that Goth was cool."

"Marilyn Manson is Goth!"

"Which explains why he's not as famous as he used to be. Zach, I think the time has come to lighten up."

He crossed his arms in front of his chest and turned back to the street. "Are you going to give me a lift or what?"

"That depends, where do you want to go?"

"My friend's brother is working the door at this new cannabis club—"

"Oh, forget it! The police already hate me, the last thing I need is for them to catch me taking a troubled teenager to his drug dealer."

"Fine, I'll walk." He reached for the door, but not before I pressed the automatic locks.

"I'll take you somewhere else."

"Somewhere that sells pot?"

I sighed and looked up at the clouds. "How about we get some ice cream."

"Yeah, now I'm really out of here." He unlocked the door, but I quickly locked it again. "You can't keep me here against my will," he whined. "That's *really* illegal."

"How 'bout an oxygen bar."

He looked at me puzzled, but he didn't reach for the lock again.

"It's a cool high," I said, encouraged. "I'll buy you a hit." The truth was I had never done the whole oxygen thing, not even when oxygen bars were all the rage, and those days had definitely passed. But for a teen who knew about The Cure and embraced Goth…well, an oxygen bar seemed just about right. "I'll even throw in a shot of hemp oil."

Zach treated me to an exaggerated eye roll. "Hemp oil doesn't do shit," he said. "It's not like smoking it."

"How do you know?" I asked. "Have you ever tried hemp oil?" Zach's silence answered my question. "Great, then it's a deal. We'll go to an oxygen bar, have some hemp and talk things over. I'm trying to figure out what's up with all these Specter Society people and you seem like just the guy who can give me the real dirt."

Zach snorted. "You're gonna need a shovel."

"Got one in my purse." I dangled my oversize handbag in front of his face before reaching in it and pulling out my cell.

"Who are you calling?"

"My friend Marcus," I said. "It's been a long time since I've been to an oxygen bar and he'll know which ones are still in business."

Marcus picked up on the second ring. "I couldn't hate you more if you were Lindsay Lohan and I was Paris Hilton," he said.

I glanced at Zach. "I don't think they hate each other anymore."

"Give them time," he said. "I had to listen to Dena bitch for an hour about Jason and about how you should have told her that he was in that Speckle Society of yours—"

"Specter Society."

"…and all of her sad little excuses for why she had to dump poor-little-vampire-boy—"

"Dena doesn't make excuses."

"Apparently it's her new thing," Marcus said curtly. "Anyhoo, the point is that I was tortured. This wasn't one of those ambiguous forms of torture like water-boarding. No, honey, this was a direct violation of the Geneva Convention. I just got off work and I'm going to get myself a cocktail immediately."

I gave Zach my best be-patient-smile and plowed on. "I know you're ticked at me, Marcus, and I do promise to make it up to you, but right now I was hoping you could recommend an oxygen bar."

There was a long silence on the other end of the line. "Honey, oxygen bars stopped being fabulous in 2001."

"I know, I know, but I'm here with a Goth teenage rebel and this is the only legal drug I can buy him."

"Really? Have you tried Wite-Out?"

"Marcus," I said warningly.

"Fine, go to Breather, it's located on the corner of Market and Church."

"Seriously, Marcus? The Castro? He's not that kind of boy."

Zach shifted in his seat and his eyes darted quickly in both directions as if he was afraid of being caught or found out...or maybe dragged out of the closet.

"Actually," I said carefully, "The Castro should be okay."

"Will it now?" Marcus asked, his interest clearly picking up. "Tell me, Sophie, what are you doing hanging out with a teenager?"

"Um, I know his mom," I said, lowering my voice as if there was any way I could avoid being overheard by a boy who was literally sitting one foot away from me.

"So what?" Marcus asked. "Wait, did this mom ask you to play chaperone for her son? Does she know you're an unapologetic sinner with a questionable relationship with a cat?"

"I am not a sinner…by San Francisco standards. And my relationship with my cat is totally normal and on the up-and-up."

"Now, now, no need to get your tail ruffled. How old is this teenage Goth boy, anyway? Is he legal?"

"No, stay away." I hung up and stuck my key into the ignition. "Ready?" I asked.

Zach shrugged his consent and within seconds we were on the road making our way toward Breather.

13

I used to go to oxygen bars, but that got too expensive so now I just try to hyperventilate over a perfume bottle.
—The Lighter Side of Death

IT TOOK A FULL FORTY MINUTES FOR ZACH AND I TO FIND PARKING AND when we did it was a parallel spot between two Harleys. I knew Anatoly adored me, but if I were to hit his bike, even accidentally, it would be hard for him to resist strangling me. So I could only imagine what reaction I would elicit from a couple of gay bikers if I ended up knocking one of these hogs over. Fortunately, I managed to avoid disaster and my parking prowess actually earned me a smile from Zach. Up until that point I had been unaware that his mouth was capable of turning upward.

As we moved through the crowd, Zach's head was swiveling back and forth so quickly that you would have thought we were at a sporting event—a really exciting one at that—because with every swivel his eyes got a little bit wider. Obviously he hadn't spent a lot of time, if any, in this part of the city. I tried to see my surroundings with the perspective of a newcomer. The Castro was…strange. It was a world-famous location, a place where tour buses designed to look like cable cars frequently drove through so that Fran and Stan from Wyoming could take pictures of Real San Franciscan Gays. Yet I always felt the neighborhood lacked a certain authenticity. There were too many restaurants and bars with names like *Hot & Hunky.* Too many rainbow flags, too many stores selling Marilyn Monroe memorabilia. It's like the Castro was where gays went to be on stage whenever they were feeling bored with their normal lives as teachers, lawyers and/or choreographers. Breather demonstrated this idea perfectly. When Zach and I walked in, I found myself wanting to shield my eyes to protect them from all the brightness. Candy-colored bar stools were arranged in clusters surrounding little oxygen machines that appeared to be lifted right out of an old Jetsons cartoon...well, okay, the Jetsons didn't have "Screaming Orgasm Flavored Oxygen," but if they had it undoubtedly would have been stored in colorful ergonomically designed containers atop contemporary kiosks with backlit bubble walls. Old Erasure songs were playing on the stereo as men milled about, gossiping, drinking nonalcoholic spritzers and sucking on their scented oxygen like it was opium. In the middle of all this was a totally gorgeous, mocha-skinned man who absolutely was not supposed to be there.

"Wait here," I said to Zach and marched over to where Marcus sat on his bright orange bar stool. "What are you doing here? I told you he's underage!"

"Is that him?" Marcus asked, craning his neck to see Zach. "My God, what's wrong with him? Is he in costume?"

"Marcus, why are you here?"

Marcus turned his twinkling eyes toward me and flashed me a blindingly white-toothed smile. "I wanted to do a good deed."

"How is picking up on a fifteen-year-old a good deed? Wait, do I even want to hear this?"

"For God's sake Sophie, that boy is hardly a masculine version of Lolita and even if he was I don't do teenagers. I play exclusively with the big boys, the bigger the better," he added with a wicked grin that made it impossible to escape his meaning. "I'm here to be a mentor to a troubled queer youth."

"You've *got* to be kidding me."

"Of course I'm kidding. I came here because I have this horrible feeling that you're about to put yourself in danger again, and as your friend I've decided that I should at least try to be around enough to minimize the risk."

"Really?" I asked, immediately softening. "Marcus thank—"

"That said, it is a given that when a Goth teenager asks you to take him to an oxygen bar in the Castro that's a huge cry for help!"

I looked over my shoulder at Zach. He was unsuccessfully trying to hide his observation of two pastel-shirt-wearing men in the corner making out. Zach's expression reminded me of Dorothy's when she initially stumbled into Oz. Give him a pair of pigtails and a small dog and he'd be all set. "He's a weird kid," I said frankly. "I can't figure out what to make of him."

"Why did you agree to chaperone anyway?" Marcus asked, his shoulders relaxing slightly as the music switched from Erasure to one of his favorite Madonna singles. "Don't tell me you're developing a maternal instinct. This has to do with the house, right?"

"Right. I brought him here in the hopes of getting some information out of him about Enrico's murder." I gave him the Cliff Notes version of what went down at the flower shop and then at Maria's.

Marcus shook his head in despair. "I can't believe you. At what point did you decide to try to turn your life into a *Fear Factor* marathon?"

"I didn't *decide*…" But then I waved my hands in the air, abandoning that line of defense. "I don't need to explain myself to you. You're not even supposed to be here. But since you are…" I reached over and toyed with one of his short and neatly groomed dreadlocks. "You could help me out with this. Maybe get him to open up about his family and Enrico Risso? He has some issues surrounding those people and I need to know what they are."

Marcus grumbled something unintelligible before rolling his eyes in defeat. "I'm in, but only because someone has to keep you in line." He then snapped his fingers in the air, grabbing Zach's attention. "Yoo-hoo," Marcus sang. "Sweeny Todd, come join us, sweetie."

I could see Zach's cheeks ripen under all that white powder, but he came over to the oxygen station that Marcus had staked out.

He looked at Marcus's smiling face and then quickly looked away, becoming very absorbed in his oxygen selection. "I think I want that one," he said, pointing to a pale orange container on the bar.

"Sex on the Beach?" I asked. "Sure, why not."

Marcus gave Zach an approving nod. "Good choice. I was around your age when I tried sex on the beach for the first time, and let me tell you that sand got into all sorts of nasty places."

"Marcus!" I snapped. "This is how you mentor the youth?"

"Don't moralize me, honey. You're the one who brought him here to get high on air."

"You know, I can hear you," Zach said. "I'm standing right here."

"Sorry," I said, plopping myself on the stool next to Marcus. "I didn't mean to—"

"What *do* you mean to do?" Zach asked abruptly. "Why was it so important that we hang out?"

I hesitated for half a second before blurting out, "Do you think Maria killed Enrico? Because the police think she did, and if they're right, then I'm not so sure I want to go to any more séances with her."

Zach chewed on his bottom lip and stared down at his shoes. "I don't know," he said quietly. "But if she did she deserves a frickin' medal."

Marcus blanched. "My, my. You are a dark little closet case, aren't you?"

"I'm not a closet case! And I don't give a shit if I'm being dark." Zach sucked his upper lip in between his teeth giving himself the appearance of a humanistic warthog. "Enrico *was* evil. I wish I could have been there when he died. I wish I could have been the one to stick the blade in. I would have made sure he saw it coming, too, and then I'd do it again and again—"

"*Hi, guys!* Can I take your order?" We all jumped as the floppy-haired waiter beamed down at us. "Oh, my goodness! I startled you all, didn't I?" he asked. "I bet I interrupted a juicy gossip session, didn't I?" He looked from Marcus to me to Zach then back to Marcus. Out of the corner of my eye I could see the bubbles in the walls of the kiosk shoot skyward only to pop from the pressure. No one said anything.

The waiter shifted from foot to foot. "Maybe I should come back in a few minutes," he offered.

"Yeah, that would be good," I said. The waiter nodded quickly and rushed off, desperate to escape an awkward moment.

"Zach," I said softly, "what exactly did Enrico do to you?" I found myself hoping that it was something truly horrible, because if it wasn't then I was about to suck oxygen with a boy who might end up being the next generation's Zodiac Killer.

Zach looked off into space. "I should just go."

Marcus leaned forward and put a hand on his shoulder.

There was no flirtation in the gesture, just a kind of platonic, almost paternal concern. "Zach," he said, "what did he do?"

Zach didn't jerk away. Instead he stared down at Marcus's hand, as if its presence was totally inexplicable, but not entirely unwelcome. "Nothing to me," he finally said. "But my sister..." His voice trailed off and his shoulders hunched over so that his body formed the shape of a depressed letter C.

"What about your sister?" Marcus pushed.

"He raped her." He was whispering now and both Marcus and I had to lean forward to catch the words. "He raped her when she was thirteen and he...he got her pregnant."

I sucked in a sharp breath. That was infinitely worse than what I was expecting, but the story had a flaw.

"Zach," I said carefully, "you don't have a sister."

"I do," Zach corrected. "At least I did. I did before she killed herself trying to abort the baby at home."

I recoiled and slapped my hand over my mouth as I felt bile sting my throat. But Marcus's hand remained on Zach's shoulder and now all the laughter that had been in his brown eyes only minutes ago had morphed into sympathy. "How did she do it?" he asked.

"Herbs and essential oils."

"I don't think I understand." Marcus's eyebrows inched lower as he tried to make sense of this.

"She tried to give herself a herbal abortion. She found the instructions online. She told me it was safe and not to tell anybody. I should have ratted her out. If I had..."

"How old were you when this happened?" Marcus asked.

"Eleven."

"Eleven-year-old boys don't tell on their thirteen-year-old sisters, not when it comes to the serious stuff."

"How did this even happen?" I asked. "Was it at a séance or—"

"We didn't belong to the stupid Specter Society then. My

dad lays floors for commercial properties, like marble floors and shit. Dad was friends with Oscar and Oscar was one of Enrico's investors, so when Enrico wanted new floors for his newest restaurant Oscar recommended my dad."

"But how did Enrico ever get any time alone with your thirteen-year-old sister?" I asked.

"My sister wanted to be a chef so my dad set it up so she could have private lessons." Zach said the last two words with the acidity that conveyed his full meaning. "Oscar knew, too. He was one of Enrico's business partners and he was always around. I know he knew. Sometimes Dad would take me and Deb to Enrico's restaurant before it was open and Oscar would be there."

Zach's hand was flat against the chrome surface of the bar, his veins pushing further and further into view as he increased the pressure of his palm. "Oscar would look at Enrico, and then he'd look at my sister and then the son of a bitch would laugh. That fucker laughed."

Marcus finally pulled back, crossing his arms across his chest. "You're right. Enrico deserved to be slashed up with a scythe."

Zach did a quick double take. What had he expected Marcus to do? Try to smother him with platitudes that couldn't possibly ease the pain? I could only imagine how long Zach had kept all of that information tucked inside. And now he was volunteering the story to us. God only knows why. Maybe because we were strangers and he could afford to alienate us. Or maybe, for some unfathomable reason, he trusted us. I looked toward the picture windows on the other side of the restaurant. It was night now and you could see the wind urging the planted trees into a violent dance.

"I knew a long time ago that I was going to—" Zach began.

"Don't say it," I said quickly. "If you want, I can get you set up with a lawyer. But don't confess anything to me or anyone else. I believe that revenge can be therapeutic, but I'm not so sure about prison."

"Why would I go to prison?" he asked. "I didn't do anything. Maria's the one who cut him up."

The waiter returned at that moment holding his pad and pencil firmly in front of him. "Sorry, but you guys really have to order something if you're going to stay. We have drinks and vegan pastries if you don't want oxygen, but the bossman here says nobody stays without ordering."

"Sex on the Beach oxygen for all of us," I said quietly, sincerely wishing that we could substitute the scented oxygen for the cocktail that was its namesake.

"We sell it for $1.50 per minute, five minute minimum per person. Each person gets their own nasal cannula—that would be a nose hose to you and me."

Under the best of circumstances this guy would have annoyed me, but now as I followed Zach down this dark path of memory, the waiter's like-me-like-me-like-me routine was almost enough to send me over the edge.

"We'll take five minutes for each of us," Marcus said.

"You sure you don't want to buy more minutes?" the waiter asked. "They say once you inhale it's hard to stop. I do it two or three times a day! I really think it's accountable for my chipper disposition."

Marcus, Zach and I all studied him for half a second before we all started talking at once, each one of us changing our oxygen order to a fruit spritzer. As it turns out, hemp oil wasn't on the menu.

Marcus looked around at the crowd in the bar. A group of men a few kiosks over burst into cheers, many of them raising their glasses as they saluted some unknown success. The environment was beyond inappropriate considering the situation, and, despite my better instincts, I wondered if I should have given in earlier and taken Zach to a cannabis club. "How do you know Maria killed Enrico, Zach?" I asked. "Did she tell you?"

"No, she's not stupid." Zach pulled gently on the lobe of his ear. "But it's kinda obvious she did it. You heard him call someone a bitch so we know it was a woman and Maria showed up at the Specter Society meeting so there's that and—"

"Wait." I held up my hand to stop him. "Why does Maria showing up at the Specter Society meeting incriminate her?"

"It's kinda obvious she came because she knew Enrico wouldn't," Zach said with a shrug. "Why else would a woman purposely go out of her way to go to the same event her ex is hanging at?"

"Ah, young Zach, women do things like that all the time," Marcus lamented. "It's one of the reasons I'm so grateful to be attracted to men. But it is possible that Maria wasn't a stalker or a murderer. Has Maria's appearance changed at all since she split with Enrico?"

Zach considered this for a moment. "She did lose a lot of weight."

"So then the attendance at the séance doesn't incriminate her," Marcus said matter-of-factly. "Anyone who has dropped a few dress sizes knows how fabulous it can be to run into an ex who dumped them before they got cozy with Jenny Craig. Do you have anything else?"

"Yeah, duh! Maria was the one who tried to set it up so Anatoly and Sophie discovered the body first. She totally knew there was a body in that condo. That story she gave you about wanting you to go over there to make sure Enrico was okay?" Zach rolled his eyes. "That was so lame and *so* obvious. Then again, you fell for it."

"No, my boyfriend fell for it," I protested. "And that's only because Maria paid him $300 to fall for it!"

"So Anatoly's naiveté can be bought?" Marcus asked. "How very disturbing."

The waiter came back with three spritzers. It seems he wasn't completely unable to take a hint because he ran off as soon as he placed the drinks on the chrome surface.

"I think we inadvertently insulted our server," I offered as I watched the waiter talk to other patrons, his back studiously turned to us.

"No," Marcus said. "There was nothing inadvertent about it."

Zach picked up his drink, which looked suspiciously like a Shirley Temple, and sipped it through his purple straw. "I don't like it. It's too sweet."

"Shocker," I said, removing the bright red cherry in the middle of my drink and placing it delicately on a napkin. "Who else knows about what Enrico did, Zach? Do your parents know?"

"No, they're idiots. They think I'm mad at Enrico because he screwed up some major gig for my dad. Dad wanted Enrico to recommend him to the Kimpton Group. Kimpton's always opening new restaurants and putting new floors into the ones they already got. That account would have made my dad's career. He even told me that as soon as he got it I would be going to private school. Like that's something I would have wanted! Enrico's a fuck-faced bastard, but he's sharp. He knew my dad's business couldn't have handled an account as big as the Kimpton Group, so he told them not to sign with him. *That's* my parents' problem with Enrico. A lost business deal! They have no fucking idea what went on under their own damn noses!"

"But your sister was pregnant when she died," I pointed out. "How did they explain that?"

Zach took a much longer sip of the drink he proclaimed to dislike. "My parents think that my sister was knocked up by

Ian, this dumb kid that Deb used to hang with. Dad even went to the school and said that they should expel Ian. Like a public school was going to kick some kid out just for taking sex ed into his own hands."

Marcus wiggled his foot under the table. It wasn't one of his normal ticks, he was trying to tell me something, but unless the message was, "check out my shoes, they're Prada," I wasn't getting it.

Zach's drink was almost gone and he was now eyeing the door. "I don't want to talk about this anymore."

"Okay," I said. "I get that."

"I'm gonna head out."

"Sure, let me just get the check—"

"Nah, I'll take the bus."

"Don't be silly. I took you here, I'll take you home."

But then something in Zach's look stopped me. Perhaps he felt he had said too much, but what was clear to me was that he absolutely did not want me to take him anywhere and I got the distinct impression that I had pushed him as far as he was willing to go.

"Zach," Marcus said, his voice determinedly light and casual, "when I was your age I was confused. That's what they call it when you're gay and a teenager. Anyhoo, I used to wish that I could have a Gay Big Brother type to hang out with. Someone who I didn't have to pretend with and who could tell me how to properly tweeze my eyebrows. If you ever feel the same—"

"I'm not gay!"

"Of course not," Marcus soothed. "But perhaps you need a queer eye to help you get things in order." He took one of his business cards out of his wallet. "Call anytime you like. I'll be your Professor Higgins."

Zach wrinkled his brow. "Who the hell is Professor Higgins?"

Marcus blinked in surprise. "You honestly don't know?

Maybe you are straight after all. But that doesn't make you any less in need of a haircut and a makeover." He pressed his card into Zach's hand. "Seriously, call. You won't regret it."

"Whatever." But I noticed how carefully Zach handled the card as he put it in the inside pocket of his jacket.

As he walked out of the restaurant I let my hands fly up to my temples. "I could never give him up," I said aloud. "Even if he did do it."

"God, no. That would be like turning in a POW child for killing the soldiers who offed his parents."

"Okay, that's a bit extreme…actually, no, I take it back. It's a good metaphor," I said, quickly correcting myself. "Maybe I could just tell Kane about the rape. No one knows about that, so I could have gotten the info from the grave."

"You're going to use Zach's dead sister's rape as a tool to keep you in that house?"

"Not *that* house, *my* house," I snapped, but my defiance wasn't quite strong enough to withstand my tugs of conscience. "No," I continued reluctantly. "But I really need something, Marcus. I can't lose, not this time."

"Well, yeah, it would be a ginormous inconvenience and financially…"

"It's more than that," I said.

Marcus tipped his head to the side, causing his little locks to point down toward the chrome bar. "You've got a real emotional attachment going on, don't you, darling?"

"To my home? Yes, yes I do."

"Lots of people lose their homes, Sophie. These days it's positively de rigueur."

"I'm not losing my home," I said stubbornly. "I won't throw Zach under a bus, but I will find something to give to Kane." I toyed with the straw in my drink. "Why were you wiggling your foot earlier?"

"You didn't catch on to the meaning behind the foot wag? I was trying to point out that Zach's faith in his parents' ignorance may be unwarranted. Maybe they figured it all out and they're the ones who are guilty."

"You were trying to say all that with a foot wag?"

"I have very expressive feet."

"Okay, fine. Maybe it was Zach's parents, but…" I let my voice trail off.

Marcus bobbed his head up and down in an understanding nod. "Throwing Zach's parents under a bus isn't really a good way to spare Zach from anything. All right, then, who do you want to be guilty? I mean, if you could choose?"

I chewed on this for a minute. "I wouldn't mind seeing Venus go down."

"You mean on something other than your ex?" Marcus laughed.

"I honestly don't care about that. She can do whatever she wants to him, but she's been on my case from the minute that she laid eyes on me, and if you met her…" I shook my head. "She's weird, Marcus, like creepy weird. I wouldn't be surprised if she did kill Enrico."

"Well, there's nothing wrong with a little wishful thinking." Marcus swiveled back and forth on his candy-colored bar stool. "Why don't you see if you can back it up with any evidence? Anybody else on your hit list?"

"Well, Kane obviously tops that list off. He's the one messing with me."

"Does he have a motive? And if he does, would it help you? You may be able to get him locked up, but he'll still have the right to sell his house to somebody else."

"I'll find the evidence and I'll use it against him. I'll blackmail him until escrow goes through and then I'll turn him in."

Marcus leaned back, his dark eyebrows tilting down toward the bridge of his nose. "Who *are* you?"

"Excuse me?"

"*Blackmail,* Sophie? You're going to blackmail a murderer instead of immediately turning him in to the police?"

"Escrow will go through in just five days!"

"Right, and what harm could a man with a lethal weapon do in five days, right?"

"Marcus, this house, it's like, it's like it's a member of my family. I need it. I need it the way I need…the way I need Mr. Katz."

"Hello?" Marcus stammered. "You're talking about your fur baby!"

"Exactly," I said. "So now you know I'm serious."

Marcus sighed and did some more swiveling. "So Venus and Kane are the preferred suspects. Well, I guess we can look into that."

"We?" I asked hopefully.

"Don't look a gift-stallion in the mouth. I said I'd help, and I will."

"Marcus, I love you."

He smiled and dropped his arm around my shoulders. "Of course you do. What's not to love?"

"I want to get into Kane's house. I've got to find a way to get him to invite me over and then, when he's not looking, I'll be able to look around and hopefully find something useful and/or incriminating."

"Won't he notice that you're searching the place while he's entertaining you?"

"That's where you come in. If you come with me then I can keep him distracted while you snoop and vice versa."

"And what's going to be your excuse for bringing me? I don't know the man."

"I'll come up with something. I'll say you're my guru or—"

"Excuse me?"

"There are worse things than having a guru...I'm not sure what they are, but I'm sure there are a few," I said. "But Kane's into weird stuff so I'll need a weird reason to explain your presence away. Guru might work, or my...my...my psychic! That's it! I'll say you're a psychic and you're helping me channel the spirits in my house! Kane will love that! We could go over there tomorrow morning!"

"So now I'm your psychic."

"You got it."

"Wonderful. Let me start by predicting that tomorrow is going to be a fiasco."

I smiled and squeezed his arm affectionately. "You see? You have a real knack for this."

14

> You probably shouldn't base an entire relationship on sex
> alone...but it might be fun to try.
>
> —*The Lighter Side of Death*

IT WAS RAINING BY THE TIME I GOT HOME. THE CLOUDS HAD BLOCKED
out the stars and the moon so now the only sources of light in
the city were artificial. These were usually the kind of nights
that made me want to head to the movies, but not this time.
This time, the only place I wanted to be was in the comfort
of my own home. I had driven around my block three times
before pulling into my garage. The cars parked along the street
were all empty and familiar: the Scion that belonged to the
teenage girl two doors down, the van painted with the insignia
of a stereo installation company of yet another neighbor, the
gas-guzzling Hummer that took up two spots and made me
want to become a guerilla warrior for Greenpeace. But there
was no sign of either the electric car driven by Venus or the
Mercedes I had seen Kane driving, and I felt confident that I
hadn't been followed. For this one night everything was as it
should be, or almost. I noticed as I flipped on the living-room

overhead lights that Anatoly's jacket remained draped over that chair under my father's picture, completely untouched from when he had left it yesterday. We had originally planned to go to a movie tonight, but I had forgotten about it until a few minutes ago and he certainly hadn't called to remind me. I took my cell from my handbag and pulled up his number, but quickly changed my mind. After he called me with an apology I would admit that I had been both harsh and overly sensitive, but until he made that call I would have to give him the silent treatment. I wasn't about to jeopardize my reputation as a stubborn, high-maintenance girlfriend by making the first conciliatory gesture.

I shrugged off my own coat and worked my way through the maze of boxes until I reached the sofa. Each unpacked box was a horrible reminder of how precarious my position was in this house. This wasn't supposed to be a pit stop. This was where I was meant to end up.

I sat on my sofa and stared resentfully at the mess around me and then, without really thinking about it, I jumped to my feet and started unpacking in earnest. I was tearing the Bubble Wrap off of vases and trinkets. I threw books into the built-in bookcases. This was *my* place. It didn't matter that I had only been here for a short while. It was mine, mine, mine, mine!

After I emptied a box I kicked it aside and went for another. More books were in there and I was determined to unpack every single one of them immediately. Unwilling to take the time to look for a pair of scissors I used my car keys to tear open the tape then tossed the keys toward the chair under my father's picture.

The keys landed with a clink, the sound you would expect if one small metal object had hit another. I looked up and discovered that Anatoly had left more than his coat. On the chair was a small metal tin. I dropped from my crouched position by the box onto my knees and sat back on my heels as I reached for it.

This wasn't Anatoly's at all. It was a tin of Strawberry Short-cake strawberry lip gloss.

I slid open the lid and sniffed. I knew that smell. I knew it from the night that I had followed Mr. Katz down the stairs.

If I had chosen to freak out at that moment it might have been justified. But the tin didn't scare me. It was entirely possible that Venus had planted it here during her last late-night visit. After all, she was probably the one trying to gaslight me. But oddly enough, even that idea didn't bother me. I rubbed my finger against the lip gloss. The surface of it was smooth and unused. Still, I shouldn't spread it against my mouth. I didn't really know who had touched it before me…and yet…

I put the lip gloss on. It smelled of childhood innocence. Maybe Anatoly had bought me this, although why any guy would buy his girlfriend a tin of Strawberry Shortcake lip gloss was beyond me. Maybe it was the new trendy hipster thing like Hello Kitty or Betty Boop. Still, I couldn't imagine Anatoly buying this.

I looked around the room again. The boxes didn't seem so offensive anymore. They would be unpacked in time and the issues with the house would be worked out, but right then, in that moment, I felt safe, a sensation so rare that not pausing to savor it would have been practically obscene. I closed my eyes and when I opened them I was looking at my father. He was smiling, the younger me happy in his arms.

"You're here, aren't you?" I whispered.

For a moment the house seemed to get quieter, which was ridiculous since there had been no previous noises. But this quiet had a different quality. This was the quiet of a paternal embrace. I closed my eyes again and as I did so I felt something, a slight pressure against my back, gentle but insistent. I caught my breath and turned around.

Mr. Katz looked up at me with quizzical eyes, his body pressed against the back of mine. He was the only other one in the house with me. So why didn't it seem that way?

That night there were footsteps in my dreams. I didn't like the sound of them and for a moment I feared that they weren't in my dream at all. They seemed somehow outside of my sleep-induced world, dragging me into consciousness. But my father told me not to worry about it. I should just relax. "I love you," he said.

And that's all I could remember when I woke up hours later. I lay there, my eyes still closed, vaguely aware of the morning light, trying my damnedest to recall that dream. But it was beyond me. The more I reached, the further removed my dream became and after a few minutes I resigned myself to making do with the crumbs of memories it had left in its wake.

I could feel the warmth of Mr. Katz lying by my side and, without opening my eyes, I moved my hand so as to place it on his back.

But what my hand touched wasn't fur. It was another hand.

I gasped and tried to jump out of bed. Instead, I got tangled in my sheets and fell with a loud thud to the floor.

It was in the midst of my descent down to whack the hell out of my funny bone that I realized the person sitting on my bed was Anatoly.

It took me a second, but I eventually got to my knees in order to peer over the top of my mattress. Anatoly was just sitting there trying unsuccessfully to suppress a grin. "Are you okay?" he asked.

"*What the fuck!* How the hell did you get in here?"

"You gave me a key."

I managed to untangle myself from the sheets enough to get back on the bed. "I still didn't invite you. I could throw you out."

"You could," he agreed, clearly not worried.

I tried to give him the evil eye, but I couldn't manage it. He was too damn sexy in his fitted black T and well-worn jeans, looking like he owned the place, or at least the bed. It was like trying to get mad at someone for putting vodka into your lemonade without asking even though you had been secretly craving the extra kick.

"Are you here to apologize?" I asked.

"I'm here to call a truce," he said carefully. "I brought you a peace offering."

"What would that be?"

He reached over to the bedside table and handed me my gift. "It's a Venti Light Mint Chocolaty Chip Frappuccino with extra whipped cream."

I couldn't help but smile as I took the cup. This was one of the big differences between Anatoly and Scott. Scott knew I liked Frappuccinos, but Anatoly knew what *kind*. Scott would have asked why I wanted a light Frappuccino if I was going to have extra whipped cream, but Anatoly understood the delicate balance I maintained between my indulgences and my justifications. Anatoly knew the details of me.

"I spoke to Maria this morning," he said.

"Oh?" I kept my eyes firmly on my drink. "Have you made any progress on Maria's case?"

"Not much. I met with her earlier this morning. She says hello."

"Hello? That's it?" I asked warily.

"Yes, what else did you expect her to say?"

"Nothing," I said, secretly relieved that she hadn't ratted me out. "I mean, it would be nice if she apologized for dragging me into her domestic drama, but hello's good. I'll take hello."

Anatoly's eyes narrowed slightly. I needed to change the subject immediately.

"We were supposed to go to the movies last night," I said quickly. "I missed you. I missed you a lot."

"I missed you, too." He let his eyes drop to where my oversize T-shirt hit my bare thigh.

"You think I'm just here to have sex with you whenever you want it?" I asked, reading his intentions.

"No, but a man can dream." I sucked in an unsteady breath as his hand touched my knee and started a slow journey up until he was slowly inching up my T-shirt.

I didn't know if he still wanted me to move out of my new house, and if he did, I didn't know how he would handle my refusal. I did know that I couldn't tell Anatoly about my latest dealings with Kane or my conversation with Jason, Zach, Maria or any of the other Specter Society members without instigating a huge fight on par with the battle of Waterloo. It was too early for all that drama. My mind wasn't fully awake yet, but my body sure was, so it seemed logical that I engage the latter first.

I put my drink down by the side of the bed. "Your shirt's dirty," I said.

Anatoly wrinkled his brow in confusion, but his hand continued to slowly push its way up. "What are you talking about?"

"It's got lint all over it. You need to take it off before it gets on my bed."

Anatoly flashed me a wicked grin before removing his hands just long enough to pull off the shirt. Now it was my turn to grin. I used my index finger to trace his beautifully defined six-pack. "We have another problem," I said.

"Do we?"

"Yeah, your jeans. Very dusty. 'Fraid those are gonna have to go, too."

Anatoly stood up and removed his jeans, revealing his fitted boxer shorts, which showcased an impressively large protruding bulge. He slipped one finger inside the elastic waistband and raised a questioning eyebrow.

"Did you really think I was going to let you get in bed with me wearing nothing but your underwear?" I asked with mock indignation. "Uh-huh, you're going to have to get out of those."

And just like that, they were off and he was standing in front of me in all his naked glory. If there was any argument for God being a woman, it was that she provided us gals with men like Anatoly to ravage.

He knelt down on the bed and this time both hands went to the edge of my T. "This is filthy," he said. "Fair's fair."

In one fluid motion he had my shirt off and had pinned me to the bed. He held my arms at my wrists above my head and he used one knee to spread my legs apart. Slowly, he let his eyes take it all in. "I meant what I said. You are mine."

"Well," I hedged, "I'll certainly let you rule me in the bedroom."

"It's a good place to start." In what seemed like slow motion he lowered himself so his lips were touching my neck. "This is mine to kiss," he said while demonstrating his point. He then moved down while still firmly holding my arms in place. "These," he said as he used his mouth to explore each breast, "are mine to touch." And then he released my wrists and moved even farther south. "This," he said, his hands seizing my hips and positioning me for his pleasure, "this is mine to taste."

I clutched the headboard and arched my back. This was the best wake-up call *ever*.

Unhurriedly he coaxed and teased me until all the anxieties of the last few weeks were pushed forcibly from my head by tidal waves of ecstasy. Trembling, I used my last vestiges of strength to push him off and then immediately rolled right on top of him. "Your turn," I breathed, and used my hand to further entice him before gently guiding him inside me. Anatoly held me by my waist and moved me to a rhythm that was purely ours. I looked down to see that his face was drawn into an expression I was intimately familiar with.

"No!" I shouted. "Not yet, two more minutes."

"Sophie—"

"Think of baseball or whatever sport you Russians are into…figure skating! Think of that!"

"That's it," he said, now rolling us both over so he was on top again. "Now you're going to get it."

"Thank God," I laughed. I closed my eyes and let myself get lost once again in our lovemaking.

In the time it took him to call out my name in the final throes of passion I had managed to squeeze in two more mind-blowing orgasms.

I relaxed under the full weight of his body, sweaty and totally satisfied.

"So we have a truce?" Anatoly asked.

"Absolutely." I felt a slight shaking of the mattress and looked over to see that Mr. Katz had jumped up and was looking at me with his feed-me-now glare.

"Oh, give me a break," I said, using one hand to wave off my pet. "Just because I got up early doesn't mean you get an early breakfast."

"I think your cat's in the right," Anatoly mumbled, his face still in the pillow beneath us. "It's got to be after 10:00 a.m. by now."

"What!" I pushed Anatoly off me and stared at my bedside clock—10:06 a.m. Marcus would be arriving any moment to take me to Kane's. If Anatoly knew that I was going over to Kane's—Kane who has been following me and might possibly be a murderer—if Anatoly knew I was going over to Kane's *house* in the hopes of finding information that I could either trick or blackmail him with, Anatoly's beautiful head might literally explode. I sat up and swung my legs over the side of the bed, but before I could even get up I heard the doorbell ring.

"Are you expecting someone?" Anatoly asked.

"No, I mean, yes. Marcus and I are…um…going to brunch."

Now Anatoly was sitting up, too. "If you're just going to brunch with your friend why do you suddenly seem nervous?"

"I'm not nervous, I'm just…shaky, you know, from all the physical exertion."

"Sophie," Anatoly said warningly. But before he could finish his thought the doorbell rang again and I was on my feet, snatching up a robe that I had draped over a suitcase. "Can't keep him waiting!" I chirped before rushing out of the room.

I pulled the robe on as I took the stairs two at a time. "Marcus," I said as I hurriedly unlocked the door, "don't tell Anatoly that—" and then I shut up because when I had the door fully open I could see that Marcus wasn't there. Instead there was a police officer.

I straightened my robe, hoping to God that I hadn't inadvertently given him a peek at what was underneath. "Can I help you?" I asked as coolly as I could manage.

The officer coughed into his hand in an obvious attempt to suppress a laugh. "Yes, I don't know if you remember me, but I'm Detective Allen. We met on the night Enrico Risso was killed."

"Is everything all right?"

Detective Allen and I both turned at the sound of Anatoly's voice. Unlike me, Anatoly had the sense to put his clothes back on before coming down. He looked past me through the door and then, seeing who was there, quickened his pace. "Good to see you again, Detective Allen," he said, proving once and for all which one of us had the better memory for names and faces. "Is everything all right?"

"I'm glad you're both here. I wanted to talk to both of you a little more about the circumstances that led you to discover Enrico's body. Do you have a moment?"

I got the feeling that he was asking us about our availability for the sake of politeness, not because he thought we really had a choice. Anatoly waved him in and I carefully closed the door behind him.

Detective Allen took a seat on the couch. "Just moving in, I see," he said, gesturing to the boxes. "Don't envy you that. Moving's a bitch."

"Mmm-hmm." I glanced back at the door, wondering if we were about to be interrupted by Marcus.

"I won't be long," Detective Allen said, reading my impatience correctly. "You said that Maria Risso went into Enrico's apartment first. Did you two wait in the hall?"

"For less than a minute," Anatoly said, stepping beside me and draping his arm around my shoulders, subtly helping keep my robe in place. "We could see Enrico's feet from our vantage point in the doorway. As soon as Maria raced inside and found him she screamed and then we both came in after her."

"So you would say she was in the kitchen with the body by herself for around thirty or forty seconds?"

"I would say more like twenty, twenty-five," Anatoly offered.

"You would concur with that?" Detective Allen asked me.

"I…I really don't know. I guess I'm not as good at estimating time as Anatoly is. I could tell you it was less than a minute."

"Enough time for her to close a kitchen window," Detective Allen noted. "Ms. Katz, you said you saw Maria earlier in the evening at a dinner party?"

"Um…well, it wasn't really a dinner party…" Mr. Katz came down the stairs with a feline glower. He swished his tail meaningfully toward the kitchen. I pretended I didn't understand and turned back to the detective. "It was more like a...a meeting."

"What kind of meeting?"

"Right, well," I hedged. Anatoly sighed and shook his head. We both knew there was no way I was going to get out of humiliating myself. "It was a séance," I finally blurted out. "I hosted a séance."

"I see," Detective Allen said, and took a little notepad out of his pocket.

"The guy who's selling me this house, Kane Crammer, he said I had to host a séance if I wanted escrow to go through," I added quickly. "He actually made it part of the contract. I could show it to you if you like."

"That would be good," Detective Allen said, as he continued to make notes.

Anatoly dropped his arm and I went to the bookshelf, reached on top of it, feeling around until my fingertips landed on a manila folder. I pulled it down and handed Detective Allen the paperwork. He read it carefully while I went to the next room to pacify my pet with Natura Tasty Herring for Kitties. By the time I came back to the living room the detective was going over the document for a second time in what appeared to be amused disbelief.

"He really *did* make it part of the contract," he said. "I didn't know you could do that."

"I didn't know anyone would *want* to do that," I grumbled.

"Good point." Detective Allen put the folder down and made some more notes. "So you had never met Maria Risso before that night, but you invited her because Kane wanted you to?"

"No, she wasn't actually on the guest list. She kinda crashed the party."

"I see," the detective said again. "And what was her demeanor?"

I considered lying for Maria's sake, but Detective Allen

would surely talk to the other people at the dinner party and I couldn't risk having my account vary radically from everyone else's. "She was agitated," I admitted. "But she said she was upset because she hadn't been invited."

"But her husband had been," Detective Allen prodded.

"Yes, but like I said before, he never showed up."

"And you were talking to him on the phone when he called someone a—" he checked his notes "—a fucking bitch, is that right?"

"Yep, that's what he said."

"And then a few hours later Maria was at your house, un-invited in place of her soon-to-be ex-husband."

It was clear that Detective Allen had already made up his mind as to who the killer was. I glanced over at Anatoly, hoping that he would say something that might take the spotlight off of his client, but he remained silent.

Detective Allen closed his notebook and offered me a smile. "That's all the questions I have for you right now. However I would like to have a list of all the people who attended that séance." He smirked slightly, unable to say the last word of the sentence with a straight face.

"I'll make one now," I offered. "Do you mind if I use your notepad?"

Detective Allen handed it over and I jotted down all the names of the Specter Society before going to get my cell phone so I could give him the numbers of the members I knew. He perused the list, thanked me for my time and left.

Anatoly closed the door after him and turned to me. "This is a first. You managed to talk to the police without falsely in-criminating yourself."

"I know!" I moved over to the couch and plopped myself down. "I don't even think I'm a suspect. I'm always a suspect!"

It had started raining again and Anatoly turned to the

window and watched as splashes of water made patterns against the glass. "Does this mean you don't have to worry about Kane not selling to you?"

"I don't know. If Kane finds out I'm off the police's radar then maybe. If it did mean that, would you be happy for me?"

The only response I got was from the rain, which had increased its tempo. My cell phone blasted out the first few lines of "It's Raining Men." "That's Marcus," I said quietly before picking up.

"Honey, I slept in, forgive me?"

"You never sleep in," I said suspiciously. "Not when you're alone."

"Yes, well, last night after we parted ways I went to this darling little bar, and at the bar was this darling little man, and—"

"Say no more. When will you be here?"

"An hour?"

"Perfect. I have my own darling little man to deal with at the moment." Anatoly looked over his shoulder and sent me a lethal glare. "Make that darling big man," I corrected quickly. "My darling, big, burly man."

Marcus laughed and we said our goodbyes before I turned my attention back to Anatoly. I was about to make a joke about Marcus's promiscuity, but something in the way Anatoly was looking at me made me nervous. He didn't say anything and I found myself wishing that Marcus wasn't running late so he could interrupt the moment.

"You're upset with me," I finally said. "Why?"

"You're lying to me. I don't know what you plan to do with Marcus today, but it has nothing to do with eating."

"You don't know I'm lying to you," I said huffily.

"You've lied to me before. All the time."

"And you've never lied to me?" I countered. "When we first met, you told me you were a contractor! You, who can't even build a house made out of Legos!"

"I thought you were a murderess at the time."

"And that's supposed to make me feel better?"

"You didn't think any better of me."

"No, but..." I sighed and threw my hands up in the air. "What are we arguing about? All this happened years ago."

"Exactly. And I was hoping that by now we would have moved past that kind of thing. But we haven't, because here you are, lying to me again."

I pressed my lips together and considered my options. "You're right," I said cautiously. "I'm not going to brunch with Marcus. I'm sorry I lied to you about that."

Anatoly nodded. "What are you planning?"

"I can't tell you."

"Can't or won't?"

"Does it matter?"

The rain had turned into a storm. Hadn't there been sun earlier, when Anatoly had climbed into my bed and caressed me with those amazing hands of his? What had happened to the sun?

"It's the sin of omission," he said coldly.

"It's not a sin if you tell people you're omitting something," I snapped. "Check your Catholic theology."

Anatoly wasn't amused. "Does this have to do with Scott?"

"What?" I asked, totally taken aback. "What? You think this is about Scott?" And suddenly I was laughing. I laughed so hard and so long that even Mr. Katz felt compelled to leave his food bowl to investigate the commotion.

"This isn't funny."

"Oh, I beg to differ. I have always been the jealous one in this relationship—and now it's you! You're jealous of *Scott!*

Scott the man who I hate more than…well, more than any person who hasn't yet tried to kill me."

"You must have cared about him a lot in order for him to make you that angry," Anatoly noted. "Now he's found you a house to buy. A house that you refuse to walk away from."

"Have you lost your mind? Scott's connection to this house is the house's only drawback! The only thing that man makes me want to do is scream!"

"I make you scream."

"I'm not talking about the kind of screaming that happened this morning in the bedroom."

"Neither am I. We have a history of driving each other crazy. I used to think that our frequent arguments would break us up, but now I understand that you are attracted to antagonism. You enjoy fighting. And you seem to enjoy fighting with Scott a lot."

"Anatoly, we've been over this. I'm not attracted to Scott. I don't want to fight with him. I want to hurt him, and if I can't do that then I want to get him out of my life as quickly as possible. And he will be out of my life once escrow closes. I just have to find a way to make that happen."

Anatoly took a second to register this. "Is that what you and Marcus are going to be doing today? Finding a way to ensure the closing of escrow?"

"Anatoly, I told you I'm not going to say anything about what I'm going to be doing with Marcus, but I will tell you that I will not be seeing Scott today or any other day that I don't absolutely have to. Can you trust me?"

Anatoly raised an eyebrow. "You've never asked that of me before."

"That's because I'm frequently untrustworthy. I know that. But not when it comes to fidelity." I stood up and walked over to him. I let my hand slip over his chest. "You make me happy,"

I said softly. "You're it for me." And all of a sudden I knew. I was totally and absolutely in love with him. But I didn't say it…I couldn't say it just yet.

Anatoly covered my mouth with his. "I trust you," he said between kisses.

He stopped and fingered the neckline of my robe before leaning in for one more kiss. Minutes after that he was gone. He didn't ask me any more questions. He trusted me.

As I showered, it occurred to me that now that I was no longer a serious suspect it was possible that none of my secret plans were necessary. Maybe Kane would relax and let me stay here without my having to prove anything.

But I doubted it. Kane was a megafreak, and you couldn't trust megafreaks to be reasonable.

Something else was nagging at me, too. I didn't *want* Maria to be arrested. I had no idea if Maria had been angry enough to kill Enrico, but I felt fairly sure that she wouldn't have used a scythe. Maybe a handgun or even a knife, but I just couldn't visualize her wrapping a curved blade around her ex-husband's neck. That required a twisted mentality, and Maria, despite her best efforts, was really just a conventional, albeit wealthy, woman with an interest in the whimsical and a chip on her shoulder.

After cleaning myself up, I managed to gather my mass of hair up behind my head and secured it with a clip. Several wavy locks refused to be confined, but I didn't argue with them. I liked what I saw in the mirror. It was the reflection of a woman in love.

Downstairs, in the guest room, which was slowly becoming my office, I found a yellow legal pad in a box labeled "paper-stuff" and brought it, along with a box of granola bars, to the dining-room table. Why I had packed granola bars in a box labeled "paper-stuff" was beyond me, unless of course I was making some kind of subconscious statement about their taste. But I was hungry and this was easy.

With a sigh I unwrapped my breakfast and wrote the names Kane, Maria, Lorna, Al and Venus all on the top of different pages. Under Kane I wrote the words *may have had opportunity to kill Enrico. May* being the operative and annoying word since I didn't really know what Kane had been doing before the séance. There was also the problem of what I was now sure were Enrico's last words. In jest, Marcus would occasionally call one of his boyfriends a bitch, but I couldn't imagine someone applying the word to Kane.

I chewed on my lip for a moment before taking my pen again to Kane's page. On it I wrote *Oscar???* Oscar definitely merited three question marks. Did he factor into this? Officially Oscar had died of natural causes, but there's a reason why they tell cardiac patients not to ride roller coasters. Had someone tried to bring Oscar's heart attack on? He was Kane's father, so surely Kane had access to his house. Kane was probably strong enough to move around the furniture, but would he do that to his own father? The thought made me want to throw up my granola. But I couldn't rule out the possibility.

But when it came to Enrico, Venus was an easier fit. I bet people called her a bitch all the time. Hell, it was probably her high school nickname. I'd have to check with Scott to see if she had opportunity. I would ask him on the phone if possible; I didn't want to do anything to compromise the trust Anatoly had invested in me.

Still, the problem was that, as far as I knew, the only people who had reason to see Enrico *and* Oscar dead were Al, Lorna and Zach. That was assuming that Al and Lorna knew the truth about what happened to their daughter. If not, that just left Zach. And if Enrico suspected, as I did, that Zach was gay, he might have thought that calling him a bitch was appropriate. It wasn't, but one couldn't expect a child-rapist to be sensitive about such issues.

I put my pen between my lips and wiggled it around like a cigar. I was getting ahead of myself. Venus and Kane might very well have fabulous motives for killing Enrico. I just had to figure out what they were, which was why Marcus and I were going to play detective at Kane's today. We would find something; we always did.

As if on cue, the doorbell rang. I dropped my project and went to greet Marcus at the door. He had on his Armani waterproof leather trench that he had to wear every time it rained in order to justify the price. That, coupled with his perfect self-confident grin, could have qualified him for the cover of GQ.

He stepped inside and dropped his umbrella in the corner. "Your psychic guru has arrived. As your spiritual leader, I demand that you supply me with a room full of DiCaprio look-alikes. It is God's will."

"Really? Because right now I think God may be telling me to smack you upside the head. He says that's what you get for attributing your hedonistic little fantasies to His will."

Marcus shook his head in mock sympathy. "Honey, I hate to be the one to break this to you, but those voices in your head? They're not God. Now go get your bag. I didn't come to chit-chat."

"My, aren't we bossy," I teased as I went to the living room to get my handbag.

Marcus took a few steps in and nodded his approval. "All right, I get it. This place is worth sitting through a few Ouija-board games."

"Are you kidding?" I asked drily. "I'd stab one of Venus's voodoo dolls of *myself* and sacrifice a chicken for this place."

"Thank you so much for the dark imagery. Now, shall we?" He opened the door and bowed slightly in mock deference. I put on my most regal expression and walked out into the wet cold. We had an adventure to get to.

15

They say that those who live in glass houses shouldn't throw stones. But if the person you're targeting is in the *same* house, and you have good aim, you might be able to get away with it.

—*The Lighter Side of Death*

"HERE'S OUR STORY," I SAID AS WE SPED TOWARD KANE'S PACIFIC HEIGHTS home in Marcus's red Miata. "I'm going to tell him that I'm on the verge of being able to spiritually commune with his parents and that you, being my psychic and all, have advised that I touch something that used to belong to the deceased. You believe that would help me make contact."

Marcus looked away from the road long enough to give me a derisive look. "Didn't your *house* belong to the deceased?" he asked. "Why can't you touch that?"

"I don't know," I snapped. "Maybe I have to touch something smaller. Something intimate that they could actually put in their pocket and keep on their person."

"There are so many juvenile things I could say to that."

"Then it's a good thing you're not juvenile." I lowered the

passenger-side window for some air. "I don't know what Kane will come up with, but whatever it is let's hope he has to look for it. Then *I'll* get to look around while *he's* looking around."

"And if he happens to know just the thing you need and hands it over in a New York minute?" Marcus asked. "What then?"

"Then you have to go to the bathroom and while you're supposed to be in there you'll *really* be snooping. Pictures of Kane with his parents would be good. Like, if you can find a picture of Kane with his mom holding a fast-food milkshake in front of a carousel, I can say that his mom contacted me and that she loved taking him to amusement parks, but regrets all the time she fed him trans fat."

"Yes, that's just the kind of message someone comes back from the dead to relay."

"I'm pretty sure that people don't come back from the dead, period. But if I'm going to pretend that they do, then I'll have them say whatever the hell I want them to say. It's my story. That's sort of why I didn't call ahead. I don't want him preparing for our visit. The only person who gets to prepare for this is me...I mean us," I added sheepishly.

"Fabulous," Marcus said as we turned onto Kane's block. "I can tell this visit is going to be a huge success. Better than *Cats*."

I smacked him lightly on the leg. "Oh, shut up and park. This is the address. Be sure that when you're playing the role of psychic you don't overdo it. You can be eccentric, but not to the point of being unbelievable."

"And if he's not home? How long are we going to wait?"

"Well," I hedged, "do you remember that time you broke into Anatoly's place for me? That was kinda fun, wasn't it?"

Marcus did a quick double take. "You want to break in," he said flatly. "To Kane's Pacific Heights mansion. Because obviously, someone as trusting as Kane would never invest in an alarm system."

"I didn't say we should pick the locks or anything. I just meant that if, I don't know, a window's open or—"

"Right, you don't want to break in. You just want to climb in an open window when nobody's looking."

"Marcus—"

"No. No, no, no, no, and…what was it that I was going to say? Oh, yeah, *NO!* I will be your psychic guru in front of Kane, but we're *not* going to be doing anything more stupid than that. My ass is way too cute to be messed with by Bubba the Bi-curious Cellmate."

"Fine," I snapped. "We'll play it safe."

"Thank you."

We both got out of the car and, hunching under one umbrella, rushed up the front steps. Out of the corner of my eye I could see that there were trees on either side of Kane's yard. Not evergreens like those of his neighbors, Kane's trees were bare with gnarled branches twisted up toward the sky like props from a spooky movie.

And then there was the double door that served as the main entrance to his home. It was practically a throwback to the time of King Arthur's court! He even had a coat of arms carved into each side! Marcus toyed with his keys and offered a bemused smile. "And you were worried about *me* overdoing it."

I laughed and smacked him again, this time on the arm. It was a harder smack than I had intended and Marcus dropped his keys. It was just as he was bending down to pick them up that the front door opened. A tall Latino man wearing a grungy T-shirt and dirty jeans looked down at him.

"I dropped my keys," Marcus explained, jingling them in front of him as evidence.

The man at the door immediately brightened. "So you're Mr. Crammer!" he exclaimed. "I was beginning to think I was going to be doing this entire job without ever meeting you.

Not that Gemma isn't great. I told her as much before she headed out of here a few minutes ago. She's very polite and very precise when giving your instructions. That's important. But still, I always like to talk to the real owner of the place I'm working on when I can."

Marcus opened up his mouth to protest, but I beat him to the punch by thrusting my hand toward the man in front of us. "Hi," I said quickly. "I'm Kane's friend Venus. Good to meet you…um," I looked to Marcus as if I expected him to know the man's name. As I had hoped the man didn't give Marcus a chance to fumble.

"Manny," he said, taking my hand in a firm shake. "I just finished redoing Mr. Crammer's cabinetry in the kitchen. Would you like to do a final walk-through with me?" he asked, directing the last question to Marcus.

Marcus gritted his teeth. "Fine," he said irritably, although I knew he was really talking to me, not Manny. "We'll do a walk-through."

Manny beamed and led us inside.

I had expected Kane's home to be in keeping with his barren trees and ostentatious door, but it was nothing of the sort. The soaring ceilings and mahogany furniture were kept from appearing overly grandiose by the moderate clutter in each room. A man's coat was draped over the sofa in the spacious living room and a large glass mug with a spent tea bag had been abandoned on the coffee table. In the formal dining room, the table was covered with mail sorted in several different piles. The whole place was livable. Or at least it would have been if it wasn't for the strong smell of varnish coming from the kitchen Manny quickly led us into.

"Your assistant told me how sensitive you are about the smell," Manny said to Marcus apologetically. "Of course I did the cabinets at my shop so what you're smelling is the island that I just refinished to match." He gestured to the island in the center of the room whose granite top paled in comparison to the gleaming wood that held it up. "It'll be a little better by the night, or are you still planning to stay in a hotel this evening to avoid it?"

"Haven't decided," Marcus said absently. He walked up to the cabinets and examined the workmanship. "Good God, these are fabulous!"

And they were. No coat of arms this time. This woodwork was more subtle and infinitely more beautiful. He had carved some rather abstract flourishes to border each hinged door and while it was clear that the work had been done by hand, it also appeared to be perfectly symmetrical. However, the thing that held my attention was the empty dog bowl in the corner. It was one thing to fool a contractor who had never met Kane, but it was unlikely that we would be able to convince a dog. But I didn't hear a dog, so perhaps Kane had taken him with him.

"So you honestly like them?" Manny asked, clearly fishing for compliments.

"Does Oprah like books?" Marcus turned to him and smiled. "You're an artist."

"Thank you, Mr. Crammer!" Manny beamed. "Looks like my work here is done." He shook my hand one more time before turning to Marcus. "If you ever want more woodwork or cabinetry done I hope you'll consider my services again."

"How could anyone not consider hiring you?" Marcus said, cleverly sidestepping the pitfall of making a promise as Mr. Crammer.

"Great! Then I better get going, I have another job scheduled."

"I'll walk you out," I offered.

As we retraced our steps to the front door I kept my eye out for a dog, but didn't see anything. Manny leaned over conspiratorially. "When I asked Mr. Crammer's assistant what Mr.

Crammer was like she said he was stylish and a bit dark. I thought she meant metaphorically dark, I didn't think she was actually talking about skin color."

I smiled without answering.

"Don't get me wrong," Manny said quickly, apparently unnerved by my lack of response, "I think it's great that this neighborhood has a little color. Really great, hope to make it here one day myself."

"Don't we all," I said smoothly, opening the door for him. "You really did a great job. Thank you...on behalf of Mr. Crammer."

Manny nodded and I closed the door as he made his way down the steps to the street. I counted to ten and then ran back to the kitchen. "We're in! We're in Kane's house! Unchaperoned! We *so* rock!"

"This is not a good idea," Marcus said, shaking his head. "What if Manny-dearest ever gets around to really meeting Kane? If Manny gives a description of you, you're toast, darlin'. You're not exactly the nondescript-girl-next-door. And in case you haven't noticed, that bowl belongs to a dog."

"But that's the beauty of this whole thing. Manny's done his job so the chances are he won't ever meet Kane, but if he does he's not going to admit that he let two strangers into his house. It will be in his interest to keep quiet. As for the dog, if he was here he would have made himself known by now."

Marcus tapped his index finger against his chin. "You may be right about that. Still—"

"We don't have time to debate this. It sounds like Kane might not be back until tomorrow, but we need to do this search quickly just in case he decides to come home to pack up some stuff."

"I have news for you," Marcus said, "I'm not staying more than forty minutes. I want to be long gone before ghost-boy even thinks about coming home. Now, what am I searching for again?"

"Anything that will give us insight into Kane's parents' life. Why don't you look around and see if you can find an office or a study or something and I'll check out the bedroom."

I left Marcus to find his way around the house while I made my way to the second floor, where I imagined Kane's bedroom would be. At the top of the staircase was a somewhat stark hallway. In fact, the only thing in the hallway was a long, narrow rug that served to mask the sound of my footsteps.

To either side of me there were rooms with doors left wide open. I spotted one bedroom so bare and pristine it could only be a guest room, and not a frequently used one at that. There was also a room that had been turned into a makeshift gym, complete with a treadmill, strength training machine and free weights. To my right there was a spacious bathroom, and in front of me, at the very end of the hall, was what had to be Kane's bedroom. The door was partially open, allowing a sliver of sunshine to shed its light on the floor in front of it.

My heartbeat picked up speed. Marcus was right, if we got caught sneaking around in this house we would be seriously screwed. But this was my best chance of getting answers. Without allowing myself to think too much about the possible consequences, I walked in.

I took a moment to absorb it all. The dark wood bed frame was both masculine and appealing. He had a wardrobe that could have easily been purchased at Sotheby's, considering the craftsmanship that had obviously gone into it. And then there was the original abstract painting he had hung on his wall which was every bit as compelling as it was disturbing. Violent sweeps of paint left textured evidence of the artist's passion and anger. Just left of center was a large, dramatic splash of red paint that had been allowed to drip down to the bottom like blood.

It was probably worth a fortune, but it begged the obvious question: who in their right mind would want something like that in their bedroom? Was Kane's goal here to covet nightmares or to simply avoid sleep altogether?

Unable to answer these questions, I let my eyes drop to an attractive but more mundane dresser. On top of it were several photos in matte silver frames. I stepped closer to get a better look.

There were no pictures of Oscar in the photos. One was of a much younger Kane, standing alone in front of one of the buildings at San Francisco State University. That surprised me a little. SF State was a perfectly respectable school, but I would have thought that someone with Kane's resources would attend a private university along the lines of Stanford or something. Of course, there was always the chance that his grades were low enough to make that impossible, but even so, SF State was rarely the backup school for the millionaire set.

The other photo was of Sutro Heights. I smiled at this. It had been ages since I had been to Sutro Heights, but as a child I had picnicked there with my family on a fairly regular basis. It was the ruins of what had once been the estate of the once powerful Sutro family, long since been made into a small national park. Not many tourists knew about it and it wasn't exactly considered a hot spot by the majority of San Franciscans, but that was what made it so wonderful. A lovely park, the ruins of a fabulous mansion, a spectacular view of the ocean and it is never overcrowded. How could you not fall in love with the place?

And yet, when I thought about it, the fact that Sutro Heights had made an impression on Kane bothered me. As far as I was concerned, the less Kane and I had in common the better.

I moved on from the photo and examined the next one. It was a picture of a woman with a thick mane of red hair that tumbled down her back. Her skin was wrinkled, but her numerous and prominent freckles made me wonder if that wasn't from sun exposure rather than age. With that in mind, I guessed her to be in her midforties. She might have looked even younger if she had been smiling. But instead, her lips were pressed together in a tight line as she blankly stared at the camera. Sitting at her side was a boy of about eleven or twelve. It was easy to identify the adolescent as Kane. His arm was around the woman and his head was on her shoulder. It had to be his mother. But if so, she didn't look like she had been the maternal sort. In the photo she barely seemed aware of her son's presence.

Then again…as I scrutinized the details I saw that her hand was actually on Kane's knee and, if the wrinkles in his pant-leg were any indication, she was squeezing it hard.

So these were the three pictures Kane chose to put on the dresser. One of him and his mom, a scenic photo of a park, and a picture of him standing in front of SF State. That seemed significant to me, especially considering that I hadn't noted any other photos displayed around the house. There were no pictures of friends or the grandparents who had apparently loved him enough to bequeath this house to him, and not a single photo of his father, whom I was supposed to summon from the grave. What was up with that?

I fingered the knob for the top drawer of the dresser and tried to decide if I was up for the trauma of going through Kane's underwear on the off chance that there was something of interest hidden among his briefs, but before I could work up my nerve something else caught my attention. What at first glance I had taken for a bench underneath Kane's bedroom window wasn't a normal bench at all, but an antique hope chest. So much more promising than an underwear drawer.

I crossed to it immediately, and was gratified to find it was unlocked. But what really made my day was what lay inside.

Stacks and stacks of photo albums and scrapbooks. A huge grin spread across my face. There would be something in here that could convince Kane that I had been talking to the dead. Lots of things. How could there not be?

With greedy hands I snatched up the album on top only to replace it quickly when I found that it was filled with nothing but shots of various landscapes. Apparently Kane had a hobby.

The next album was more promising. There were pictures of Kane as a child, usually in the arms of his mother. A few of them were at the beach, and, in the photos from Kane's later elementary-school years, there were pictures of him and his mom at Sutro Heights.

I made a mental note of this. *Your mom spoke to me,* I imagined myself saying. *She liked the beach and parks.* This was about as convincing as the horoscopes included in the Sunday paper, but it was a start. I continued to flip through the pages, memorizing some of his mother's outfits and her various hairstyles through the years. Oscar must have been the designated family photographer because he wasn't in any of the shots. At least that was my assumption, until I got to the second last page. This one was taken at the San Francisco Zoo. Oscar, Kane and his mother were standing in front of the polar bear exhibits. Oscar was standing behind both mother and son, one hand on each of their shoulders. It would have been a typical family photo except for one small problem. Oscar only had half of a face. Someone had scratched out the other half from the picture.

I ran my index finger over the destruction. Had Kane done this? Maybe his mom? Even if it had been his mom, certainly Kane hadn't fully disapproved of her actions, otherwise he wouldn't have kept the ruined picture, would he?

Carefully, I closed the album and with a little trepidation

picked up the next one. When I opened it up my heart plummeted down into my stomach.

These weren't pictures of Kane's family.

They were pictures of mine.

16

When I wanted to lose weight I forced myself to go sky-diving, handle dangerous animals and walk the inner city at night. Terror is a wonderful appetite suppressant.

—*The Lighter Side of Death*

THERE I WAS AT TEN, THROWING A FRISBEE WITH MY DAD AT SUTRO Heights. There was another of Leah at eight holding both my mom's and dad's hands as they led her across the street toward the studio that held her dance classes. There was another of my dad, taken from a far distance...so far that even I had to hold the photo close to ensure it was really him. In this one, he was standing by a car that had been parked on the street. It looked like there might have been glass by his feet, but that could have been a trick of the light playing off a puddle or something. What was clear was that he was staring in the direction of the photographer, and, while it was hard to make out, that his hands were in fists by his side. He had always done that when he was struggling to control his temper. I did it, too.

I swallowed hard and forced myself to turn the page. There he was again, this time looking perfectly content. He was standing in his office, his beard and mustache neatly trimmed, his arm loosely thrown around the shoulders of Kane's mom— Kane's mom, who in this photo, unlike all the rest of them, looked totally and completely happy.

I dropped the photo album and backed away from the chest. There was a pounding in my head and I pressed my fingers to my temples in an effort to make it stop. But there was another pounding, too. Footsteps coming toward the room. I turned around just in time to see Marcus throw open the door.

"Kane and Scott are here!" he announced between labored breaths. "I saw them outside from the window, and they have a horrible beast with them! It may be a dog, but it's entirely possible that it's *el Chupacabras!*"

"Do we have time to get out of here before they come in?"

But the sound of the front door opening and then slamming closed answered that question.

"'Gemma? Gemma are you here?" Kane called. Then I heard Scott's voice, too low for me to make out the words, but it didn't really matter what they were saying. I had fifty million questions swirling around in my head, but one thing I was clear on was that this situation was very, very bad.

"Any ideas?" I asked.

"Plenty," Marcus whispered. "Many involve strangling you, but for now I think we should just hide."

"Follow me," I heard Kane say, his voice much closer this time. "I have the papers in my room and there's a painting I would like to show you."

Marcus's brows shot up. "Come up to my room, I have a painting to show you?" he whispered. "Is Kane making the moves on Scott?" But before I could respond he shook his head hard enough to make his locks act as little whips against his scalp. "Doesn't matter, we still need to hide. We need to hide *NOW.*"

There was a big part of me that didn't want to run. Who did this asshole think he was anyway? What gave him the right to store pictures of my dad! Particularly pictures of my dad with his skanky mom! I had half a mind to confront him on the spot, but for once in my life the logical part of my brain won over. I had no real proof that Kane had committed any crimes, but he would have no such problem if he discovered me snooping around his house uninvited.

Marcus was looking around the room, frantically trying to find a place that would conceal us. He opened a door that I had assumed led to a closet. The room was actually a bathroom and without a word Marcus grabbed my hand and yanked me inside. After silently shutting the door behind us, he pulled back the shower curtain and lay down flat in the bathtub, pulling me on top of him. I struggled to close the curtain from my position and only achieved success as I heard Kane and Scott enter his bedroom.

"Interesting painting," I heard Scott say. "Where'd you pick it up?"

"It's the work of my mother," Kane replied. "She made it for a man she loved. He never did see it."

"Huh. Your mom was a talented lady. What's it called?"

"Love in Death."

"Yeah?" This time Scott's voice sounded a bit more uncertain. "Well, that's um…creative. What kinda paints did she use? Are those all oil colors?"

"Mostly. Except for the red. It's magnificent, isn't it? It's the red of life, or death, if you prefer."

"I don't think I follow you."

"It's my mother's blood. She slit her throat right over this painting. This was her last work."

Marcus slapped his hand over my mouth just in time to stifle the sound of my dry heaving.

From the bedroom there was a long silence followed by the sound of Scott clearing his throat. "Can I use your bathroom?"

That was followed by a shorter pause before Kane reluctantly replied, "It's right through that door."

A second later the bathroom door was opened and closed and I heard Scott whisper, "What the fuck!" At first I was afraid that he had somehow discovered Marcus and me, but then I remembered Scott's tendency to talk to himself and there was certainly another WTF situation going on at the moment that had nothing to do with me or the guy I was lying on top of. The sound of the faucet filled the bathroom and I knew that Scott was in the process of splashing water on his face. I felt a slight tickle on my wrist. Crawling up my arm and toward my sleeve was a large brown spider. Reflectively I flicked my wrist to get it off and accidentally touched the shower curtain. The curtain didn't move much, only a slight jiggle, but when the faucet was abruptly turned off I knew we were in trouble. Marcus stopped breathing and so did I. The curtain was jerked back and there was Scott, staring down at us, his mouth slightly open and slack.

He squatted by the side of the tub. "What the fuck?" he said again.

"There's a very good explanation for this," I said in a tiny whisper.

Scott narrowed his eyes. "I find that highly unlikely."

Marcus smiled apologetically, unwilling to add his own voice to our conversation.

Scott shook his head, and for once I really had no idea what he was thinking or what he planned to do.

"Scott..." I started.

"Tell me later," he said. And before I could react he pulled the curtain back closed. I heard the bathroom door open and close again and then Scott's muffled voice talking to Kane. "You know," he said, "Venus recently bought a painting at auction that I think you'll appreciate. It's titled *Destruction of Everything*. It's way up your alley. Why don't we go see it now?"

"I'm not up to seeing Venus today," Kane said, his voice filled with sarcasm. "I'm out of antacids."

"I hear ya," Scott said. I could hear the forced joviality in his voice, but perhaps Kane couldn't. Few people knew Scott's tones as well as I did. "She's not going to be home for a few hours, though. So you won't have to deal with her. Or maybe we should take the…um…dog for a walk."

"The whole reason I put Avernus in the backyard is so I could avoid a walk. It's pouring outside."

"Hey, I love the rain. It's good for the sinuses."

"No, it's not," Kane countered. "Rain brings mold. That's horrible for sinuses, and you hate my dog."

"I don't hate animals, Kane," Scott said flatly. "And how can someone who loves the paranormal as much as you do not appreciate a dark and stormy night?"

"It's early afternoon."

"What's the deal? Does everything have to be perfect for you? Let's just take the dog for a walk!"

"The painting makes you uncomfortable."

"Well, what did you expect?" I heard Scott say, echoing my thoughts. "Your mother killed herself, bled all over a canvas. Not only did you keep the canvas, but you hung it on your fucking wall! Kane, you know I like you, man. But that's seriously messed up."

"I know it's hard to understand," Kane said slowly. "But if you think about it, this painting is a part of my mother, literally and figuratively. I'll never lose her as long as I have this."

"Yeah, that's great. Can we get out of here? I have houses to show and you have a hotel to check into so—"

"I canceled my reservation."

Marcus's eyes went back into his head. If Kane had nowhere to go what was to keep him from hanging out here for the rest of the day? How long before he discovered us?

"Why'd you do that?" Scott asked. "I thought you couldn't stand the smell of varnish."

"I've decided that it's a matter of control. The smell will only bother me if I let it bother me, you know?"

"No, but that's me. Well, then, if you're not going to a hotel and you won't go on a walk then can we at least have this meeting downstairs?"

"You need to learn about control, too," Kane said. "You can't let your fear of a picture determine where you feel comfortable."

"I'll work on it, but not now, all right?"

"Fine, but first…"

Kane let his sentence hang there unfinished and I heard the sound of a drawer opening and closing. "This is why I called you here today. You may sit in the study while you read it over if you like."

"Great, let's do that—wait a minute, what is this? You're re-writing the terms of Sophie's escrow?"

I gasped and started to rise, but Marcus held me tight, making movement impossible. "Shut up and keep still," Marcus said in a barely audible whisper.

"I doubt the changes will surprise her," I heard Kane say as I tried to constrain myself. "You already told her how I felt about selling to her before she was able to make contact."

"I told her what you said, but are you really going to try to make it a legal stipulation?" Scott sounded incredulous, perhaps even indignant. "You might as well start making out a check for twenty grand because there's no way she's gonna go for this. It's crazy."

"Are you saying that I'm not in my right mind, Scott?" There was something in Kane's voice that made me shiver.

"No," Scott faltered, "I think you're as sane as…Freud."

During my marriage to Scott he had used this expression a lot. The people he used it on never knew what to make of it. None of them realized how whacked Scott thought Freud was, no one except me. It was our inside joke, and he was using it now. It shouldn't have made me smile, but it did.

"But I do think that she might object to this, Kane. I know Sophie, you can only push her so far."

"She wants the house. She's connected to it," Kane proclaimed.

"Have you ever actually heard her say that?"

"No, but if you ask her I'm sure she'll admit it. Even when her boyfriend urges her to leave she insists on staying. It's rather odd that she can't explain that connection…that she doesn't know…but perhaps she'll figure it out in time."

"You're losing me, dude."

"It's nothing you need to worry about. Go make yourself at home in the study and read it all over. I'll join you in a moment."

"Why just me? Why don't we both go to the study?" Scott asked, perhaps a bit too quickly.

"If you must know I'm going to use the bathroom. I'll only be a—"

"Don't do that," Scott said.

"Why?"

"Because…because I…because…"

"What's in the bathroom, Scott?"

"Nothing! I—"

But before he could continue the door swung open.

There was another silence and then I heard slow footsteps approach the tub. Marcus started mouthing the words "Oh my God, oh my God, oh my God" over and over again and then the footsteps stopped and I could see Kane's shadow standing on the other side of the curtain...and then I heard the sound of someone throwing up.

The shadow withdrew instantly. "What's wrong with you?" Kane exclaimed.

"I don't know," Scott said hoarsely. "I think this must be the sudden onset of the stomach flu." Then I heard him gag. "I literally just felt it coming on, like, a minute ago."

"Why didn't you want me to come in here?" Kane asked, but now his voice was strained with what sounded like disgust. I was feeling a little disgusted, too. Whatever Scott had up-chucked he hadn't yet flushed down and the smell was quickly getting bad.

"I was trying to tell you that I was going to need to use it first, that's all—" another gag "—I just...couldn't...get...the words...out, oh, man, here I go again—"

"I'll use the bathroom down the hall," Kane said quickly. I listened to Kane's footsteps make a fast retreat as Scott managed to regurgitate a little more.

The moment the door closed Scott flushed the toilet and pulled back the shower curtain again. "There!" he whispered, glaring down at me. "I literally made myself sick trying to save your ass. *Now* do you believe that I'm sorry about the shit I pulled ten years ago?"

"Are you really trying to say that you vomited just for me?" I asked, wriggling against Marcus in an attempt to look up at Scott. "I've never known you to be able to make yourself sick on demand, Scott."

"Have you ever known me to try? Jeez, Sophie! Are you ever going to give me credit for anything?"

"Ladies," Marcus interjected, "perhaps this isn't the best time for a catfight seeing that Norman Bates is just down the hall."

"Right. Should we stay in the bathroom?" I asked.

"God no," Marcus said. "Kane might come back to ensure that Scott didn't contaminate his monogrammed Lauren towels with his bile...then again, Kane might see that as an artistic expression. Either way, we need to skiddoodle."

Scott nodded and reached out his hand to help me up. For half a second I hesitated, a fact that was not lost on Scott.

"Sophie, I know you hate it, but right now you need me."

He grabbed my hand and I didn't resist. Carefully, I climbed off of Marcus and out of the tub. Marcus came out a second later. "C'mon, we don't have a lot of time," he pointed out. "And by the way, you two can stop holding hands now."

I looked down in horror to see that I had forgotten to jerk my hand away from Scott. An oversight I quickly corrected. I looked up at Scott's face expecting to see a smirk, but his expression was completely grave.

"Kane has a high bed and it has a bedskirt," he said. "Let me check to make sure the coast is clear and then you two hurry under there. When you hear us go down the stairs go to the door and listen for another two minutes. I'll do everything I can to get him and keep him in the study. If I can't do that, I'll be loud about it so if you *don't* hear anything after those minutes have passed you two run *quietly* downstairs and out the front door. Got it?"

"My, my, look who has an efficient side," Marcus said with a cluck of his tongue.

"Yeah, I'm very efficient when it comes to basic survival. Stay here." He cracked open the door and then slipped out and tiptoed to the bedroom door as Marcus and I peeked after him. After seeing that Kane wasn't in the hall he waved for us to come out and Marcus and I crawled across the room and dragged ourselves under the bed. As soon as we were completely under, I stuck my head out from behind the bedskirt. "What does Kane want to do to my escrow?" I asked urgently.

"Later!" Scott whispered, and leaning down shoved my head back under the bed just as we all heard the sound of a toilet flushing in the distance. A moment later there was the brief sound of running water before a door opened and Kane's voice carried down the hall. "Ah," he said. "You're done."

"Yeah, I think I'm okay now," Scott said. "Let's go down to the study and look this stuff over."

"Are you sure you're up for that?" Kane asked, although I couldn't detect any real or even fake concern in his tone.

"Yeah, I need to stay put for a little while anyway. Don't want to be throwing up while on the road. Plus there's no way I'm going to talk to Sophie about this new escrow agreement until you and I hash it out."

My fists clenched at my side at the very mention of those papers, and Marcus put a hand on my back, as if to keep me from lunging out and attacking Kane's ankles.

"There's nothing to hash out. Either she agrees or she's out." Now his voice was getting fainter. Scott and Kane were moving farther down the hall. Marcus and I listened intently as the footsteps and voices moved down the stairs until we couldn't hear them at all. A moment later Marcus and I rolled out from under the bed and crouched by the door, both of us silently counting the seconds until two minutes were up.

"Now," Marcus said, getting up and pulling my arm.

I tried to pull away. "I want to grab one of his photo albums."

"Are you crazy?" Marcus asked. "We don't have time for this!"

"A second, Marcus," I insisted, rushing over to the window and lifting the lid of the hope chest. "The pictures he has in here...I just need them."

"Sophie, if you take anything from this room—"

"I have to do this, Marcus!"

"—Kane will think Scott took it and he'll come after him."

My hand froze on top of the album I meant to seize. These pictures were of my family! Kane had no right to them. But then there was Scott, the man who had screwed me over in more ways than I could count. The man who I had imagined torturing on more than one quiet night. The man who had just, to use his words, saved my ass. I withdrew my hand.

"Okay," I whispered. "Let's go."

Without waiting another second, Marcus yanked me out of the room and down the stairs. Just then we heard a dog barking excitedly in the backyard and then Kane's voice coming from the study. "Relax, Scott. I'm just going to find out what Avernus is upset about." But it didn't matter anymore, because Marcus and I were quietly closing the front door. And then we were running. Marcus jumped in the driver's seat of his car while I quickly took my place beside him. With what must have been enormous restraint against adrenaline, he slowly pulled out of our parking spot and drove down the street. His speed was steady and inconspicuous. I watched Kane's house get smaller and smaller in the side mirror. I was furious with Kane and relieved as hell to be away from that house.

And, to my great annoyance, I was scared for Scott. He was now alone with Kane, and Kane was clearly out of his mind. Scott's well-being wasn't my concern. Or rather, his lack of well-being had long been something I had hoped for, and yet now, when there was the real potential for danger, I only wanted Scott to be safe.

And perhaps that was the biggest danger of all.

17

Some people drink to forget. I drink in hopes of finding the courage to remember.

—*The Lighter Side of Death*

MARCUS STARED MUTELY AT THE RAIN AS IT HAMMERED DOWN ON HIS windshield.

"We did get out without getting caught," I pointed out timidly.

"By Kane," Marcus corrected coolly. "We were absolutely caught by Scott, and if he hadn't decided to be decent for once in his life, we would both be wearing orange jumpsuits right now. Do you know what I look like in orange, Sophie? *Do you!*"

"But he didn't turn us in." Marcus was driving too fast now and the colorless buildings that lined California Street were a blur, indistinct from the gray sky that encased them. "He said he was sorry."

"Are you going to get mushy just because he had the courtesy to vomit? Mother birds do that for their chicks all the time, and you know what they do the minute their chicks start looking old? Abandon them and get replacements. Don't be Scott's chick. Let him regurgitate on somebody else."

"Please! I have no interest in being Scott's chick! I'm just surprised, that's all. I thought he…or that he didn't…it doesn't matter." I pressed the base of my palms into my forehead in an attempt to press back the confusion. "What does matter is that Kane has been stalking my family for years. And I mean *years,* Marcus!" I told him about the pictures I had found. By the time I was done he was turning the car onto my street, his speed having decreased as if in complement to his dissipating anger.

"Honey, I know you love that house, but this Kane guy is mental. Like Manson-mental. Can't you buy a different house? You know, sane people sell property, too."

"I'm not leaving my—wait a minute, that's Leah's car."

Marcus pulled up to my house and squinted at the two figures huddled inside the Volvo that was backed into my driveway. "She brought Mama Katz with her," he said with a smile. "I smell a guilt trip coming."

"Why would she spring Mama on me?" I muttered.

Marcus shrugged and leaned over to give me a kiss on the cheek. "As much as I'd love to catch up with your brood, last night's darling little man only lives ten minutes from here and he's a massage therapist. And after the stress of this afternoon, I need a good rubdown."

"Lucky you." I started to open the door, but stopped and turned to give him another hug. "What Scott did for me was nothing compared with what you did today. I know you didn't want to go into that house, but you did, and you held me still when I wanted to spring out and kill Kane. You are the best friend a girl could ever ask for."

"You're just figuring that out now?" Marcus asked sarcastically, but I knew he was touched. He gently shooed me out of the car. "Your mother went through nine hours of labor to bring you into this world and now you keep her waiting? Did she raise you to behave like this?"

I smiled and waved as I slammed the door behind me and then rushed over to the Volvo where Leah, wearing an A-line hooded cloak, was already out and opening the door for Mama. She held an oversize black umbrella in place to protect our mother from the torrents of rain. The umbrella served more for effect than anything else since Mama was already bundled up in her cheery yellow raincoat, her wild, white curls tucked into a clear plastic bonnet. The look was the antithesis of chic and that bothered me some. My mother used to care about fashion when my father was alive.

Now the two women were standing there, looking at me with determined expressions. Instantly I knew I was in trouble.

"This," Leah said, "is an intervention."

My mind raced through the various addictions I had indulged over the last few months. I hadn't had that much alcohol or sex lately, which meant there was only one vice left.

"Studies show there are health benefits associated with drinking five cups of coffee a day," I said. "According to a recent Japanese study I could even kick it up to eight."

"This isn't about the caffeine, mamaleh," Mama said and then clucked her tongue. "Look at you, you're not even wearing a decent coat! You'll catch pneumonia at this rate. Come, let's bring this intervention business inside."

Leah nodded sagely and she and Mama led the way up to my front door. As I fished for my keys I noticed that Mama's hand was on the doorknob, her arthritic fingers caressing its curvature.

"Do you want to open it?" I asked, unsure why that might appeal to her, but nonetheless certain it would. She smiled and took the keys. It seemed to take an hour for her to twist it in the lock, although it was probably less than thirty seconds. As she opened the door she sucked in a sharp breath before stepping over the threshold. Leah and I followed her. Unlike my more practical relatives, I was wearing a totally-adorable-but-not-all-that-waterproof coat. It took considerable dexterity and strength to pull the waterlogged fabric from my body.

"For God's sake, hang it over a shower rod," Leah instructed as she put her own coat on the rack by the door. "It's dripping so much that if you hang it in here you'll have a river running through your living room and you'll absolutely ruin these hardwood floors."

That was all the encouragement I needed. I went to the nearest bathroom and tried not to wonder at my mother, who seemed to have gone into some kind of trance as she fixated on the darkened fireplace.

When I came back, Mama had moved on to the bookcase. "Such nice books you have here," she said as she fingered the various titles by Alice Walker, David Sedaris and Chaim Potok. "I always told him these shelves were too pretty for academia. Such a waste that would have been."

"You told who?" I asked, now standing only a few feet behind her. "Oscar? Did you know Oscar?"

"Okay, that is it!" Leah slapped her hands on her hips and positioned herself between us. "I always knew you were the master of repression, but this is unseemly. As your sister I insist that you pull it together and deal with your multitudes of issues. I have Jack with the Slaters' nanny. She's twenty-two dollars an hour and I've only budgeted forty-four dollars toward the task of making you sane."

"Leah, what the hell are you talking about?"

"You have to remember this house!" she said, her voice rising in both volume and pitch. "I mean, *I* don't remember, but I was too young. Plus, *I* am not the one who decided to jump through a million hoops to buy this place!"

"I told this story to your sister earlier today, and now I tell you."

"Leah, you're not making sense. Of course I remember this house. I live here!"

"So did we," Mama said, her eyes twinkling now. "Surely this house was built from the wood of the tree of life, no? How else could it have made us all so vibrant?"

"Again, I have no idea what either one of you are talking about."

She took a step forward and for the second time in three days I felt her wrinkled hands against my cheeks. "Sit down, mamaleh," she said gently. "For once you're going to let your mama do the talking."

On any other occasion I would have taken that as a cue to remind her that she *always* does the talking, but not this time. Instead I let her lead me through my various boxes to the sofa, and I let her hold me as she told me the story of a past that I had chosen to forget.

The first part of the story was familiar. I knew about my mother's first husband, Sheldon Kleinstein, although I never thought of him by that name. To me he would always be Mr. Decent. That was the only description of him I had ever really gotten. Her family liked Sheldon's family and vice versa and they were all for the marriage, but what made up my mother's mind for her was that she knew that Sheldon was the kind of guy you could count on. He made a decent living by running the family business in Brooklyn, and he would make a perfectly decent husband and eventually a perfectly decent father. All of that was true, except the latter. It wasn't that Sheldon had some kind of deep-seated hatred of children, but no matter how hard they tried my mother couldn't get pregnant. Every night before going to bed she would try to strike a deal with God. If only she could be *schwanger* (pregnant) she would start going to *shul* every week. She would keep kosher, light candles on Friday night, the works! But God was having none of it.

So, eventually, my mother resigned herself to being a decent childless wife to a decent sterile husband, her only consolation being that she could still eat bacon and go to the movies on Friday night. Of course, my mother didn't know decent Sheldon had a low sperm count. She thought the problem lay with her.

All this decency came to an end when Sheldon was struck down by a drunk driver at the young age of thirty-nine. My mother, who had never been truly in love with Sheldon, still mourned him. He had become a dear friend and deserved so much better. She also mourned the loss of her own prospects. At thirty-eight and presumably barren, what were the chances of her ever finding another husband? After a little too much Manischewitz she decided that without children to be a role model for, or a husband to provide a home for, the only thing left to do was to stop being so decent and go have a little fun. So that night she told her landlord she was moving, and less than a month later she was in San Francisco, which, according to all reports, was where people went when they wanted to have some indecent fun.

The men she dated in the city of love would never have met the approval of her friends back in Brooklyn, but that was just fine. Approval, shamoval, she was having a blast. And that's when she met my dad. He wasn't like her other San Francisco beaus; he wasn't a Bohemian or an aged beatnik trying to fit in to the new hippy movement. This man was a smartie! A distinguished professor, at San Francisco State University no less! For a man of color to achieve such a position, surely he had to be a genius!

They came from totally different worlds, but they were able to join those worlds together, not in a melting pot, but in the way you would put together two pieces of a puzzle. Two different and distinct shapes that managed to fit together perfectly to make a picture. They had only been dating a few months when she became pregnant with me. She knew that it was a miracle. God wanted her to make a family with this man, and she was only too happy to oblige.

I knew that story. I tended to embellish the last part. In my version, she knew she was madly in love with my father before the pregnancy and he had already been shopping for a ring. But those details weren't all that important, really. What mattered was that we all lived happily ever after until fate unjustly made my mother a widow for a second time.

"But mamaleh," my mother said, when I offered her my conclusion. "This is not how it was. Life is not so easy."

I pulled back from her slightly, slowly becoming aware of the flat-screen TV and energy-efficient lightbulbs that forced me out my revelry of the last century and into the new millennium. "What do you mean it wasn't like that?" I said. "You and Dad made it. He embraced Judaism, changed his name from Christianson to Katz and you learned to love Otis Redding and soul food. It was a win-win for everybody and you two were totally and absolutely in love. What wasn't easy?"

"It's like I said, we were puzzle pieces. You know what happens to puzzle pieces when they get old? When you take them out and expose them to the elements? I tell you what, they start to curl up in the corners. They lose their shape. All of a sudden they don't fit together so easily and when they are together the picture they create has faded. It's not so brilliant anymore."

"You and Dad were happy," I said firmly. I looked over to Leah for support. She was standing by the window, looking out at the rain instead of at us.

"We were happy," Mama assured me, leaning down to stroke Mr. Katz as he nuzzled her ankles. "But there were times that were not so great. We had so much to learn about one another. My family was not so happy that I married a black man, and his family thought I was a demon—a witch who could turn a gentile into a Jew! All this we could have dealt with, but still, it takes some getting used to living with a man from a different world and I didn't always make it so easy for him, either!"

"Why are you telling me all this, Mama?" I asked, trying not to sound as uneasy as I felt. "What does that have to do with this house?"

"Always in such a rush." She tsked.

"Well, seeing as this story is costing Leah twenty-two dollars an hour I thought a little rushing would be considerate," I retorted, again, trying to catch Leah's eye. She blushed slightly, though I only saw it in profile since she still wouldn't look my way.

"Twenty-two dollars an hour is small potatoes," my mother insisted. "The wisdom of a mother is worth a million! Now, as for me and your father, we went through some turbulence during the year after Leah's birth. It had been hard before that, and after one too many fights we decided to call it kaput."

"What!" I was on my feet now. "How could you have even considered leaving Dad? He was our center, he held our family together!"

"By the time you were in grade school, yes, he did. But when you were a preschooler? Not so much."

"So what happened?" I demanded. "How did he talk you out of it?"

"Sophie," Leah said, her voice sounding more tired than it had been in a long time, "she didn't talk him out of it. *He* left. He left willingly."

"What are you talking about?" I have never considered myself a foot-stomper, but the moment seemed to call for it. They were attacking my childhood memories and it would take childlike behavior to defend them! I glared at Mama, my arms tightly folded across my chest. "Dad didn't leave us. He wouldn't have done that."

"Maybe not if I had asked him to stay," Mama said quietly. "You were so angry, mamaleh. Barely four years old and you were filled with all this *moloreziche*. All day long all I heard was *'where's my papa, when's Papa coming home, give me Papa back.'* You visited him in his apartment all the time, but it wasn't enough for you. Always the stubborn one you were. But that year you were also the scared one. You had been my brave little Sophie and all of a sudden you were afraid of the dark! It didn't help that I got appendicitis on top of everything else."

"That's when you got your appendix removed?" I asked.

"Yes, but I didn't tell your father anything about it. I was stubborn like you. But you, you were too young to see your mama in so much pain. You tried to be such a grown-up, making nice to your sister and feeding her spoonfuls of applesauce, but it wasn't right. It was all too much for you, mamaleh."

"I don't remember this," I whispered. But flashes of memories were popping up. Shouting, a door closing, cries in the middle of the night, my cries, cries for someone who wasn't there. From her seat my mother reached out and took my hand in hers. I knew my mother's hands so well. Long before they had become puffy with arthritis I had watched as they expertly wove threads through my torn pant legs and applied extra lace to Leah's dresses.

But now I knew that those hands had also taken off the ring my father had given her. At one point they must have held the door open for him as he prepared to walk out of her life.

"Thank God I was too young to know what was going on," Leah said with a shudder. "It might have hampered my ability to be in a healthy relationship."

Both Mama and I stared at her. "Bubbala," Mama said to

her, "you know I love you, but your late husband was a number-one schmuck."

"Oh, him," Leah said dismissively. "He doesn't count."

"Why not?" I asked. "He was the father of your child, after all. I don't think anyone would have granted you an annulment if he had lived."

"He wasn't Jewish," Leah said with a sniff. "According to Israeli law the marriage was never legal."

"Oh, I'm sorry. I was under the impression that you were an American citizen."

"Enough with the fighting already. Sophie, stop giving your sister a hard time. Leah, Bob's religion wasn't such an issue. A pig is a pig no matter what house he prays in. As for the problems between me and your father, well, they were exactly that. Problems between me and your father. It's not my fault that you two don't know a good man from a *bohmer!*"

Leah wrinkled her nose. "Do I want to know what that means?"

I gave her a meaningful shake of my head. I didn't know exactly what it meant myself, but I could hazard a guess.

"And your father and I, we worked it all out. He invited me to lunch one afternoon, and I was healthy by then, so off I went. Then there was another lunch and another and then one day he met me at the Cliff House with a dozen roses, if you can imagine! Lunches turned into dinners and then long walks on the beach and always we were talking. Until we were blue in the face we talked! That father of yours may have driven me crazy, and I may not have understood all of his ways, but his soul—that I knew. No matter how different our backgrounds our souls still fit together like two pieces of a puzzle. I cared for Sheldon, but your father? Him I loved."

I relaxed instantly, all my childhood assumptions reconfirmed. Sinking back down onto the couch I let out an audible sigh of relief as Mr. Katz jumped from his position at my mother's feet onto my lap.

"So we decided we'd start over. Right from the very top. Your father had an assistant, Andrea. Her and her husband, Oscar, were moving to their summer home in San Diego. Can you imagine? Having a different home for different seasons?"

"Wait," I said, some of the anxiety creeping back in. "Kane's mom was my dad's assistant?"

"For a time," my mother confirmed. "So here they are, all their furniture is moved or sold off, and Andrea, she says we should use the house to renew our vows."

"To start fresh," I said.

"Exactly! So we have a ceremony. You wanted to dress up like a grown-up, so your papa, he bought you Strawberry Shortcake strawberry lip gloss. Very fancy!"

"Strawberry lip gloss?" I whispered.

"You were smacking your lips through the whole cere-mony!" Mama laughed. "All our friends were there and this time no one gave us any trouble. Everyone saw the love we shared. And there were flowers, and the food! You've never seen so much food! You know, Sophie, it wouldn't kill you to take some cooking lessons like your sister—"

"Mom, stay focused. What happened after the vows?"

"Our family came back together, that's what! It was in this house that you got your papa back, and all of a sudden you weren't so scared anymore."

"I was safe," I said. Leah stiffened and wiped her hands on her skirt. For all her bravado, I had always been her protec-tor. She had come to my rescue on occasion, but we had both seen her efforts as an act of altruism or the expression of sisterly love. For me it was a job requirement, and while she frequently reveled in pointing out my imperfections, it was still disconcerting for her to hear me talk about my own need to feel safe.

"And so your father," Mama continued, "he decided that since this was the house in which our family came back together, this was the house we should make our home."

"Dad wanted to buy this place from Oscar and Andrea?" I asked.

"Want to? It was practically all he talked about! And Andrea was all for it, telling us to move our things in whenever we like—"

"Kane basically told me to do the same thing," I murmured.

My mother watched me silently for a moment, the creases in her forehead deepening in concern. "You watch out for that one. He could be a crazy like his mother."

"His mother was crazy?" I asked. Then I remembered the painting and realized what a stupid question that was.

"She was one of those artists, always getting passionate about the wrong things. Unfortunately, that husband of hers was getting passionate about the wrong woman! Here we all were, your father and I already looking at paint chips and then, all of a sudden, Oscar snaps his fingers and says the deal's off. He's moving back in, without Andrea! Almost everything of hers she had sold while planning for her move. The houses had been Oscar's since before the marriage. I tell you that man left her with nothing! Your father wanted to help, but what could he do? So Oscar moved back into this house and we had to make our home somewhere else. That would be the home you remember growing up in. It was a good home, with its yard and big fancy bathrooms, but your father, he never fell in love with it the way he fell in love with this house here."

"And now," Leah chimed in, no longer so concerned with the rain or the ticking of the clock, "you've literally joined a group of poltergeist-loving lunatics and reacquainted yourself with your womanizing, irresponsible ex-husband all for the privilege of living in *this* house. We all know you're good at denial, but this is taking it to a whole new level."

"*Really,* Leah?" I asked. "How many years were you married to Bob? And how many women was he sleeping with? Don't talk to me about denial!"

"I'm the younger sister," she seethed. "If I have problems it's because I learned them from you."

"Right. Besides, your marriage didn't count because you're a wannabe-Israeli. Give. It. Up."

"What is this?" Mama asked, raising her hands in protest. "Jerry Springer? So Sophie didn't know exactly why she liked this house so much. She had just turned five when Papa and I renewed our vows. What do you want from her? The important thing is you know now," she said, patting my hand affectionately.

"Tell her about Andrea," Leah said curtly.

"Ah, yes, a real harlot that one turned out to be. As soon as Oscar left her she turned to your father. Support, he could give her. They were friends, after all. But I could tell she wanted more. A woman can sense these things. Soon everybody could see it. She called the house at all hours of the night. She would try to sneak pictures of herself into his coat pockets. Dirty pictures! There she was with her *tuchas* hanging out right in front of the camera!"

"It's perverse," Leah spat.

"You're telling me! And did she drink! Always with the drinking! Your father had to fire her, but did that stop her from following us around? Everywhere we turned there she was. We were able to protect you *kinderlach* from her crazy antics, but she had me worried."

"I'll bet," I breathed.

"But then we found out that Oscar had been threatening to

have Andrea locked up in the loony bin and have Kane taken away from her. So your father tells her that if she doesn't stop bothering us he'll help Oscar do it!"

"Did it work?" Leah asked.

My mother nodded. "It took some time, but eventually your father found the ammunition he needed to convince her. She wasn't so worried about losing Kane, but being locked up in a hospital? That she couldn't handle. She had a tough time of it, that one. I'm not sure what happened to her, but she did stop bothering us, and that's the important part."

"How old was I when she finally left us alone?" I asked.

"No more than six, mamaleh."

My mind raced back to the photographs I had found of my family at Kane's. Had Kane's mother taken all those? But that picture of Leah was taken when she was at least seven. So was my mother wrong? Had Andrea stalked us right up to the point when she decided to take her life?

But these were questions that neither Leah nor my mother could answer. I stroked Mr. Katz, envying the simplicity of his life. All I had wanted was a nice home with central heating. How had everything gotten so weird?

"Do you remember any of this now?" Leah asked.

"I remember the lip gloss," I said. "Strawberry Shortcake lip gloss in a tin. I remember that part perfectly." I looked up at the picture of me and my father, and for reasons I wasn't willing to acknowledge or explain, I mouthed the words, *thank you*.

18

When a spy is captured, he takes a suicide pill, believing
it's better to die than be tortured. By that reasoning shouldn't
those same pills be issued to anyone foolish enough to fall
in love?

—*The Lighter Side of Death*

LEAH AND MY MOTHER DIDN'T STAY LONG AFTER THAT. MY SISTER
wanted me to rethink my decision to buy the house. Vague senti-
ments from the past should not be the basis for financial decisions
that could affect my future, she reasoned. It was very practical
advice, except for one caveat. I was getting the house for an
insanely low price. If I could cut through the drama being foisted
upon me by Kane and Scott I would be able to count this sale as
the best investment of my life. Unfortunately, the drama was
getting almost Oedipal in both tone and scale. I suppose a reasonable person might wonder whether any real-estate investment
was worth the hassle. The cost of a Victorian, three bedroom?
Nine hundred eighty thousand dollars. The cost of my sanity?
Priceless.

And yet I knew I wasn't going to move. Outside it had

become dark and the rain was heavier than ever, pounding against the pavement as if applauding my decision to stay. Of course, making a decision was one thing. Coming up with a plan to make that decision work was a whole other ball game. In order for me to do that, I was going to have to find a way to outsmart Kane, because I was now convinced that he had no intention of selling to me. He was undoubtedly out for revenge, using me as an instrument to avenge a mother so justly rejected by my father.

As I had walked my mother and Leah out to the car, I asked Mama exactly what ammunition Dad had used against Andrea.

My mother had smiled at me from under her plastic cap. "Your father was a clever one. He agreed to meet with Andrea. He got her to talk about all the crazy things she had been doing. What she didn't know was your father was getting it all on tape! When he told her *that,* she knew she was kaput! I may still have that tape somewhere if you want it."

And for about an hour I thought I had it all figured out. I would get the tape, splice it up and hand it over to Dena or Marcus. One of them would then hide in the house and play Andrea's answers to my practiced questions. Kane, not knowing about the tape or my hidden friend would hear his mother's "ghost" answering my questions and would then give me the house! And Dena was dating a DJ who liked to remix! Kim could splice the tape for me!

And then reality hit me like a punch to the gut. Kane was crazy, not stupid. He would hear that the voice of his mother was coming from another room and he would inevitably follow the sound. In short order he would discover my ruse and then he…well, God only knew what that freak would do.

I also couldn't try the trick of getting Kane to admit something on tape the way my father had with Andrea. For one thing, Kane didn't have a crush on me. He wasn't going to admit to anything no matter how much I batted my eyes. For another, my father's blackmail had worked because he was threatening to give the tape to Oscar and maybe a few men in white coats. But if I got Kane to admit to some illegality, the only people who would be interested in hearing his taped confession would be the police, and they were the only people who absolutely *couldn't* listen to it. Taping someone without their knowledge, without a warrant, was illegal. Kane's confession would be thrown out as inadmissible, and I would go to jail for getting it in the first place.

I was mulling all this over with a Cosmopolitan in hand when there was a knock on the door. At first I thought it was the wind, but when it gained in force and rhythm I knew someone was there. Mr. Katz and I looked at one another. With everything that was going on, another unexpected visitor was not a positive development. I took a large chug of my drink before getting up to go press my ear to the door. "Who is it?" I called.

"The man who saved your ass."

I experienced the unexpected rush of relief. I hadn't even realized that I had still been worried about Scott, but now that I knew he had gotten out of Kane's place in one piece I felt like doing a little happy dance.

I threw open the door and took a step forward, ready to give him a big hug. And then I stopped short. What the hell was I doing? Scott was the bad guy I loved to hate. Sure, he had his moments, but hugging was definitely out. Silently, I stepped aside as he walked in.

He waited until he heard the door click closed before he turned back to me. "You can't ever do that again."

"I know it was rash, but—"

"Ever!" he thundered.

I stood there with my mouth hanging open like an idiot. I

wasn't used to Scott being this forceful or this serious. He looked over at the filled bookcase and then down at the half-filled box of novels that had yet to find a place. Without a word he walked over and started to take the books out of the bookcase and put them in the box.

I ran over to him and grabbed his arm. "What the hell do you think you're doing?" I demanded.

"You're not going to buy this place," he said simply, shaking me off and grabbing another armful of books. "Start packing up your stuff."

"Wait, who says I'm not buying this place? *Kane?*"

"No, me. I'm not brokering this deal for you. It's off. I reserved a suite for you at the St. Francis hotel. You can stay there, figure out what you want to do. My treat. It's the least I can do."

"The least you can do is stop manhandling my things and help me buy this house! It's mine, Scott!"

"Wrong! It's Kane's, and that guy is dangerous. If I had known that before I would never have gone through with any of this!"

"Any of what?"

"The sale, of course." But before he said that there was a moment of hesitation. There was more to this.

"Scott, what aren't you admitting to?"

"Look, this plan to have you buy Kane's house? It's *over!* The writing isn't just on the wall, it's written in blood! There is no more negotiating. No more escrow. No more anything! Start acting like you have half a brain and start packing!"

And just like that I slapped him. The sound of my palm smashing against his cheek almost had a musical quality to it. Like the first lone beat of a song that was destined to rock.

"You slapped me!" he whined. "You never slap me."

"That was then. This is now. So why don't you stop insulting me and tell me what it is you're not saying."

Scott ran one hand over his cheek, the other still holding one of my books. "I just want to protect you. That's all."

"That's not your job anymore."

We stood there in a face-off for what seemed like an eternity. Then Scott finally looked down at the book he was holding. "*The Great Gatsby.* I always wished I was more like him."

"Who? Gatsby? You know he doesn't get the girl, don't you? He ends up alone in his big old mansion without any real friends."

"Yeah, but in the end you love him despite all his shit. Everybody loves Gatsby." He looked up at me. "Kane doesn't care if you killed Enrico or not. He never did. He just wants you to prove to him that you can contact ghosts."

"I realize that lying to me is par for the course with you, but why did you lie about this?"

"I knew that if I had told you that Kane wasn't going to sign over the house unless you proved your abilities as a medium you would have pushed me to tell you why Kane was so certain you were a medium to begin with," he babbled. "Sure, you knew he had his suspicions based on his own whacked beliefs, but that he was certain of it…that would have required an explanation. But by telling you that he didn't want to sell to a murder suspect and the only way I could imagine overriding that concern was if you convinced him you could talk to ghosts, well, I thought you would take that as an opportunity to win Kane over by faking him out."

Scott was being borderline incoherent now. A sure sign that he was hiding something.

"I didn't think you would go out and try to solve Enrico's murder," he went on. "But then again we've been out of touch for a while and you seem to be the kind of person who, with every year of age, becomes a little more comfortable with risk. By the time you're ninety you'll be jumping out of airplanes and eating blowfish."

I stepped back and gave him a critical once-over. "You buried the lead."

"Excuse me?"

"Why should I be suspicious, Scott? Why is Kane certain that I'm a medium?"

"Who knows? Maybe he thinks it was predicted in one of the rare texts of Nostradamus. Or maybe…" His voice trailed off.

"Maybe what, Scott?"

"Maybe he's certain you're a medium because I told him you were."

"Goddammit, Scott!" I yelled, sorely tempted to slap him again. "Why would you do something that stupid?"

"After his dad died, Kane wasn't going to sell you the house, Sophie! I knew you wanted it and I knew Kane wasn't going to go for it, not for the price you wanted to pay for it."

"I would have found a way to pay more!"

"And so would have a lot of other people. Look around you, Sophie. The housing market in this country is a mess, but not in San Francisco. Houses like this in this city are like diamonds in South Africa. People will kill for them."

"So what are you saying? That out of the goodness of your heart you decided to lie to Kane and later to me so I could get the house on the cheap?"

"Pretty much."

"And now you not only expect me to believe that you lied for my own good, but that you actually have a heart. Talk about suspension of disbelief."

"Like I said, I owe you and I…I don't hate you."

"Wow, Scott. I'm touched."

"Well, you hate me, right? I screwed up, and you decided to hate me, end of story. I'm not like that. Love and hate have never been the flip side of the same coin for me."

"What makes you think they are for me? Just because I once told you I loved you doesn't mean I meant it."

"Ouch! That's cold!" But he was grinning, a sure sign that he wasn't buying my line.

"Better cold than stupid. Stupid would be telling a man that the woman he's about to sell a house to is a medium when she's not."

"Right, well, it doesn't matter anyway. Kane wants to put it in the escrow agreement that you have to come up with some suitable evidence that you have been able to contact the ghost of a former resident, preferably his mother. Now, I don't think he can legally do that, but what he *can* do is just back out of escrow, and, I gotta tell you, I think that's for the best."

"Why?"

"Why?" Scott slammed *The Great Gatsby* back on the bookshelf. "You were there, right? You heard him when he talked about that painting. We all need to dissociate from this guy and pray that he leaves us alone."

"I will…as soon as I get the deed. Tell me, what are the chances that Kane is the one who killed Enrico?"

"You think so?" he asked. "I don't know why he would, but I guess anything's possible. We could talk to the police about it."

"No, not yet. Now, if I understand our agreement correctly, as soon as he signs something saying I have been respectful of the house he no longer has the right to take it away from me, even if he does pay me $20,000, right?"

"Well, we did change the word *respectful* to *good caretaker,* although the term is just as ambiguous and he can't just sign something. It's a specific document that we had drawn up, but for the most part, yes, that's basically how it works. Before that, he can also kick you out whenever he wants if he signs another specific document saying your caretaking abilities aren't so hot. I'm paraphrasing, of course."

"Right, so this is what we're going to do. We're going to convince Kane that I have been talking to his evil mommy. As we work on that, we are going to figure out if it was Kane who killed Enrico and if he had anything to do with what happened to Oscar."

"Why would we do something like that?"

"Because deed or no, I'm going to have to get rid of Kane. He has it in for me big-time. In fact, I think he may have it in for my whole family, and as you pointed out, he's a whack-job. But if I can prove that he's been killing people then he'll go to prison and I won't have to worry about it for another ten to twenty, if ever. So the two objectives are get the house and then get Kane, in that order."

Scott walked over to the fireplace and peered into the ashes. "There are so many problems with this plan I don't even know where to begin."

"It'll work."

"No, I do know where to begin. How are you going to prove to Kane that you can commune with ghosts? You think you can bullshit him? Or have you recently been in touch with the dead?"

I walked to his side and picked up the tin of lip gloss that I had left on the mantel. "It's easy to convince people of something they want to believe."

"And you expect me to help you with this?"

"I do."

"And why would I do that?"

Smiling, I put down the lip gloss and placed a hand on each of his shoulders. "You'll do it because you don't hate me, Scott. And because if you don't help me I can, and will, kick your ass."

"Don't tease me with your sexy tough talk, Sophie. I'm a man of very little willpower." In one swift move he pulled me close. I groaned and was all set to pull myself away and scold him. But I didn't do that because I was distracted by the door. It was opening.

I still should have pushed him away, but the shock of seeing Anatoly glaring at me froze me in place.

He turned around and walked right back out. The sound of the door slamming was louder than any clap of thunder. It was that sound that spurred me into action.

"I have to go after him," I said, quickly freeing myself.

"Why? Because he caught us hugging? Give me a break!" He grabbed me by the waist, holding me back as I attempted to leave. "Sophie, it's pouring out there. You can't go out without a jacket."

"Let me go!" I yelled, reinforcing my request with a very effective backward jab of my elbow. As Scott yelped in pain I rushed from the house, into the rain. But it was too late. Anatoly was gone.

"He'll come back," I heard Scott call from my doorway.

"What if he doesn't?" I asked, just loud enough to be heard.

"Well, you always have me."

I was soaked now, but all the water in the world wouldn't have been enough to wash away the sense of horror that last statement left me with. Slowly I turned around and reentered the house, stalking past Scott, ignoring the puddles of water I was leaving in my wake.

"I don't know if you remember this," Scott said, taking a step up behind me, "but I never walked out on you. Not when I was in a bad mood, not during a fight, never. If Anatoly is going to tuck his tail and run the minute there's a conflict, maybe he's not the right guy for you."

"Anatoly left because it was the only way he could resist beating you to a pulp," I said flatly. I turned to him, pulling a drenched lock of hair from my face. "And you didn't walk out because you never allowed yourself to be pulled into a conflict that would warrant it. You changed the subject, tried to calm me down with a drink, tried to smooth it over with sex, anything but talk about what was really going on."

"Are you trying to say you didn't like my drinks, or... well..." He grinned and moved forward, but I put my hand up to block him.

"Go home, Scott. I'll call you when I figure out what I want you to say to Kane."

He reached for the hand that I had held up to impede him and kissed my palm. "All right, I'll go. I've already waited ten years, so what's another few days."

I didn't even bother to respond. Instead I walked him to the door, holding it wide open so there was no mistaking my message. "I do want to thank you," I said, "for not giving me up to Kane."

"I would never do that," Scott said seriously.

"Mmm, well, as a token of my gratitude I'm going to share a juicy tidbit."

"And that would be?" Scott asked, his grin back and his eyes exploring all the places where my clothes still clung to me.

"A tidbit of *information*," I clarified. "Venus broke into my house. Remember that brooch we found in Oscar's dead hand? She planted it or its duplicate in my bedroom and then she returned to deliver a few thinly veiled threats before taking it back. I just thought you should know that if Kane isn't a murderer your girlfriend probably is. Good night."

Scott's face was the picture of shock and confusion as I shoved him out of my house and closed the door in his face. It had been one of the most trying days of my life and that was saying something. I desperately wanted Anatoly's arms around me all night long. But something Scott had said had hit its mark. Anatoly shouldn't have walked out. Maybe I had been right about his leaving to avoid the temptation to start a fight, but I *wanted* Anatoly to fight for me. I didn't want him to leave me.

I went into the dining room and found Mr. Katz resting his head and front legs on my purse. "Sorry about disturbing you, but my handbag is not a pillow."

Mr. Katz glared.

"Be nice," I said as I gently pulled my purse out from under him. "I need a friend right now."

At that Mr. Katz turned around and left the room. Well, if I couldn't count on my guys, I would just have to turn to my girls. I pulled my cell out from my bag, dialed Dena's number and waited.

"Hey, Sophie, good timing," she said upon picking up. "I just finished untying Kim from the bed."

"Does he have rope burns?" I asked.

"No, I used satin ropes."

"Satin ropes?" I paused for a moment, marveling at how Dena could make a good knot with a fabric that slippery. "Does this mean you're not mad at me about Jason anymore? I was going to tell you that he was in the Specter Society. It's just been so crazy lately," I said, not bothering to note what a huge understatement that was.

Dena sighed heavily. "I'm the only one I can legitimately be mad at."

"Why?" I asked, surprised.

"Hold on a second," Dena instructed. I heard her muffled voice tell Kim that she would be right back, then the sound of a door closing. "I've missed him," she said into the phone.

"Who?"

"Jason, you idiot. I've been thinking about him. I've been thinking about him a lot."

"Seriously!" Mr. Katz reentered the dining room and disappeared again into the kitchen, his determined gait an unmistakable indicator of the hunger that was driving him. "How long has this been going on?" I asked, following my pet. "Days? Weeks?"

"Since the very moment I broke up with him. Can you believe that? I'm breaking my own cardinal rule!"

"The one about loving and leaving?" I asked as I reached for a new can of gourmet kitty food.

"Lusting," Dena corrected. "Lusting and leaving...or actually, lusting, satisfying and leaving. That's the order it's supposed to go in. I love my friends. My men are supposed to be disposable."

"But Jason isn't, huh?" I felt myself relaxing. Clearly Dena was having an emotional crisis. It was nice to know I wasn't the only one. Mr. Katz nudged my ankle to remind me of the task at hand.

"He's so different," she said irritably. "He doesn't conform at all and he's seriously kinky. I mean, that guy taught *me* things."

"No way!" I shoveled out some stinky brown stuff into the food bowl and left Mr. Katz to his meal as I hopped up on the kitchen counter. "So why don't you go for it? I know you're a commitmentphobe, but..."

"I am not a commitmentphobe. I just don't believe in commitment, that's all."

"And the difference is?"

"I don't believe there's a multitude of gods, but that doesn't make me afraid of Hindus. That's the difference. I don't believe, but I'm not afraid."

"Because you're not afraid of *anything?*"

"I'm a little creeped out by acid-wash jeans and neon nail polish, but that's it."

"Dena?"

"Yeah?"

"You're full of it. You're scared to death. You are always in control, and I mean *always*. But if you let yourself get involved with some guy you actually care about all that control goes bye-bye. Then you'll be doing the *does-he-love-me-does-he-not* just like the rest of us."

"Wrong! I know Jason loves me. He told me so, right before I kicked him to the curb."

"No, you didn't! Dena, how could you be so mean?"

"Because the other option was to tell him I loved him, too."

This was enough to shock me into silence. Dena was in love...with a vampire named Jason. I peered out my sliding glass door half expecting to spot a pig flying through the air.

"Dena," I finally said, "it's been years since you've seen Jason, and if he's been on your mind all this time...well, that's something. I mean, you've dated how many men? And he's the first one to get to you?"

"Well..."

"There have been others!" I shouted. "Why am I just hearing about this now?"

"There haven't *been* others. There *is an* other. I'm really digging Kim."

"What!"

"Not in the same way I dig Jason, but Kim is so much damn fun. And he's open to everything. You know how cynical Jason is about our puritanical society. I like that about him. But I also like that Kim's not cynical and he's completely unaffected. He actually gets giddy about new experiences! He's like a kid at the circus for the first time."

"And you're the freak show?"

"You better fucking believe it. The freaks are the only cool people in the circus. Or at least they used to be before the PC Police made the circuses stop featuring them."

"How do you mean?"

"See, clowns and animal trainers join the circus because they want to run away from something. That's why they say, *he ran off and joined the circus.* But when freaks joined the circus they were making a statement. They were saying, *yeah, I'm different, now watch me capitalize on that!* They showed off their abnormalities like a badge of honor that everyone else was privileged to see. Those are my kind of people and Kim gets that. He likes me freaky."

"It's hard to imagine you any other way," I admitted truthfully.

"So the bottom line is that I'm not ready to give up Kim. I know what we have can't be permanent because I don't do permanent, but it definitely hasn't run its course, either. And even if it had, I couldn't have an exclusive relationship with Jason. If I can't have my rainbow coalition of studs I'll lose it."

"So if I'm hearing you right, you're going to continue to blow off Jason, the first man you ever loved, because you don't want to give up your Dick of the Month Club."

"Nuh-uh, don't get self-righteous with me. Your entire life story consists of one questionable decision after another. At least my decision here has to do with physical reality."

"Meaning?"

"Meaning I have a massive libido that craves diversity. It was programmed into my DNA. I'm not going to neglect that for a love affair with some guy who used to wear velvet pants!"

Mr. Katz swished his tail, his way of telling me Dena had a point. I've always wondered if she wouldn't be better off if she settled down a bit, but should I really be pushing her to commit to Mr. Velvet-Pants?

"If you don't think Jason will fit well into your life, then don't fit him in," I said. "You're the judge on this."

"Damn right I am. I'm moving on like I always do and Jason needs to be a man and do the same."

"I think he may be on his way to doing that. There's another

Specter Society member named Amelia. She works in a flower shop south of Market. There are definitely sparks between Jason and her."

"Oh…that's good," Dena said haltingly. "Let him be some-one else's problem." She hesitated before asking, "What flower shop does she work for?"

"O'Keefe's, why?"

"No reason." I heard a man's voice in the background. "Wait, I'll show you," Dena called out. "Kim's found my rubber ducky vibrator. He wants to know how it works."

"You can't put a rubber ducky up there!" I gasped. "It couldn't possibly fit!"

"Not a dildo, a vibrator. You hold it against you and his little beak massages your—"

"I don't want to know," I said quickly.

"Suit yourself, but you don't know what you're missing. Speaking of which, what am I missing? We've spent this whole phone call on me and my issues. What's up with your new digs and all that?"

There was so much to tell, but suddenly the timing seemed all wrong. How could I burden her with my issues when Kim had just taken possession of her ducky? "Everything going fine," I said.

"Lying."

"Yes, but I'm not going to talk about it tonight."

"Right. I'll call you tomorrow then?"

"Sounds like a plan. Have fun with your duck."

"How could I not?"

I hung up and stared at my cat, who was still busily lapping up his mystery meat. "Dena ties busboys to the bed," I said.

Mr. Katz swished his tail again as if to say, *this is news?*

It wasn't news, of course, and that's why I had clung to that part of the conversation and pushed aside the rest. Dena was changing, I was changing, my place of residence was changing. It was just nice to know that there were some things that stayed the same.

But I wasn't able to linger on that thought because suddenly there were footsteps upstairs. One after another, I heard them make their way down the hall.

At least I thought I did...could it be the storm? A tree knocking against a wall or something?

I heard it again. It certainly *sounded* like footsteps. I reached down to the drawer that lay behind my dangling legs and pulled out a carving knife. Much better than a plunger. I got to my feet and dialed 911 on my cell. My finger rested lightly on the send button as I slowly made my way out of the kitchen, through the dining room and living room and then up the stairs.

I turned on the hall light when I got to the second floor. Nothing there. I took a few steps forward and the light went out. I told myself it had to be a short, but my pulse picked up speed anyway. This was so different from when I had followed Mr. Katz down the stairs accompanied by the scent of strawberry lip gloss. I had been oddly calm then, nothing about the experience had alarmed me...not until I had heard the footsteps. Plus this time Anatoly wasn't here. He couldn't claim that the sound had come from him.

I held the knife in front of me. I had always liked this knife. I had used it to cut through the flesh of many a chicken without having to apply much pressure at all.

The lights inexplicably went back on. Still nothing there. Again I checked each room. Again, I checked under my bed. Nothing, nothing, nothing.

"I am alone in the house," I said, as if hearing the words would help me believe them.

Mr. Katz entered my bedroom doorway and blinked at me,

reminding me that *alone* was a relative term. I sighed and sat down on my bed and Mr. Katz jumped up next to me, nuzzling my arm that held the knife. I could be holding a bazooka and Mr. Katz would still see me as nothing more than a source of cuddles and food.

I sat there with him for over an hour, but there were no more footsteps and no more blinking lights. Just me and my cat, and eventually I gave in to my exhaustion and went to sleep.

My knife and my cell phone both were within easy reach.

19

I'm very good at reading people. The only person I know who I haven't really figured out yet is…me.
—*The Lighter Side of Death*

THE NEXT MORNING, I WOKE UP, THINKING OF SUTRO HEIGHTS. I THINK I had dreamt about it, but I couldn't be sure of that. Perhaps it had been recent events that had placed the images of long-passed family picnics in my head. My father used to bring bottles of bubbles on those picnics. Dad had been one of those people who could blow a bubble inside a bubble using both big and small wands and broad strokes of his hand. They would land on the grass, resisting the initial pierce of the individual blades and Leah and I would count the seconds until they popped, always wondering how something that looked so fragile could be so strong.

Those moments hadn't seemed important at the time they happened. It's funny how death can give weight to what was once trivial.

I stretched my arms above my head…and that's when I saw the knife, placed carefully on my bedside table next to my cell phone that still had the numbers 911 on its screen. The noises of the night before…for a brief moment I had forgotten about them. But they had just been noises, most likely of the storm. If it had been otherwise, I would have had to use that knife.

Still…it had *really* sounded like footsteps.

I swung my legs over the side of the bed, already thinking about the coffee I was about to make myself. And then my cell rang. No one I was close to would call at this hour. I leaned over to check the caller ID. Maria Risso. I considered this as my phone danced around my bedside table. Maria was the kind of person who would be difficult to deal with before the intake of caffeine. But God only knew if I'd be able to reach her later, so reluctantly, I picked up.

"Sophia?" she asked.

"Sophie."

"Of course, Sophie." She paused as if uncertain on how to proceed. "I met with Magnum yesterday, about the case."

"He told me," I said.

"But I didn't tell *him* that I spoke to *you*. Friends must never give away one another's secrets."

I smiled at her lack of subtlety. "I haven't told anyone about our conversation, either," I assured her.

"Because we're friends," Maria pressed.

"Mmm." It was the only answer she was going to get on that question because the most honest answer was no. I didn't know Maria and I hadn't fully made up my mind if I liked her or not.

"Would you like to have breakfast with me, Sophie?"

Another easy no. But she knew Kane and maybe she had some information that could help me beat him. "Where shall I meet you?" I asked.

I could almost feel Maria's smile on the other end of the line. "You've been to Mama's?"

"Washington Square, North Beach. They're closed on Mondays."

"Oh, of course." I waited as she came up with another option. "Zazie!" she proclaimed. "That's right around the corner from you, you could walk."

"Zazie, then," I said, rubbing my eyes and stifling a yawn. At least that would give me some extra time to wake up as she made the journey from the Embarcadero to Cole Street.

"Wonderful, I'll be there by 9:30 a.m. I...I want to thank you, Sophie. I need to get out today. I need to rejoin the world, but I'm having such a hard time of it."

"Not a problem," I said guiltily. "It'll be fun." I hung up and looked at Mr. Katz, who was swishing his tail at me like a wagging finger.

"I know," I moaned. "She's a mess and I'm using her. I'm a horrible person."

Mr. Katz blinked in agreement before jumping off the bed and leaving me to my shame. With another sigh I got out of bed and got myself ready for breakfast.

I got to Zazie at 9:30 a.m. on the button, but Maria was already there. She waved to me from her small brown table pressed against a brick wall. She was wearing a long-sleeved, cowl-necked jersey dress with exquisite draping and absolutely no jewelry. The camel color of the fabric perfectly complemented her tan skin. Two glasses of ice water and menus adorned the table along with the standard condiment tray and utensils.

"How long have you been here?" I asked as I slid into the seat opposite her.

"Twenty minutes." We could hear the various noises from the semiexposed kitchen and the conversations around us rose slightly so that the words blended together into a cheery roar.

"I was ready to go when I called you," Maria went on. "I

was planning to go out by myself, but..." She shook her head. "I wish I hadn't found him. I think I could cope better if I hadn't seen him...like that."

"I'm thinking maybe we shouldn't talk about this before we eat," I said as I carefully unfolded the napkin in my lap. "Have you ordered?"

As if in answer to my question our waitress appeared at our table. "Welcome!" she said, her dark brown ponytail bobbing as she talked. "Can I get you something to drink while you two look over the menu?"

"OJ and coffee," I said with a smile and then turned back to the menu as she went to fill my request.

"I love this neighborhood," Maria said wistfully. "And I've always loved that old house of Oscar's. I'm rather amazed that Kane sold it so quickly. I wasn't at all sure he'd let it go."

I made my food selection and snapped my menu shut. "How long have you known Kane?"

"Years. Oscar and Enrico were friends."

I let my eyes drop to the mint-and-white-checkered floor. "Kane is an interesting guy."

Maria laughed. "One of the things I love about the English language is its euphemisms. Yes, Kane is...shall we say, a *horribly* interesting man. He has a darkness about him that is positively foreboding, but I can't say I dislike him."

"Yeah? What is it that appeals to you about him?"

She shrugged. "The enemy of my enemy is my friend. It's one of my favorite expressions."

"Who was the common enemy? Enrico? Not that Enrico was exactly your enemy," I added quickly, "but during a divorce..."

Maria waved off my stammering. "Kane knew Enrico wasn't a believer even though Enrico said otherwise. So Kane wanted him out of the Specter Society. But Enrico wasn't really Kane's enemy. Venus was. If Kane is dark and foreboding then Venus is a black hole. I personally can't stand the bitch."

"Why's that?" I asked, instantly warming to Maria. The waitress chose this moment to come back with my drinks and Maria and I quickly gave our orders: Eggs Fontainbleu for her and gingerbread pancakes for me.

"She is one of those people who liked Enrico's fame," she said once we were alone again. "She used to be reasonably nice to me, but as soon as she realized that my marriage was in trouble she never missed an opportunity to be condescending. The only person I think she's ever had any genuine fondness for is Scott."

"That won't last," I said confidently as I poured a packet of Splenda into my coffee. "Scott's not all that into her. He's made that pretty clear. Eventually he'll leave her or he'll do something to piss Venus off enough to throw him out."

"It would take a lot to get Venus to throw Scott out. He's already cheated on her. Everyone knows it. But still, she keeps him. She paid off all his debt, and from what I understand it was a considerable amount. But you're right about Scott eventually leaving. From all accounts he's making a very good living as a Realtor these days and now with his debt taken care of, the incentives to stay are dwindling. He'd probably be gone already if she didn't keep buying him cars and other trinkets."

"Why do you think she likes him so much?" I asked, although I had an inkling. Scott could be incredibly charming and he had this vitality to him that was kind of addictive, like a drug. Problem is when you've had too much of any drug it makes you sick.

"Scott has his charms," Maria said, as if reading my thoughts. "But I believe the main reason Venus is so attached to him is merely because he's still there. She has difficulty hanging on to her men. I imagine she's impossible to live with, and there are other problems. I overheard one of her previous lovers complain about her modesty in regards to sex."

"Venus is modest?" I asked. I had a hard time believing that.

"In the bedroom, missionary position, lights out. That's what he said. Although I also overheard him say she knows how to give a good blow job."

I squeezed my eyes closed against the image and tried to redirect the conversation. "So Kane has always hated Venus?"

"Always. Venus believes in ghosts, but will sacrifice a successful séance for a celebrity guest like Enrico. Kane doesn't care about the guest list. He just wants to talk to the dead. He's very single-minded that way. When Venus convinced...or should I say *intimidated* everyone into keeping Enrico as a Specter Society member and throwing me out, Lorna and Kane came to my defense. At first to no avail and then, something happened."

"What?"

"I don't exactly know. Kane called me and said he had discovered one of Venus's secrets and if she wanted him to help her keep it she was going to have to do what she was told. The first thing he told her to do was let me back into the Specter Society."

"But when you came to my séance..."

"You weren't told to invite me," Maria said coolly. "Yes, my readmittance was short-lived. Somehow Venus got the upper hand again. Don't ask me how, but Kane called and told me I couldn't come anymore. He clearly didn't want it to be that way, but he said he no longer had any leverage." She rapped her French manicured nails against the table. "With Kane I do believe it's always about leverage."

I nodded. So Kane once had leverage over Venus and she found a way of turning it around. As much as I hated to admit this, Venus had something to teach me. I took a sip of my orange juice. It was fresh squeezed and totally fantastic. "Do you come here a lot?" I asked.

"Not a lot. Never before on a weekday morning. I'm usually at work at this time."

"Oh? I didn't know you worked."

"You didn't think I was the type," she said matter-of-factly. "You imagined that I wrapped myself in the security of Enrico's hard-earned fortune while I set my mind to more amusing pursuits."

"No…I mean…well…"

"It's all right. I love nothing more than being underestimated. When Enrico met me, I was a tour guide in Salerno. My childhood friend, Giovanni, was my partner. I had never traveled farther than France, but I did speak English, the Queen's English. And I can speak French, too, and Spanish and enough German to get by, although I hate the language. It lacks…whimsy."

I sat back in my chair. "I'm having a hard time believing that English is your second language or even that you learned to speak with a British accent. You sound like you could have been born right here in the city."

"I find that the only way to truly know a language is to study its poetry and its lyrics. From those, you can learn the language's nuance and humor in a way that you could never get from a textbook."

Maria glanced up at the framed French art deco poster hung against the exposed brick wall. Her eyes lingered on the foreign words that the artist had included to explain the scene. "I love words. And accents, I adore accents. Each has its own unique taste and texture. I'm obsessed with them in a way. So it was only natural that I would start a business that played into that. I'm a translation service provider."

"Really?" I asked. Maria was becoming more impressive by the second.

"I have a staff of linguists and some very powerful clients.

Fortune 500 companies, law firms, and I usually have at least one government contract at any given time...or at least I used to."

"The investigation into Enrico's murder has probably put a damper on that," I noted.

"Yes. At first I worried that he would haunt me, but he doesn't need to. The nature of his death has made him victorious."

"How exactly is Enrico victorious now?" I asked. "He is dead, after all."

Maria's painted red lips drew up into a forced smile. "Yes, he's dead and I'm alive, so I suppose that makes me better off. That's easy to forget these days." She looked down at her ice water and drew a circle in the moisture that clung to the outside of the glass. "The police came to visit me last night. This afternoon I will be meeting with a lawyer."

"If they haven't arrested you they must not think they have a very strong case." *Yet,* I added silently. But Maria seemed to hear the unspoken qualification. It hung over our table like a bad odor.

"I'm not scared," Maria insisted. "Not like I was in Italy. Giovanni got involved with some people who, as the Italians say, had their hands in the pasta."

"Hands in the pasta? Is that some kind of sexual innuendo?"

Maria laughed. "No, we don't have as many clever sexual innuendos in Italian as you do in English. We prefer our sexuality to be more explicit. To have your hands in the pasta means that you are involved with the mafia."

"Seriously?" I asked. "How the hell does a tour guide manage to get mixed up in something like that?"

Maria gave me a withering look. "Incredibly easily. The mafia's influence in the south of Italy is enormous. Whether you're a small business or a large company with multinational ambitions, you simply must give the mafia a percentage or pay a horrible price. A few years ago the police tried to rein it in, but more often than not the government has looked the other way."

"Okay," I said, "so your partner got involved with the God-father. If everyone does it then why was it so scary?"

"Because Giovanni did something to make them mad."

"Oh. That's not good."

"No, it's very, very bad, and I was right there in the cross fire. The fear was paralyzing. I was like a child looking for someone to take care of me. And then Enrico walked into my office, bro-chure in hand, ready to see the Greek temples at Paestum. He was a true American success story. I showed him everything there was to see and by the end of the tour he had me in his arms. He didn't mind that I was so vulnerable. He said it made me alluring."

There was something very disturbing about that statement and I tried to gauge Maria's expression to see if she was aware of it.

"Yes," she acknowledged, "it's very sexist and condescend-ing. But what I saw was a man who was willing to open his heart to a woman in need. In less than forty-eight hours he told me he loved me, and in less than three weeks we were married and off to America. He was my savior. How could I not love him?"

"Uh-huh." I took another sip of my orange juice. "What happened when you stopped being so needy?"

Maria cocked her head to the side. "You're rather clever, aren't you? What happened is my marriage began to unravel. It took a while. I was so desperately grateful to him that I was willing to play the wallflower for a while. But people started making a fuss. They praised the ease in which I mastered American colloquialisms and accents and my ability to adapt to a new culture…Enrico didn't like that. He grumbled when I started up my business, and when it began to succeed he hated it."

"So he thought there was only room for one star in the family?"

"Yes. He said that a husband is like an entrée and his wife like a fine wine. Wine is meant to complement the meal, not overpower it."

"Wow, that's just...wow."

The food came and Maria and I were quiet for a few minutes as we tasted our dishes. She didn't seem to have much of an appetite, but I had no problem devouring what was in front of me.

"People think our marriage ended because I'll eat things like this," Maria tapped her eggs and cheese, "and not something like that." At this she waved her fork at the decadent pile of carbohydrates on my plate. "It's not true."

"Obviously," I mumbled, my mouth full of roasted pears. "Your marriage was chock-full of more serious problems from the start."

"But I owed Enrico everything...possibly my life. I would have found a way to make it work. But then Lorna came to see me."

The pear stuck in my throat. "What did Lorna have to say?"

Maria toyed with her unused spoon, turning it around and around so that it lightly clicked against the wood of the table. "She told me that when her daughter, Deb, killed herself she had been pregnant. That would have been when I was first starting up my business. Enrico had been giving Deb cooking lessons as a favor to her father who was working for him at the time. I was rarely at home. Lorna told me that...she told me..." Maria shook her head fiercely. "It's not true," she whispered. "When I confronted Enrico he was so offended and...and shocked!"

"You think Lorna was lying?" I asked incredulously. "Why would she do that?"

"Not a lie, but a misplacement of blame," Maria corrected. "She needs someone to blame for her daughter's death. She needs for there to be a reason. I know it's not true. But for a moment I *didn't* know that and if I could believe something so horrible about my husband for even a second then the problems with my marriage were no longer surmountable. Enrico kicked me out. It was the right thing to do."

I placed both my hands flat on the table. "Maria," I said slowly, "has it ever occurred to you that Lorna is the one who killed Enrico?"

"I've considered it. But when she told me…when I believed her…well, I took out my gun."

"You have a—wait a minute—you were going to *shoot* him?"

"I thought it was true, Sophie. I thought he had hurt that innocent little girl and then dared to come to my bed at night, dared to play the role of the hero and the protector. How could I not have at least considered it?"

I wanted to say that I wouldn't have considered it, but that was a stretch.

"But Lorna had other ideas," Maria said. She took a large bite of her eggs, her appetite apparently returning. "She said that the greatest punishment is not death, but to live to see the people you love leave you over and over again. I think that's Lorna's life. She dreams about her daughter and then in the morning…" Maria held up her empty hands to show me exactly what Lorna had when she woke up. "She was afraid Enrico would find peace in death. She wanted him to live and suffer. She talked me out of shooting him."

"That was probably a good move on her part."

"Yes, particularly because Enrico didn't do those things," Maria said stubbornly. Too stubbornly. We were the only people at the table and she was trying to convince both of us. "So I doubt it was Lorna. Besides, she didn't know about the bird."

"What bird, you mean the parrot? What does he have to do with any of this?"

"I told you Enrico had trained that bird to do some amazing things. Did you notice the perch built into the wall, right next to the door frame? Perhaps you thought it was a hook."

"I didn't notice," I admitted, not adding that there had been more dramatic things to see at the time.

"Enrico had trained that bird to chain lock the door. He just picked the chain up with his beak and slid it in while sitting on that perch. He wasn't as good at unlocking it, which proved to be a serious problem. One day Enrico and I sat outside that door for forty-five minutes with our faces pressed up against a sliver opening waiting for that silly bird to figure it out. But he did know how to lock it on command. Enrico and I were the only ones who knew the command. Lorna didn't even know about the trick."

"Did you tell the police about this?"

"Tell them what? That in addition to having motive and opportunity I also knew how to get the bird to chain lock the door behind me?" Maria asked with a cold smile. "No. Would you?"

20

Man cannot improve on God's creations. When we try, we get things like hairless dogs and "cheese" that you squeeze out of a can.

—The Lighter Side of Death

BY THE TIME I LEFT ZAZIE, I FELT CERTAIN THAT I HAD JUST DINED WITH A murderer. Unless of course the killer was Lorna. The weird part was that I wasn't at all sure if it mattered anymore. It was getting harder and harder to work up any sympathy for Enrico, and unless the person who killed him was Kane, finding out who did it wasn't going to help me in my quest to hold on to my home.

I was walking back to that home now, and I kept my coat off so the cold weather could enhance the effects of the two cups of coffee I had already consumed. I had so much to figure out. How should I handle Kane? Was Venus a real threat? How could I repair things with Anatoly? It was all giving me a humongous headache. I needed help and maybe just a moment of peace.

I stopped short of the front door. Leaning against it was a large, bulky manila envelope with my name written across it in Leah's hand. Leah was usually a very careful person. She wouldn't have left a large envelope by my door in plain view from the sidewalk unless she had felt disoriented, upset or flustered.

I picked it up and tore at the seal. Inside was a small, rather outdated, minicassette player/recorder and inside that was a small tape labeled Andrea.

I put the recorder back in the envelope and pulled out a white piece of paper. It was a note from Leah. It read:

What's going on? You're never out this early! Anyway, Mama wanted me to drop this off. Be forewarned, it's a little hard to listen to. I almost wish I hadn't.
Love,
Leah

I put the note back and then, on a total whim, turned away from the door and went to my garage. I wasn't sure where I was going when I stuck my keys into the ignition of my car. I just knew that I had the urge to escape. I put the manila envelope on the passenger seat. I would listen to the tape later. Not now. I couldn't take it now.

I had only driven a block when I realized I was kidding myself. I simply had to know what was on the damned tape. I pulled over into the first parallel spot I could find and after several deep breaths pulled the recorder out of the envelope and pressed Play.

"You don't love her," a female voice said. It was small and distant as if the recording device had been placed far from her mouth. "I know you don't. You can't."

"Andrea, I love my wife very much."

I pressed my fingers against my lips to prevent myself from crying out. It had been so long since I had heard his voice!

"But we are fated to be together!" Andrea went on. "I went to a Tarot card reader yesterday. Do you know what she said?"

"Andrea, I'm telling you that we are never going to be a couple. You need to stop harassing us."

"But even Kane knows we were meant to be. Kane, my own son! He understands! Why can't you?"

"What has happened to you? You used to be more sophisticated than this! Now you take your advice from Tarot cards and eight-year-olds!" There was a muffled thump in the background and I knew it was the sound of my father's fist hitting a table or some other solid surface. He always did that when he was struggling to make a point. "You broke the window of my car, Andrea!" he continued. "You've been stalking my family!"

"I'm sorry." The tears were now audible in her voice. "About the car that is. But Martin, I had to do it. They told me to do it!"

"Who told you?"

"I love you so much, Martin!" she said as if she hadn't heard his question. "I didn't see it at first, but Oscar's leaving me was a blessing! And when you get your divorce that will be a blessing, too! Your children can live with us. I'll take care of Leah and Sophie. Sophie is such a special girl. I'll watch out for her. You just have to believe in me!"

"Andrea, you just admitted to vandalizing my car. How can I possibly believe in you?" His words were only mildly biting, but his tone...I had never heard him use that tone before. It was acidic.

"Why are you being so cruel?" she asked, more softly this time. "Don't you see? It's not just the Tarot card readers. The voices of my ancestors speak to me. The dead know what's important and they tell me. They tell me what I need to do to hold on to you. They care about *us*, Martin. You and me!"

"Andrea—"

"That's why I follow you. I'll always be there, watching, waiting for you to do what's right."

There was a long pause and then my father spoke again. "You are an incredibly tragic figure, and yet, I can't find it in me to feel sorry for you. You've threatened my family. I love them Andrea. I'll never love you."

"You don't mean that," Andrea insisted. "You're confused."

"I'm tape recording this conversation."

There was another long pause. "I...I don't understand," Andrea finally responded.

"If you don't back off I'll give the tape to Oscar. It's all he needs to have you committed. You could lose custody of Kane, Andrea."

"How dare you!" This time it was a screech and I found myself wondering where they were. Surely if Andrea had raised her volume to that degree in a public place she would have attracted attention.

"I won't give it to him if you leave me and my family alone, although I probably should. You need help."

"Martin—"

"Goodbye."

"NO!"

"Get off of me!" My father yelled and then there was a crash...then a cry of a little boy.

"What did you do to Mommy!" the boy sobbed.

"Go back to your room, Kane," my father said. "Call your dad to pick you up. Unless you'd like me to take you to him now. Maybe that would be best, Andrea."

"NO!" Andrea screamed again.

Her voice was quickly followed by the young Kane's. "Don't worry, Mommy, I'll stay with you! I won't leave!"

But Andrea didn't seem to be acknowledging him. "Martin! Martin, please come back to me! Don't let him lock me up, Martin! Martin, please!" But now her voice was becoming fainter as she or the tape recorder moved farther into the distance. There was a sharp click. And then there was silence.

I rested my head against the steering wheel and closed my eyes. Now I knew why Leah had been unwilling to wait for me to get home before dropping off the tape. This was not the father she wanted to remember. She didn't want to know that our dad had been capable of hate.

But there was another way to look at it. Our father had done what he had needed to. To protect us. He kept us safe. Now, when my family needed protection, they looked to me.

I started the ignition again, but this time I knew where I was going. Within ten minutes I was within sight of Sutro Heights.

I parked the Audi behind the high brush that partially hid the park from the Edwardians positioned across from it. There were hardly any cars on the street. A bus drove by, not bothering to slow as it passed the empty bus stop not ten feet in front of me. Across the street a commercial van pulled to a stop in front of one of those Edwardian houses ready to provide it with whatever services. To my right I could see a muddy path and a bit of the well-manicured lawns that we used to picnic on. An overwhelming sense of nostalgia washed over me, the kind that you feel when you see an old movie that was popular when you were a child, or hear a song that was played at your first rock concert. I took out the tape and put it in my coat pocket before getting out. I found my way to that path and as I walked it I started a conversation with my father. In whispers only I could hear, I asked him how he was, if he was happy, why he had left me. It was a one-sided conversation, but that didn't bother me. What shocked me was that I had found the courage to ask the questions.

Ignoring the way the mud was sucking at the bottom of my boots, I followed the path up to the ruins of the Sutro mansion.

When I climbed the stairs, I stopped to admire the spectacular view of the ocean. It was wild and unpredictable under the
cloudy sky, hinting at another storm that hadn't yet announced
its arrival. My father loved the ocean when it was like this. I
wanted to share this with him and there was a little part of me
that wondered if I already was. "Can you see it?" I asked.

"Can I see what?"

I whirled around to find Kane staring at me. He held the
leash of a hideous dog that was completely hairless save for a
blond Mohawk streaked across its narrow skull. That styling
detail only served to bring attention to the dog's ears, which
stuck straight up like exclamation marks.

"He's a Peruvian breed," Kane said. "The Inca believed they
could help their masters find their way to the world of the dead."

"Maybe that's because they look like canine zombies," I
suggested.

Kane smiled, his eyes moving past me to the waves. The dog
strained at his leash and yipped a greeting, or perhaps a warning.

"You're following me, Kane."

"Did Scott tell you what I want you to do?"

"You want me to contact a ghost. But I was thinking, maybe
you should stop with all the insane demands and just sell me
the house for the agreed-upon price. In return, I won't have
you arrested for stalking."

"It's a public park, Sophie."

"And when I saw you across from Amelia's flower shop?"

Kane shrugged. "We were on a public street. It's a small city.
You gotta assume that we're going to bump into each other
now and then."

"I swear to God, Kane…"

"Why won't you let them in?" he asked.

"Who?" The wind was picking up and the dog seemed to
shiver at Kane's side.

"I'm talking about the dead, Sophie. Why won't you open your mind to the dead?"

"How can you be so sure I haven't?"

"You won't even acknowledge the spirit of your own father and he's *trying* to contact you! What chance does my mother have of ever getting through to you? Why are you closing yourself off?"

He hadn't raised his voice or even changed his tone, but his anger was projected by the stiffness of his posture and the narrow slits of his eyes. He was dangerous. The dog wagged his tail in anticipation.

"There have been signs," I said, reaching for something to placate him with. "The lights in my room went on and off by themselves. My doorbell rang when no one was there to push it. There were footsteps in the hall and—"

"A bunch of meaningless shit!" Kane snapped. "Those are the kinds of signs that are supposed to spur you into action! You should have sat down immediately and tried to make contact! You should have spoken to her by now, but you are so determined not to see what you don't understand! You have this extraordinary gift and yet you throw it away in favor of the mundane! Why? Why should I let you move into that house, *her* house! Why should I let another nonbeliever desecrate my mother's home?"

"The other nonbeliever being your father?"

Kane didn't seem to hear me. "They said she was schizophrenic, but she wasn't. The voices she heard weren't in her head—they were of the dead. She had a gift, but unlike you she embraced it. I have the gift, too. But I can't hear *her!* You have to help me hear her. You *can* do that, but you *won't!*"

"You hear voices?" I asked.

"Don't look at me like I'm crazy. I'm gifted! I'm fucking gifted!"

Right, gifted like Charles Manson. Aloud I said, "I have spoken to a spirit. I think it was your mother. Was her name Andrea?"

Kane didn't say anything.

"She was in love with my father. She was going to sell him her house, but…"

"Your family told you about this."

"Did not," I lied.

"Don't try to fool me, Sophie. I'm smarter than you. And for the record, the only reason my mother offered to sell the house to your dad was because at that time she didn't know what a complete womanizing asshole he was."

"You son of a bitch." I advanced upon him, my fist raised, but the hound of hell growled and bared its teeth, doing its duty of protecting the Antichrist.

"You can talk to her," he insisted again. "I know you can."

"Yeah, and who told you this? The voices?"

"Don't forget that I can still stop this deal anytime I want to. Maybe I can't legally insist that you use your gift, but I can raise the price of that house to five million if I see fit."

"It's not a five-million-dollar house."

"But I can try to sell it for that. I can put it all beyond your reach and throw you out on the street. And it won't stop there. I can make you suffer every bit as much as your family made my mother suffer. You, Leah, and that hag you call Mama all owe me, and I'll collect. It's just a matter of how."

"Are you threatening me?"

Kane smiled. "That would be illegal." He leaned down and patted the dog on its lonely strip of hair. "Escrow is up in three days. You have 'til then to contact her. I'll know if you're lying, so don't try it."

"It doesn't matter if I lie to you or not," I shouted. "No matter what I say you're planning on throwing me out, aren't you! This whole thing was a setup!"

But Kane was walking away now, tugging the dog along as he went. I watched him retreat down the stairs, the wind at his back, pushing him away from me.

"How do I negotiate with a crazy person?" I muttered. The fact that I was the one talking to myself didn't faze me. At least *I* wasn't hearing voices.

Except at the séance. But that hadn't been madness...had it? I looked up at the sky and suppressed the urge to scream. I needed someone to point me in the right direction, or any direction for that matter.

As if on cue, my cell phone started vibrating in my handbag. I pulled it out to see who was calling only to see the word *restricted* flash across the screen.

"Yes," I growled as I picked up.

"Is this Sophie Katz?" asked a meek, familiar voice.

"Yes," I said again.

"This is Lorna, Zach's mom? I was wondering if maybe, possibly you might have heard from Zach today?"

"Why would I have heard from Zach?" I asked. I looked down and spotted an empty bottle discarded on the ground, ugly and out of place. Lorna shouldn't have been calling me. Not unless she suspected something was very, very wrong and had nowhere else to turn.

"I know we don't know one another very well, but he seems to have taken to you, and now, well, he seems to be missing. He didn't show up at school and I found this poem in his room...at least I think it's a poem. It may be a note."

A chill spread to my lungs, making it hard to find the breath I needed to ask the next question. "What kind of note?"

Lorna choked back a sob. "Please, I need to find him. I'm afraid he may be planning on leaving me like his sister. I can't lose both my children, Sophie. It can't happen!"

I reached my hand out, hoping to find something to steady

me, but nothing was there. "I haven't heard from him," I said. "But I'll help you look."

"I don't have my car." Each word of Lorna's shook more than the last. "It's in the shop and I can't tell his father—"

"What are you talking about, you *have* to!"

"But it could be nothing, and his father will be so angry. Please, you have a car. You offered Zach a ride that afternoon. Couldn't you give me one, too? We could go to all of his favorite places and look for him. I'm sure I can find him. I'm his mother," she said, as if being his mother gave her some kind of advantage in the search. But it wouldn't, because Zach would know where she would look, and if he really didn't want to be found he'd be somewhere else.

"I'll pick you up. But on one condition. You have to tell his dad what's going on. We need as many people looking for him as possible. Time could be of the essence here."

She whimpered what sounded like a word of agreement. She then proceeded to give me her address, and as soon as I had it I hung up and called Marcus.

"Sophie, darling," he cooed after the fourth ring. "I'm sure you have some fabulous new crisis to relay, but I'm about to wave my magic brush and turn a brunette into a blonde. Call you back in an hour?"

"Marcus, Zach is missing. His mom found something that may be a suicide note."

There was a moment's pause before Marcus responded. "Tell me where to look and I'm there."

Less than forty-five minutes later, I had both Lorna and Marcus in my car. "Al blames me," Lorna said dully as we slowly drove down Haight Street, only a few blocks from where I lived. Apparently, Zach had loved the neighborhood. Funny that I wouldn't know that, but then again the things that I loved about my new neighborhood wouldn't be the same things he found appealing. I liked the Victorians, the close proximity to Golden Gate Park, the restaurants on Cole Street. Now we were cruising the tattoo parlors, the head shops, the dive bars on Lower Haight that may have "forgotten" to check Zach's ID. It was easy to forget that this world merged with my own. I didn't see it because it didn't belong to me. What scared me was that it belonged to Zach, a fifteen-year-old with a grudge and a significant sense of self-loathing.

"We need to get out," I said once we had gone up and down the block three times. "Go to every shop. Do you have a picture of him?"

Lorna numbly pulled out her wallet and flashed me a photo of Zach. "I can't lose both my children," she said for the second time that day.

"He looks like…well, think The Cure's Robert Smith meets Marilyn Manson and you got Zach," Marcus was saying into his cell from the backseat. It had been his idea to give Breather a call in case he had decided to give Sex on the Beach a try after all. "But he's young. A teenager, so he's Robert Smith meets Manson meets a Mouseketeer… Right now he's only got one toe out of the closet so he may seem a bit out of his element…"

"What are you talking about?" Lorna asked. "My son's not gay! He's a good boy! A decent boy!"

Marcus ignored her and continued talking into his cell. "Are you sure, he wasn't in there at all today? Did you ask all your waitstaff?" He listened for a moment and then made eye contact with me via the rearview mirror and shook his head.

I whipped the car off Haight and started barreling west down a side street. "Forget the shops. He can only get in so much trouble there. We need to be driving along the beach."

"But Zach hates the beach!" Lorna cried.

"Doesn't matter. If he is really planning on trying something he'll want to go where no one else is around," I explained, "and no normal person is going to be at the beach on a day like this. And considering the riptide, it's a good way to…well, we'll just look there. After that we'll try the park."

Marcus tucked his cell into his jacket pocket and let out an audible sigh of frustration. "The park's right here, Sophie. Let's try that first. You know better than anyone how easy it is to commit a crime in the park without being caught," he said, referring to the time I had stumbled upon a mutilated body while going to the park to meet a friend.

"My son would never commit a crime," Lorna said. "He tries to act tough, but he's not. He's vulnerable and…"

"Last I checked, taking your own life was a crime," Marcus said, a bit too abruptly. "And just so you know, your son is good and decent and probably gay. Zach might be a little less vulnerable if you could acknowledge that those things aren't mutually exclusive."

"Really not the time, Marcus," I said as I pulled into the park. But where to start? This wasn't the neighborhood playground, this was Golden Gate Park! It was the size of a small town for God's sake! My eyes flitted from the soccer fields to the volleyball courts to the winding walking paths. "I guess I'll just park anywhere and we could just split up?"

"Yes," Lorna said quietly.

"Did you call all his friends?" Marcus asked as I slowed down to look for a spot big enough for my Audi.

"He didn't have a lot of friends. He didn't trust people. He did seem to trust you…and he liked Scott. Zach seemed to admire him, and Al encouraged their friendship. Scott took him out a few times. They'd go to ball games and things like that."

Scott liked it when people looked up to him, so I could understand his willingness to take Zach under his wing, but trying to visualize Zach at a ball game was difficult. "So you called Scott?" I asked.

Lorna hesitated. "I should have, but...I really don't like Scott. I think he's a bad influence."

I did a quick double take. "Are you kidding? He's a horrible influence, but if there's a chance that he knows where Zach is you've got to call him. What the hell is wrong with you?"

"Sophie, there's a spot," Marcus said.

I backed my car into the parking space, my teeth clenched so tight my jaw actually ached. What *was* wrong with Lorna? Didn't she get it? Didn't she know what was at stake?

Before I even had the chance to turn off the car engine, Marcus had his door open. "We'll split up. Everybody keep your cell on and ringer up. Sophie, you call Scott while you look. I'm going to explore the area around the soccer field."

I watched as he trotted off. Zach had gotten to him somehow. Maybe because Zach's life was so horrifically distressing. Maybe that's why he had gotten to me, too.

"Are you going to call Scott?" Lorna asked, still glued to her seat.

I nodded curtly. "Walk back that direction, toward Haight. Be sure to look behind every bush and tree. I'll go toward the De Young. Call if you find anything."

"And you'll do the same for me? You'll call?" The notes of escalating panic were seeping into her voice.

"I'll do the same for you. Now go." It took Lorna a lot longer to get out of the car than it did me. I had to fight the urge to open the door for her, pull her out by her hair and hurl her in the direction of where she was supposed to be searching. But instead I let her get out at her own slow pace. She stopped and stared at me as I tapped my foot impatiently, anxious to call Scott and find Zach. "Did you want to say something?" I asked.

"You think I don't care enough," she said slowly. "You think that's why I didn't call Al right away, why I didn't call Scott, why I'm not running around the park screaming Zach's name."

"I think," I said, "that we need to start looking."

"Maybe the problem is not how much I care, but how scared I am. I failed my daughter, Sophie. I tried to give her a good life, but the one time she came to me for help I...I simply didn't understand. She died knowing that I failed her and she still believes that, I know it. Betrayal like that can't be forgotten in death. Maybe I can't call Al or Scott or search for my son with the same sense of urgency as you and your friend because I can't face another failure."

"Oh," I said. The wind was picking up again, whipping through her already disheveled bob, making her look wild and desperate. "So this is about you."

Lorna's mouth dropped open as she struggled to respond, but I didn't give her a chance. I turned on my heels and started toward the De Young, purposely steering off the beaten path. I called out Zach's name and then I called Scott.

"Sophie!" he said, "I'm so glad you called. Listen, I found the receipt for the brooch, it's from some antique store in Marin. Apparently it used to belong to some psycho Victorian chick or something. I confronted Venus, but she says she gave it to Oscar before he died and didn't see it again until you said it was on your pillow. I think she was telling the truth, but—"

"Tell me later," I interrupted. "Lorna called me. Zach's missing and he may have left a suicide note."

"Wait a minute...Zach...how do you...when did..." Scott sputtered through a few more incomplete thoughts before he was able to pull together a sentence. "He *might* have left a suicide note? What does that mean?"

"It could have been a really dark poem à la Sylvia Plath."

"Sylvia Plath stuck her head in the oven."

"Right, so no matter how you look at this, it's not good."

"Where have you looked?"

"I'm in the park right now. I thought if he wanted to be alone—"

"Okay," he interrupted. "You search there, I have some other ideas."

"Like?"

"Like, I'll talk to you later."

"Scott, wait! Don't hang up!"

"Why, what else is there?"

I stopped and bit down on my lower lip. By my feet a small flowering shrub trembled as some burrowing animal pulled on its roots. "There's nothing else. I just...I don't want to find another body. Not Zach's. I don't think I could handle that."

And there it was. I was just as cowardly and self-centered as Lorna. Zach could be dead and all I cared about was my own emotional health. The shrub sunk lower as I waited for Scott to reply.

"Soapy," he said gently. "Unlike me, you can handle anything."

I smiled and breathed in the damp air. "You think you know me so well."

"Every inch of you, sweetheart. Now, let's find Zach."

I nodded, knowing somehow that Scott would pick up on my agreement without my having to say a word.

"I'll call soon," Scott said, and when I didn't try to hold him on the line he hung up. I slipped the phone back in my purse and called Zach's name again.

Fifteen, twenty, thirty minutes passed without finding anything. My phone remained silent. I thought of calling Anatoly. After all, he was the private detective. But realistically could he do much more than what I was doing now? Unlikely.

When I reached the steps of the De Young I started questioning the few tourists that were around. I described Zach over and over again, searching their eyes for a glint of recognition, but it wasn't there. He had disappeared.

By the time my phone rang again I was near tears. The fact that the number on my cell's screen belonged to Scott didn't cheer me. "I haven't found him," I said when I picked up.

"I have."

"Is he...is he..." I said, trying to articulate the question that I didn't want answered.

"If you're trying to ask, *Is he drunk?*, then the answer is yes."

"Drunk?" I asked with exuberance. "He's drunk? Like he's alive and loaded?" I was jumping up and down now. The people around me must have thought I had won the lottery. "Where are you?"

"I took him back to my place. Venus is making him some coffee."

For the first time I actually felt some warmth toward Venus. "I'll call his mom. I'll bring her over."

"Right, well, you might want to tell her that Venus has already called Al to tell him Zach's here."

"Great! One less phone call we have to make."

"Yeah, but he's pretty pissed at Lorna."

"He can't really put all the blame for this on Lorna. Teen-agers get themselves into trouble sometimes and—"

"Zach has more reason to act out than most teens. Lorna has tried to kill herself twice since her daughter did it four years ago. That's why Al is always breathing down her neck, insist-ing that she tell him where she is every moment of the day."

"Oh, shit."

"Yeah, that's what I said. Anyway, he's coming over and Venus says he's already ranting about how Lorna has ruined their son. So, you know, be prepared."

"Scott," I said slowly, "is everybody in the Specter Society this messed up?"

"If I say yes, will you be mad at me for getting you involved in it?"

"You know I hate you, don't you?"

"You've mentioned it before. I'll see you in a bit." He hung up and I did one more little jump for joy before I dialed up Lorna and then Marcus to tell them the news.

21

They say insanity is doing the same thing over and over again while expecting a different result. Replace the word "thing" with "man" and I think we can all agree that there are a lot of crazy women out there.

—The Lighter Side of Death

NO ONE SPOKE ON THE WAY TO SCOTT AND VENUS'S, BUT OUR MUTUAL relief absorbed the silence and turned it into something wonderful. Of course I realized that things weren't all hunky-dory. Zach may very well have started this morning off with the intention of offing himself. But he didn't do it, and that decision, no matter what had motivated it, was worth celebrating.

It didn't take long to reach our destination. Venus and Scott lived in the Seascape area; their home was nestled between the Bay and Robin Williams's mansion. Marcus took it in with a low whistle, but made no further comment. It wasn't until we actually entered the house that the peace was broken. Scott was the one who let us in and as soon as he cracked the door open I could hear Al shouting.

"What were you thinking?" he bellowed. "Do you know

what they do to kids who drink and drive? They put them in juvie, that's what!"

He was answered with drunken laughter. "You can't drive a bike, Dad! I was drunken riding." Zach seemed to think he was being incredibly funny because he burst into another fit of giggles.

"Welcome to the party," Scott said sarcastically as Lorna rushed past him. Marcus and I followed Scott into the living room. Al was hovering over Zach, who was sitting in a leather armchair, a cup of coffee at his side and a bucket clutched between his hands.

Lorna fell to her knees at her son's feet. "I thought…I thought—"

"You thought what?" Al spat. "You thought he was as pathetic as you?"

Lorna didn't seem to hear him. She reached out her hand and gently touched Zach's arm as if testing to make sure that he was really there.

"What would you have done?" Al continued. "What if he had tried to kill himself the way you've tried? What if we had lost both our kids? Would you have tried to call him back from the dead the way you're always trying to do with our daughter? Would you try to redeem yourself by being a good mother to a goddamned ghost? How many times do I have to tell you? When people die, they die! You can drive someone into the grave, but you can't call them out of it."

"Al."

I looked up to see Venus standing in the entryway on the other side of the room. She was wearing a charcoal-gray shift that gently brushed against her slender hips. "Al," she said again, "I understand that you are upset, but I simply cannot allow this energy to be in my house. I'm afraid the three of you will have to leave now."

Lorna jerked her head in Venus's direction, as if she had just remembered that there were people in the room that weren't Zach. "Thank you," she said quietly. "Thank you for taking care of him, and thank you," she said, turning to Scott, "for finding him."

"Course he found me," Zach muttered. His white powder was wearing off and the black lines he had painted around his eyes had smeared down his cheeks. "I went to Eddie's bar, right, Scott? What'd ya call him when ya introduced us? No ID Eddie? Eddie, Eddie…Eddie, Eddie bo beddie, ba nana fanna foe—"

Scott stepped forward and tried to ruffle Zach's hair, which had been gelled into immobility. "He's wasted, and doesn't know what he's talking about…. And he's just a kid. Don't be too hard on him," he said quickly, directing the last comment to Al who was sending little invisible daggers his way.

"You told my son where he could go to get drunk?"

"No, no. We just ran into Eddie at a game and I may have said I would take Zach to his bar when he turned…okay, I may have said eighteen, but I did tell him to wait until then. I swear."

Al was turning a bit purple, but fortunately for Scott, Zach was the one who needed attention. So, as a team, Lorna and Al pulled Zach to his feet and, with great effort, led him toward the door.

"One last thing," Venus said in a voice that managed to sound both calm and demanding. "Lorna, I know that you are a true believer, but it's clear that your husband is not, and non-believers are not allowed to be members of the Specter Society. If you choose to attend any further meetings it would be best if you came alone. Gina Priestly, that wonderful woman who hosts *Haunted San Francisco* on the History Channel, she has shown an interest in our séances. We'll give Al's slot to her."

"Oh, come on, Venus!" I snapped. "This family has been through hell and back today. Do you really need to lay into them with your stupid Specter Society rules?"

Venus took two steps in my direction and stopped. The space between us was charged with our mutual antipathy. "You're upset that I didn't tell you about how I was the one to buy that brooch. As I told Scott, I gave that piece to Oscar because he lived in the same house as Cecile. I certainly didn't put it on your bed. But I suggest you be careful before you attack the rules of the Specter Society," Venus said sharply. "Kane may not like me, but I do have his ear. How would he react if he knew you had referred to his spiritual practices as stupid?"

"*Enough.*"

The word was said with such vehemence that it took me a moment to realize that it was Scott who had spoken. He was glaring at Venus.

"That's enough, Venus," he said again. "Lay off."

I swallowed hard and looked away. Later Scott would probably try to tell Venus that he had been defending Lorna and her family, but everyone in the room knew he was really standing up for me.

Lorna was the next one to speak. She looked scared again. Even more frightened than when Zach had been missing. "Al believes. He's just upset, Venus, he believes—"

"That everyone here is full of shit," Al spat. "Don't worry, Venus. I won't be at another Specter Society meeting. None of us will be. Come on, Lorna. Let's get our son home."

Lorna was shaking, although that could have been from the effort of holding Zach up. Slowly the trio made their way out of the room and then, eventually, out the front door.

"You should leave, too," Venus said, leveling her gaze on Marcus and me.

Marcus, who had been uncharacteristically quiet, took my arm and led me out. It was when we were standing out on the sidewalk, feeling the day's first drops of rain, that he finally found his voice. "Being a gay teen...it sucks. Doesn't matter how liberated San Francisco is supposed to be, straight teenage boys are evil. They won't let you be one of them. There's no place where you can belong. It's almost too much to deal with. But Zach, he has to deal with all that—two psychotic parents who hate each other and a dead sister. What chance does the poor boy have?"

"He'll make it through," I said, although I wasn't sure I believed it.

Marcus shook his head. "I need to get back to the salon and see if I can salvage some part of my day."

"I'm so sorry I dragged you away."

He held up his hand, signaling that I shouldn't worry about it. I smiled, grateful that for once he wouldn't be lording the huge inconvenience that I had put him through over my head. Together we went back to my car. When we both had our seat belts on he turned to me again.

"I do have one question for you," he said.

"What's that?"

"Why didn't you tell me that Venus used to be a guy? Whoever did the surgery did a great job. I wouldn't have even known if I hadn't spotted that little scar where her Adam's apple used to be. And of course her hands. Guess the doctors couldn't do much about those."

A damp leaf blew onto my windshield and plastered itself there, exposing each one of its veins and discolorations for scrutiny. I turned to Marcus and said the only two words that would come to mind, taking care to enunciate each syllable:

"Holy shit."

I dropped Marcus off at Ooh La La and then immediately called Jason. "When you went over to Amelia's the other night, did she say anything more about Venus?" I demanded as he picked up the phone.

"Who is this?" he asked.

"Sophie!" I swerved to miss a pedestrian as I left Fillmore Street. I was headed straight for O'Keefe's.

"Whoa, I didn't recognize your voice. You sound pissed!"

"What did Amelia say about Venus?" I asked again.

"I don't think she said anything about Venus that night."

"You don't think?"

"Hey, we got pretty high, some of the details are kinda fuzzy."

"Are you kidding me! You said you were going to question her and then you got so high that you can't even remember if she answered you?"

"Yeah, it happens, but I'd like to think that I never asked the questions to begin with. Amelia's amazing. Not in the way Dena is, but she really knows how to give of herself without any of the conventional solicitude to societal hang-ups. I don't want to use her, even for a good cause, you know?"

"*What I know* is that I'm freaking out right now!" I screeched to a halt as the yellow light I had been racing toward turned red. "Remember all that stuff Amelia said about Venus's brother having surgery or have you completely destroyed your short-term memory?"

"I remember her talking about that."

"Okay, well, I have a feeling that Venus's brother didn't die so much as transform."

"You talking reincarnation?"

"I'm talking sex change, you idiot! I think Venus *is* her brother. And I'm thinking that Venus may be so insecure about having once had a penis that she's killing off all the people who threaten to out her."

"Wow, Sophie, you need to drop the prejudices that have been fed to you by the mainstream media and embrace some scientific realities. If Venus did get a sex change, all that shows is that she's willing to do what it takes to be true to her inner self. It doesn't mean she's violent. All studies show that transsexuals are no more or less well-adjusted than the rest of us."

"The rest of us?" I scoffed. "What *rest of us* are you referring to? Would the four people who have tried to kill me in the past few years qualify as the rest of us? The world may be filled with well-adjusted transsexuals, but Venus is clearly not one of them. She's a fucking voodoo priestess for God's sake!"

"Yeah, you may be onto something there," Jason said begrudgingly. "Are you gonna talk to Amelia?"

"I'm going to O'Keefe's right now."

"She'll be more comfortable opening up if I'm there," he said. "I'll meet you out front."

As I rolled through stop signs and swerved through lanes, I tried to get a handle on my excitement, but it was impossible. I realized that there was no more urgency now than there was before, but I felt like this new revelation was the key to everything. And it was shocking. I mean struck-by-a-lightning-bolt shocking. Scott, the world's biggest womanizer, was living with—*sleeping with a tranny!* Maybe Jason was right; maybe I needed to be more open-minded about these things, but I knew that Scott never would be, which meant he didn't know. And with a little luck I would be the one who would get to tell him.

By the time I arrived and found parking Jason was already standing in front of O'Keefe's. He was chewing on a toothpick. A bright green dragon glared at the world from the front of his black T-shirt.

"Does Amelia know you're here?" I asked, once in earshot.

He shook his head and glanced behind him. "I caught a glimpse of them through the window, but they didn't see me."

"*They* didn't see you? Who's they?"

"Amelia, Dena and that sorbet-asshole! What the fuck are they doing here? Did you call Dena?"

"No...wait, well, sort of."

"What's that supposed to mean?"

If we had been in a commercial I would have bought myself a moment by stuffing a Twix candy bar in my mouth. "I may have mentioned this store to her," I said carefully.

"Since when does Dena care about plants?"

"I think it was the name. Dena's a big O'Keeffe fan, you know. She says some of her paintings inspire her in her line of work."

"Yeah," he said begrudgingly, "she does love O'Keeffe. I love her, too. Her paintings of flowers made me want to be a gynecologist."

"Right...well, I have to talk to Amelia about Venus," I said, glancing at the door leading into the shop. "If you don't want to come in that's totally fine, but I'm not waiting."

"I'm going in." His voice suggested that of someone ready to infiltrate the fort of a heavily armed enemy.

As I entered, Amelia looked up from a perfectly tended orchid and beamed, not at me, but at the man behind me with the toothpick in his mouth. Dena stood with her finger linked through Kim's belt loop, ready to drag him wherever it was she wanted to go.

"I didn't expect you!" Amelia said. She turned to Dena and Kim and shrugged her shoulders in a halfhearted apology for the interruption. "Jason and Sophie are friends of mine," she explained. "And they're flower lovers, too. Perhaps *they* could make a suggestion about what floral scents work as aphrodisiacs."

"Sophie's my friend, too," Dena said coolly, her eyes glued on Jason.

Kim cast a nervous glance in Jason's direction before quickly deciding to focus on me. "Hey, Sophie, what's up?"

I took a deep breath, ready to spill my new information. "Well—"

"*And* I know Jason," Dena interrupted. "He and I do have similar tastes, so why *not* ask for his opinion? Let's have it, J. Is there something here that turns you on?"

Jason finally removed the toothpick from his teeth and laid it in his palm, clearly unsure of what to do with it.

"Whoa, I'm picking up on some really amazing energy here." Amelia stepped forward so she was positioned between Dena and Jason. "Are you into Jason?" she asked without the slightest hint of malice.

"That's over," Dena said definitively, but her eyes stayed with Jason. Kim shuffled his feet. It was a small shuffle; Dena really did have a tight hold on him.

"Why?" Amelia prodded. She stepped back slightly and the leaves of a hanging plant touched her hair. "He's so sweet and such a generous lover and you seem really cool. Why close yourself off to him?"

"Are you trying to pimp him out?" Dena asked, finally giving Amelia her full attention. Kim cast a longing glance in the direction of the door.

"No, I just believe in passion. And sexuality and tenderness, and I think those are things to be celebrated, not just with one person, but with lots of like-minded people. You know, free love." She grinned at Dena and then turned her smile on Kim.

Kim's eyes got so wide they seemed to take up the entire top half of his face. "No way!" he sputtered. "Are you suggesting what I think you're suggesting?"

"I'm sorry," I said, putting my hand up in the air to stop them. "But is this a setup for a porno? *Hothouse Flower Makes Greenhouse a Gas* or something equally stupid? I didn't come for that. I came to talk to you about Venus."

"Oh." Amelia looked up, apparently becoming aware for the first time of the plant above her. She quickly stepped beyond its reach. "I don't have much else to say about Venus."

"What about her brother?" I used my fingers to make imaginary quotation marks around the word *brother.*

Amelia fingered an arrangement of daisies. "I'm supposed to make some more bouquets."

"Amelia, did Venus really have a brother?"

No answer. Dena looked at me questioningly.

"Um, hey." Kim awkwardly waved his hand in the air in an attempt to get everyone's attention. "Can we get back to what we were talking about before? You know, the stuff about the free love?"

"Not now, Kim," I snapped.

"Sophie, please don't ask me about Venus or her brother," Amelia pleaded.

I took a step toward her. "Amelia—"

"It's not like his...her...um...their choices...are any of our business," she persisted. "Live and let live, that's what I always say."

I took another step forward. "Amelia—"

"One of the things I love about this country is that men...and women...and...well, everyone...we all have the right to make our own decisions about our body. We can get tattoos...piercings...bigger boobs...we can have things removed..."

"Amelia." I was in her face now and Amelia was looking at the floor, the ceiling, the plants, anything but into my eyes.

"I mean moles, of course. We can get moles removed."

"Amelia!" I shouted. "This...person, Venus, has threatened me. She's broken into my house. She wants to do me harm. I need to get a handle on what I'm dealing with. Now, I'm going to ask you—"

"Oh God, please don't ask me!"

"Amelia, did Venus used to be a guy?"

Finally Amelia met my gaze. "She said she'd kill me if I told anyone."

Dena's finger dropped from Kim's belt loop. "You're serious?"

Amelia nodded. "I think she might have been, too…about killing me, that is. She pushed me against a wall and she put her hand on my throat." Amelia's fingers fluttered to her neck as if to protect it. "She didn't have to get so upset. I respect her lifestyle choice and I totally respect her privacy. She didn't have to be so…so…violent about the whole thing."

"Who else knows?" I pressed. "Did Oscar know? Enrico?"

Amelia shrugged. "I doubt it. I would never have known if I hadn't tried to get some more information on what had happened to her brother. It's not like I knew him well or anything, but he had seemed healthy. I was just curious, but I guess I should have minded my own business."

"So you seriously think everyone else was in the dark?" I asked. "I doubt that. Didn't I hear that Enrico and Venus were close?"

"Yes, but so are Scott and Venus and I know Scott's clueless," Amelia pointed out. "I think Kane and I are the only ones who knew up until now."

"Kane?" I asked, surprised. "But he hates Venus. If he knew, wouldn't he tell everyone?"

"Speaking of telling everyone," Dena said, "when are you telling Scott, and can I please, please, PLEASE be there when you do it?"

"Dena…"

"Pretty please?"

"I think Kane may be blackmailing Venus," Amelia said quietly.

I blinked and then took a step back. That was the leverage! But what could Venus have later gotten on Kane that would trump *that*?

"See, when I figured out who Venus was, I decided not to

confront her with it," Amelia continued. "Why would I? She obviously didn't want me to know or she wouldn't have made up that story about her brother being dead. But then she had that séance at her house. I was one of the first guests to arrive. Except for Kane."

Jason broke the toothpick in half and stepped up to Amelia's side. He draped one arm over her shoulders, then thought better of it and lowered his hand to her waist. "I remember that séance," he said. "I got there at the same time Scott was coming in with the candles. You were a mess, but—"

"But you couldn't get me to talk about it," Amelia finished. "I've tried really hard to block that whole thing out. See, her door was open, and she didn't hear me come in. I heard her and Kane, though. They were in the kitchen and Kane was freaking out, as usual."

"About?" I asked.

"Venus was going on about how Scott still had feelings for some woman. I don't know who Venus was referring to. All I know is Venus saw her as a threat. She said she didn't want Scott anywhere near her."

"And what did Kane say?" Kim asked. I started. He had gotten so quiet I had nearly forgotten that he was there. But now he, too, was caught up in Amelia's story and was anxious to hear more.

"Kane told Venus that if Scott was still interested in this woman he wouldn't have let ten years go by without contact, and that if Venus wanted to keep her secret she better make sure that Scott called her. He said something like…what was it? Oh, yes. He said that she was the key to avenging his mother's death."

Fury is a funny thing. Sometimes it hits you like a gale wind in that it can't be controlled, but it can be escaped. Other times, like now for instance, it creeps into your circulatory system and rushes through your veins until it becomes an intrinsic part of you. My mind sped this process along as I recalled all those phone calls Scott had placed to me starting six months ago, seemingly out of the blue. He wanted to talk to me about something, he had said. But it was Kane who had wanted to talk to me all along. Once again I had found myself beginning to trust him, or if not fully trust at least soften toward him. And once again he had betrayed me outright.

Amelia was still talking. She was telling me how she had interrupted Kane and Venus's argument, that Kane had then left the room and how she had tried to comfort Venus, telling her that she knew about the sex change and that she shouldn't be ashamed of it and certainly shouldn't let Kane use it as a tool of intimidation. It was then that Venus had flipped out, pushing Amelia to the wall, her hand wrapped around her neck, threatening her life if she dared to tell anyone. Amelia had tried to excuse this behavior by telling herself that, thanks to Kane, Venus's nerves were shot to hell. It was understandable that she might behave irrationally. Still, Venus scared her. And while Amelia spoke, Jason slowly drew her closer and Dena watched them, not with jealousy this time, but curiosity. I absorbed all this information the way a computer does, which is to say I understood it and filed it away, but I didn't have an emotional reaction to it. All my emotion was tied up in my hatred of Scott.

"...I stopped going to the Specter Society meetings for a while after that," Amelia went on. "But I missed the free food from Enrico and...honestly? I missed Jason, a lot."

Everyone was quiet for a few moments after that latest admission.

"Sophie," Dena said in a low voice, "let's call Scott now."

I couldn't answer. Anger was weighing down my tongue.

Dena stepped away from Kim and held out her hand. "C'mon, we'll tell him to meet us at your house and then you'll lay it on him. You want revenge? Wait until you tell that asshole that his girlfriend's kahunas aren't metaphorical."

"I'm going to tell him," I finally managed to say. "I'll get revenge. But this time I'm going to do it alone."

22

I always confess my worst sins to those who think I'm a liar.
—*The Lighter Side of Death*

SCOTT DIDN'T ASK WHY I WANTED TO SEE HIM AND I DIDN'T VOLUNTEER
it. But it was clear by the excitement in his voice that he had
drawn his own incorrect conclusions. I was at my house now,
sitting on my sofa and just…waiting.

The house was totally quiet and yet it seemed to be speaking
to me. *Don't be too hard on him,* it said. *He brought you to me.*
But while I got the message I absolutely refused to acknowledge it. I was like a little kid with her hands over her ears
singing, *la, la, la, la, la, I'm not listening to you!* I would not suffer
the kind of bullshit that Scott had been pulling without retali-
ating. I was, after all, still me.

When the doorbell rang I reached into my pocket and pulled
out a Goody rubber band and pulled my hair into a ponytail.
I wanted him to see me. I wanted him to be able to look me
in the eye when I made my accusations. I went to open the
door and there he was, in his Armani shirt, Diesel jeans and
that stupid, self-congratulatory smile of his. He was so sure he

was going to get lucky. It didn't matter that I hadn't given him any reason to hope. It didn't matter that he should be riddled with guilt for luring me into a meeting with Kane. All he cared about now was getting into my pants.

Well, that wasn't going to happen.

Scott's smile faded somewhat when he saw my expression. He walked past me and draped his coat over the rack. "What is it this time?" he said with a sigh.

"Your girlfriend, Venus." I slammed the door shut and followed him into the living room.

Scott nodded. "The brooch thing was definitely weird. I called the store where Venus bought it. Venus was telling the truth about it having belonged to some woman named Cecile and the whole drama surrounding it. But like Venus said, she *gave* it to Oscar, so it's not like it got here on its own."

"This isn't about the brooch." I sat down on the couch, careful to angle my body toward Scott so my words could deliver a direct blow. "Venus is not what you think she is."

"Sophie, I know how much you hate her, and you have good reason. What she's been doing, the way she acted today…completely inexcusable. But that doesn't make her a murderer."

"No, but it doesn't make her a woman, either."

Scott stared at me for a moment. "What?"

"That little love goddess you're shacking up with? She used to use a urinal."

Scott continued to stare. And then he laughed. Scott buckled over with laughter.

"I knew you were jealous, Sophie, but this? This is beautiful! Only a mind as awesome and deviant as yours could make up something like this."

"You think I'm *jealous?*" I asked.

His laughter relaxed into a good-natured chuckle. "I didn't

mean to be insulting. It's not like I wasn't jealous of Anatoly, but now that he's out of the way—"

"Anatoly and I are not over. Not by a long shot. And I didn't make this stuff up about Venus. Ask her, see how she reacts."

"You want me to ask her if she used to be a man?" The first flash of doubt crossed his features.

"I know what you're thinking," I said coolly. "She's gorgeous."

"Like a supermodel," Scott said quietly.

"Right, just like a supermodel. She's tall. She's got those narrow hips and those broad shoulders that make her waist look tiny. She'd be a regular Linda Evangelista if it weren't for those man–hands of hers."

Scott swallowed hard.

"What about her boobs, Scott. Do they feel real?"

"Lots of women get implants," Scott said, but now his voice was shaking.

"Has she ever gotten her period?"

"She takes those birth control pills. The ones that keep you from ever getting a period."

"Really? How amazingly convenient."

He shifted his weight from foot to foot. "My girlfriend is not a man."

"No," I confirmed. "She's a woman. She just wasn't born that way. And that brings me to another question. We know about Venus's metamorphosis, but I was wondering, when your mother gave birth to you, were you a normal human being? Or were you always a lecherous, lying, backstabbing leech?"

"What?" Scott asked distractedly. "I'm sorry, but I think I need to sit down."

"Then you can sit on the floor like the dog you are," I snapped. "When were you going to tell me that Kane was the one who initially told you to call me?"

A new wave of comprehension washed away the little color Scott had left. "It was complicated," he said. "Kane had wanted me to get you over to Oscar's house when Oscar wasn't around, and he offered to get me some awesome listings if I managed it. He said he had been reading about you in the papers and wanted to meet you. Kane's always eager to connect with people who have been around death or have had near-death experiences, so I didn't question it. When Oscar told me he was selling and then that same day you came to that Marina open house…it was like a sign, Sophie! And it wasn't just Kane who wanted me to call you, Venus thought it was a good idea, too, and I…"

"*When* were you going to tell me, Scott?"

"Sophie, please—"

"Wait, let me guess," I said. "Never. You were never going to tell me."

"You're not being fair," he said stiffly.

"No? You *didn't fucking set me up?*" I was on my feet now. Scott had a good half-a-foot on me, but at that moment I felt so much taller. "I can't believe I was ever stupid enough to give you the benefit of the doubt."

"What are you talking about?" He growled. "In your entire life you have never given ANYONE the benefit of the doubt, least of all me!"

I felt a slight breeze coming from the foyer. Apparently, I hadn't closed the door all the way, but I couldn't be bothered with that now and I kept my eyes glued on Scott. "You just didn't have the guts to tell me what was really going on, did you?" I asked. "You have absolutely no balls! You're a eunuch just like your stupid girlfriend!"

"Give me a break!" he snapped. "You thought I got you a deal on this house because I still wanted you. Not that I loved you, but that I wanted to get you into bed. You actually thought one night with you was worth over $20,000 of lost commission! Who the hell do you think you are? Angelina Jolie?"

And then I felt him, not Scott, but the one who I had heard in my foyer. Anatoly.

He was behind me, then in front of me, and then he was punching Scott in the jaw and Scott was falling to the floor. Anatoly stood above him, his chest heaving. "Angelina," Anatoly said, "has nothing on Sophie."

I literally hadn't seen anything so awe inspiring since Cirque du Soleil.

Scott lay on the floor, his hand firmly clutching his chin. "You could have broken something!"

"Is that an invitation?" Anatoly asked. "That punch was to make a point, but I have been trained by both the Russian and Israeli army, so if you would like to bring this fight to the next level I'm more than ready."

"Russian and Israeli..." Scott sputtered. "What the hell, Sophie! You're dating a mercenary?"

"Yeah." I sighed. "And he's cute, too."

Anatoly took a step back, keeping Scott in his line of sight while coming to my side. "I spoke to Maria's friend Lorna. She told me you questioned Maria and Zach. I explicitly told you not to do that. You are the most irresponsibly reckless woman I have ever met."

"Gee, Anatoly, is that your way of saying you missed me?"

He slipped his hand into the back pocket of my jeans. "Yes."

Scott managed to get himself to his feet and he glared at both of us.

"I don't have anything else to say to you," I said. "Feel free to leave."

"Where! Where would you like me to go, Sophie? It's not like I can go back to Venus!"

"Why?" I asked sweetly. "A lot of people in this city would

tell you that women are women. It doesn't matter how we start out. And it's not like she's going to reverse her sex change operation. So nothing's really changed. You just have to find a way to make peace with her past."

"Sophie——" Scott growled.

"Of course there are other problems," I added, pressing myself a little closer to Anatoly. "I still think that part of Venus's past involves murder. She said she gave that brooch to Oscar. Why? Did she like him that much? Or was she using the brooch as a threat, the way she tried to do with me? Oh, and did I tell you that Venus tried to strangle Amelia when she found out she knew about the sex change?"

"Venus tried to strangle who?" Anatoly asked.

"Long story," I said, still smiling at Scott. "Anyhoo, I think we have reason to believe that Venus killed Oscar and maybe even Enrico to keep them quiet. That might make it a little harder for you to accept her for who she is."

"Oscar died of a heart attack," Scott said as he continued to rub his jaw. "Threatening people is Venus's thing. She gets off on it. But killing people? I just don't see it."

"It seems to me there's a lot of things you have failed to see about Venus. But if you want to go back to playing house with her, go ahead. I don't really care. Just remember, you owe me."

Scott tapped his sore jaw gingerly. "I'm not sure I do."

"You have done nothing but stab me in the back and I still took the time to warn you about Venus. So yes, you owe me, and the first thing you can do for me is get out."

"Sophie, don't be like——"

Anatoly took an advancing step on him, his fist clenched.

Scott threw his hands up in the air. "Fine!" he shouted. "I'm outta here. Just remember, Sophie, you don't know what I was going to say when I first started calling you again because you wouldn't pick up the damned phone! And when I did get a chance to talk to you I tried to tell you why I had been calling, but you didn't want to hear it! It's kinda hard to betray the trust of someone who perpetually holds you in suspicion!"

He started to leave, but he didn't notice that Mr. Katz had moved under his feet. Scott stumbled, grabbing onto the fireplace mantel to keep himself from falling. "I hate this cat!" he yelled.

I pointed dramatically at the front door. "Out!"

Scott grumbled, snarled at Anatoly and stormed out.

There was a long, awkward silence that followed. Anatoly and I were frozen in our respective places, contemplating different aspects of what had just transpired and what was to happen next. It was Anatoly who spoke first.

"So Venus had a sex change?"

"It would seem so." My mind was still focused on Scott's parting words.

"Interesting."

"Kane asked Scott to bring me to this house. It was a setup from the beginning. Scott would never have told me," I said firmly, "even if I had given him the chance."

"I don't know about that." Anatoly stretched his neck to the right and then left side before taking a seat on the couch. "I think Scott's the kind of guy who will do the right thing if you make it easy for him."

"And I didn't make it easy."

"You never do. You're a challenge." He smiled. "I love a challenge."

It was getting cold, but I didn't move to turn on the heat or light a fire. Nor did I go to Anatoly and wrap myself up in his arms. I was afraid that one clumsy misstep might erase the implications of his last statement. So instead I reached out to him with a question. "Do you love all challenges? Or just me?"

KYRA DAVIS

His brown eyes were so intense. I loved the way they penetrated me, like Superman looking through my clothes and examining the woman underneath. "I love you," he said simply.

I half expected a celestial choir to start up, but instead the only response came from me. "I love you, too."

It had been so long since I had said those words, and this was the first time I had said them to the right man. But there was still a shadow cast over this reunion. "Last time you saw me here with Scott you walked out."

"You were in his arms."

"Did you think…"

"Sophie, I've never killed a man outside of combat. I had to walk out in order to maintain that record."

"You wouldn't have really killed him."

"You were in his arms," he said again.

"He grabbed me when I wasn't expecting it. It meant nothing…not to me, at least."

"I know that now. But right then I wasn't thinking straight."

"And now that you're not so befuddled, do you still trust me?" I asked.

Mr. Katz, who had been moving aimlessly around the room, finally settled on the sofa cushion beside Anatoly. His claws extended and retracted as he kneaded the fabric beneath him. "I trust you. With some things."

I laughed. "Considering our history, I suppose that's as much as I have the right to expect."

"Considering our history, you should have expected a lot less."

I raised my eyebrows tauntingly. "And yet."

"And yet," Anatoly repeated. He held his hand out to me and when I accepted it he pulled me onto his lap.

"Can I ask you something?"

"Anything," he said.

"Did you buy me a tin of Strawberry Shortcake lip gloss?"

"No, why would I do that?" Anatoly pulled back and looked at me quizzically. "Am I missing something?"

"No," I said quietly. I glanced up at the photo of my father, studying the laugh lines around his eyes. *A real prankster,* my mother had called him.

"I'm going to check into your accusations against Venus," Anatoly said, bringing me back to the here and now. "I'll find out what she's guilty of, if she's guilty of anything at all. I would like to trust that you'll leave the rest of the investigation to me." He planted a kiss on my neck before adding, "Too bad I can't do that."

"Yeah, it's a shame."

"I don't think Maria's a killer." He was nibbling my earlobe now. "Unfortunately, I haven't been able to prove that yet. Most of the evidence still points to her. Even the chain locked door."

"You know about the bird trick?"

"Maria told me. I take it she told you, too?"

I nodded. "Parrots are smart."

Mr. Katz, apparently feeling jealous, hopped on my lap, making us a stack of three.

"You want to tell me the details of what you and Scott were talking about? When and why did Kane and Venus tell him to call you?"

I sighed heavily. We had just admitted that we loved each other! The girly part of me wanted to dissect that. I wanted to examine every aspect of what had brought on those declarations. I wanted to think about what all this meant for now and the future. And just for a moment I wanted to pretend that this love, now fully acknowledged and appreciated, would make everything in my life easier.

But the part of me that knew better pushed the girly part of me aside so I could answer Anatoly's questions. I told him about my latest conversation with Kane and what I had found out from Amelia. Anatoly listened quietly, his index finger idly moving up and down my outer thigh.

"Something's not right," he finally said when I had finished.

"I think that's what they call an understatement."

Mr. Katz blinked in agreement.

"Kane dismissed everything you said about the lights flickering?"

"Yes."

"*Did* the lights flicker?"

"More than flicker, actually. They turned on and off on their own and then the doorbell rang even though there was no one there to push it. And yes, I did hear footsteps and no, I'm not crazy. I'm just telling it as it is."

"And none of that impressed Kane?"

"No."

"And the information you had about his mother and her feelings for your father, did your family give you that, like he suggested?"

"Yeah, they told me this whole long, convoluted story about Kane's mom and her relationship with my family. It's seriously twisted."

"Where did they tell you about this?"

"Where?"

"Yes, where? Did they take you out to lunch? Were you at Leah's place?"

"I was here, why?"

Anatoly paused. "No reason." He pushed both Mr. Katz and me off his lap and pulled a small notepad and pen out of the inside pocket of his leather jacket. He put his finger to his lips to hush me and then wrote the words, *in which room did your family tell you about Kane's mom?*

Confused, I started to ask him what the hell he was doing, but he quickly put his hand over my mouth and then, when he knew I got the hint, moved his hand back and gave me the pen and paper, urging me to write my response.

In this room, I wrote, *why can't we talk?*

Anatoly looked at what I had written and nodded. But instead of answering he got up and started feeling around the fireplace mantel. He found the Strawberry Shortcake lip gloss I had left there and held it up, questioningly.

"It's a long story," I said aloud. I got up and took it from his hand and shoved it into my pocket. "Anatoly…"

"I've never seen you in pink lip gloss," he said, cutting me off. His hands continued to explore the fireplace and then he moved over to the bookcases. "Your lips are perfect the way they are."

"Why are you talking like that? You're never that corny."

"I'm paying you a compliment, Sophie." He was running his fingers over each bookshelf, taking extra care to explore the corners.

"Anatoly, why are you…"

"Why am I undressing you? I'll give you three guesses."

I looked down at my clothes that were all perfectly in place. Anatoly took that moment to cross back to me and he picked the notepad back up.

Do you have a ladder? he wrote.

Yes, in the laundry room. WHY ARE WE WRITING NOTES?!?!

Again, Anatoly didn't answer. Instead he said, "I'm going to make us some drinks. I'll be right back."

"Wait," I said. "What…" Again Anatoly put his hand over my mouth and with his free hand he wrote, *just say okay.*

"Okay?" I said, and then he turned on the only lamp I had in the living room, turned off the overhead light and left the room. I sucked in a sharp breath and wrote another note in anticipation of his return. It read:

Tell me what's going on or I will hang you from a flagpole by your jockstrap.

When Anatoly returned he was carrying my ladder. He was extra careful to make sure that it didn't bump into anything. Even with his heavy load his movements were stealthy and precise.

I tried to thrust my note in his face, but he ignored me and put the ladder under one of the built-in light fixtures. After taking out a penlight from his pocket he climbed up. I watched as he moved his light this way and that so as to examine every angle. Then he froze, and from my spot on the floor I thought I could see the veins in his neck bulge. He silently climbed down and took the notebook from me. He read my comment dispassionately and then underneath gave me the answer I sought.

Your house has been bugged.

23

A therapist once told me couples shouldn't try to solve their problems with sex. I stopped dating her after that.
—*The Lighter Side of Death*

IF YOU REALLY WANT TO TORTURE SOMEONE, MAKE THEM SO FRUSTRATED that they want to scream, and then force them to hold it in and make idle small talk. That was the task Anatoly gave me as he led me from room to room, identifying bugs as we went. In addition to the living room there was one in the dining room, one in the kitchen, my makeshift office, my bedroom...Kane had actually listened to Anatoly and me having sex! And I knew it was Kane. It explained so much. I had never told him that I didn't believe in ghosts; in fact, I had suggested the opposite. Yet he knew the truth. He knew exactly what my mother had told me about his family, and while I had been hiding in his bathroom with Marcus, Kane had told Scott that Anatoly had urged me to move. The man knew everything! By placing those bugs he had stolen my privacy, but worse yet—he had violated my home.

But Anatoly wouldn't let me speak of these things. As he searched for the electronic devices we talked about politics, the proposed suicide barrier for the Golden Gate Bridge, the strangulation of a child that Anatoly read about in the *New York Times:* subjects that allowed me to touch upon my anger and pain without ever revealing its true source. And as I railed against Putin and the people who would use a national monument as a means to take their own life I was really, secretly telling Kane how much I hated him. When I said I wanted to rip child abusers to shreds, I was really telling Kane what I was planning to do to him.

After checking the upstairs hallway thoroughly, Anatoly muttered something to himself and then carefully closed the doors to the bedrooms and bathroom that lined the corridor. "It looks like this is the only room in your house that isn't bugged, that and the closets and the laundry room."

I leaned against the wall and trailed my toe against the floorboards. "Wouldn't it be ironic if I took up one of these floorboards and used it to beat Kane to death with? You know, like, you fuck with my house and I'll make sure it fucks with you?"

Anatoly stared down at the floorboards. "This is where you heard the footsteps?"

I nodded. "I know this isn't the worst thing that's ever happened to me, but it's making my top ten. I feel so—"

"I saw some tools in the laundry room. I'm going to get them."

"Why?" I asked.

"I'll explain later."

Anatoly went downstairs while I stayed in the hallway. Long hallways are usually the rooms that give children nightmares. They imagine monsters jumping out at them from invisible doors. But my hallway had suddenly become my sanctuary. The monsters were in the other rooms, hiding in the light fixtures.

Anatoly came back with his arms full of tools that I had never used. An electric drill, a large hammer (not the cute little Ikea hammer that I had become accustomed to), a wide chisel that I don't remember buying, and a tire iron that I had purchased a few months earlier when Leah and I decided to learn to change our own tires. We hadn't actually taken the time to figure that out yet, but we both had the equipment and we liked to pretend that meant something.

Anatoly got down on his knees and started knocking on the floorboards.

"What are you doing?" I asked.

"Shh!" He tapped on another few boards. At first they all made the same basic noise until one sounded just slightly different. Anatoly stood up. "The bugs aren't powerful enough to pick up sounds in the next room, but as an extra precaution I would still like to put a towel under each of these doors." He waved his hand toward my bedroom, the guest room and the hall bathroom. "I also think you should plug your iPod into the portable speakers and play it full blast in your bedroom."

"Anatoly, what exactly are you going to do?"

"Sophie, I need you to trust me with this."

I rolled my eyes, but did as I was told. When there was a towel under each door and my iPod was blasting the latest Linkin Park single, Anatoly started drilling into one of the floorboards.

I dropped to my knees by his side. "What are you doing to my floor?"

"Just one floorboard," he said as he finished with his last hole. "You can get it fixed."

"I don't want to get it fixed! I want it to stay as it is!"

But Anatoly already had the wide chisel out and was using the hammer to wedge it between the board he was working on and the one adjacent to it. Then, using the tire iron like a crowbar, he pulled up the board. I was seriously considering using the tire iron on Anatoly's head when I looked down and saw what it was that he was trying to get to.

Underneath that floorboard was a speaker.

"I bet there's more of these," Anatoly said. "Just enough to project footsteps moving through your hall."

My rage had a rhythm now. It throbbed inside my temples like a drum. "How could he do this?" I asked. "He's turned my life into a bad episode of *Scooby-Doo!*"

I sat back against the wall and Anatoly put the board down and took his place at my side. For a few minutes we didn't say a word. We just sat there as the edgy and bittersweet notes of Linkin Park filtered into the hallway.

"You know what you have to do, don't you?" Anatoly finally said.

"No," I said honestly. "I don't have the slightest clue."

"You have to call the police, Sophie. Kane can't record your every move without your permission, even if he does own the house. This is enough to have him put away."

"But then I'll lose the house."

"Yes, you will."

"My father wanted to buy this house, did I tell you that?"

Anatoly shook his head.

I reached down and rubbed the small bump in my pocket where the lip gloss was. "He was barely sixty years old when he died," I whispered. "I wasn't prepared for it. And this house…it's like my connection to him, you know?"

Anatoly kept his gaze straight ahead. "I lost my father when I was five," he said.

I looked up at him sharply. "You never told me that. You just told me your family was in Israel now!"

"My mother and brother are in Israel."

"How did he die?"

"I don't know if he did. He just disappeared."

"You mean he just up and left?"

"Maybe. You have to remember that I grew up in the old Soviet Union. Outspoken people sometimes disappeared."

"Wait a minute. You're telling me that the Soviet government may have taken your father from you and then, once you were of age, you joined their army?"

"The Soviet Union was about to fold when I enlisted, but yes, and I had my reasons."

"You're not going to tell me what those reasons are?"

"Not now. I just wanted to tell you that I lost my father. The circumstances were different, but I know what it's like to miss someone who's supposed to be there."

"Oh." Again we both fell into a brief silence. I wanted to be irritated, but who was I to judge him for keeping his secrets when I had so many of my own?

"Living in this house isn't going to bring him back, Sophie. The only people it connects you to are Kane and Scott. You need to let it go."

I put my hands flat against the floor, hoping to find some kind of stability there. "I can't call the police now. Not tonight. You have to let me wait until tomorrow."

"Tomorrow then. Why don't you pack up an overnight bag? You can stay at my place tonight."

I nodded and with an enormous amount of effort got to my feet. Once I had packed up some things, Anatoly escorted me down the stairs, immediately bringing the conversation back to politics. I couldn't respond this time. I could barely breathe.

Anatoly took my keys from me and locked the door behind us although it seemed like a pointless exercise. Kane was already in my house and nothing short of an exorcism was going to get him out.

As I followed Anatoly back to his place I kept the music off so that the rantings of the pop stars wouldn't mingle with my own ranting thoughts.

I had to park three blocks away from Anatoly's apartment, and when I got to his door he was already there, waiting patiently. The streets on Russian Hill are never entirely quiet, but the fog was thickening, making everything a bit more muted. He reached out his hand to me, his other arm supporting a helmet that he had tucked under his arm. "You're upset."

"Good call," I said with a bitter laugh.

"Let me make you happy."

My inner voice was screaming for revenge, revenge against Kane, revenge against Venus, revenge against Scott. I pressed my mouth up against Anatoly's and let the taste of him consume me, muting the screaming the way the fog muted the sound of the passing traffic.

He pulled his key out of his pocket and slipped it inside the lock, quickly pulling me in and then leading me upstairs. As we entered the apartment I stood by the door as he dropped his helmet on the coffee table and his jacket on the floor. "Make yourself comfortable," he said casually. "Take off your jeans."

I smiled despite myself and leaned up against the wall. "Why don't you help me?"

In three large steps he was in front of me, then on his knees. I dug my fingers into his thick black hair as he removed my jeans and then my panties. He then raised himself up so he could dispense with the rest of my clothes. He ran his fingers lightly up and down my body as I waited for him to devour me. "You are the sexiest woman I've ever seen," he said, and again I smiled.

And then we were on the floor. Anatoly pushed his fingers up into my core as the tip of his tongue made the journey from my neck to my breast. I thrust my hips forward, allowing myself to be lost in the moment.

Anatoly had said that we belonged to each other. I wasn't sure I believed that, but I did know that he was part of my world in a way that no other man had ever been. He was still unpredictable and somewhat mysterious, but I had learned to trust him and that trust had completely erased my inhibitions. I lifted one leg and draped it over his shoulder as he continued to caress and tease me with his tongue. "Right here," I moaned. "Right now."

It was more of a mantra than anything else, but Anatoly took it as a request. He was immediately on his feet and in an instant he was pulling me up, as well, and pushing me back against the wall. I fumbled with his jeans, but he pushed my hands away and swiftly took them off himself before lifting me up. With the first thrust he managed to push out all thoughts of the house and Kane. I clung to him, my thighs wrapped around his waist, my hands clinging to his shoulders. I didn't know anything about the dead, but I did have my ideas about heaven, and this was it. My heaven was the feeling of Anatoly inside me. It was the smell of our sweat and the sound of his voice as he whispered my name, and most of all it was the knowledge that all of this passion and carnal pleasure was wrapped up in love. It wasn't dirty any more than it was innocent. It was just fantastic.

And when I reached that moment when all my muscles contracted and the shivers of pleasure shot through every vein in my body, then it was even more than fantastic. It was perfect.

And that was the word that shot out of my mouth as Anatoly finally released himself, lowering us both back to the floor where we lay together, breathless and satiated.

"Perfect."

24

Throughout our lives we are tested so it really helps if you know how to cheat.

—*The Lighter Side of Death*

I DID SLEEP WELL THAT NIGHT. I THINK MY BODY UNDERSTOOD THAT AS long as I slept I would dream of making love to Anatoly. But as soon as I awoke I would have to steel myself against a devastating loss.

But eventually I did have to open my eyes. Anatoly was already up. On the large plastic storage box he used as a bedside table was a travel mug. It smelled of coffee and chocolate. I picked up the mocha and brought it to my lips, confident that it was meant for me. How nice it would be if I could just stay in bed all day and pretend everything was okay.

Reluctantly, I got up and shifted through the pile of Anatoly's clothes that lay on the floor until I found a T-shirt that was neither stained nor smelly and slipped it on. I found Anatoly in his living room, already shaved and showered and writing something on a large legal pad. His laptop on the coffee table revealed a Google search he had done on Venus.

"What are you working on?" I asked. I sat down next to him on the couch, still cradling my drink. If I had slept so well why was I so incredibly tired?

"I'm making a list of all the things I need to look into today. I'll be meeting Maria in about twenty minutes. I want to see if she had any inkling about Venus's sex change or if she thinks Enrico knew. I still think you were on to something when you suggested Venus was the one who killed him."

"I'm totally over that theory now. It was Kane all the way."

"Because he bugged your house?" He got up and picked his leather jacket off the floor.

"Well, yeah. That, and the painting in his bedroom."

Anatoly stopped. "What painting in his bedroom and how do you know about it?"

"Oh, right, well…on your way out? I don't want to keep you."

"When were you in Kane's house, Sophie?"

"Um…maybe two days ago?"

"He invited you over?"

"Not exactly," I hedged.

"So you initiated the visit and he invited you in?"

I scooted a little lower in my seat. "Not exactly."

Anatoly's jaw jutted forward. "You broke into Kane's house."

"It seemed like the thing to do at the time."

He cursed in Russian. "Do you know how lucky you are that you weren't caught?" Anatoly demanded.

"Luck had nothing to do with it," I snapped. That was sort of true. The thing that had gotten me out of that situation un-scathed was Scott, but I didn't feel like sharing that at the moment. "I handled myself well, and Kane didn't find out a thing, which I think is pretty impressive since the guy is totally up my ass."

"You didn't talk about the break-in while in your house?"

"Not even once."

"So what did you find?" Anatoly asked irritably.

"You know, you don't get to lecture me just because...wait a minute...you're not lecturing me."

"No."

I hesitated a moment. "I don't know what to do with that. It's so out of character for you."

"I would prefer it if you didn't consistently risk your life, but I'm not going to argue with you about something you've already done and can't change."

"Oh, um, okay." Anatoly was *always* arguing with me about things I had already done. This was a totally new approach for him.

His computer blinked to sleep mode and Anatoly stared moodily into the blank screen. "What did you find, Sophie?"

"Right, well, I actually found a lot. The grossest being his mother's blood."

"I'm sorry?"

"His mom slit her throat and bled all over a canvas. Kane has it hanging over his bed."

Anatoly's mouth dropped open and for a rare moment he was actually speechless.

"I know," I said, "it's so much more disturbing than strangling kittens or any of the normal psychopath stuff."

Anatoly shook his head. "I've seen some horrible things while serving in the army but...his mother's blood?"

I nodded.

"That might be the thing to give me nightmares."

"Yes, well, welcome to my world. But wait, there's more."

I went on to tell him about the pictures of my family I found in the hope chest. Anatoly stopped me briefly to ask what a hope chest was and then marvel at the fact that a single man would have one in his bedroom, but other than that there were few interruptions. By the time I was done, Anatoly was sitting beside me, rapping his fingers against his knee. "I'm glad you didn't call the police on Kane last night."

"You are?"

"Yes. Assuming Kane doesn't sign off on your escrow agreement, and he won't, it will fall through tomorrow. I'm going to find a way to get him over to the house and then I'll confront him for not selling to you or for some other made-up issue."

Made-up issue. The words assaulted my ears like a high-pitched whistle.

"Hopefully, I'll get him angry. Sloppy angry. I want him to say something self-incriminating. Normally a taped confession isn't admissible, but he can't claim that he didn't know he was being recorded if he's the one who bugged the house."

"No, he certainly can't," I said slowly.

A new idea was taking shape in my head.

Anatoly got up and gave me a light kiss. "I made some pancakes—they're in the oven keeping warm. Stay as long as you like. Move in if you want. Tomorrow, before I deal with Kane, we'll get everything moved out of the house and back to your apartment. Do you want me to contact a moving company?"

"I'll take care of that," I said. My plan was taking shape now, all the details falling into place.

"All right." He went to retrieve his keys from the top of his boxy old TV set. "Think of it this way—tomorrow you will be $20,000 richer."

"Yay, me."

Anatoly leaned over and gave me another, more lingering kiss and then went to leave. He paused for a second while standing in the doorway. "You're going to be okay, Sophie."

"I know." When the door closed and I was alone, I allowed my lips to spread into a grin. "I will definitely be okay."

And immediately I was on the phone. Dena picked up on the fourth ring. I heard a male voice in the background.

"Is that Kim?" I asked eagerly after she had greeted me. "I need a favor from him."

"Actually, that's Jason."

"Jason," I repeated. Notes of bewilderment and vague panic played on my emotions. "Um, obviously I want you to do whatever it is that makes you happy, but I kinda need Kim."

"No worries, he's here, too." And as if that wasn't shocking enough, she added, "and so is Amelia."

"Dena," I said slowly, "orgies are like cocktails. You're not supposed to start up until it's past noon."

"This is better than an orgy. I'm having a relationship with two men and I'm sharing them with Amelia. This is as close to monogamy as I'm ever going to get."

"You...wait...what?" I stammered.

"Here are the rules—my two boys aren't allowed to sleep with anyone but Amelia and I can't sleep with anyone but the two of them. It's rather restrictive, but I think I can make it work."

"Wow, that's just...wow." I tucked my feet underneath me and tried to come up with something more coherent, but it was hard. Dena's life could be Bravo's new reality TV series. "Okay," I finally said. "I'm sorry to interrupt your...um, relationship, but I need help."

"Name it."

"I'm hoping Kim will agree to splice up a recording that's currently on an old minicassette tape. I'll need it done by tonight. Like, six, at the latest."

"A minicassette tape? What's on it?"

"It's a long story."

"It always is with you," she said with a grunt. "You're in luck.

Kim only has two classes today and one's at night. I'm sure he'll help you out. Can you bring it over now?"

I hesitated. "Is everyone going to be wearing clothes if I do?"

"If that's important to you, I can probably arrange it."

"That would be good. See you in a bit."

As soon as I hung up I practically ran to the shower. I had an enormous amount to do and less than eight hours to do it in.

It was inevitable that when I got to Dena's she would push to find out what I had planned. I absolutely refused to tell her. The fact was that the warnings of my friends and family had begun to take on a rather redundant quality. *Get out of the house, find another place, nothing's worth having to deal with Kane.* I knew it was all very well-meaning, but it was becoming painfully clear that none of them understood how important this was to me, and if they couldn't understand that then I couldn't confide in them. This time I really was on my own.

Anatoly called four times between 10:00 a.m. and 4:00 p.m. Each time it was "just to check in." He suspected something, but I left him in the dark just like everybody else. Finally, I had to tell him that I was going to the Castro film festival with Marcus to lift my spirits. Of course that meant he wouldn't be able to call me.

By six o'clock I had everything I needed. Kim had done a brilliant job with the new recording. The tinny quality of the old cassette tape was negligible on the small digital device it was now on. Amelia had also lent me a great book that I had spent a good two hours of my day skimming. It was titled *Reaching the Dead*. After that I went shopping for everything I would need.

The only thing left to do was go home.

When I got there it was almost six and the entire city had been swallowed up by the thick fog. It blurred the outlines of everything substantial from the planted Monterey pines to the houses lining the street, and gave everything a vague and abstract quality. I took a deep breath and walked in my door, a shopping bag full of goodies in hand.

Mr. Katz greeted me immediately and his resentment was palpable. I had given him extra food and water before I left the night before, but nothing since. I put my bag down by one of the many half-full boxes and went to the kitchen to feed him. I was careful to make sure that I talked to him and banged around in the same clumsy and tired manner I would normally take on if I had been out for the day. Kane would not hear anything that would hint at my agitation.

Nor would he hear the way I was going around the house, checking the locks on each and every window along with the back door. If Kane decided to burst in on me—which, with what I had planned was a likely scenario—he would have to use the front entrance. I couldn't afford him sneaking in from an unexpected opening. Maintaining complete control of the situation was going to be of the utmost importance tonight.

When I was done with that I stepped into the living room. On the bookcase I placed an empty glass. "All right, Andrea," I said, tilting my head up toward the light fixture. "Let's see if you're really here."

And then I turned to my bag of tricks. The first thing I pulled out was a tablecloth, which I draped over the coffee table. I then placed five red candles on top of that. Red like the color of Andrea's hair and the color her blood must have been when she spilled it. I carefully lit each wick, and then I pulled out a piece of sage and set that on fire before dropping it into the fireplace.

I was doing it by the book, Amelia's book, and it looked authentic. Kane would appreciate that. There were only two things left in the bag now. I pulled out the digital recorder and held it firmly in my right hand. And then I retrieved the switchblade. The man in the store had assured me that it was legal in California, but I wasn't so sure. The fact that he hadn't charged me sales tax was one of the tip-offs. Nonetheless, it would fit in my pocket and if I needed protection it would do the job. I sat on the floor and took another steadying breath.

"Thirty-two, thirty-one, thirty…" I was counting back from my age, another suggestion from Amelia's book. After every three numbers I paused before continuing. Mr. Katz crept into the room and stared at me then found a seat by the fireplace. His yellow eyes lifted to the image of my father.

"Zero," I finally said. Then, projecting my voice even more, "I summon the spirit of Andrea Crammer. I summon the spirit of Andrea Crammer, I summon the spirit of Andrea Crammer!"

I could hear a car drive by outside and I thought about how I wanted to be in it, driving away from the very idea of making an idiot out of myself for Kane's amusement. "I have felt your presence. I know your spirit is within these walls. Please, allow me to see you…or hear you. It would be great if we could just talk."

The book hadn't specified how formal one's speech should be while questioning the dead, so I was winging that part. "Your son, Kane, has asked me to live here," I said, raising my voice again as if volume could mask my embarrassment. "Please, let me be your medium, let me bring the two of you together again. He still needs you, Andrea."

I paused for a minute before quietly standing up and going over to the empty glass on the bookcase. I lifted it and held it at arm's length. And then I simply let go and let the fragments of glass fall where they may as I scurried back to my spot by the coffee table. "Andrea," I said with what I hoped sounded like awe, "did you do that? Did you make that glass move?"

Mr. Katz swished his tail in disdain and walked out. I couldn't blame him. This was the worst dialogue and acting since the last *Godzilla* movie. "Andrea," I said again, "can you hear me? Is there a message I can deliver to your son?"

And this time I pressed Play on the recorder. I kept the volume as soft as I could without making it imperceptible to the bug in the light fixture.

"Kane, my own son!" Andrea's voice said. "We are fated to be together!"

"Are you really here?" I exclaimed, my finger now on the stop button. "Why couldn't I hear you before?"

"You just have to believe in me!" Andrea said.

I didn't hear him until he was already on the front steps, and then there was the jiggling of the doorknob, and when it didn't turn the sound of keys clinking together on a key chain.

Wherever he had been listening from it had been closer than I had thought.

I lunged for the couch and was able to stuff the recording between the cushions and get back to my seat by the coffee table before he found the right key and threw open the door.

"She's here!" he exclaimed excitedly.

I kept my seat and looked at him coldly. "I knew it," I said icily. "She didn't speak to me at all, did she? You set this up? Tell me, Kane, how the hell did you get that glass to fall off the bookcase?"

"What?" he asked. His head swiveled from side to side as he searched for something that wasn't there. "I didn't set this up! I heard her voice! You heard it, too! You spoke with my mother!"

"I spoke to a female voice," I snapped and got to my feet. "I have no idea who the voice belonged to, but I bet you do."

"You can't think I'm behind this!" Kane said desperately. He walked over to the bookcase and, bending down, scooped up a handful of glass.

"What are you doing?" I shouted.

Fresh lines of blood crossed his palm, but Kane ignored his injuries. Instead he looked up at the ceiling, his eyes wild and frenzied. *"Mother!"* he shouted. "I'm here! It's me! *Please, talk to me!"*

"Are you trying to frighten me?" I asked. I had planned to say that. It was part of the act. The problem was that I no longer felt like I was acting. Kane was really crazy and being in the same room with him was beginning to scare the shit out of me.

"Sophie," he said, finally bringing his gaze to me, "I need you to believe me. I didn't have a hand in this. You spoke to my mother. You reached out to her with your gifts and it worked! Now please, *please,* get her to speak to me!"

I took a step forward, my hands clenched into fists. "You want me to believe you?" I asked. "How can I do that, Kane? How do you explain the way you barged in here? I didn't call you. I haven't told you anything about what just happened and yet, you seem to know."

"I…" Kane looked around the room again and for the first time he was the one who looked scared. "I was listening in. You can be mad, that's okay, and I'll make it up to you, but please, don't take her away from me again! You contacted her! You called her to you! Please, Sophie! Call her back for me?"

"Listening in, how?"

Kane swallowed hard. I had wanted to revert him to the role of a child and I had succeeded. He was lost and he wanted his mommy.

"I have this place bugged," he admitted. "And the footsteps and the doorbell and the lights…that was all me, too. I had an electrician rig the whole house right before you moved in. It's still my house so I can do that. See, I needed you to believe, to spur you into action…and it worked! I didn't do the glass that broke, though—so it worked!"

I opened my mouth to speak, but before I could he did something totally unexpected. He actually fell to his knees. "It was wrong, I know it was wrong but, God, Sophie, I had to know if she would come to you…if you reached out to her! She always liked you! She said you were creative and smart… Martin's firstborn."

"Enough, Kane."

"No, you have to tell her that I'm worthy of her now. You have to bring her to me."

I took a step back and then, out of the corner of my eye I thought I saw something lurking outside the window…a shadow that didn't seem quite right. But when I turned my head to get a better look, there was nothing there. I was nervous and it was entirely possible that my mind was playing tricks on me. After all, the danger was right here, inside the house.

I turned my attention back to Kane. "You need her?" I asked coolly.

"Yes!"

"Well, I need this house."

"Fine, it's yours."

I walked over to the couch where I had left my cell phone.

"Who are you calling?" he asked.

"Scott," I said. "I'm going to tell him to bring over the necessary paperwork because your word just isn't good enough."

Kane was still on his knees, his eyes wide and unseeing. I took a step backward.

"Sophie," Scott said, as he picked up the phone. "I knew you couldn't stay mad. Listen, last night I said some things I didn't mean and——"

I turned my back to Kane, no longer able to stomach the sight of his bleeding hand. "Bring over the escrow agreement in triplicate," I said. "I'm at home and Kane's here, too. He says I respected the house and he's signing it over to me."

"You've got to be kidding me."

"I'm not."

"How the hell did you manage that?"

"Just bring the papers over, Scott, and if you have one handy, a witness."

"The only witness you'll need is me," he said. "By the way, I broke up with Venus. I just couldn't deal, you know what I mean?"

"I know that I don't care. Bring the contract. Now."

I hung up the phone and reluctantly turned back to Kane. He was still on his knees and now he was staring at his hands as if he had just realized the harm he had done to himself. "Call to her?" he said. I think he had meant it to be a command, but it had come out as a question.

"I'm sorry," I said, almost meaning it at this point. "I'm going to wait until you sign the papers. Even then I'm going to insist that Scott go to a post office and put it in the mail before I do anything else."

Kane looked confused. "But don't you want him to take it personally to the courthouse to file it?"

"Of course, but one copy will be sent to Anatoly and it will remain sealed. That way if you try to destroy it there won't be a problem. There also won't be a problem if you try to claim that I altered the date and signed it after escrow was set to expire. I'll have the document in an envelope with a postmark that will prove otherwise."

"You've thought of everything," Kane observed, the flash of suspicion crossing his features. "Impressive since this has all happened in the last few minutes."

"I think quickly on my feet," I said, refusing to let him fluster me.

Kane got up without saying anything.

"You should clean your hand," I said, gesturing to his injury. "Do you want some Neosporin and maybe a tweezer?"

"I didn't hear what she said to you right before I came in," he said softly. "Did she say anything more about me?"

"She said..." I let my voice trail off and then shook my head furiously. "No, I can't...I misunderstood I'm sure."

"What?" Kane said, now alarmed. "What did she say?"

My phone rang and I looked down at the screen half expecting to see either Scott's or Anatoly's name. Instead it was Marcus. I clicked Ignore and put the phone in my pocket. It made a slight clink as it hit the knife.

Kane gave me an odd look and without saying another word walked over to my little makeshift office and peeked inside. He then started moving room to room. Whether he was looking to see if he could find evidence that I was faking him out or whether he was actually looking for the ghost of the notorious Andrea was anybody's guess.

My phone buzzed again—this time Marcus had sent me a text. It read:

WTF?! Came 2 cu. Saw Kane go in but heard ur voice in unlocked van. Am in van now, lots of equipt, can hear u. want me 2 call cops?

I immediately replied:

No! Stay where u r!

His response was:

This very crazy. Do u have death wish?

To which I told him to: call cops when I say the words "I need 2 call Andrea." Not a sec before. And no more txts!

I shoved the phone back in my pocket as I heard Kane's

approach. When he was back in the room he gave me a strange look. "I don't feel her," he said.

"Neither do I," I admitted. "But when I reach out to her again I'm sure she'll respond. She said you were fated to be together."

"I heard that part. What else did she say?"

And then there was a knock on the door. It was Scott, with a small stack of papers in his hand. I let him in, greeting him only with a nod. No one said a word as the contract was laid out by the rapidly diminishing candles on the coffee table. Scott wrote an X where he needed Kane to sign and then handed him the pen.

"Once you sign this saying Sophie has met the terms of the escrow there's no backing out," Scott said. "The place will be hers."

Kane held the pen like it was a magic wand that he wasn't at all sure he wanted to use. "How do I know you won't back out?" he whispered.

"Either you trust me with this or the whole deal is off," I snapped. "I lose the house, you lose your last chance to talk to your mom."

"What are you talking about?" Scott asked.

"What's it going to be?" I asked, totally ignoring Scott. "Are we going through with this or not?"

Kane hesitated, but only for a moment. Then his pen flashed across the signature line. A short triumphant laugh burst from my lips.

And then Kane handed the pen to me. I took the ink-filled magic wand and added my name to the document. The house was mine! I had refused to give up and now I had won! Scott gave me an approving smile, and it was everything I could do not to give him a huge hug. Hell, at that point I was ready to hug Kane!

"Quickly," Kane said, his voice hoarse, "get it to a post

office. Leave me here with Sophie, we need to…to call someone."

Scott's expression changed from approving to worried. "Why don't I send this out tomorrow," he suggested. "I have some things I want to talk to Sophie about now."

"You need to go, Scott," I said, still fondling the pen. I had originally planned to go to the post office with Scott because I knew being alone with Kane was risky. But now that I knew Marcus was around I felt safer. Safe enough to add a stage two to my plan.

However, Scott had no such sense of security. He took a step closer to me. "I really think I should stay," he said in a low voice.

"The post office," I repeated. "Kane's right. And remember to send one copy to Anatoly. As for me, well, I need to call Andrea." I took extra care to enunciate the last three words so Marcus could hear his cue clearly.

"Kane's *mom* Andrea? But she's—"

"Go, Scott. Call when the contract's in a secure mailbox." I then turned my eyes to Kane.

After another moment of hesitation, Scott left.

And again I was alone with Kane. He stood above the candles, allowing the flame to cast a frightening pattern of light across his face. "I won't try to contact her until Scott tells me that the contract's in the mail," I said.

"I know. Now tell me what she said as I ran to get here. What was it that you think you misunderstood?"

I inched a little closer to the door. The police would be on their way now. I only had a few minutes to get him to confess to the worst of it. "She says she knows what happened to Oscar. She knows what you did."

A manic smile lit up Kane's face. "She knows? Did it make her happy?"

Again I hesitated. "You thought what you did…would make her happy?"

"Yes! Oscar destroyed her life! He threw her out on the streets and left her to take care of me all by herself! She wanted him dead. He had no right to live here in *her* house while I mourned her!"

Kane was confessing to murder and it was being recorded. Kane knew that…and yet I had a feeling that Kane didn't know anything at the moment.

"How did you do it?" I asked. "Everyone thought Oscar had a heart attack."

"He did," Kane said, his eyes once again traveling the room. "I switched his heart medication for a placebo. Then I started gaslighting him the way I did to you. When I finally changed the furniture to match the old photographs I knew I had him. I switched the medication back so the police would find the right thing and then I just waited for Oscar to come home. He did and, well…" Kane shrugged his shoulders in lieu of finishing.

"You killed your own father."

"I did," he said. "Maybe you should think about that as you decide whether or not to keep your promise. I want to talk to my mother now, Sophie."

"Did you kill Enrico?" I asked.

Kane cocked his head to the side. "Why would I do that?"

"I don't think I really understand why you do anything."

He smiled wistfully and began to pace the room. "My mother was unpredictable, too. I got it from her."

"Do you know why you killed Enrico?" I tried again. "Was it just for fun? Did he know something, maybe something about Venus? Did you kill him to protect her secret?"

Kane started laughing. If chaos had a sound I was hearing it now. "I would never do anything for her…or should I say him? The pronoun issue is confusing in these cases."

"How did you find out about her surgery?" I asked.

"Who cares how I found out, the only thing that matters is that I did. I needed something on her. She wouldn't let Scott call you and I needed him to contact you because I knew…" He stopped and took an advancing step toward me. "I knew you would reach her. I knew she would speak to you."

He was no longer talking about Venus, but I wasn't ready to let the subject go. "Did she help you kill your dad, Kane?"

"She helped me move the furniture, that's all. For a while there she was doing everything I asked in order to protect her secret. I even got her to hand over that cameo she paid so much money for. Forgive the mixed metaphor, but I think finding that brooch on his bed was the straw that broke Oscar's heart. Of course, when she found out that Oscar died she put everything together. She knew I had worked to bring about his death. She stopped doing what she was told and threatened to reveal my secrets if I tried to reveal hers. It was a stalemate. She even had the nerve to ask for her brooch back. But," he said with a wicked grin, "I gave it to you instead. Pinned it right on your pillow. Sorry that bitch took it away from you. It wasn't very nice of her."

He took another step forward. "Call her now, Sophie."

I inched a little closer toward the door. "I know that I NEED TO CALL ANDREA," I said, praying to God that Marcus had remembered the code, "but I won't do it until Scott calls. I told you that. In fact, maybe we should just call her tomorrow when you're in a better place…mentally that is."

"You don't want to stall, Sophie. Not with me."

"Okay, so now you *are* threatening me, right?" I asked. I glanced at the door. I'd have thought that the police would have come in by now.

"No, Sophie. I've never threatened you. I never threatened my father, either. Like I said, I'm unpredictable. If you're scared of me now then you're probably safe. It's when you feel safe that you'll have a problem. Then again, it may not be you personally who is in danger. Maybe it will be someone else in your fucked-up family who will get hurt. Your sister, your mother…how old is your nephew again? Pretty easy to sneak up on a toddler."

"You fucking asshole!" I reached into my pocket and fondled the handle of my switchblade. But Kane wasn't looking at me anymore. He was looking at the cushions on my couch.

"What's this, Sophie?" he asked, zoning in on a corner of silver.

"Nothing, I—"

But he had it. He was pulling out the digital recorder and his finger was on the play button.

"I NEED TO CALL ANDREA!" I yelled, but it didn't drown out Andrea's voice.

Kane threw the recorder down and it smashed against the hardwood floor. "You lying little cunt!"

He lunged at me, but I managed to step aside, fumbling with my knife as I did so. It wasn't opening like it had in the store. Now I knew why it was legal—it didn't fucking work! He lunged again and I turned and ran for the door, which almost knocked me out as Marcus swung it open. Unlike me, his weapon was already drawn. He pointed the bottle right at Kane's face and pressed down on the nozzle.

It wasn't until Kane had his hands pressed against his eyes and was screaming in agony that I figured out what it was Marcus had just assaulted him with. Aerosol hairspray.

And it was at that moment that the cavalry arrived. The police with their guns drawn had us all put our hands up as Marcus and I tried to babble explanations and Kane moaned in pain.

"The van!" Marcus finally sputtered. "Freak-boy here has

this whole place bugged. Everything that happened is recorded in the van."

The police looked more than a little incredulous, but when two more squad cars arrived one of the officers went to check it out. Another escorted Kane to the bathroom where he could flush out his eyes.

"I'm so glad you came," I whispered to Marcus as we stood side by side, our hands still on our heads.

"How is it that you always get me into these situations, and why do I let you?"

"I know, but I'll…I'll send a troop of male strippers to your apartment to make it up to you."

"Please, men don't have to be paid to get undressed for me."

"Found the van."

We turned to see that the officer who had left had now returned. "You can put your hands down now," he said, and then to the other officers, "The van's right across the street. It's got an ad on the side of it for some bogus stereo equipment store, but it's clearly some kind of mobile surveillance unit. It's registered to one Kane Crammer. I listened to a few minutes of what went down here tonight."

Kane emerged from the bathroom with his police escort, his face dripping with water.

"Cuff him," Officer I-found-the-van said. "We're bringing this guy in."

And when they were halfway through the Miranda rights, Scott called me. The contract was in the mail. I had won in every sense of the word. I turned to Kane, ready to taunt him with some words of triumph, but something in his expression stopped me. He wasn't looking at the officers who were in the process of arresting him. He was staring at me. "I'll get out," he said. "And then we will be continuing our conversation."

The cop who had just finished reading him his rights wrinkled his nose. "I've gotta remember that one. It'll make a good talking point in court when the judge is deciding whether or not to grant bail."

Another two police officers entered and Kane was dragged out the door. I knew what these new officers had for me. Questions, questions and more questions. But for the first time in weeks I had some answers. I didn't even blink as more and more police showed up. Nor did it bother me when they started wandering around my house collecting bugs, taking photos and finding Kane's hidden speakers. In fact, I didn't get flustered until Anatoly showed up. He wasn't happy.

25

The people who love us frequently hurt us when they're trying to help us. The people who hate us are much more reliable.

—*The Lighter Side of Death*

HE ARRIVED A LITTLE BEFORE ELEVEN WHEN THE LAST OF THE POLICE WERE leaving. He didn't come to the front door at first, so it wasn't until I was walking Marcus out the door that I spotted him. He was standing on the sidewalk, and while it was too dark and foggy for me to really see his eyes, I knew that he was glaring.

"Ooooh, you're in trouble now, honey!" Marcus laughed.

I slapped him lightly on the arm. "It's not funny."

"Wanna bet? I'll skidoodle so you two can have your little tête à tête."

"Thanks...I mean, really, thank you." I reached for his hand now and held it in both of mine. "You saved my life today."

Marcus smiled and gave me a kiss on the cheek. "Anytime, sweetie." He jogged down my front steps and paused only long enough to say something to Anatoly before popping into his own car and taking off.

And then there were two. Anatoly didn't even bother to say hello as he stormed past me into the house.

"I thought we agreed on what we were going to do," he snapped.

"No," I said, "*we* didn't."

"Do I even want to know why the police were here? Do I want to know what suicidal game plan you came up with this time?"

"Probably not. But you might want to know that Kane's been arrested for bugging my house and killing his father. He'll probably get convicted for Enrico's murder, as well, so next time you see her be sure to tell Maria a thank-you card is in order. Oh, and I got Kane to sign the house over to me, so that's all taken care of, too."

For the second time in two days Anatoly's mouth was hanging open. "You did it," he finally managed. "You saved the day without screwing anything up."

"Pretty amazing, huh?"

"And you don't want to tell me the details of how you pulled this off?"

"To be honest, no, I really don't. You'll just get mad again and I'm too tired to get into a heated debate. Besides, you decided we shouldn't argue about things I've already done and can't change."

Anatoly smiled and shook his head. "I knew I was going to regret that one."

"I did, too, but you are the one who said it."

He nodded and fell back on the couch. "All the bugs are gone?"

"The police took every last one as evidence."

"And this house is really yours."

"Kane signed the papers."

"This is before or after you had him arrested?"

"Before, of course."

"Of course. So, now what?"

"Now," I said as I sat next to him, "I finish unpacking and we go furniture shopping. Just so you know, your pool table isn't coming anywhere near this living room."

He studied me for a moment and Mr. Katz stuck his head out from where he had been hiding in a semifilled box. "You want me to move in."

"Yes. As soon as possible."

The corner of his mouth curved up into that sexy little half smile of his. "We drive each other crazy, Sophie. I'm still reeling from what you pulled tonight."

"A little craziness is good. It makes life interesting."

"A *little?*" He laughed. "We also can't keep our hands off each other. If we're around each other every day how will we get anything done?"

"It'll be good," I said as I reached over and traced the outline of his pecs. "I hate going to the gym and if I can do you daily I'll be able to work off all those Frappuccinos."

"So I'd be like your personal trainer."

"More like a good, strong workout partner."

Anatoly smiled and moved both his hands to my face. He kissed me deeply and then pulled away and stood up. "I need to think about this," he said.

"What's to think about? You said not too long ago that you wanted to live with me."

"I know what I said. But honestly, I'm still a little pissed."

I swallowed and clasped my hands in my lap. "Will you get over it?"

"Yes, I have to. I'm in love with you."

If we had been in a movie there would have been some fantastic song playing in the background, extolling the bittersweet virtues of romance. But our soundtrack was Mr. Katz. Somehow that felt right for us.

"You'll call me tomorrow?" I asked.

"I'll come by. We'll have breakfast."

"I'm a little tired tonight. But tomorrow, if you really promise to forgive me, I'll give you a great blow job."

He smiled. "I should get going. You'll be okay here alone for the night?"

"I'll be fine. This is my home, after all."

He nodded and went to the door, but just like this morning he paused once he had opened it. "Sophie?"

"Yes?"

"All your blow jobs are great."

And then I was alone. In *my* house. I started walking around the room, touching the walls, the moldings; at one point I even bent down and touched the floors. This place had been worth every bit of trouble it had caused me. Its history of love, lust and loathing only made it more complete. This wasn't a fairy-tale house. This place had substance. I stopped in front of the photo of my father and this time I didn't just look at it, I actually touched it, my hand falling just right of the child-hand that caressed his cheek.

"I actually thought you were here with me," I said quietly. "Even after all these years. But that was Kane, wasn't it? He planted the lip gloss, he did everything. You…you're just gone."

I kissed my free hand and put it against his chin and for a split second I thought I could feel the tickle of his beard against my fingertips. "Goodbye, Dad," I whispered. "I've finally decided to let you go."

I turned around and there was Mr. Katz watching me approvingly. "Come on," I said, leading him up the stairs, "let's go to bed. Our bed in our house." I laughed at the way that came out. "Our house," I said again. "Soon it will belong to Anatoly, too. I guess I'm going to have to give up on my dreams of becoming a spinster cat lady."

I took my time preparing myself for bed, knowing that the lights wouldn't be turning on and off. Strange brooches wouldn't be showing up on my bed. Everything was calm. When I finally tucked myself under the covers, Mr. Katz was already asleep on the pillow beside me. Anatoly's pillow.

If I kept thinking like that I would make myself giddy, and then I would never get to sleep.

So I stopped thinking altogether.

I felt my body get heavier.

Then lighter.

And then I was dreaming.

26

What you don't know can not only hurt you, it can kill you.
—*The Lighter Side of Death*

HE WAS WITH ME, HOLDING MY HAND. I WAS AN ADULT AND HE WAS... ageless. He wasn't human at all anymore, I could see that now. The outline of his form was blurred by a brilliant illuminating light that seemed to come from his center.

"You don't need to hold my hand anymore, Dad," I said. "I've already let go of yours."

"Tonight I do," he replied. "Before I go, I need to stand beside you one more time. That means you need to stand up, too, Sophie. Stand up right now."

I felt a tugging on my arm and I cracked open my eyes, but I couldn't have been fully awake because I could still see him and feel him. That was impossible. He was dead.

And then I smelled the gasoline.

The image of my father was gone. I was alone in the room with a very awake, very alarmed-looking Mr. Katz, and there was someone downstairs moving around, and there was gasoline.

I ran toward the living room, my bare feet pounding out a

rapid rhythm down the steps as my inner voice screamed the obvious: *Kane's back.*

I was ready for him when I got down there. His mommy fixation was his weakness and I knew how to use it as a weapon against him.

Except it wasn't Kane. Standing in the middle of my living room holding a can of gasoline and a lighter was Lorna. At her feet was another gasoline can, but that one was empty, which explained why my feet were now wet.

"Lorna," I said, hoping that saying her name would help me readjust to this new and unexpected enemy. "Are you trying to kill me?"

She stared at me blankly for a moment. Her eyes had been lined with a sky-blue eyeliner and her mascara had clumped, turning her eyelashes into minidaggers. "No," she finally answered. "You can leave."

I put my hands on my hips, now more indignant than frightened. "I can leave?" I repeated. "Gee, how nice of you to let me get out of here before you BURN DOWN MY HOUSE!"

"I have to burn it down," Lorna said. "He hurt her here. She told me. She said that he sat her down on the couch in this room and he kissed her."

"Are we talking about your daughter?"

"But I didn't believe her," Lorna went blankly on. "I told her that Italians kissed all the time, that it didn't mean anything. And so she stopped telling me things. And then she died. It all started here."

"Lorna, I'm really sorry about your daughter. Seriously, I can't even imagine what I'd do. That said, I think maybe it's time to talk about all this with a psychiatrist."

She looked down at the gas can still in her hand. "I came by earlier. I looked through the window and you were talking to Kane. Is Kane still here?"

"No."

"That's good. I don't want to hurt him, either. When you talk to him next, please tell him that I killed Enrico. The bird locked the door behind me. Enrico taught me how to get him to do that. He didn't know I was there to kill him."

"And the scythe?" I asked. "Where'd you get that."

"Maria took it back from Arizona. She didn't tell you that part. She didn't tell you that it was in that condo. She didn't take it with her when she moved. Isn't that strange? I know why she didn't tell you, though. She didn't want you to think she was guilty. Maria's not guilty of anything but being nice. I really like Maria."

That was it. I didn't care what it said in my escrow agreement, I was going to find a way out of being a part of the Specter Society.

"Lorna," I said carefully, "give me the lighter."

"My daughter came to me after that...I didn't see her, and I couldn't hear her, but I could sense she was near. That's when I knew she approved. She wanted me to purge the earth of the sins that were committed against her. You can commit a sin against someone, can't you? Or should I say crimes?"

"Lorna, the lighter. I need it now."

"I'm going to be with her now, after I do this one thing. You better leave. She doesn't need me to hurt you."

"Lorna! You need to come out of your trance and listen to me! Do you have any idea what I had to go through to get this house? Kane is in jail right now for all the shit he tried to pull. Venus is probably sticking pins in a Sophie doll as we speak, and my ex-husband has spent the last few weeks alternating between lying to me, whining to me and trying to get in my pants. It's been like being married to him all over again and that is *not* a good thing. So no, I'm not going to just walk away and let you destroy the whole place just because you have some sick notion that it's going to make things right with your late daughter. And by the way, you have another kid and it would really suck for him if you burned yourself alive!"

Lorna held up the lighter. "This is your last chance."

I knew I needed to be scared, but I was just so incredibly angry! I was going to have to walk away! All my dreams were literally about to go up in smoke and there was nothing I could do about it!

But I couldn't risk being burned alive, not even if it meant I had a chance to save this house. That had to be where I drew the line. I gritted my teeth and took a side step toward the door. And then it hit me. Something very important was missing.

"I have to get my cat." It hurt my throat to say the words. I was admitting defeat. I was giving up.

"There's no time for that, you have to leave now."

Well, that *really* wasn't going to happen.

"You're going to have to wait until I get my cat."

Lorna shook her head and this time she dumped the remaining gas on the floor. The lighter was still held high in front of her.

"Sorry, Sophie."

I opened my mouth in a last-ditch attempt to reason with her, but then there was a sudden shift in her expression. It went from psychotic calm to confused to totally awed. Her eyes were glued to something behind me, but I didn't turn around. I was focused on the lighter and when her grip loosened I rushed her. She went down with a crash and the lighter flew from her hands, but she wriggled free from beneath me using the smelly slickness of the gasoline to slide forward. She grabbed the lighter at the same time I did and we rolled around, wrestling and grunting as we tried to breathe without inhaling. With a sickening feeling I realized that this fight could go either way.

I was yelling at her, yelling so loud I didn't hear the door open, didn't hear the footsteps approaching, but I did feel the hands.

Strong masculine hands with long manicured nails wedging between me and Lorna and pulling the lighter away from both of us. Lorna and I both stopped and looked up at Venus.

Venus glared down at us. "Lorna," she said, choking on the name, "were you trying to burn this house down with Sophie in it?"

Lorna curled up in a ball and started rocking back and forth.

"You were trying to kill her," Venus continued. "And now you've put me in the position of having to save this slut's life! I came here to make her miserable! She found out about me and she told Scott. This…this cunt took him from me and now I have to fucking save her life! Is this some kind of *joke?*"

Lorna didn't say anything and continued to rock.

I cleared my throat. "Um, Venus, I think we should call the police."

"Shut up!" she screamed waving the lighter at me like a pointer. "This does not make us friends. You know that, right? I hate you and I will spend the rest of my days trying to make your life a living hell!"

"But you're not going to set the house on fire, right?"

Venus gave me a withering look and handed me the lighter. "Call the police."

"Thank you," I whispered. "You saved my life. And my home! And my cat's life!"

"Fan-fucking-tabulous! Call the damn police!"

"Right, okay, but…um…my cell's upstairs. Can I use yours?"

"I really hate you," Venus snarled as she handed me the phone.

"Yeah, I, um, got that." I dialed 911. "Hey, this is Sophie Katz. You guys were here earlier this evening and I was hoping you might be willing to swing by again. I have another murderer on my hands and it would be great if you could take care of her."

I continued to give the 911 operator information until I could hear the sirens wail down the street. As I hung up Lorna looked up at me with misty eyes. "That picture moved by itself, just as I was about to set the fire. It just…moved!"

I turned around and there it was. The picture of my father and me at a complete diagonal and underneath it was the lip gloss, just sitting there on the mantel of the fireplace. I knew damned well that wasn't where I had left it.

The police barged in. This time they didn't have their guns drawn; they had smelled the gas. "We all need to get out of here right now."

Speechless I looked up and saw Mr. Katz watching me from the top of the staircase. If I didn't know better I would have sworn he was smiling.

27

Nature loses its beauty when we try to perfect it. The same can be said about the ones we love.

—*The Lighter Side of Death*

EVERY ONCE IN A WHILE THE WEATHER COOPERATES WITH WHAT IT IS you want it to do, and this was one of those days. Not that it could have stopped us. Nothing was going to keep my family from having our Sutro Heights picnic. But the fact that the clouds were high and dispersed sparingly around a blue sky certainly made the experience more enjoyable.

Leah sat on her knees, ready to spring up if Jack took off running. At the moment, he was entertaining himself by pulling up small weeds and sticking them down his pants. I can't imagine why anyone would want to do that, but Jack had always been something of an enigma.

Mama, who reportedly hadn't sat on the ground in decades and didn't intend to start now, was in a portable lawn chair, and I was sitting cross-legged on a blanket as green as the grass beneath it, spreading hummus on a rice cake.

"How long before your floors are finished?" Leah asked as she plucked a grape from its stem.

"Another week," I said with a sigh. Only a week had passed since both Kane and Lorna had been arrested and it was fair to say that the dust was still settling. In fact, that was a rather literal truth since Lorna's decision to wash my floors in gasoline had effectively destroyed them. I was staying with Anatoly in the meantime. He still hadn't agreed to move into the house with me, but I was confident he would.

"Such a mess," my mother said with a click of her tongue. "And to kill a man with a scythe, no less. Not that I blame her for wanting to do him in. If any man had dared to lay a hand on my girls I would have fixed him good! Believe you me! But a scythe? What's the matter, a gun isn't fancy enough for her?"

"She bought into Kane's whole thing about how everyone in the séance had to be a believer," I said. A ladybug landed on my knee and I tried to keep still so as not to disturb it. "She figured that if she could make it look like Enrico was killed by a ghost she would have her revenge, and if she was lucky her husband, Al, would start to buy the whole ghosts-walking-among-us deal and the two of them would be able to make contact with their daughter."

"Good God, it's amazing she wasn't committed years ago," Leah said. "Have you heard anything about her family? She has a son, doesn't she?"

"His name's Zach. Al's not doing so well and he doesn't really know how to help Zach with all this. Then again, he's never been very good with Zach from what I understand. But Zach's found himself a big brother of sorts."

"Oh, do you know him?"

"Well, yeah, it's Marcus."

Leah leveled me with a stare. "Marcus is going to be chaperoning a fifteen-year-old? Isn't that like telling your child to make a role model out of Charlie Sheen?"

"Marcus is being a very good influence. He's vowed not to pick up men while he's with Zach and he's already convinced Zach to dye his hair back to its natural color and stop wearing makeup."

"Marcus told a boy to *stop* wearing makeup?"

"Give Marcus a break. He's playing Professor Higgins, minus the weird sexual undertones that existed between Higgins and Eliza."

"Ah, but what about the sexual undertone that existed between Higgins and Colonel Pickering, hmm?" Mama asked. "If you ask me those two were up to some hanky-panky!"

"Mama!" Leah exclaimed as I bent over laughing.

"Relax, I'm just teasing," Mama said with a wicked grin. "Marcus is doing a good thing. So what about that no-goodnik ex-husband of yours? What's he up to now?"

I shrugged. "I haven't really talked to him. I know it's over between him and Venus, and I think he's found an apartment in the Marina, but that's the extent of my knowledge. There's only one man I need to keep track of these days."

"Unlike Dena," Leah scoffed. "How many boyfriends did you say she's faithful to these days?"

"Only two. For her, that's downsizing. And you know what, it really seems to be working for her."

"Two men!" Mama said. "Who ever heard of such a thing? How does she find the time?"

"Well, she shares them with this girl, Amelia. I mean, I couldn't handle the arrangement, but I'm not Dena."

"Yes, there's only one Dena, and thank God for that," Leah mumbled. I smiled and spread some more hummus. Leah and Dena would never be best friends, but beneath the acidic rhetoric they had a begrudging respect for one another. It was just another weird way in which my world seemed to fit together.

"Do you have to go to the Specter Society anymore?" Leah asked.

"By contract, I'm required to attend at least two meetings a month for the next twelve months, but all the other members of the Specter Society are either going to prison, a mental hospital or they've just quit. So yes, I have to go to the meetings, but that's kind of a moot point since I'm now the only member."

Leah laughed appreciatively. "My therapist says that people who believe in ghosts are often people who don't know how to fully connect with the living."

"I'm not so sure about that," Mama said as she stretched her legs out in front of her. Jack tried to stick a dandelion up her sandal, but Leah managed to get it away from him.

"You believe in ghosts, Mama?" I asked.

"I believe there are things that we don't understand, but unlike some people I'm not in such a big hurry to understand everything. A little mystery is not such a bad thing."

I smiled and ran my fingers over my lips. For the first few days after the incident with Lorna I had worn the Strawberry Shortcake lip gloss, but then I had tucked it away in a keepsake box and gone back to Clinique. I didn't need to wear a child's lip gloss to feel the presence of my father.

I knew Dad could no longer be the linchpin that held our family together, but I was okay with that now. In my dream he had told me that he was going to stand by me one last time. It was possible that Lorna had been the one to mess with my father's picture and put the lip gloss on the mantel. She was crazy enough to have done that and then convince herself it had been a supernatural event. But I chose to believe something else. As far as I was concerned that was my father's last stand on earth. He was free now. *I* had finally set him free. Every once in a while I could think about him and miss him, but I didn't have to obsess over his memory any more than I had to deny it. I could move on with my life. With my family. *This* family, composed of a colorful Jewish mother, a sister with a *Good Housekeeping* fetish and a nephew, who my friends had justly nicknamed the Destroyer. And then there was my cat, who liked to sleep on my head, and my man, who I was constantly arguing with. It was, as far as I was concerned, the best family in the world.

Mama regarded Leah and me thoughtfully. "Such beautiful women you two grew up to be. And smart! Your father would be proud."

"You know what?" I said, "I'm proud of us, too." I lifted a can of Hansen's soda. "To us!"

Leah and Mama lifted their cans, too. Jack held up a clod of dirt. "To us," Mama and Leah chimed in.

"And to Sophie's new dream home," Leah added.

I chugged down the rest of my soda. It really was a perfect day.